THE ORCHID TRILOGY

Jocelyn Brooke was born in 1908 on the south coast, and took to the educational process with reluctance. He contrived to run away from public school twice within a fortnight, but then settled, to his own mild surprise, at Bedales before going to Worcester College, Oxford, where his career as an undergraduate was unspectacular. He worked in London for a while, then in the family wine-merchants in Folkestone, but this and other ventures proved variously unsatisfactory.

In 1939, Brooke enlisted in the Royal Army Medical Corps, and re-enlisted after the war as a Regular: 'Soldiering,' he wrote, 'had become a habit.' The critical success of *The Military Orchid* (1948), the first volume of this trilogy, provided the opportunity to buy himself out, and he immediately settled down to write, publishing some fifteen titles between 1948 and 1955, including the successive volumes of this trilogy, *A Mine of Serpents* (1949) and *The Goose Cathedral* (1950). His other published work includes two volumes of poetry, *December Spring* (1946) and *The Elements of Death* (1952), the novels *The Image of a Drawn Sword* (1950) and *The Dog at Clambercrown* (1955), as well as some technical works on botany.

Jocelyn Brooke died in 1966.

JOCELYN BROOKE

• • •

THE ORCHID TRILOGY

THE MILITARY ORCHID

A MINE OF SERPENTS

THE GOOSE CATHEDRAL

• • •

INTRODUCTION BY

ANTHONY POWELL

A KING PENGUIN

PUBLISHED BY PENGUIN BOOKS

Penguin Books Ltd, Harmondsworth, Middlesex, England
Penguin Books, 625 Madison Avenue, New York, New York 10022, U.S.A.
Penguin Books Australia Ltd, Ringwood, Victoria, Australia
Penguin Books Canada Ltd, 2801 John Street, Markham, Ontario, Canada L3R 1B4
Penguin Books (N.Z.) Ltd, 182–190 Wairau Road, Auckland 10, New Zealand

—

This edition first published by Martin Secker & Warburg Ltd 1981
Published simultaneously in Penguin Books
Reprinted 1981

—

—

—

Made and printed in Great Britain by
Cox & Wyman Ltd, Reading
Set in Baskerville

Contents

JOCELYN BROOKE

By Anthony Powell

In 1949, a moment when I was editing the novel pages of the *Times Literary Supplement*, a book came in called *A Mine of Serpents*, author Jocelyn Brooke. The name was familiar on account of a previous work, *The Military Orchid*, which had appeared the year before, and received unusually approving notices. I had not read *The Military Orchid*, partly because there was a good deal to do reviewing other books, partly because (being in that respect like Wyndham Lewis's Tarr, for whom 'the spring was anonymous') I thought a work much concerned with botany sounded off my beat.

Quite fortuitously, I reviewed *A Mine of Serpents* for the *TLS* myself, treating it more or less as a novel, which it was only to a very limited extent. There was some excuse for that, as a note at the beginning stated the book was 'complementary' to *The Military Orchid*, rather than a 'sequel', and certain ostensibly fictional characters occurred in a manner to suggest later development of a contrived plot. I did not grasp that here was the second volume of a loosely constructed autobiographical trilogy, slightly fictionalized. The review now strikes me as a trifle pompous, but I recognized Brooke's talent at once, and remarked that the epigraph from Sir Thomas Browne – 'Some Truths seem almost Falsehoods and Some Falsehoods almost Truths' – contains 'in a sense justification of all novel-writing'.

I knew nothing of Jocelyn Brooke himself, except what was to be gathered from this book. He was, in fact, then just about forty, and had recently emerged from the ranks of the Royal Army Medical Corps, in which he re-enlisted two years after the end of the second war. A collection of poems by him had appeared in 1946, but *The Military Orchid* was his first published prose work.

In the same year, 1949, Brooke brought out *The Scapegoat* and *The Wonderful Summer*, neither of which came my way at the time – nor were part of the trilogy – but in the spring of 1950 I reviewed his Kafka-like novel, *The Image of a Drawn Sword*, and, in the autumn, the trilogy's third volume, *The Goose Cathedral*. By that time I had marked Brooke down as one of the notable writers to have surfaced after the war.

In those days reviewing on the *TLS* was unsigned, so there was no question of Brooke having known about my liking for his work, when in 1953 an article by him appeared in one of the weeklies praising my own first novel, *Afternoon Men*, published more than twenty years earlier. *Afternoon Men* had, as it happened, been reprinted about a year before, but, when I wrote to Brooke expressing appreciation of this unexpected bouquet, he turned out to be unaware of the book being in print again, having merely reread his old copy, and rung up a literary editor on impulse. In due course we lunched with each other, met from time to time afterwards (though never often), and continued to correspond fitfully until Brooke's death in 1966.

All writers, one way or another, depend ultimately on their own lives for the material of their books, but the manner in which each employs personal experience, interior or exterior, is very different. Jocelyn Brooke uses both elements with a minimum of dilution, though much imagination. However far afield he goes physically, his creative roots remain in his childhood. He was by nature keenly interested in himself, though without vanity, or the smallest taint of exhibitionism.

Brooke might, indeed, be compared with a performer at a fair or variety show (perhaps to be called Brooke's Benefit), who arrives on the stage always with the same properties and puppets. The first backdrop is certain to be the landscape of Kent, into which the author is wheeled in his pram by his nurse, his mother in attendance. Soon he is lifted out of the pram, and presents himself as child and schoolboy. There are botanical effects; sometimes fireworks. Soldiery of the Royal Army Medical Corps wait in the wings to provide mainly comic relief. Occasionally the scene is changed, though rarely for long: a London pub; the houses and flats of perhaps rather dubious friends; a camp in the Middle East or Italy; but sooner or later we are back among the hopfields, with the neighbours and the family wine business; the bizarre antitheses of a highbrow childhood in unhighbrow surroundings. In short, the facts of Brooke's life are more than usually relevant.

Bernard Jocelyn Brooke was born 30 November 1908, third

child and second son of Henry Brooke and his wife May, *née* Turner, the youngest of the family by ten years or more. Both his grandfathers had been wine merchants, also his father, who had started life as a solicitor. Brooke's elder brother, after ten years as a regular officer in the Royal East Kent Regiment, The Buffs, joined the firm too, and for a while Brooke himself.

Earlier generations were parsons, in the professions, yeomen farmers. A less run-of-the-mill heredity is suggested by the portrait (1826) of Great-Aunt Cock with her two little dogs (reproduced in one of Brooke's books); also by the box containing the literary remains of a great-grandfather, crony of Thomas Hood's, Joseph Hewlett, a tipsy vicar with eighteen children, who kept body and soul together on a minute stipend by writing facetious novels under the name of Peter Priggins.

The Brookes' wine shop – always known as the Office – was at Folkestone. They themselves lived at Sandgate, a more socially eligible strip of coast to the west. They also possessed an inland cottage at Bishopsbourne in the Elham Valley, where in the summer they retired to 'the country'. Bishopsbourne was the neighbourhood to provide Brooke earliest memories, most beloved centre for imaginary adventure in childhood, hunting-ground for flowers, the very heart of the Brooke Myth.

From earliest days Brooke used to overhear grown-ups muttering that he was 'not strong', a condition that must have caused specially uncomfortable concern to parents who were converts, though not fanatical ones, to Christian Science. At a later date Brooke's childish problems would no doubt have been looked on as largely pyschological. The household, without being in the least professionally intellectual, was not without all literary contacts, not on visiting terms with Conrad, who had a house by Bishopsbourne, but the two elder children used to attend the parties of a Mr Wells, who turned out to be H. G.

Brooke's nanny (from some early mispronunciation always known as Ninny), by creed a Strict Baptist, was a preponderant figure in his life, and (like the country round about) remained so virtually to the end of his days. He was an intelligent child, painfully sensitive, and, like many such, quick in some directions, slow in others:

'Often, but not always the botanophil is precocious. A family legend relates that myself, at the age of four, could identify by name any or all of the coloured plates in Edward Step's *Wayside and Woodland Blossoms* ... not content with the English names, I memorized many of the Latin and Greek ones as well. Some of these (at the age of 8) I conceitedly incorporated in a school essay ... The headmaster read the essay aloud to the school (no wonder I was unpopular).'

A consequence of the touch of crankiness in the Brooke home, which went side by side with a good deal of conventionality, was that Brooke was not allowed to eat meat in childhood (Ninny asserted it 'caused sand in his water'), a curtailment which, when he first went to school, nearly resulted in death from starvation, as nothing was added to his plate of routine vegetables, a component of the menu at its lowest ebb in school fare during the first war.

Thought of being sent to school had in any case clouded Brooke's early days, and, when the blow fell, the reality confirmed his worst fears. A day-school was just tolerable, but he was not at all happy at a local preparatory school, which sounds little different from most prep schools of the time. The real disaster came when he entered King's School, Canterbury (alma mater of Christopher Marlowe, Walter Pater, Somerset Maugham, Patrick Leigh-Fermor), from which Brooke ran away in the first week. He was sent back. The second week he ran away again. The latter withdrawal marked the termination of his residence there, which had lasted less than a fortnight.

Brooke's parents – whom he more than once designates as long-suffering – accordingly decided to transfer their younger son to Bedales. In this milder atmosphere, co-educational and 'progressive', he found relief; indeed was surprised by his relative contentment. He has left some picture of life at Bedales, where sex was condemned as 'silly' (I remember a female Old Bedalian, the late Julia Strachey, telling me that in her time one girl was so 'silly' she had a baby), and Brooke does not disguise that this doctrine did not provide a complete answer to all sexual difficulties.

At Bedales (in face of some official discouragement) Brooke first read Aldous Huxley, deciding he was himself a disillusioned Huxley character, though the requirements of that stance were not always easy to maintain at school. 'The Huxleian poison continued to circulate in my veins for the next ten years or more: indeed, I think I have never succeeded in finally excreting it from my system ... I idolized him when young, and if I find his later work hard to 'take', my difficulty is partly due, perhaps, to the immense expectations which his earlier books aroused in me.'

Brooke, like his novel-writing clerical forebear, Peter Priggins, was up at Worcester College, Oxford, where he often felt lonely, but seems to have lived the fairly typical life of a Proust-Joyce-Firbank-reading undergraduate. Oxford memories soon became blurred for him, but he remembered sending an article on the subject of Oxford Decadence to the *Isis*, which was accepted by the then editor, Peter Fleming, but no meeting took place, a record of which might have been enjoyable.

On coming down from Oxford, the Twenties now moving fast towards their dissolution, Brooke, prototype (as he himself always emphasizes) of the all but unemployable young man of the period, came to London. He worked for two years in a bookshop in the City. When for one reason or another that job terminated he decided to try the family business, from which his father had by then retired, the Brooke parents now living at Blackheath. Brooke found himself dreadfully bored writing out invoices for wine orders, nevertheless he drudged away at that; in a general effort to take life more seriously also attempting to grow a moustache. The family business turned out not to be the answer, nor various other employments, and he had some sort of breakdown.

Brooke, as this account of his beginnings shows, was very much a Child of the Age, anyway a highbrow child. The curious thing is that he did not, like so many young men of that category, bring out a first novel telling a hard-luck story. It is difficult to believe he could not have achieved publication had he wished. On the contrary no book by him appeared before the war, and, when his own kind of autobiography went into print, though its roots were in a richly self-pitying epoch, it was entirely free from that element.

To what extent Brooke returned from the war to an accumulation of notes for books is not clear, but the fact that his eventual output included fifteen works published – some separated by only a few months – between 1948 and 1955 suggests he had at least made up his mind about a lot of literary possibilities. Among these later volumes was another collection of poems (Brooke's verse was competent rather than inspired), an Introduction to the Journals of Denton Welch (that gifted *petit maître*, as Brooke calls him, who died at the age of thirty-three), some technical writing on botany (though Brooke always insisted he was only an amateur among real botanists), and a surrealist *collage* in the manner of Max Ernst.

In various thumbnail sketches of himself taken from different angles during early London life, Brooke sardonically presents a typical young intellectual of the period, toying rather ineffectively with the arts, writing poetry intermittently, trying to fit himself in among the homocommunists (a useful portmanteau word Brooke coined, later adopted by Cyril Connolly in *Horizon*), but Communism proved wholly unpalatable, and, like efforts to grow a moustache, Brooke gave up politics. He might, perhaps, in his own manner, have been called an existentialist, disliking the pressure of all abstract idea, but he preferred to define himself as a futilitarian.

When war came in 1939 Brooke enlisted in the Royal Army Medical Corps as soon as that was possible. The army, recurring throughout most of his books, was to provide some of his best material. Again, though his military service must often have been far from comfortable, he is without the least self-pity. In fact, feeling after a time that life was too easy, he volunteered for the branch of the RAMC treating venereal disease –in army parlance the Pox-Wallahs – returning to the VD branch when he rejoined after the war, and managing to get posted to Woolwich, conveniently near the family home at Blackheath.

The success of *The Military Orchid* with the critics, the possibility stemming from that of finding employment in the BBC, the newly allowed permission for a soldier to 'buy himself out', combined to bring an end to Brooke's second round of soldiering, though, like the man in the Kipling poem, Brooke felt the army pulled at his heartstrings. He had found it much changed after the war, and the National Service men were impressed by his five medal ribbons, even if unable to understand this second voluntary acceptance of barrack routine.

From the moment of returning to civilian life again Brooke settled down to write, in due course retracing his steps to Ivy Cottage, Bishopsbourne, where he lived with his mother and Ninny, neither of whom died a great many years before Brooke himself. He was therefore in the end established as nearly as possible to childhood circumstances, at the very focus of the magical world he had himself created.

The Military Orchid is the opening Act of the Brooke variety show referred to earlier. All the basic Brooke constituents are here introduced in his search for the rare orchid of this name (with its closely related fellows, some almost equally rare, some relatively common), its very designation giving a hint of the link it was to make with war, and all sorts of unexpected people and places. Brooke has the gift – just as some musicians can write of music in a manner intelligible to the unmusical – of making botany intelligible to the unbotanical. Early childhood, school, the army, all come into *The Military Orchid*, but not yet Oxford.

The title, *A Mine of Serpents*, refers to a firework, thereby introducing another preoccupation of Brooke's, second only to botany. He was obsessed by fireworks until at least the age of fifteen (relations beginning to raise eyebrows as 'too old for that'), and he never lost his love for *feux d'artifice*, one of the best displays he ever saw being in Italy at the end of the war, when the Italian crowd abandoned itself to a delight as uninhibited as his own.

A Mine of Serpents, without losing sight of life in Kent, recalls Brooke's Oxford, fictionalizing some of his contemporaries. He glances at an Italian holiday; then returns to days in the army. Brooke is not, I think, at his best as a writer in projecting undergraduates, a hard enough assignment, and these friends, even after they come down from the university, never quite take on substantial enough shape. It is the occasional autobiographical passage, however brief, that holds the attention.

Brooke always appeared to have satisfactorily resolved his own homosexuality in life, but in his books, perhaps because at that date some discretion had still to be observed, he is at times less at ease, veering between satire and a kind of embarrassed uncertainty, in a theme that recurs, the hearty queer, perhaps an army officer, who pretends to be otherwise, but has designs on the narrator. This is perhaps to say no more than that Brooke was simply more skilful at his own particular art than in the give-and-take of the traditional novel.

The Goose Cathedral, third volume of the trilogy, continues to lean towards the novel-writing end of Brooke's method, with some amusing vignettes, though again I prefer the straight autobiography. The book is named after the lifeboat station at Sandgate, a small grey neo-gothic building by the shore, which in childhood marked one of the limits of Brooke's daily walks with

Ninny. An Oxford friend came to stay when Brooke was older, and, on account of the flock of geese that made a habit of pottering about on the shingle in front of the lifeboat station, the two young men named the place the Goose Cathedral. Later the Goose Cathedral was for a time inhabited as a seaside cottage, then transformed into a tea-room, cropping up again at intervals throughout Brooke's life, a typical symbolic landmark in Brooke lore.

One of the few books by Jocelyn Brooke which, though the action takes place in Brooke's familiar Kentish countryside, can unquestionably be listed as a novel, the story being told in the third rather than first person, is *The Image of a Drawn Sword*. Even here a form of autobiography is not entirely lacking, because in place of Brooke's physical experience, a kind of vision of the phantasies that sometimes haunted his mind is set out, especially phantasies about the army.

Reynarde, the hero – perhaps rather anti-hero – has been invalided from the army during the war, and, living in a cottage with his widowed mother, works in a bank in the neighbouring town. Places like the Roman Camp, Priorsholt, The Dog (a pub) in the neighbouring village of Clambercrown, which occur in Brooke's other works, are mentioned in the story.

A young regular officer, who has lost his way, comes to the cottage. He has something to do with the local Territorials. There is the faintest suggestion – better handled than in some of the other books – of mutual sexual attraction. He and Reynarde become friends. The officer tries to persuade Reynarde, who is not wholly unwilling, to join the Territorials. Later Reynarde attempts to speak with this army friend on the telephone, who for some reason seems never available.

Reynarde continues his efforts to get in touch, and, while he does so, finds it assumed that he himself has already in some manner gone back to the army. Not only that, but a war has broken out in the neighbourhood, though no one seems to know who are the enemy. Reynarde's friend is constantly rising in rank, while Reynarde suddenly finds himself treated as a deserter. The book ends with his arrest, facing sentence of a hundred lashes and fortnight's field-punishment.

The Image of a Drawn Sword, in its way not inferior to Kafka (though Brooke had read no Kafka at the time the novel was written), has a haunting sinister quality very well maintained. One wonders if the whole theme came to birth when Brooke was in truth trying to make up his mind whether or not to join the army again. *The Dog at Clambercrown* (1955), perhaps Brooke's best book, defines some of these emotions, crystallized by a fellow-private remarking: 'Anyone'd think you *liked* the army.'

'As it happened, Pte Hoskins' unlikely hypothesis was perfectly correct: I did like the army – though "like" is hardly an adequate word to describe my feelings about it. "Love" would perhaps be nearer the mark, though here again the word required qualifications, for my liaison with the armed forces (and I use the word in its erotic rather than military sense) was by no means a starry-eyed, spontaneous affair which the word love too easily suggests. It resembled, rather, the kind of relationship described by Proust, in which love itself is apprehended, so to speak, only in its negative aspects – the pain of loss, the absence or infidelity of the loved one, the perverse satisfaction of possessing (like Swann) some woman who isn't one's type, whom one doesn't even like, but with whom one has become so fatally obsessed that life without her is unendurable.

'Soldiering had become a habit with me – out of uniform I felt lost, uprooted, a kind of outlaw with no fixed place in the scheme of things. During the two years since my demobilization I had suffered from a growing sense of loss and self-betrayal: I had cast off my mistress – glad enough, at the time, to be free of her thraldom: yet I knew that, despite her tantrums, her cruelty and her possessiveness, I loved her still. Sometimes, passing a recruiting office, I would feel the old nostalgia creeping over me, and I would experience a masochistic impulse to throw myself, once again, at the feet of my lost love. She would, I knew, be ready to take me back – exacting and possessive as ever, but prepared to let bygones be bygones.'

Brooke's taste in writers was essentially that of his generation – the debt to Proust freely acknowledged in the above passage – and the writers he knew, he knew well. There is acute literary criticism scattered about in his own books, some of which may be quoted. For instance, on James Joyce in *The Dog at Clambercrown* which opens with Brooke reading *Ulysses* in the plane on the way to a holiday in Sicily. '*Ulysses*, I suppose, is the most fascinating and the most devastatingly boring novel ever written ... I remember, many years ago (at the period when *Finnegan* was appearing serially in *transition*), reading a poem by an undergraduate in some university magazine or anthology in which the poet describes Joyce as hunting in a drain for the "lost collar-stud of his genius". The image still seems to me – as it seemed at the time – an apt one; for Joyce's genius was, I believe, of a minor order – he lacked the power and range of the great novelists, and his later work is chiefly distinguished by an infinite capacity for taking pains.'

When Brooke arrived on this journey at Syracuse he stayed in the house of a (female) friend, whose library was stocked with English books published between 1905 and 1925. As the weather was wet and cold Brooke embarked on a re-read of D. H. Lawrence. '*Aaron's Rod* (much praised in its time) struck me, quite simply, as an abysmally bad novel ... *The Rainbow*: the first chapter seemed magnificent; after all, I decided, Lawrence had everything – a genius for evoking landscape, a sense of character, a marvellous apprehension of human relationships. Yet after a further chapter or two I was firmly bogged down: the prose became more and more turgid: more and more repetitive ... Yet there are magnificent passages in *The Rainbow* – as there are in *Women in Love*, its sequel. If only, one feels, he could keep it up! But he couldn't ...'

'Lawrence's "secret" – if one can call it that – was, I suppose, that he was profoundly homosexual: but his lonely, puritanic, lower middle-class upbringing prevented him from coming to terms with his own homosexuality ... *Sons and Lovers, The White Peacock*, a few of the short stories, and a handful of memorable poems – it is these out of Lawrence's enormous output, which seem most likely to survive.'

In *The Military Orchid* Brooke reviews the capabilities of famous writers and poets in the field of botany. Here Lawrence, who loved flowers and knew about them, comes in for high praise. Oddly enough, Proust knew about flowers too, though he rarely described them for their own sake, liking to use them as analogies for human behaviour, for instance (in the context of 'hermaphroditic plants'), the moment when M. de Charlus first grasps that the ex-tailor, Jupien, is homosexual, and himself gets to grips.

Matthew Arnold, usually accurate in his botany, slips up by calling the convolvulus blue, though he corrected that to pink in later editions of the poem. Keats, admittedly unable to see what flowers were at his feet, nor what soft incense hung upon the boughs, was inclined to confine himself to vague generalizations about violets and eglantine; Shelley equally equivocal in botanical imagery. Clare and Crabbe are justly famous in the realm of Flora, though Brooke doubts whether Crabbe's 'dull nightshade hanging on her dead fruit' in Suffolk, was indeed Deadly Nightshade; in that county more likely to be the harmless Black Nightshade, or even Bittersweet.

Shakespeare comes out with high marks for being explicit, though Elizabethan nomenclature has sometimes changed.

> . . . long purples,
> That liberal shepherds give a grosser name,
> But our cold maids do Dead-men's fingers call them.

Millais, says Brooke, painted the Purple Loosestrife in his picture of Ophelia, which was never called Dead-men's fingers, nor for that matter by any grosser name. 'Dead-men's fingers, in fact, refers to one or other of the palmate-rooted orchises, and is also loosely used for the *Orchis mascula*, one of the round-tubered species, all of which are given "grosser names", not only by liberal shepherds, but by the early herbalists; the reason being that the two tubers suggest a pair of testicles.' One is glad to learn that as in the days of King Lear samphire may still be gathered on the Dover cliffs.

I was never a close friend of Jocelyn Brooke's, but we corresponded quite often, and he was one of the people to whom one wrote letters with great ease. He speaks more than once of his own liking for that sort of relationship, a kind that did not make him feel hemmed in. There are several incidents in his books when the narrator refuses an invitation from someone with whom he is getting on pretty well so that it was no great surprise when, a few months after Brooke had stayed with us for a weekend, he politely excused himself from another visit on grounds of work. The reason may have been valid enough, writing time always hard to conserve, but one suspected his sense of feeling 'different', unwillingness to cope with face-to-face cordialities of a kind that might at the same time be agreeable in letters.

Brooke liked a fair amount to drink, and, after lunching with one, was inclined to say: 'Shall we be *beasts*, and now go to *my* club, and have another glass of port?' In 1964, less than two years before his death, my wife and I were staying in Kent, and went

over to see him at Bishopsbourne. We lunched at The Metropole
in Folkestone. All this territory was the hallowed ground of
Brooke legend. Writing of Beatrix Potter, Brooke says that as a
child the world of *Mr Todd* and *Jemima Puddleduck* had seemed
'indistinguishable from the landscape of our own village.' Ivy Cottage, where he had lived with his mother and Ninny, was indeed
almost uncannily like Mr Jeremy Fisher's 'little damp house'.

In appearance Jocelyn Brooke was tall, pale, not bad looking,
with an air of melancholy that would suddenly leave him when he
laughed. Photographs give him a haggard air, a stare as if mes-
merizing or mesmerized (perhaps assumed for fun), that hardly
does him justice. He often reminded me of George Orwell, not in
feature so much as a kind of hesitancy of manner, thinking for a
second or two of what had been said, but he had none of Orwell's
wish to set the world right, and his laughter was quite un-
Orwellian.

As a writer I think Brooke completely realized himself, in spite
of dying comparatively young. He had said what he had to say in
the form he wished to say that. No doubt his critical views would
always have been of interest, but he had already marked out his
own magical personal kingdom, one that makes him different (in a
sense, what he himself felt) from any other writer.

Jocelyn Brooke quite often quotes A. E. Housman, half-respect-
fully, half-deprecatingly, as if finding the shared rural images,
shared homosexuality, both a shade too lush for his own taste,
while all the same admiring the poetic mastery. Nevertheless, one
feels a suitable epitaph might be provided by only the smallest
adaptation of Housman's often quoted lines:

> Far in a Kentish Brooke-land
>   That bred me long ago
> The orchids bloom and whisper
>   By woods I used to know.

JOCELYN BROOKE

THE
MILITARY
ORCHID

To Jonathan Curling

Contents

Author's Note

THIS BOOK is not, strictly, an autobiography, and the author has taken a novelist's liberties both with persons and institutions. I hope that 'St Ethelbert's' and schools of its kind have long ceased to exist; as for the *dramatis personae*, so far as they impinge upon reality at all, they are to be considered as caricatures rather than characters.

Acknowledgements are due to the Editors of *Penguin New Writing* and *The New English Weekly*, in whose pages certain passages from this book have previously appeared.

J.B.

'Souldiers Satyrion bringeth forth many broad large and ribbed leaues, fpred upon the ground like unto thofe of the great Plantaine: among the which rifeth vp a fat ftalke full of fap or iuice, clothed or wrapped in the like leaues euen to the tuft of flowers, wherupon doe grow little flowers refembling a little man, hauing a helmet vpon his head, his hands and legs cut off; white upon the infide, fpotted with many purple fpots, and the backe part of the flower of a deeper colour tending to rednes. The rootes be greater ftones than any of the kinds of Satyrions.'

GERARDE, *Herbal*, 1597

'I have found it during the last four years very sparingly. It only appeared in a barren state in 1886.'

DRUCE, *Flora of Oxfordshire*

'*Orchis militaris* shows its close affinity with *O. purpurea*, perhaps, by sharing its sterility, though this appears to be less pronounced on the Continent . . .'

EDWARD STEP, *Wayside and Woodland Blossoms* (3rd Series)

'Rare in Spring. Grows in chalky districts only and not always there.' J. S. E. MACKENZIE, *British Orchids*

'Now nearly extinct.'
GODFERY, *Monograph and Iconograph of Native British Orchidaceae.*

PART ONE

A Box of Wormseed

'Thou art a box of wormseed, at best but a salvatory of green mummy.'

DUCHESS OF MALFI

I

Mr Bundock's function, so far as my family was concerned, was to empty the earth-closet twice a week at the cottage where we used to spend the summer. This duty he performed unobtrusively and usually late at night: looming up suddenly in the summer-dusk, earth-smelling and hairy like some menial satyr, a kind of Lob. (Perhaps the maids left a bowl of cream for him on the threshold.) He became of sudden interest to me one June evening by asserting, quite calmly, that he had found the Lizard Orchid.

Now the Lizard, at that period, had just made one of its rare appearances in the district: mysterious and portentous as the return of a comet, but, unlike a comet, unpredictable. A photograph of its extraordinary bearded spike had appeared in the *Folkestone Herald*; the finder was an elderly Folkestone photographer, who had subsequently exhibited the plant in his shop-window, where I had been taken to see it. Very kindly, he had detached two florets from the spike and presented them to me. (I heard, many years afterwards, that he was suspected of importing plants from the Continent and naturalizing them on the hills near Folkestone. The story recalls Gerarde, who glibly asserted, in the 1597 edition of his *Herbal*, that he had found the Wild Peony in Kent; a statement corrected in the 1633 edition by Johnson, who explains that Gerarde 'himselfe planted the Peonie there, and afterwards seemed to find it there by accident.')

Mr Bundock seemed to think nothing of finding the Lizard. One might have supposed it was an everyday occurrence with him. He promised to bring me specimens the next evening. I waited with immense excitement. He duly arrived, and presented me with several specimens of the 'Lizard Orchid'. Alas! it was not the Lizard at all, but the Green Man Orchid, *Aceras anthropophora*: a rarity, certainly, but not to be compared with the almost mythical Lizard. Besides, I had already found it myself.

My disappointment was immense, but mitigated by the other orchid which Mr Bundock had brought me. This was unfamiliar: a tall, handsome spike of purple-brown and pink-spotted flowers. Obviously, I thought, it came under the desirable category of Very Rare Orchids. But which was it?

I must have been about seven years old at this period; and besides being a keen (if somewhat erratic) botanist, I had already begun to specialize: I was bitten with the Orchid-mania. Up till this time, the only 'flower-book' I had possessed was Edward Step's *Wayside and Woodland Blossoms*: adequate for the amateur, but not of much service to the specialist. On my seventh birthday, however, I had acquired a book on the Orchids themselves: *British Orchids, How to Tell One from Another*, by a certain Colonel Mackenzie. I still possess the book: produced in a rather sub-arty style, it bears no publication-date, and must have been long out of print. It is illustrated with a dozen rather ladylike watercolours, mostly of the commoner species; the sole exception is the very rare, almost extinct, Lady's Slipper, which I am prepared to wager the Colonel had obtained from a florist.

For the Colonel was an amateur, and not a very enterprising one, either. In his foreword he naïvely confesses himself baffled by the ordinary Flora, with its scientific classification of species; and in the subsequent text, invents a system of classification entirely his own. About the rarest orchids, which he had evidently not seen, his tone becomes almost sceptical; one feels that he doubts their very existence.

Poor Colonel Mackenzie! His book was not the best of introductions to its subject. Yet he was a true orchidomane, and I salute him across the years. I imagine him living in comfortable retirement in Surrey, in a red house with a drive and spiky gates, among pine-trees; pottering on the downs above Betchworth and Shere, but not often venturing further afield. Probably he did possess a copy of Bentham and Hooker; but he could seldom have looked at it. It is a pleasing thought that another retired officer, Colonel Godfery, has since written the standard Monograph[1] on the British *Orchidaceae*. (He also lives in Surrey.)

1 *Monograph and Iconograph of Native British Orchidaceae*, Cambridge, 1933.

So, with Colonel Mackenzie and Edward Step open before me, I addressed myself to the identification of Mr Bundock's new Orchid (he had no name for it himself). Now, according to Colonel Mackenzie, the plant was none other than *Orchis militaris*, the Military Orchid. But according to Edward Step, it might equally well – more probably, in fact – be *Orchis purpurea*, the Great Brown-Winged Orchid, which the Colonel didn't even so much as mention. The discrepancy provoked in me a moral conflict; for I wanted, very badly, to find *Orchis militaris*.

The Military Orchid ... For some reason the name had captured my imagination. At this period – about 1916 – most little boys wanted to be soldiers, and I suppose I was no exception. The Military Orchid had taken on a kind of legendary quality, its image seemed fringed with the mysterious and exciting appurtenances of soldiering, its name was like a distant bugle-call, thrilling and rather sad, a *cor au fond du bois*. The idea of a soldier, I think, had come to represent for me a whole complex of virtues which I knew that I lacked, yet wanted to possess: I was timid, a coward at games, terrified of the aggressively masculine, totemistic life of the boys at school; yet I secretly desired, above all things, to be like other people. These ideas had somehow become incarnated in *Orchis militaris*.

But alas! according to Edward Step, the Military Orchid occurred only in Oxfordshire, Berkshire, Buckinghamshire and Hertfordshire, and I lived in Kent. True, there was said to be a subspecies, *O. simia*, the Monkey Orchid, 'with narrower divisions of the *crimson* lip, occurring in the same counties as the type, with the addition of Kent'. But if Mr Bundock's orchid was not the Military, still less could it be the Monkey; its lip was not crimson, but, on the contrary, pale rose-coloured or nearly white, and spotted with purple. Moreover, the sepals and petals were striped and stippled with dark purplish-brown, which fitted with Step's description of *Orchis purpurea*. Furthermore, the Great Brown-Winged Orchid was said to grow in 'Kent and Sussex only'. Judging by Edward Step, Mr Bundock's orchid was, beyond the shadow of a doubt, *Orchis purpurea*.

And yet ... and yet ... if only it could be *Orchis militaris!* After all, if one could trust Colonel Mackenzie, it *was* the Military. So far as he was concerned, there was no such thing as a Great Brown-Winged Orchid. All I had to do was to ignore Edward

Step, and pin my faith to Colonel Mackenzie. The Colonel, more-over, provided an additional loophole for my conscience: in *his* description, there was no nonsense about Oxfordshire and Berk-shire; he merely contented himself with saying that the plant was 'rare in spring', and grew 'in chalky districts only and not always there'. Consequently, since Kent was chalky, the Military Orchid might be expected to occur there ...

I repeated to myself the statements of each writer, till they sang in my mind like incantations. 'Rare in spring: in chalky districts only, and not always there.' The words beckoned like a far bugle, remote and melancholy beyond mysterious hills ... Yes, it *must* be the Military ...

So Edward Step was firmly closed and put away, and I basked in the glory of having found (or at least been told where to find) the Military Orchid. Another book which was presented to me at this time – *British Wild Flowers*, by W. Graveson – confirmed my decisnon, the author relating how he had found the 'Military Orchid' in the Kentish woods. (No doubt, like Colonel Mackenzie, he considered *O. purpurea* to be the same as *O. militaris*.)

Conscience, however, triumphed in the end, and I had to admit that Mr Bundock's Orchid was not the Military but the Great Brown-Winged. Edward Step, after all, could hardly have inven-ted *Orchis purpurea* out of sheer malice. No, the Military Orchid, alas! was still unfound.

And it still is – at least by me, and, I imagine, for the last forty years, by anybody else. For *Orchis militaris* is one of several British plants which have mysteriously become extinct, or very nearly so. The last reliable record for it dates from 1902, when it was found in Oxfordshire. An unconfirmed report does, indeed, state that it occurred near Deal, in 1910. But botanists are sceptical about Kentish records for *O. militaris*; Edward Step, after all, was prob-ably right ...

As for Colonel Mackenzie, I am prepared to bet that he had never seen either the Military or the Brown-Winged – nor, for that matter, the 'subspecies known as the Monkey Orchid' which nowadays, raised to the status of a species, and more fortunate than its Military relation, still survives in a single locality in Ox-fordshire: the exact spot being a closely-guarded secret, known only to a few botanists.

The Colonel, of course, was partly justified in his omission of the Brown-Winged and the Monkey; his list of species, no doubt, was based on early editions of Bentham and Hooker, and consequently (more or less) on the original classification of Linnaeus, who 'lumped' *O. militaris, purpurea* and *simia* together as a single species. So I could have said, had I but known, that in identifying Mr Bundock's orchid as the Military, I was merely following the example of Linnaeus. I am still, I must confess, in my less conscientious moments half-inclined to yield to the temptation.

II

No psycho-analyst, so far as I know, has yet attempted to explain the love of flowers in Freudian terms. Art has long since been reduced to its true status – a mere function of the neurotic personality; the young Mozart presents a perfectly clear clinical picture. Even the scientist can be explained away, I suppose, in Adlerian terms, as a victim of organic inferiority. But the botanophil – the unscientific lover of flowers, as opposed to the professional botanist – remains a mystery. It may be that his singular passion is a relic of totemism; flowers, perhaps, provide a lodgement for the External Soul, thereby rendering the body invulnerable against all perils, magical or otherwise. Doubtless, the matter will be cleared up before long; but – happily, perhaps for its adherents – the cult of botanophily has been so far neglected by investigators.

Often, but not always, the botanophil is precocious. A family legend relates that myself, at the age of four, could identify by name any or all of the coloured plates in Edward Step's *Wayside and Woodland Blossoms*. For the truth of this I cannot vouch; but my own memory testifies to the fact that I could perform this disgustingly precocious feat two or three years later. By that time I had learnt to read; and, not content with the English names, I memorized many of the Latin and Greek ones as well. Some of these (at the age of 8) I conceitedly incorporated into a school-essay at the day-school in Folkestone which I attended. The headmaster read the essay aloud to the school (no wonder I was unpopular); but this flattering tribute was mitigated by his pronunciation of the names. My knowledge of Latin had scarcely

progressed beyond the present indicative of *Amo*; for flower-
names I had my own pronunciation, and the headmaster's version
of them came as a shock. I still utter the specific name of the Bee
Orchid – *apifera* – with a slight feeling of flouting my own convictions. I realize now, that the accent *is* on the second syllable, but
my own inclination would still put it on the third.

Why, without any particular encouragement, should flowers,
rather than stamps, butterflies or birds' eggs, have become my
ruling passion? True, I flirted, throughout my childhood, with
butterflies, tame grass-snakes, home-made fireworks; but flowers
were my first love and seem likely to be my last.

Here I had better confess (since this book is largely about
flowers) that, not only am I not a true botanist, but that even as a
botanophil I am a specialist in the worst sense. Whole tracts of the
subject leave me cold: certain Natural Orders or Genera frankly
bore me, and always will – the *Chenopodiaceae*, for example, or
those tedious *Hieracii*, or the Chickweeds. Recently I went with a
real botanist to the Sandwich Golf-links, celebrated for a number
of rare plants; it was a chilly afternoon in spring, and no weather
to dawdle unless for a very good reason. My friend was in pursuit
of a rare Chickweed – or one, at any rate, that was rare in Kent –
and every few yards would throw himself flat on his face and
remain there, making minute comparisons, while the glacial sea-
wind penetrated my clothes and reduced me to a state of frozen
irritability. I could almost realize, on this occasion, how boring
botanists must be to non-botanists. Yet had the elusive Chickweed
been, say a rare or critical Marsh Orchid, I would have risked
pneumonia with as much enthusiasm as my botanist friend. A rare
Broomrape – *Orobanche caryophyllacea* – was indeed said to
grow half-a-mile away, and I was as anxious to see it as my friend
was to identify his Chickweed. Why? The Broomrapes are not
notably beautiful. The Clove-scented one is very rare, certainly;
but mere rarity is not enough – the Chickweed was rare, too. If the
love of flowers itself is hard to explain, still harder is it to account
for the peculiar attraction of certain plants or groups of plants.

Most obvious, of course, is the appeal of the *Orchidaceae*. It is
easy enough to see the attraction of those floral aristocrats, with
their equivocal air of belonging partly to the vegetable, partly to
the animal kingdom. Myself yielded to their seduction at an un-

naturally early age. But Broomrapes? Chickweeds? There seems no reasonable explanation.

For non-professionals, like myself, such prejudices condition the extent of such little true botanical knowledge as we may possess. I know something about the flower-structure of the Orchids, because I happen to like them, and a minimum of technical knowledge is necessary to identify the more critical species. But ask me to explain by what similarities of internal structure a Delphinium is placed in the same Natural Order as a Buttercup, and I am stumped. Yet I like the *Ranunculaceae*. To find either of the two Hellebores is always a major thrill – particularly *Helleborus foetidus*, the Setterwort, that august and seldom haunter of a few south-country chalk-hills. One of my cherished ambitions is to see the truly wild Monkshood in the few places where it is still said to survive; and another is to find in England the wild Larkspur which I have seen growing as a cornfield-weed in Italy. The *Ranunculaceae*, however, as a family, just fail to excite me sufficiently to overcome my ignorance about their internal affairs. I admire them as I once heard a certain French lady, at Cassis, confessing that she admired the proletariat: '*J'adore les ouvriers*,' she declared, '*mais de loin, de loin*.'

III

I suppose for many people, as for myself, some childhood-scene tends to become archetypal, the hidden source of all one's private imagery, tinging the most banal and quotidian words and objects with its distinct yet often unrecognized flavour. For me the village where we spent my childhood summers, where Mr Bundock lurked like a wood-spirit in the warm, tree-muffled evenings, has this quality of legend. Certain basic, ordinary words such as 'wood', 'stream', 'village', in whatever context I may use them, will always, for me, evoke a particular wood, a particular stream, almost always in the immediate neighbourhood of our summer-cottage.

For some people, I suppose, such words have become entirely abstracted from any such archetypal images – mere generic names for natural features. One might divide the human race into those who develop this power of abstraction and those who don't; it would probably serve as well as a good many other artificial categories. I have read somewhere that the more primitive languages have no generic name for, say, a tree or a camel; each individual camel or tree has to be given a name of its own as required. Children, like other savages, develop the 'abstracting' faculty slowly; many, like myself, never fully develop it at all.

A word which, more than most, evokes for me that Kentish village, is the word 'afternoon'. The cool, green, slumberous syllables refuse to be detached from the cottage-garden, drowsing among its trees, the tea-table laid in the shade, the buzzing of wasps busy among the fallen plums – a subdued, perpetual bourdon orchestrating the shriller melodic line of birdsong and the voices of children. In memory, the village seems held in a perpetual trance of summer afternoons: possibly for no better reason than that we seldom visited it in the winter. Half-hidden by trees and (in those days) remote in its valley, the little street with its scattered houses, its squat-towered church and its slate-roofed Victorian pub was still comparatively 'undiscovered'. A celebrated Jacobean divine had ended his days in the rectory; in the closing years of my childhood, an eminent novelist inhabited the dower-house, a pleasant early-nineteenth-century building near the church; these were the village's only claim to fame. But even in my earliest childhood the bourgeois invasion had begun – my family, indeed, formed part of the vanguard – and nowadays the number of cottages inhabited by land-workers is in a small minority. The lanes and hedges, today, have become scrupulously tidy; the grass in the churchyard is punctually cut; the cottages have sprouted new wings, carefully disguised by expensive 'weathered' tiles; the dower-house is to be pulled down; and the eminent novelist is commemorated by a bogus-Tudor porch tacked on to the parish Hall. The village, in fact, is fast becoming a garden-suburb.

But it was not only words which were to become permanently associated with that particular childhood background. Whole tracts of experience – certain types of landscape, certain phrases and passages of music, innumerable smells, particular ways of speech became for me (and remained) imprinted indelibly with the same atmosphere of a summer afternoon. The process of identification began early: when my Nurse read Beatrix Potter aloud, and still more when I had learnt to read myself, the landscape of *Mr Tod* and *Jemima Puddleduck* seemed indistinguishable from the landscape of our village. I knew the track which Tommy Brock took through the wood, when he made off with the rabbit-babies: it was none other than the path, fringed with bluebells, through the copse which we called Teazel Wood. The hillside where Cottontail lived with her black husband was the park behind the big Queen Anne manor house ... 'The sun was still warm and slanting on the hill-pastures' – how well I recognized the description! Tommy Brock's abduction of the baby rabbits, the agonized pursuit by Benjamin Bunny and Peter Rabbit – the whole long-drawn and tragic tale was for me bound up (and indeed still is) with a landscape which I knew and loved. Reason (and Miss Margaret Lane[1]) tell me, nowadays, that the scene of Beatrix Potter's stories was really Westmorland; none the less, the path through Teazel Wood is still haunted, for me, by Tommy Brock and the foxy-whiskered gentleman.

I have wondered, too, lately, why when re-reading Ronald Firbank, I should so often be reminded of Miss Trumpett; and can only conclude that the peculiarly gushing, late-Edwardian conversational style which characterizes so much of his dialogue (especially in the early *Vainglory*) is for me an echo of tea-parties at the cottage where, like an exotic bird, plumed with crimson or scarlet, Miss Trumpett would suddenly appear and hold me spellbound by such a vision of sophisticated elegance as I had never beheld before in my life.

If Mr Bundock haunted the village-evenings with his mops and buckets and disinfectants, it was Miss Trumpett who was the presiding genius of the afternoons. Tea-time was her hour: I cannot believe that I ever saw her in the morning, though in the nature of things I must have done. Of Creole extraction, her mother had married a well-off English solicitor; the Trumpetts had, indeed, become more English than the Royal family: their very Englishness was excessive, and served to enhance their innate exoticism.

Miss Trumpett, as I remember her, was (perhaps consciously) slightly Beardsley: full-lipped, with powdered cheeks of a peculiarly thick, granular texture, and raven-black frizzy hair. She affected clothes, too, which put the village in a flutter: on summer

1 *The Tale of Beatrix Potter* by Margaret Lane. F. Warne, 1946.

afternoons she would appear in gowns worthy of Ascot, and wearing an immense hat of crimson or vermilion, and scarlet shoes (like Oriane de Guermantes). A scarlet umbrella completed the ensemble; or, at other times, a paper parasol which I was assured in awed tones, was authentically 'Burmese'. (The idea of Burma is associated for me, to this day, with the curious 'tacky' texture and resinous smell of Miss Trumpett's parasol.) Her whole personality seemed to have a velvety bloom which, with her richly-powdered cheeks, suggested to me an auricula. I was entirely fascinated; all the more so, since Miss Trumpett had a slight flavour of forbidden fruit.

Nothing very scandalous; but rumour (and something more than rumour) said that she had settled in the village to 'catch' a certain well-off bachelor who owned one of the two 'big' houses. Poor Miss Trumpett! She never caught her man; but she remained, for my Nurse, who strongly disapproved of her, 'that naughty Miss T'. Her naughtiness, I fancy, consisted chiefly in her clothes and her general air of 'smartness'; she was, ever so slightly, 'fast'. I should conjecture that she was, in fact, completely virtuous; she was certainly extremely conventional in her tastes, with a passion for bridge which was sometimes indulged in the company of my parents (for the most modest of points – she would never have consented, any more than Mrs Hurstpierpoint in *Valmouth*, to play for '*immodest*' ones).

No, there was nothing very 'naughty' about Miss Trumpett; but the word, with its tang of Edwardian gaieties, is fitting enough. She was my first contact with the exotic: her clothes, her Latin-American ancestry, her putative wickedness, contributed something to the effect she had upon me; but what I remember chiefly is her voice – rich, resonant, with the same velvety, powdery texture as her outward appearance. Her conversation was enlivened with the *argot* (already rather dated at this period) of Edwardian *chic*. Phrases like 'too divine' or 'divvy' – unknown in my family circle – fell on my ears with an effect of alien and slightly immoral elegance. She would speak slightingly of something or somebody as 'very *mere*'. Once, at tea, when I announced that I was 'full', she pulled me up sharply: it was rude to say that, she told me. If I *must* announce the fact, I ought to say '*Je suis rempli*'. She was free with her French phrases; and this, my first contact with the language, was to confer upon it, for all time, a certain imprint of

exoticism, something of the elegant, powdered, auricula-like quality of Miss Trumpett herself.

She was a great reader; in her cottage were ranged (among
palms and fire-screens and unseasonable flowers) the complete
works of Meredith; a little later it was Henry James; later still,
Galsworthy. She played the piano, too, and sang: rattling off *The
Vision of Salome* or some new and fashionable tango with great
spirit, or singing *Every Morn I Bring Thee Violets* or *Sweetest Li'l
Feller* in a voice which invested the songs with an air of *mondain*
luxury and splendour, an atmosphere of plush, mimosa and the
Edwardian jollifications of Homburg or Monte Carlo.

One night, greatly daring, I walked round the garden with her
by moonlight: it was my first romantic encounter. Had it been the
Jersey Lily herself or la belle Otéro I could not have been more
thrilled. I paid for the experience in the acute embarrassment
which I suffered on returning to my Nurse. Contemptuous, she
said nothing; but her disapproval was all too obvious . . . I did not
repeat the exploit. Obscurely, perhaps, I felt that I wasn't cut out
for such as Miss Trumpett; her world was too alien, too romantically remote.

Nor, it seemed, was I cut out for her young nephew and niece
who, with their parents, took a cottage in the village that summer
or the next. They were pretty and well-behaved children, excessively polite and even more conventional than their aunt. I loathed
them. In vain did our respective parents seek to engineer an al-
liance: I would have none of it. In the company of the little Trumpetts I became more shy, more ill-behaved and in general more
unpleasant than I was by nature. I preferred the children of a local
farmer, Mr Igglesden; they were, indeed, my only friends, and I
was happy with them. The little Trumpetts showed no inclination
(fortunately for me) to fraternize with the Igglesdens; so I was
able, in time, to avoid the bourgeoisie entirely and to throw in my
lot with the working-class. This phase in my political evolution
was speeded-up considerably when, at one of my unavoidable encounters with the Trumpett children, their mother overheard me
explaining to Mary Trumpett the difference between a male and
female tiger-moth. Thenceforth I was considered a corrupt
influence, and encouraged no further.

But before the final split, the Trumpetts did prove of some value
after all. One evening, coming back from a picnic in the woods,

they showed me an unusual flower they had found. It was a year or two since Mr Bundock had brought me the orchid which had provoked in me such an acute moral conflict; moreover, I had never managed to find it for myself. Now, in the plant found by the little Trumpetts, I recognized Mr Bundock's mysterious orchid. This time, I received exact directions about the locality; and shortly afterwards, in a copse only half a mile from the village, I was able to find it for myself. It was not the Military Orchid – I had long ago, reluctantly, abandoned that idea, in spite of Colonel Mackenzie. But it *was* the Brown-Winged – or, as it is more pleasantly called, the Lady Orchid; the most regal of British orchids, and perhaps the loveliest of English wildflowers: its tall pagodas of brown-hooded, white-lipped blossoms towering grandly, like some alien visitor, exotic as Miss Trumpett at a village tea-party, above the fading bluebells and the drab thickets of dog's-mercury, in a wood which I had known all my childhood, but whose distinguished inhabitant I had never before discovered.

IV

If the village of our summer holidays was an afternoon-land, tranced in a perpetual and postprandial drowsiness, our real home, at Sandgate, was by contrast matutinal: my memories of it are bathed in the keen, windy light of spring mornings, a seaside gaiety and brilliance haunted by the thud of waves on the shingle and the tang of seaweed. At the time, Sandgate lacked romance, being merely the place where we lived (my father had his business in the neighbouring town of Folkestone); during the autumn and winter, the village became for me a Land of Lost Content, the symbol of a happiness which would only be renewed again in the spring. (With most children, this state of affairs is reversed: it is the seaside which enshrines the memory of summer-happiness, not, as for me, the country.) Later, in adolescence, Sandgate too would become part of the legend of the past, the private myth; but in childhood, it was the village in the Elham Valley which, alone, possessed the quality of romance. When I began to write, at about fifteen, I naturally turned to the valley-village for the background of my stories. But that country-legend had, after all, grown up with me; from earliest days I had surrounded the valley landscape with an aura of sentimental nostalgia, and in consequence, my adolescent recollections of it were apt to seem rather second-hand – mere memories of memories; my attempts to write about it seemed over-stylized and at the same time too facile. Some small episode, trivial as Proust's madeleine-dipped-in-tea, must have accidentally evoked Sandgate for me at about that time and the whole atmosphere and flavour of our seaside home was recalled as Combray was for Proust: vivid and immediate, springing nakedly from the past without the swaddling of conscious sentimentality which had obscured my recollections of our country village.

Our house was on the Undercliff: behind it, the cliff rose steeply to the Folkestone Leas; below, a garden descended in terraces to the beach. The house, from the road, presented an undistinguished façade of grey cement; at the back, however (on the seaward-facing side), it was faced with white stucco, and the windows were fitted with green *persiennes*, giving to the house an oddly Mediterranean air. The tamarisks in the garden (and an occasional stone-pine) added to this illusion of meridional gaiety. Had I but known it, the rest of the flora, too, provided curious parallels with that of the Mediterranean seaboard. Stationed at Ancona during the War, I was repeatedly struck by the number of plants which I remembered as growing at Sandgate: Horned Poppy, Bristly Ox-tongue, Tree-mallow, Henbane. (The maritime flora is, in fact, singularly uniform from Northern to Southern Europe.) Walking on the cliffs by the Adriatic, I might have fancied myself back at Sandgate: till the scattered stars of pink anemones, or a glimpse of an outlying cornfield carpeted with wild red tulips, recalled me to a sense of reality.

One summer – I think it was 1916 – a miracle occurred: the cliffs above our house were carpeted, in July, with the brilliant blue spikes of Viper's Bugloss. The plant was common enough on the cliffs, but had never occurred in anything like such quantity: nor has it ever done so since. The other day, travelling up by the Portsmouth line from Petersfield, I saw near Liphook, for only the second time in my life, the miracle repeated: a field covered, as thickly as if with bluebells, by that noble and stately flower. The blue is of a brighter shade than that of bluebells: in the July sun it seems positively to sizzle and splutter, like a blue Bengal light.

I know of no reason for these occasional displays by the Bugloss: they appear to be as irregular and unpredictable as (in Southern latitudes) the Aurora Borealis. But the year 1916 was, I suspect, something of an *annus mirabilis* for botanists; or do I imagine so merely because I myself was lucky? Henbane was one of my finds that year: not a great rarity, but often appearing sporadically, and disappearing again completely from the locality for a period of years. Its creamy flowers, veined with purple, and the clammy, corpse-like texture of its leaves, impressed me at the time with an agreeable sense of Evil. The Mandrake itself is a fairly harmless-looking plant; it is a pity that the name, with all its Satanic associations, cannot be transferred to the Henbane. (Is Henbane the 'Hebanon' of *Hamlet*? Nobody seems to know.) In practice, if not in theory, flower-names are oddly interchangeable. Many non-botanists, for instance, are convinced that they know the Deadly Nightshade when they see it; but in nine cases out of ten, the plant they are thinking of proves to be the Woody Nightshade, or Bitter-sweet. It is useless to tell them that the Woody Nightshade, that first-cousin of the potato, is not only not deadly, but scarcely even poisonous at all: they are convinced that it is lethal, and if shown the true Deadly Nightshade, a rare-ish plant of southern chalk-down, will refuse to believe you. It is a mistake that never fails to irritate me, detracting as it does from the sinister dignity of a plant which has a good claim to be the chief villain of the British Flora: a plant 'so furious and deadly' (as Gerarde remarks) that it is just as well it is not commoner than it is.

Another 'find' of 1916 was the Coltsfoot: it seems incredible that I had not found it before. But I had formed the mistaken idea that it was a rarity, and therefore, presumably by a kind of in-verted wishful-thinking, was simply unable to see it. The mistake arose through a mis-reading of Edward Step's account of the plant, which refers to a dubious variety recorded by Don from 'the high mountains of Clova'. This statement was taken, by me, to refer to the common Coltsfoot; and doubtless because of the romantic sound of the 'high mountains of Clova', I conceived a passion for the plant. I dreamt of Coltsfoot, I insisted on my Nurse purchasing some Coltsfoot-rock at a chemist's, I copied Edward Step's plate of it in washy watercolours.

Then one day a teacher at my first day-school happened to mention that it grew on the foreshore at Seabrook, near Sandgate.

On a March morning I set out to look for it: not really believing that a plant hailing from the 'high mountains of Clova' could grow half-a-mile from my own door. But there, on the shingle-flats by the beginning of the Hythe Military Canal – there, no more than a stone's throw from the sea, in a spot I must have passed a dozen times before – there was the Coltsfoot, its golden ruffs wide-spread in the morning sun, abundant as any dandelion and per-fectly at home. I was delighted; the discovery made me happy for weeks afterwards. But somehow, after that, the Coltsfoot lost some of its romance. Like a new and unusual word, encountered for the first time, which one is sure to meet again within a day or two, I soon began to see the Coltsfoot everywhere.

Yet Coltsfoot has not, even today, entirely lost the romantic aura with which I at one time invested it. Seeing it from a train, precociously ablaze on some chalky embankment, or even straying up the sidings to the edge of some suburban platform, I still find myself cherishing a superstitious belief that the seeds must have blown there from the romantic heights of Clova.

I have never been to Clova: I don't even know where it is. For me it belongs in the same category as the Zemmery Fidd and the Great Gromboolian Plain. Similarly, I am inclined to be sceptical about the existence of Mayo and Galway. Here I think Colonel Mackenzie is to blame again; for those romantic-sounding counties were for me merely the home of *Habenaria intacta*, or, as it is called nowadays, *Neotinea intacta*, the Dense-spiked Orchid. Unlike the Coltsfoot, *Neotinea* preserved its romantic aloofness, and refused to oblige me by occurring at Sandgate. But having found the mysterious denizen of Clova almost, so to speak, at my backdoor, I saw no reason why the Entire Habenaria (thus it was crudely Englished) should not turn up too.

I lived in hopes: the 'Habenaria' shared some of the glamour of *Orchis militaris*. It must have been in the year 1916 that Mr Bun-dock brought me the Lady Orchid; and it was in 1916, too, I am almost sure, that I was first taken to The Hills.

They were referred to as 'The Hills' – those low downs behind Folkestone, knobbly and broken in outline by barrows and earth-works – rather as dwellers in the plains of India speak of Simla, though not (at least by my family) with any desire to visit them. Indeed, my mother insisted that they were 'very dull', and the long-promised expedition to Sugarloaf or Caesar's Camp was for one reason or another delayed from year to year. Our walks took us almost to the foot of them: they loomed grey and austere against the sky, ringed with their concentric terraces trodden by grazing cattle. Beyond them lay The Country – a country which, in fact, I knew, but which, cut off by that high, forbidden barrier, seemed immensely romantic and mysterious.

At last I heard from somebody that the Bee Orchid grew on Sugarloaf. I refused to be baulked any longer, and one June morning we set off: taking the scarlet East Kent bus from Coolinge Lane, traversing the Sandgate Road and the mean streets beyond the Town Hall, till at last we began to climb the Canterbury hill. The bus dropped us at the Black Bull – a pub which in those days marked the fringes of the town. A sign hung from it, inscribed with the magical words 'Nalder and Collyer's Entire'. Entire what? I still don't know. The adjective seemed to flap, mysteriously, in the air, demanding its appropriate substantive. I soon supplied one. Nalder and Collyer's became linked, for me, with *Habenaria intacta*, the Entire Habenaria. The Black Bull sign seemed a good omen. (Alas! the Black Bull, today, is 'Entire' no more, and the sign, unromantically, announces the ownership of Messrs Ind, Coope and Allsopp.)

We walked up the hill through the hot June morning, the air heavy with chalk-dust and petrol. Just beyond the Black Bull, a farm with a thatched barn and outhouses huddled among the raw new villas, its smell of dung bravely combating the town-smells – the stink of petrol, dust, pubs; an outpost of the country overtaken and nearly submerged by the licking tentacles of suburb. We left the main road by the track skirting the foot of the hills: there was a sudden muffling of traffic-noises, a country-silence murmurous with the hum of bees and the scraping of grasshoppers. We crossed a field, climbed a stile, and entered the Promised Land at last – the mysterious, hitherto-forbidden land of The Hills.

Against the hot blue sky, the terraced knoll loomed enormous, its summit lost in a shimmering heat-haze. The grassy flanks seemed to radiate a reflected heat, enfolding us in a weighted, thyme-scented silence, enhanced rather than disturbed by the monotone of a thousand insects. On the banks at the hill's foot, the cropped turf was gemmed with the small downland flowers, many of which I had never seen before: rockrose, milkwort, centaury. In that moment, I encountered a new Love – the chalkdown flora: a Love to which I have always remained faithful. Most botanists have their ecological preferences; and though I have had brief spells of infidelity with peat-bogs, with sand-dunes or even with wealden clay, the downs remain my Cynara, and I still return to them with some of the pristine delight of that first visit to The Hills.

A miniature chalkpit dazzled our eyes a little way up the hill. Running ahead, I paused near the edge of it: a plant had caught my eye, a flower with pink petals on which a bee seemed to be resting. Suddenly I realized that this was the goal of our pilgrimage; like Langhorne,

> 'I sought the living bee to find
> And found the picture of a bee.'

Yes, there was no doubt of it: a single plant, standing stiff and aloof, bearing proudly aloft its extraordinary insect-flowers, like archaic jewels rifled from some tomb; I had found the Bee Orchid.

As it happened, I added, that day, a greater rarity to my collection than I suspected. True, I had found the Bee Orchid, which was exciting enough. But years later, looking through pressed specimens of 'Bee Orchids' labelled 'Sugarloaf, 1916', some of them proved, beyond a doubt, to be not the Bee Orchid at all, but the Late Spider (*Ophrys arachnites*) – one of the rarest of British orchids, confined to a few localities in East Kent. Like the Lady, the Late Spider was not even mentioned by Colonel Mackenzie; Edward Step did refer to it, in passing, as a 'subspecies', but I was bored by such hair-splitting. To have found the Bee Orchid was good enough for me.

The Late Spider, nowadays, is of course considered a 'good' species; but it has, unfortunately, become much more rare. It resembles the Bee, but has a fuller, more swollen lip, and the 'sting' (supposing a spider to have a sting) projects forward, instead of being recurved, as in the Bee. It was not surprising that I failed to recognize it: I have known botanists who have lived near the Late Spider localities all their lives, and yet are unable to distinguish the two species.

Another insect-orchid was said to haunt the Folkestone hills – the Drone Orchid, a variety of the Early Spider; I must have first

read about it in one or another of the works of Anne Pratt. I found
the Early Spider in due course, but the Drone eluded me. No
wonder: for it is no longer 'accepted' by most botanists as a good
variety and is probably a myth.

How many people, nowadays, remember Anne Pratt? She is
hardly to be included among the 'classical' botanists; yet, if less
illustrious than Brown, Babington, Hooker and other of her contemporaries, she scarcely deserves the oblivion into which she
seems to have fallen. So far as I know, no memoir of her exists; one
still comes across her works in second-hand bookshops, but they
must all have been long out-of-print. Her *magnum opus* in four
volumes, *Flowering Plants, Grasses, Sedges and Ferns of Great
Britain* is certainly somewhat out-of-date from a strictly botanical
point of view. But it is still an excellent bedside-book. It is leisurely
and discursive; the botanical literature of several centuries is ran-
sacked for tit-bits of plant-lore; there are innumerable excursions,
often extremely entertaining, into folk-lore, herbal medicine and
so on. Nor are the Arts forgotten: the verses quoted, in praise of or
in connection with plants would, if collected, form an instructive
anthology, not only of botanical verse, but of forgotten minor
verse in general. Bishop Mant (who was he?) is perhaps the most
often quoted; but many of the poems were written, so the author
tells us, 'especially for this work'.

Erudite and allusive as she is, however, it is in her more personal
moments that Miss Pratt is at her best. Hearing, for instance, that
'the root of our native Catmint, if chewed, will make the most
gentle persons fierce and wrathful', she decides, with a com-
mendable scientific curiosity, to verify the statement. 'The writer
of these pages, who, with a friend who joined in the experiment,
chewed a piece of this bitter and aromatic substance, of the length
of a finger, is able ... to assure her readers that for at least four-
and-twenty hours after taking it, both she and her companion
retained a perfect equanimity of temper and feeling.'

It would have taken more than Catmint, one feels, to impair the
equanimity of Miss Pratt. One pictures her as middle-aged, sensible and humorous, immensely energetic, and quite undaunted by
the weather, gamekeepers, spiked fences and other such obstacles
to the pursuit of her profession. From internal evidence, it appears
that she lived at or near Dover: there are innumerable references

to the Flora of the Dover Cliffs, and a number of the plants she mentions as growing there can still be found in the same locality – for example, the wild Cabbage and Nottingham Catchfly. (Others, such as the Dwarf Orchis, have alas! become rare since her day.)

Miss Pratt, in fact, emerges as a glorified (and professionalized) version of a type: the Victorian lady-botanist. She was more industrious, more energetic than most, and turned her knowledge to professional use; but she remains an amateur, none the less: a cultivated lady of the period, with an eminently suitable and 'educational' hobby.

Her book has a special charm for those who, like myself, have a taste for odd and mainly useless scraps of information. It is pleasant, for instance, to learn that Antonius Musa, physician to the Emperor Augustus, 'wrote a whole book setting forth the excellences of Betony, which he said would cure forty-seven disorders'; or, of the Roman Nettle, that Julius Caesar's legionaries, 'having heard much of the coldness of our climate, thought it was not to be endured without some friction that might warm their blood; they therefore used this nettle to warm and chafe their benumbed limbs'. And again, of the ordinary Nettle (not the Roman one): 'We have ourselves in childhood often supped off a dish of nettle-tops boiled for about twenty minutes and eaten with salt and vinegar.' The authoress remarks that they 'seemed delicious', but cautiously adds that 'their flavour may have been improved by the fact of their having been gathered during a long country walk, and by our having watched them during the process of cooking'.

Miss Pratt is a great one for local nomenclature; and, not content with English names, she more often than not supplies half-a-dozen foreign ones as well. Thus Herb Paris, she tells us, is in France called *Parisette* (a name which somehow suggests Mistinguett and the old Moulin Rouge), *Raisin de Renard* and *Etrangle Loup*; in Germany it is *Einbeere*, and in Italy *Uva di Volpe*. Of the Sun-spurge, she remarks that the old herbalists called it Sun Tithymale, while the Dutch name for it is Wolfenmilch; and in England it is known variously as Churn-staff, Wartweed, Cat's-milk, Wolf's-milk and Littlegood.

Here is a specimen of the occasional verse 'written for our volume' – in this case by Calder Campbell:

> 'October winds were drifting yellow leaves
> From wintering trees – October waves rose high
> Against the barren shores of Calais, where
> I stood and mark'd the stormy sea that frown'd
> 'Neath frowning skies. "Is there no hope?" quoth I . . .[2]

And so on for a further twenty-eight lines, in which the poet's melancholy is finally cheered by the discovery of the Sea Buckthorn.

One would like, too, to try some of Miss Pratt's less-familiar herbal beverages – for instance, Wild Marjoram Tea, which she tells us 'is very grateful and refreshing, and doubtless is wholesome, though its efficacy in preserving health may be somewhat overated by country people'. Less successful, among her experiments in country-recipes, was the use of the Lesser Celandine as a vegetable. The leaves, she tells us, were 'formerly boiled and eaten; but the author, who has tried their worth, cannot say much in their favour'.

But if Miss Pratt was prepared to experiment with the gastronomic uses of plants, her attitude to the darker side of plant-lore was one of rational but pious scepticism. Quoting Ben Jonson's Witches' Song, in connection with the Horned Poppy, she cannot resist a slightly complacent reference to the decline of superstition. 'The light of Revelation,' (she writes) 'which has dawned now on every British village, and brought its teachings to hall and cottage, has dispelled fancies and practices which were sanctioned in other times, and none dream now of gathering the poppy for incantations.'

Pious, cultivated, sensible, immensely energetic – one would like to have known Miss Pratt. One imagines her setting forth, on some summer's afternoon in the 'fifties, perhaps escorted by some frock-coated clergyman, or by the friend who shared in the Catmint experiment, sensibly-clad, minutely observant, humorously deprecating the vestiges of superstition among the villagers, and always ready, by an appropriate word here or there, to assist in spreading the Light of Revelation. Toiling over the Dover Cliffs for *Silene nutans* wading through the marshes about Sandwich for the Greater Spearwort, or searching 'in the woodlands or on the bushy hill' for *Orchis purpurea* – one sees her, indomitable but incurably lady-like, pursuing her purposeful way through the Kentish countryside, her tweeded figure bathed in the warm, golden light of a Victorian Sunday afternoon in summer. One almost feels that, like the Scholar Gipsy, she may yet haunt, at sunset, the hillsides of Kearsney and Alkam, behind Dover, or those remoter woodlands about Nonington or Womenswold; laden, no doubt, with a 'store of flowers'—

> the frail-leaf'd white anemone,
> Dark bluebells drench'd with dews of summer eves,
> And purple orchises with spotted leaves . . .

Or possibly some rare fern or rush, or Herb Paris ('which the French call *Parisette*') or Hemp Agrimony which is called in Russia *Griwa Kouskaja*, or Marjoram to brew a 'grateful and refreshing' tea . . . And it is not improbable, either, that

> Far on the forest-skirts, where none pursue,
> On some mild pastoral slope . . .

she may have stumbled, quite accidentally, in the darkening shade, upon the Military Orchid itself.

v

1916, if it was an *annus mirabilis* for botany, was also, for me, the end of a Golden Age; for in this year I started to go to school. It was the beginning of a process which was to last nearly twelve years, during which I certainly suffered more acutely than I ever have since. The best thing one can say, I suppose, for the (bourgeois) English educational system is that it immunizes one to a great extent against subsequent horrors. I had cause to be grateful for it, at least, in the Army, where one saw the State-educated soldier, uprooted from the home-environment for the first time in his life, suffering all the torments of homesickness which I had endured – and more or less come to terms with – at the age of eleven.

My initiation into school-life, however, in 1916, was sufficiently mild: I was not sent to a boarding-school, but merely to a Kindergarten attached to a large and flourishing local girls' school, called Gaudeamus. This, moreover, I attended only in the mornings; so that Gaudeamus, for me, exists in memory as a morning-world, its rooms bathed perpetually in the early sunlight. I cannot imagine what it looked like in the afternoon: I am inclined to think that, like E. M. Forster's cow, it simply wasn't there.

The school stood beneath the cliffs, and the garden and playground, fringed with glaucous, billowing tamarisks, abutted on the beach. Within, the rooms seemed enormous, their high windows and polished floors reflecting the morning glare of sunlight, and echoing perpetually with the thud and hiss of the waves on the shingle.

Gaudeamus, as its name implied, inculcated a breezy and strenuous optimism. Miss Pinecoffin, its founder, had 'advanced' ideas, and had even been heard to speak in favour of co-education; but there was nothing revolutionary about Gaudeamus, and co-education was confined to the Kindergarten. The girls might wear djibbahs, but there was no nonsense about Montessori or the Laboratory system: their education was soundly based on the School Certificate, the Higher Local and the Church of England. With such a firm basis of orthodoxy, Miss Pinecoffin could afford to spread herself a little in the matter of environment; and the interior decoration of Gaudeamus represented all that was most respectably artistic and 'progressive' at the turn of the century. Corot and Greuze hung on the walls, and Rossetti's *Beata Beatrix* in muddy monochrome; in the green-tiled fireplaces stood bulging jars of beaten copper, filled, in summer, with yellow flags or foxgloves. The singular flora of *Art Nouveau* – sprawling water-lilies and *fleurs-de-lis* – burgeoned unexpectedly in corners; the chairs were all of an exceedingly uncomfortable, neo-Morrissy pattern, with high backs bored, in the centre, with curious heart-shaped holes. The heavy oak doorways (opening by means of enormous and cumbrous wooden latches) were provided with latticed panels of thick green glass. The rooms seemed always cold; yet, despite the supplies of fresh air, a faint but characteristic odour haunted their draughty spaces: a mingled taint of floor-polish, dried ink and yesterday's meals.

It was all very inspiriting and healthy. Perpetually, it seemed, little girls in sage-green djibbahs were tearing breathlessly to and fro, as though the school were run on the lines of a military detention barracks, where all orders are carried out at the double. I was terrified: the tempo was too fast for me, and my hours in the

Kindergarten were spent mainly in unlearning, in a daze of unfamiliar words and objects, all I had learnt in the nursery.

Miss Prendergast, who taught in the Kindergarten, was kind but rather overwhelming. When she kissed me on the first morning, her hair smelt of dandruff. I detested being kissed, anyway, but worse was in store. The French mademoiselle, by way of enlivening her French classes, insisted on playing kiss-in-the-ring. When my turn came, I firmly refused to be kissed. Threats, persuasions, appeals to my vanity – all proved useless. I remained mutely but firmly rebellious. Finally it was decided that I should be allowed to shake hands instead of kissing. The fact of being made an exception increased my agonies tenfold; none the less, I had won my point.

Sometimes Miss Prendergast took us for a botany ramble. (It was she who had destroyed my illusions about the Coltsfoot.) I should have liked these rambles, but my pleasure in them was entirely destroyed by a paralysing fear that we might encounter some member of my family. Within the bounds of the school itself, I was prepared to suffer any amount of indignity or humiliation; I had already learnt to expect it. What I dreaded was that my family should be witnesses of my shame. Even at home, when visitors came to the house, I was overcome by an appalling self-consciousness; my every word and movement became automatically awkward and ridiculous, and I was tortured by the thought that my family were silently laughing at me. To have been seen, by my mother, on a botany-ramble, seemed to me the lowest pitch of degradation. I tried to hide myself as much as possible behind the other children; I even had the courage to suggest a route which would take us as far as possible from our home. Mercifully we never did pass it; nor did we ever meet any member of the household. Once we had covered what I hoped was a safe distance from the house, my self-consciousness left me, and I was able to surprise Miss Prendergast by my precocious knowledge of botany. It was my first success: and her flattering comments did much to assuage the agonies of that first term at school.

In my memory the image of Miss Prendergast is wreathed about with that squalid and uninteresting weed *Lepidium draba*. It was Miss Prendergast who told me its English name – Pepperwort. An alien, introduced into Kent comparatively recently, it has spread further inland, nowadays: and seeing its dirty white tufts in some railway-cutting, I am transported immediately to the high, empty, sunlit rooms of Gaudeamus; I hear again the thin adolescent voices chanting the daily psalm at Morning Prayers; the smell of floor-polish and seaweed is in my nostrils; and I see again the tall, wide-flung windows giving upon the shingle playground, the hedges of tamarisk and the pale-blue summer sea.

I was more interested, at that time, in flowers than in people. Indeed, except in particular cases, I still am. Yet the social flora of the Sandgate Undercliff, where we lived, was perhaps worthy of study. I devoted to it approximately the same amount of attention as I did to bird-life – a subject which I found less interesting than flowers or butterflies, but not without a certain attraction.

It was seldom, in the social milieu frequented by my family, that I encountered anything so exotic and orchidaceous as Miss Trumpett. None the less, some of our neighbours might have been described in the language of the Floras as 'local', if not, 'very rare'. Occasionally a true 'exotic', an 'adventive' species would make its appearance, as when a certain Maharajah, with his suite, took one of the neighbouring houses for a few months. Like some Himalayan cistus or saxifrage escaped from a garden, he enlivened, for a whole summer, the sedate paths of the Undercliff ... Then (an indigenous but distinctly flamboyant species) there was Mrs Croker, the Anglo-Indian novelist, who sometimes came to tea with my mother. And – better-known to myself – there was the portentous figure of Sessquire: tall, snowy-haired, with a monocle, he was a figure straight out of a du Maurier drawing. Peering into my pram (or mail-cart), and booming a greeting in a voice which had once held London audiences spell-bound, he seemed to me like some tall and very robust species of cotton-grass, with his white bush of hair, and his mysterious, sibilant name which seemed to rustle like dried stalks in the wind ... One day my sister, turning a corner on one of the cliff-paths, encountered Sessquire, inadequately concealed by a bush, obeying an importunate call of nature. Much tact was shown on both sides, but the episode doubtless left its mark; for me it has acquired a slight period interest, now that I realize that Sessquire's real name was Sir Squire Bancroft.

Eriophoroid, too, was 'Salvation' Hall, an ex-evangelical preacher with an immense white beard. He was also a botanist, and used to bicycle for miles in search of specimens. Once he showed me a pocketful of Thrift, which he said he had gathered on Romney Marsh. It was a plant I had never found, and perhaps I showed myself over-interested. At all events, he didn't offer me a specimen; remarking, with a cackle of laughter, as he remounted his bicycle, that when I was grown-up I should be able to go out to Romney Marsh and get some too. It was pleasant, after that, to discover that Thrift grew abundantly on the cliffs above our house; I can only hope that 'Salvation' Hall never discovered it.

Few grown-ups realize how subtly insulting their assumptions of superiority can be to a child. Indeed, one suffers more in childhood from wounded vanity than ever in later life. Once, I remember – I had left Gaudeamus, and gone to a day-school in Folkestone – I returned from a school botany-ramble with a bunch of woodland flowers: Bluebells, Wood-spurge, Weasel-snout, Bugle. A lady – she must have been a parent visiting the school – professed a gushing interest in what I had found, and proceeded to ask me the name of each plant. All went well till I came to Bugle.

'Bugloss,' she corrected me.

'Bugle,' I insisted.

'No, no. You mean *Bugloss*, dear.'

'But I don't. It's *Bugle*.'

'Bugloss,' she corrected me.

The lady began to look cross.

'Bugloss,' she repeated.

'Bugle,' I retorted, impenitently.

We parted unamicably: doubtless she thought I was a rude child. But I happened to be right, and she wrong. My plant was Bugle. I could have probably told her the Latin name – *Ajuga reptans*. Yet I was helpless, I had no redress. She was a grown-up, and must therefore know better than I.

It is perhaps worth putting on record, for the benefit of the curious social historian, that when my family first went to live on the Undercliff, they were socially ostracized. A stigma attached to them only less black than that associated, in those days, with *divorcées*, inverts and card-sharpers. At tea-parties, when the question arose whether my mother should be 'called on', it was whispered that my father was *in trade*. That, of course, settled it. One wasn't a snob, of course, but . . . well, there it was.

There it was: the dreadful truth was out. My father was 'in trade'. True, he was a wine-merchant, and one's wine-merchant even in those days ranked only a little below one's solicitor. If he had confined himself to having an office in London, he might have enjoyed the glorious privilege of being 'accepted' by the Undercliff. But alas! he actually had a *shop*. There it was, as large as life, in the Sandgate Road, Folkestone. True, it looked more like a Bank, and was always called the 'Office'; but the fact remained, you could go into it and buy a bottle of wine (or even, for that matter, a bottle of beer) over the counter.

In later years the ban was apparently lifted: whether because our neighbours became less snobbish, or because they feared that my father, provoked beyond endurance, would put arsenic in their wine, I have no idea. The shadow remained in the background, at any rate: for when I first went, as a day-boy, to a Folkestone preparatory-school, I remember being haunted by a feeling of shame. Secretly, the 'Office' in the Sandgate Road had for me some of the sinister glamour with which, it may be assumed, Mrs Warren's daughter invested her mother's profession.

One day, at about this time, I was leaning out of the window with my brother, watching a column of soldiers marching past on their way to Folkestone Harbour, to embark for France. My brother asked me if I would like to be a soldier. I said I would. 'But of course,' he assured me, 'if you were in the Army, you wouldn't be just one of those Tommies. You'd be an officer.'

This prophecy, at least, was not to be fulfilled; when I did join the Army, twenty-four years later, I joined as a private, and remained one: a circumstance which would doubtless have prevented me from being 'called-on' by the Undercliff – supposing I had still lived there, or that there had been anybody else left to 'call'. Alas! the social ecology of Sandgate must have changed out of recognition, these many years; and the indigenous 'rarities' of my childhood have no doubt been long swept away by a weedy overgrowth amid which my own so-bourgeois family, had they remained there, might have enjoyed the prestige of a colony of orchids (or, shall I say, ranunculi?) surviving among a thicket of docks and nettles.

VI

Les seuls vrais paradis, said Proust, *sont les paradis qu'on a perdus*: and conversely, the only genuine Infernos, perhaps, are those which are yet to come. After the post-Munich period, with its atmosphere of slowly-gathering crisis, the outbreak of war itself was like a sudden holiday, bringing a sense of release, almost of relief: the kind of relief which an invalid feels when a definite disease has declared itself, replacing the vague, indefinable malaise by a set of recognizable physical symptoms.

I remember, chiefly, at the time of Munich, re-reading Beatrix Potter and Ronald Firbank; or playing the piano-music of Erik Satie – cool and impersonal as plainchant. In those small and civil duchies one could forget, temporarily, the expanding suburbs of the mad capital, the smooth, ribbon-developed *Autobahnen* to the lands of violence and darkness. Or when these failed, there was the stoic's pleasure in occupations at once scholarly and useless: in my own case, writing a paper – with a rather conscious pedantry – on the distribution of *Orchis simia*, for the *Journal of Botany*; assuming, rather jauntily, the pose of the detached, the touch-line observer – an ostrich-defensiveness, like Housman with his footnotes to Manilius.

And lying awake in the small hours of those hot, rainy nights, hearing a plane drone overhead like the muttered presage of disaster, one's mind leapt to a sudden, annihilating consciousness of the future; the weak guts responded with a colic spasm, the ignominious grip of fear; and the feeling was suddenly oddly familiar, there was the sense of a duplicated experience reaching back to the remotest past. Where had one felt precisely this sensation before? And then the vision came of a corner-seat in a train, hard-boiled eggs, the *Strand Magazine*; the journey to a new school at the end of the summer-holidays.

And one realized that the War would be like this: like the end of the holidays, going back to the red, unfriendly house with its laurelled drive and empty, polished rooms, smelling of ink and varnish, loud with jokes about bums and farts. Wake up, brace up, be keen, put your back into it: school is the world in miniature, Life is a football-match ... The hearty games-master showing off his muscles in the changing-room – 'Gosh, Sir, you must be awfully strong' – and the smell of the bogs: locking oneself in to indulge the nostalgic tears, living only for the holidays.

Yes, the War would be like this. But at this school, of course, the holidays might never come ...

Thank goodness none of it was true. Life is not like a football-match, even in war-time: the War was certainly uncomfortable, but not to be compared with the horrors of an English prep. school. And for me, happening to be lucky, the holidays have come again.

My first boarding-school was in Sussex, and I went there because it was popular with Christian Scientists. My parents, at about the time of my birth, had exchanged a rather tepid Anglicanism for the more up-and-coming doctrines of Mrs Eddy. So to St Ethelbert's I was sent. The Headmaster himself was not (as the jargon of the cult used to phrase it) 'in Science'; he was, as a matter of fact, in Holy Orders. His wife, however, was, as they say, a 'keen Scientist', and every facility was given for the proper celebration of the rites. Every morning before breakfast we 'Scientists' congregated in a sort of catacomb in the basement, where the day's 'lesson' was read to us by one of the assistant-masters, Mr Learoyd, a 'keen Scientist' himself. His 'keenness' showed itself at times in other ways: he had a singularly well-developed knack of twisting arms and ears during his arithmetic classes. However, as he believed that pain was an Error of Mortal Mind, he could afford to laugh pleasantly at the tears of anguish and humiliation which his 'keenness' too often provoked. I myself was slightly prejudiced in his favour by the fact that, on the day of my arrival, he wore a spike of *Orchis morio* in his buttonhole.

But St Ethelbert's, like the War, was never quite so bad as one expected it to be. The threat of being 'sent to boarding-school' had hung over me, vaguely, for years – just as the War itself was to do later on. Whenever I was more than usually ill-behaved, I was threatened with this dread banishment. After a time, since the threat was never fulfilled, 'boarding-school' began to seem no more terrifying than the world of ghosts and goblins – things which one was assured didn't exist, but which one still half-believed in. Then, one day, out of the blue, came the news that I was to go to boarding school the very next term. My first reaction was a deep sense of injustice: I hadn't been particularly naughty, and the announcement had not been preluded by any of the usual threats. My mother made it suddenly one day: more in sorrow than in anger, as it were – rather as Chamberlain announced the outbreak of war in 1939.

A Munich-period of anticipation ensued – the thing was inevitable, but not yet quite real. Then trunks appeared, and lists of clothes; hairbrushes were washed, toilet-articles were labelled ... When the day came, we made the journey by car; it was the first week in May, and the country was unfamiliar. I realized for the first time that there might be compensations for my exile: I should at least find some new flowers. And when we drove up the laurelled drive to the slate-roofed, red-brick building, there, sure enough, was that nice Mr Learoyd to welcome us, with the Green-winged Orchid in his button-hole.

My first new 'find' was Cross-wort, which was rather rare – and still is – in East Kent. *Orchis morio* grew in the school playing-field. I botanized semi-secretly, with a sense of shame. Not that botany was actively discouraged: it was tolerated, but rather as religion is tolerated today in the USSR. As a botanist, at St Ethelbert's, I was in a similar position to that of a priest in Russia – I could botanize, but my activities had, so to speak, no legal status, they didn't fit into the ideological framework. It would have been different if I had been 'keen' on the things that really mattered: football and cricket. But I not only intensely disliked games: I was silly enough to say so. One afternoon my fielding was such a disgrace that Mr Wilcox (another keen Scientist) degraded me from the Third Game to the Fourth, which consisted of the 'babies' of eight or nine (I was eleven). I was put in to bat ... It was the one and only athletic triumph of my life-time: I scored, I believe, about sixty-odd runs. The school was divided, for competitive purposes, into 'sets', and every day at tea-time a senior boy came round the tables noting down our scores for the afternoon. On this occasion, instead of the usual 'duck', I proudly announced my enormous and unprecedented score. The note-taking senior stared, as well he might. The matter was referred to Mr Wilcox; and it was decided that, as I had been degraded to the Fourth Game, the score didn't count ... After that, what little 'keenness' the system had managed to instil into me, withered in the bud. I gave up pretending. I loathed cricket with a pathological loathing, and I still do.

Scouting was another occupation in which I showed insufficient keenness. At last things came to such a pitch that Mr Wilcox, who was the scoutmaster, told me I might as well give up scouting altogether. I was a disgrace to the Troop, he said, and he never wanted to see me on parade again. Highly delighted, I put the good news into a letter home. My father, scenting some irregularity, wrote to the Headmaster; and, shortly after my 'expulsion' from the Scouts, I was amazed to be taken aside by Mr Wilcox and offered a sweet. He began to talk to me in a voice of such mellifluous friendliness that I thought I must be dreaming. I seemed (he began) to have misunderstood something that he had said . . . Surely I never imagined that he had *really* said I was to leave the Scouts? Why, he hadn't even thought of such a thing, much less said it. (Another sweet.) I didn't really *still* think he'd said anything of the sort, did I?

I remained in the Scouts; I tried to be keen – but with little success. Once, when we were out on a field-day, marching down a sandy lane, I saw some foxgloves growing in the hedge. Foxgloves, for me, were almost a rarity – they are not common on the chalky lands of East Kent. Without a restraining thought, I broke from the ranks and ran across to the hedge . . . The foxgloves once in my hand, I realized what I had done. But Mr Wilcox, surprisingly, remained calm and even amiable . . . Perhaps he was afraid I might write home again.

Miss Amphlett, one of the woman-teachers, was something of a botanist; she taught the 'babies', and only the babies were supposed to be interested in flowers. I was the sole exception – a bourgeois, as it were (according to the caste-system of school-life) bent on declassing himself. In some respects I came to prefer the proletariat: they were not expected, for one thing, to be quite so keen.

Poor Miss Amphlett was not, after all, very reliable: she shocked me one day by identifying Betony as Purple Loosestrife. I might have argued with her as I had argued with the lady at Folkestone about Bugle and Bugloss. But I had become more soph- isticated (and more dishonest) by this time. If Mr Learoyd and Mr

Wilcox had not taught me to be keen, they had at least taught me that it was not always wise to tell the truth.

At St Ethelbert's one heard a great deal about Honesty. The word was uttered in the reverent tones in which one spoke of Jesus. We were all understood to be perpetually 'on our honour' not to misbehave. There was no fixed scale of punishments: they were assumed to be unnecessary. To break the rules was dishonourable, and therefore unthinkable.

The emotional strain produced in children by such a system has to be experienced to be believed. Petty misdemeanours – failing to put one's gym-shoes away in the racks provided, talking after lights-out, being late for a class – these assumed the awful complexion of mortal sins. The appalling sense of guilt thus engendered can be imagined: to talk after lights-out was equivalent to fornication, to tell a deliberate lie or to swear was only less sinful than the amusements of the Marquis de Sade.

Periodically, of course, this atmosphere of mass-guilt and persecution-mania found official outlet. On a Sunday evening after tea, it would be announced that the Headmaster wanted to see us all in the Big School-room. Dead-silent, and consumed by an agonized apprehension, we waited, penned in our rows at the scarred, ink-stained desks. Presently the Head made his entrance: not Hitler entering the Reichstag, after the unmasking of some plot against his life, could have created a more profound effect ... Softly the Head began to talk. 'As you know' (he would begin) 'I do not approve of using THE STICK ...' The word fell heavily, like an expected thunderclap, upon our taut, hypnotized minds ... 'No, I never, if I can avoid it, use The Stick. But I'm sorry to say that some of you have been found guilty of conduct which I view as DISHONOURABLE ...' Another thunderclap: we wriggle in our seats ... The soft voice continues, gradually mounting to a crescendo of horror. Somebody has broken a rule – we are on our HONOUR to observe the rules. If our Honour will not prevent us from breaking them – then there remains only one alternative ... The voice ebbs: the alternative is not mentioned, the expected clap, the storm's peak, fails to break over us. But we know and mutter to ourselves the unutterable word: THE STICK. And then, like a preacher turning to the East, and gabbling 'And now to God the Father, God the Son ...' the Head's voice suddenly drops its dramatic tones; he glances at a little list – 'I want to see the following in my study immediately afterwards.' We listen, with a final and increased straining of attention, to the names ... *No, I'm not on it* ... The Head sweeps out, and we disperse: hysterically laughing, jostling, catcalling in an ecstasy of relief ... except, of course, for those whose names were on the list. These trail slowly, outcast and without hope of reprieve, towards The Study, where the Head is already preparing for the sacrifice: bending, testing in his white, rather podgy hands, the *malleus maleficarum*, the long, lissome, willowy shape of THE STICK.

VII

ONE morning, half-way through that first summer term at St Ethelbert's, a small parcel arrived for me. I undid it, and with difficulty choked down my tears. It contained orchids found by my old Nurse near the cottage, whither the family had already repaired for the summer. Not for years – not till I had left school – should I ever be able to find these orchids myself again: the Lady, the Green Man, the Early Spider – none of them grew near St Ethelbert's. For the months of May, June and July I was condemned, for what seemed all eternity (and at that age, there is little difference between five years and eternity) to an unhappy exile, if not in a flowerless, at least in an orchidless world. I realized it for the first time, that morning; and the yellowish spikes of the Man, the purple-spotted pagodas of the Lady, awoke in me a nostalgia which was no ordinary homesickness, but a sense of greater loss. I realized, at last, that my childhood was nearly over.

Hurrying to be in time for Prayers (with the dread word 'Honour' echoing in my ears) I stuffed the orchids into my toothglass in the dormitory – as usual, with a sense of shame and embarrassment, rather as a priest in Russia might prepare to celebrate Mass before an assembly of keen party-members ... Yet, like the priest, I was secretly assured of the validity of the rite; privately I despised my tittering companions, recognizing the shallowness of their school-bred, conventional enthusiasms, knowing them incapable, in nearly every case of even a moment's genuine emotion.

I hurried down to Prayers; but not before I had noticed, among the other orchids, an unfamiliar one: pale pink, almost white, with a crimson lip narrowly divided into four tendril-like lobes ... Later in the day, I unpacked Edward Step from my play-box, and once again turned up the passage about *Orchis militaris*. Had I found it at last – the Military Orchid? Again the annihilating, impotent nostalgia swept over me: the orchid had been found quite near our cottage, in the park in which I, myself, had found the Green Man, the Bee, the Pyramidal, for many a summer ... And now, in the very first year of my absence, this distinguished stranger had elected to turn up there. Was it the Military? Once again, as when Mr Bundock had brought me the Lady, the old conflict was revived: I wanted my plant to be the Military, and knew that, by accepting Colonel Mackenzie as my authority, I was justified in so calling it. But alas! there was that qualifying clause in Edward Step about 'a sub-species known as the Monkey Orchid ... with narrower divisions of the crimson lip ... occurring in the same counties as the type, with the addition of Kent'. I looked at the plant again: the divisions of the lip could not well have been narrower; moreover, they were indubitably crimson. And the plant had been found in Kent ... Reluctantly I decided that it was, after all, the 'sub-species known as the Monkey Orchid'. (Perhaps St Ethelbert's had already purged me of that mental dishonesty which had enabled me, years before, to label Mr Bundock's orchid the Military.)

So the Military was, after all, still unfound. It was nice to have the Monkey; but there seemed to me something slightly inferior about a 'sub-species'. The very phrases of Edward Step sounded faintly derogatory – 'a sub-species *known* as the Monkey Orchid' ... it suggested the subtly insulting phraseology of the police-court: 'a woman *described* as an actress'. I could not know that my old Nurse's 'find' was to prove one of the more important plant-records of the century.

A year or two later, the season was early, and the summer term must have started late; walking across the Park, on the last day of the Easter holidays, I found a single plant of the Monkey Orchid. By that time, I had a better idea of its importance: I had discovered that it was promoted, nowadays, to specific status, and could be ranked with the Military on equal terms. Later, I heard that one or two other people had found it in the same place at about this period: a lady staying in our village had drawn it, and the drawing was hung – and still hangs – in the Canterbury Museum. But after 1923 – when I found it myself – it seems to have disappeared entirely from the district. It was not till many years later that I realized how portentous its appearance there had been. Colonel Godfrey, I found, in his immense and erudite *Monograph* on the British Orchids, could quote only one record for the Monkey Orchid in Kent – it had, apparently, been found, in the early nineteenth-century, by the Rev S.L. Jacobs, near Dover, and never re-discovered since. Colonel Godfrey, indeed was sceptical even of this single appearance, attributing it to an error of identification, or to a windblown seed.

I wrote to him, enclosing a floret of a pressed specimen, which had fortunately survived the years. He agreed that it was undoubtedly the Monkey Orchid. And so, in the warm, rainy days of Munich I wrote the story of the Kentish Monkey for the *Journal of Botany*: remembering that morning at St Ethelbert's – the tittering boys, the sneers of Mr Wilcox, the hustle to be ready in time for Prayers; and the delicate, aristocratic flower, one of the rarest and most beautiful in the British Flora, stuffed hurriedly and ignominiously into a tooth-glass.

The other day, I made the pilgrimage to Oxfordshire to visit the Monkey in its sole remaining locality: a chalky hillside overlooking the river, within too-easy reach of a popular boating-resort. There it was: half-hidden among the rough grasses, smaller than its Kentish fellows, but the same charming and exquisitely-formed flower that I had stuffed into my toothglass at St Ethelbert's some twenty-five years before. The botanist who accompanied me pointed out that I was possibly the only living person who had seen the Monkey Orchid growing in two separate British localities. If so, it is perhaps a small claim to fame: but one of which I am extremely proud.

Round about us stretched the gentle hillsides of the Thames Valley, hung with woods which, long years ago, had harboured the true Military Orchid. Perhaps one day it will again be found there; there seems little reason why it should have so totally vanished. Why, in any case, should the Lady survive in Kent – abundantly, in some districts? And why does the Monkey linger in Oxfordshire?

A botanist of my acquaintance recently told me of an experience of his which occurred some years ago. He had heard that a single plant of the Military still grew, carefully protected, on a private estate. He made a special journey in order to photograph it; when he arrived, however, he found that the flowers had begun to wither, and he postponed his photographing till the following year. He duly revisited the place: but the single plant – perhaps the last Military Orchid to survive in this country – had vanished, and has never since reappeared.

> Behind the drum and fife
> Past hawthorn-wood and hollow
> Through earth and out of life
> The soldiers follow . . .

And *Orchis militaris* has presumably gone with them – gone with scarlet and pipe-clay, with Ouida's guardsmen and Housman's lancers; gone with the concept of soldiering as a chivalric and honourable calling.

VIII

Mr Learoyd, that 'keen scientist', would sometimes give little extempore talks in the basement room at St Ethelbert's. On one such occasion, I remember, he was poking fun at some of the more flagrant errors of Mortal Mind. How silly it was, he remarked, that if one got one's feet wet, one should get a cold in one's head. That, he said, was typical of Mortal Mind . . . I tittered, obsequiously, with the other little 'Scientists'; but even then I realized, I think, that Mr Learoyd's play on words was typical, not so much of Mortal Mind, as of Mrs Eddy's peculiar and paranoid theology.

But though I might sometimes be faintly critical, I was a pious enough adherent of the cult. At home, I had been a 'Scientist' merely out of deference to my family, and because they expected me to be one. At St Ethelbert's I embraced the Faith as one who was starving in the wilderness. The familiar, incantatory passages from *Science and Health* were (like the parcel of orchids) a breath of home; I had heard them from the lips of my family, and now, in the mouth of Mr Learoyd, they assumed a fresh and poignant significance.

*

Threatened by an attack of 'flu or measles, or terrified by my inability to work out an algebraic equation (in which Honour was, of course, once again involved), I would make strenuous efforts to give myself Treatment, or, as we used to say, to Know the Truth. I invented for myself a series of Christian Science Theorems, which I visualized as neatly set out in the manner of Euclid:

> God is All (this was an axiom)
> ∴ All is God
> If All is God, I must be part of God.
> But God is Good (another axiom);
>
> Therefore I must be Good – i.e., I cannot be ill
> (or be bad at maths.)

QED

The fact that my temperature rose yet higher, or that the equation worked out wrong (as the case might be) didn't seriously discourage me; it was merely, I supposed, that my 'theorems' – like the equations themselves – hadn't worked out correctly. In any case, it was all very comforting; though alas! when the holidays came, there was, I regret to say, a noticeable falling-off in my pious practices.

Mortal Mind might be prolific of illusions such as Mr Wilcox and endless afternoons of cricket. But the holidays did arrive eventually, and I found myself once again at the cottage. Everything at home, I told myself firmly, was as it had been. Yet I was aware of subtle, indefinable changes ... I might refuse to admit them, and I was certainly unable to analyse my sensations; but the awareness set up a state of irritation and depression, I felt unsettled, possessed by a vague, irrational anxiety. Such visible, tangible changes as did occur produced in me a disproportionate unhappiness: a new wallpaper in my bedroom, some minor rearrangement in the garden. Since going to school, I clung with a ferocious conservatism to the Past: it had already become a *vert paradis*, a Land of Lost Content.

Arriving home for that first summer-holiday, I visited the Igglesden children. They told me that they had found a strange plant, an orchid they thought, up in the Park. They had dug it up and planted it in their garden. I went out to investigate. The plant was withered, but recognizable – an orchid indeed, two feet high, with an inordinately long flower-spike. I looked again. Yes, there was no doubt of it. The Igglesdens had found the Lizard Orchid.

Once again a surge of bitterness swept over me: if only *I* could have found the Lizard! But untold ages of school – an eternity of cricket, of Mr Wilcox, of equations – lay between me and the time when I should be able, myself, to walk across the Park in June and July. The Monkey, the Lizard – both had chosen this year of all years to make their portentous appearance; and I was not there to see them. Why should the Igglesdens be thus privileged, when I was not? *They* went to the village school; *they* were not exiled for nine months of the year at St Ethelbert's; and as if this were not enough, they must needs find the Lizard Orchid, which assuredly they didn't fully appreciate. The whole system seemed to me grossly unfair.

I consoled myself by making fireworks. At the local chemist's I obtained little packets of saltpetre, charcoal, sulphur, strontium nitrate, potassium chlorate. My mother lived in hourly terror of my blowing myself and the entire family to smithereens. Once or twice I nearly did; and a year or two later, quite unwittingly, I nearly blew up Professor Joad.

I was at Bedales by that time, and had become friendly with Julian Trevelyan, to whom, in the holidays, I sent a parcel of my home-made fireworks. Mr Joad, who was staying with the Trevelyans, was detailed, it seems, to ignite one of my maroons. Either Mr Joad was too slow, or the fuse was too short: the maroon, at any rate, exploded with an annihilating report within a few inches of the eminent philosopher's nose. Had the distance been only slightly less, the BBC might have been a different (and doubtless inferior) institution.

PART TWO

Du Côté de Chez Prufrock

I should have been a pair of ragged claws
Scuttling across the floors of silent seas.
T. S. ELIOT

I

The roaring twenties ...! But the label, perhaps, is a mistake. The true voice of the epoch was, surely, not so much a full-throated roar as a kind of exacerbated yelping; a false-virile voice tending, in moments of stress, to rise to an equivocal falsetto – half-revealing (like the voice of M. de Charlus) behind its ill-assumed masculinity a whole bevy of *jeunes filles en fleurs*. The authentic note in literature is sounded by Mr Mercaptan – whose laughter was said to resemble an 'orchestra of bulls and canaries'. In fact, Mr Mercaptan, with his eighteenth-century bric-à-brac, his nigger sculpture, his editions of Crébillon and Proust – Mr Mercaptan, if anybody, may be said to epitomize the period. His ineffable flat in Sloane Street surely deserves a plaque: and while they are about it, perhaps the LCC will bestow a similar honour upon that other house, nearby, where 'under the name of Monna Vanna, Mrs Shamefoot kept a shop'.

The War, the Boom, the Slump – events did conspire to isolate those years with a curious completeness: justifying, for once, perhaps, the slick reckoning of the gossip-writer, too ready, for the most part, thus to pigeon-hole a period neatly between two noughts. The world of the Twenties existed in a kind of historical parenthesis: a timeless St Martin's Summer, in which the past was forgotten, and the future, as far as possible, ignored. No wonder that those of us who grew up during that extraordinary decade are apt to suffer from an incurable nostalgia. The typical Man of the Twenties – Prufrock or Theodore Gumbril – was but poorly adapted for the earnest, drab salvationism that came in with the Thirties; he might learn to call himself a communist or even an Anglo-Catholic, but he remained, at bottom, an impenitent Futilitarian, whose only ethical slogan (if any) was Intellectual Honesty.

By the time I left school in 1927, the epoch had, alas! already passed its peak: legends were forming, even then, of the Heroic Age, the 'post-war' years of Dada and the *Boeuf sur le Toit* ... By the end of the decade even the music-halls had 'gone nostalgic' with highly-successful revivals of Edwardian or war-time tunes: *A Bicycle made for Two, If you were the Only Girl in the World* ... Lawrence died; Prufrock was already a High-Anglican; Mr Mercaptan was well on the way to becoming a hollywood Yogi or a Constructive Pacifist.

In 1930 appeared the first edition of Auden's *Poems*. It was the death-knell of the decade, a call to order. Next year came the National Government, and with it the New Seriousness. A steady stream of expatriates began to flow homeward (second-class) from their artificial paradises in the South. Nepenthe and Trou-sur-Mer were abandoned. A cry went up from the Dôme and the Rotonde, and was echoed from a hundred delicious night-boxes. (Even the rue de Lappe felt the pinch.) Weeping, weeping multitudes drooped in the Fitzroy (lately refurbished, incongruously, with chromium stools from the wreckage of the Blue Lantern). The intellectual *chichi* which had marked the vanishing era was sternly rebuked; and the strident war-cries of homocommunism echoed from Russell Square all the way to Keats Grove. A number of ageing Peter Pansies wisely fled to the country, there to cultivate their Olde Worlde Gardens among the pylons and the petrol pumps; and an epoch which had begun with a bang came to an end, all too appropriately, with a whimper.

For myself, the period did indeed start with a bang, which, besides almost liquidating Professor Joad, shook me into an uneasy awareness of other worlds outside the green paradise which I was soon to leave. But the Whimpering Thirties were a long way ahead: in 1920 I was still at St Ethelbert's, and was to remain there for two more years. Towards the end of that time my life was overshadowed by the propsect of yet a further remove from my *paradis perdu*: in the autumn I was to go to a Public School.

And to a Public School I duly went; King's School, Canterbury, was my father's choice. I stayed there a week before I ran away; I was sent back, and at the end of another week, ran away again.

Thus my Public School career lasted a fortnight, which may, for all I know, constitute a record. No doubt I was more-than-usually sensitive, and less-than-normally plucky; but a friend of mine, who had accompanied me (with a scholarship) from St Ethelbert's and who, on both occasions, ran away with me from King's School, was to all appearance perfectly normal. He even, I seem to remember, enjoyed cricket. Unlike me, he was sent back to the school after our second escape; and as he – as well as most of our contemporaries, apparently – survived the normal four years there without going mad, I can only conclude that the system was not much more ferocious than in most places of the kind. But for me, at least, that fortnight was the final stage in a long process of prophylaxis, of immunization against the age in which we are still living. The worst I had to fear from the War was that it would be as bad as going back to King's School again: but it never was.

Far too much has been written already about public schools, and I have no intention of adding to the literature of the subject. My experiences, I suppose, were quite usual: the ferocious initiation ceremonies, the petty cruelties and indecencies, the perpetual sense of injustice and irrational guilt. I had never thought that I should live to look back, with nostalgia, upon St Ethelbert's; yet even St Ethelbert's seemed a heaven-on-earth compared with King's School.[1] I was taken away and with a belated wisdom, sent to Bedales; but my fortnight at a public school, if it immunized me successfully against any possible horrors which the future might hold in store, bred in me also an intolerance of tradition, a hatred of all authority and a deep-seated distrust of all institutions from which I am only now slowly beginning to recover.

Reading the innumerable accounts of the experiences by refugees who have escaped, either before or during the War, from a totalitarian to a democratic country, I have felt, over and over again, a sense of familiarity with the emotions they describe. For this was precisely my own experience when I left King's School and went to Bedales. Here, from the very first day, I was made to feel happy, and as much 'at home' as it is possible to feel at any boarding-school. Nearly everybody was pleasant to me: not merely because I was a special case, but from habit, as I learnt when other new boys (and girls) arrived in subsequent terms. The perpetual cloud of fear and suspicion – which I had known at St Ethelbert's as well as

[1] I am told that, since those days, the school has been radically reformed.

at Canterbury – was suddenly, miraculously, lifted. I had not thought it possible to be 'happy' at school: but at Bedales I learnt, to my astonishment, that it was not only possible but easy.

I could make many criticisms of Bedales; co-education, as it was practised there, is possibly, I think, a mistake: for, like all small unorthodox communities which attempt to live within the framework of the *status quo*, a school has to make too many concessions to the principles of the outside world. Such concessions are bound to react upon and modify to some extent the principles of the small group: and so it was at Bedales. Plainly, sexual activity couldn't be encouraged; equally plainly, in a close community of adolescents of both sexes, the sexual element must be dealt with somehow. At Bedales, the problem was solved, not exactly by ignoring sex, but by minimizing its importance. To be attracted to a girl or boy and to show it was considered *silly*. In cases where 'affairs' seemed likely to have serious developments (and there were surprisingly few of these), the two parties concerned were treated to serious and sympathetic lectures in which it was pointed out that 'all that' was mere silliness; that the aim of co-education was to promote a 'healthy, natural comradeship' between the sexes, and that any deviation from this 'healthy attitude was a kind of disloyalty to the Headmaster. How such 'comradeship' between a young man and a normal adolescent girl could be 'healthy' yet entirely sexless, was not explained. Nor did one gather why 'all that' presumably ceased to be 'silly' when (at the age of eighteen or nineteen) one left school.

I think the usual accusation levelled against co-education – that it makes girls into tomboys and boys into pansies – has little justification. The effect is more insidious. Most of the girls at Bedales were perfectly feminine; the boys, far from being effeminate, tended as often as not to assume a rather over-emphatic clod-hopper kind of virility – probably as a protest against so much feminine influence. What *did* happen was that the perpetual minimizing of the sexual problem created a sort of emotional vacuum in the mind of the average Bedalian. I have compared Bedales to a liberal-democratic state; but this antisexual atmosphere, created as it was by a combination of fear and self-hypnotism, had something rather fascist about it. The German in Nazi Germany, who was repeatedly told that the Jews were sub-human criminals, may have begun by doubting the assertion; subsequently he found it convenient to pay lip-service to official opinion; in his own mind, he would learn to avoid the subject of the Jews: better not to think than to harbour 'dangerous thoughts'. Finally, in most cases, his own former opinions were replaced by the official attitude.

I don't suggest, of course, that sex at Bedales was regarded as the Jews were in Germany. But, if Hitler had taken it into his head to convince the German people that sex was 'silly', it is conceivable that he might have succeeded: there is something in common, after all, between the chronic idealism of the average German (especially when canalized completely by the State) and the state of mind of an English adolescent in a large boarding-school.

But if the atmosphere at Bedales was anti-sexual, if inconvenient facts were gingerly skated over, the school was, I think in other respects, a successful experiment. Spartan as it was, the Spartan element was combined with humanity and kindness. Bullying was very rare; athleticism was encouraged, but not exalted above other activities. One was, indeed, adjured to be 'keen', just as at St Ethelbert's; but I soon found, to my astonishment, that one was allowed to be keen on other things besides cricket – for instance, botany. As to the school work itself, there were, admittedly, serious weaknesses in the system: it was too easy – at least during one's last year or two at school – to avoid doing more work than one wanted to. The curriculum itself was a hybrid product, which had grown out of a series of experiments: the Dalton System, the 'Laboratory' plan, Montessori, and what not. When I first went to Bedales, the 'Individual' system was in operation: for so many hours a day one was free to work at whatever one liked – Geography, Drawing, Latin, Mathematics. A teacher was posted in the appropriate class-room to oversee and encourage such 'individualists' as chose to turn up. Naturally, some forms of 'individual activity' were more popular than others: the Carpentry shop, the Book-binding room, the Studio were usually crowded out. I remember that my first two or three days at school were spent almost entirely in the Studio. Later on, the system was tightened up, and by the time I left, was not very different from that of an ordinary school. Even so, it was possible to slack almost to one's heart's content. Once I had passed the School Certificate and

Responsions, nobody cared a hoot what I did – with the result that, when I got to Oxford, I was totally unable to construe a simple bit of Latin prose, and consequently distinguished myself by failing in the Law Prelim. at the end of my first year.

II

Mr Bickersteth, the biology master, was rather a misfit, I fancy, at Bedales; he was terrifically 'keen' – so much so, that I was uneasily reminded of Mr Wilcox and Mr Learoyd at St Ethelbert's. Fortunately for me, however, most of his keenness was centred upon botany, and in particular upon orchids. Every summer a 'Show' was arranged in the Biology Lab. – rows of labelled plant-specimens in jam-pots. The 'Show' soon became my particular province. I began slowly to realize that botany, which for me had been up till now a semi-secret and rather shameful hobby, was in fact a recognized science; and I was appalled by my ignorance. I set about, energetically, to repair some of my worst omissions; Edward Step was discarded (reluctantly) for Bentham and Hooker or Hayward's *Botanist's Pocket-Book* (edited by the redoubtable Dr Druce), and I was surprised at the number of plants I had never heard of.

None the less, I was able to impress Mr Bickersteth by some of my Kentish 'finds', and the Lady Orchid, the Spider and the Green Man were duly exhibited in the show. Parcels of plants, too, would arrive from other parts of the country, and even from abroad, for Mr Bickersteth's enthusiasm was not confined to the local flora. One morning a parcel arrived from, I think, Switzerland. Mr Bickersteth opened it in considerable excitement: I think he knew what was inside. He peered beneath the enveloping moss, and a hoot of joy escaped him as his suspicion was confirmed. Tenderly, he lifted the plant from its packing, and held it out for my inspection.

It was the Military Orchid.

True, it was a foreign specimen, and I had not found it myself; but there it was, *Orchis militaris* beyond a doubt: not Edward Step, not even Colonel Mackenzie could have called it anything

else. It was not unlike the Monkey, but with a longer, more cylindrical spike, and broader divisions of the lip. There was nothing
very military about it after all: the name presumably refers to the
helmet-shaped 'hood' of the flower, or possibly to the faintly-
anthropoid, reddish lip, but the resemblance to a soldier was hard
to detect.

More realistic in its mimicry was the Lizard Orchid, which my
old Nurse discovered, that same season, in the locality where the
Igglesdens had found it a year or so previously. Mr Bickersteth's
enthusiasm, when the parcel arrived, was noisy and prolonged. To
exhibit the Lizard and the Military in his show, in a single season,
exceeded the scope even of his wide-flung ambition. Not content,
however, with these two prizes, he had obtained, before the end of
the term, specimens of the Red Helleborine and the Lady's Slipper, as well as *Orchis laxiflora*, the Jersey Orchid, from the Channel Islands.

To myself, the assembled orchids, in their jam-pots and potted-
meat jars, were so many symbols of a happiness which was so
acute, so consciously enjoyed, that it filled me with a kind of superstitious fear. To be so happy at school seemed to me against
nature; I could only marvel, as the exciting, sunlit weeks slipped
by, that I had actually forgotten to look forward to the holidays.
Of course, it would be nice when they came ... but my half-
hearted anticipation was largely a matter of habit and schoolboy
convention. I had never been so happy or felt so well in my life
before: not, at any rate, since I first went to school. My school-life,
up till now, had passed in an uninterrupted longing for the holidays: and in the holidays, my happiness – itself based mainly on
the fact of not being at school, rather than on any more positive
emotion – had been invariably tainted with the prospect of the
coming term.

I had become, in fact, a different person. Even my physical and
social timidity had largely been cured by the tolerant, easy-going
atmosphere of Bedales. I learnt to swim; and I began to make
friends. My stupidity at Arithmetic, instead of being regarded as a
breach of Honour, or an insult to the Master concerned, was
treated with helpful kindliness. Even cricket and football came to
seem merely boring instead of a source of terror. I had gone to
Bedales in the Christmas term, after leaving Canterbury; by the
following summer, I had become transformed from a 'difficult',

neurotically-timid and generally unsatisfactory child, into something approaching a healthy, normal schoolboy.

On Saturday and Sunday afternoons we would set off on our bicycles – Mr Bickersteth, myself, and one or two other enthusiasts – for Harting or Selborne, or over the downs towards Winchester, in search of some unfound rarity. And after the long, torrid hours spent wading through marshes, or climbing over chalk-downs, we would arrive back, sweating, our vascula crammed with specimens. Perhaps we had found the Frog Orchid on Wardown, or the Violet Helleborine on Selborne Hanger; or I had seen Sundew or Bog Asphodel for the first time in Woolmer Forest. It was seldom that the vasculum didn't contain something which made the journey worth-while and exciting. Arriving back at the school, we would bathe, then eat an enormous tea; and happiness would blossom in my mind like some brilliant, alien flower which has established itself in homely surroundings, where its splendour is still a source of surprise, almost of suspicion. It was as though one should suddenly come upon the Military Orchid on a waste patch in some dingy suburb, among Mugwort and Goosefoot and all the squalid weeds bred by indifference and neglect.

After tea, I would return to the Lab., to put our specimens in water, and to gloat, once again, on the fabulous lineaments of the Military and the Lizard. And later (if it was a Sunday) there was 'Jaw'.

This was the disrespectful name bestowed, by staff and children alike, on the Sunday evening service, at which, in rotation, some member of the staff gave an address. The service was held in a building imitated, I think, from some mediaeval tithe-barn or Hall of Justice: arched beams of unvarnished oak supported the roof, and through the narrow, latticed windows, the evening sun fell softly upon the piano, the school orchestra, and the assembled school. The service was strictly undenominational: the music ranged from plainchant or the Agincourt Song to the brighter, more uplifting melodies of Hymns A. and M. The words were as varied as the tunes; and the prayers had a tentative, rather apologetic air – God, one inferred, was addressed rather hypothetically: at mention of His name, the speaker would usually pause, ever so slightly, as though adding, silently, the cautious qualification: *'If You exist.'*

After the service, the entire school filed past the assembled staff, shaking hands: a ritual in which the staff – like officers in the matter of saluting – had the worst of it. At the end of the row stood the Headmaster, J. H. Badley – the pioneer of co-education in England: tall, broad-shouldered, with grizzled hair and beard, his eyes kindly but grave behind his spectacles; attired invariably in a grey flannel suit, gym-shoes, and a scarlet tie.

And coming out of the Hall, the school-buildings, the tall, high-windowed rooms, the echoing, glass-roofed Quadrangle – all the quotidian background of the school-life, seemed transfigured, fringed with a romantic haze of happiness – a happiness tainted, already, for me, with a fore-knowledge that it could not be lasting. For my sense of the past was too strong to allow me to surrender, for long, to such a calm and sunlit contentment. Try as I might to forget, memories of Canterbury or St Ethelbert's would recur; I would remember, too, that once I had been happy before; and images of Sandgate, of Gaudeamus, of our country-cottage would merge with the symbols of my present happiness, infecting them with melancholy; and my eyes would prick with tears, as I realized suddenly that this summer-evening, too, would pass at length into the hoarded repository of my memories, irretrievable, never to be repeated: a picture to be placed alongside other pictures – evenings at the cottage, Mr Bundock bringing home the Lady Orchid, my moonlight romance with Miss Trumpett, or our home at Sandgate, with the sound of the sea stealing, like a muted plain-chant, through windows opening upon the summer-garden.

Such moments seemed to demand some form of outward expression, and I decided to embark upon a love-affair. It began almost by accident: I was sitting in the Library, where one was not allowed to talk; a girl was sitting at the same table, and for some innocent reason – probably I wanted to borrow her pencil – I passed her a note. Later, when I left the Library, there were titters: Brooke had been passing notes to Dorothy. Evidently it was an 'affair': the dormitory that night could talk of nothing else.

I was painfully embarrassed, but at the same time rather excited. It would be rather fun, I thought, to have an affair. As it happened, I had scarcely noticed the girl; but the next day I contrived, once more, to sit at the same table during prep. More notes were passed. Dorothy seemed to approve, in a rather negative way; at least, she didn't object. That evening, after prayers, we stood together for five minutes under an archway in the Quad., saying good night: this was the prescribed nightly ritual for those who 'had a girl', and our liaison was thereby recognized, put on an official basis, like an engagement announcement in *The Times*.

Dorothy (a very suitable name) was a plump, pasty-faced girl, two years older than myself; besides being quite unattractive, she was monumentally boring. I cannot remember a single word of the conversations we exchanged: I preferred passing notes in the library, anyway, since this required less effort, and appeared agreeably conspiratorial. The whole thing soon bored me to tears: the excitement of 'having a girl' began to pall, and I sensed that the elder boys and girls – and probably the staff as well – were deprecating my 'silliness'. Silliness it undoubtedly was in my case: there was about as much sex involved as there had been in my 'romance' with Miss Trumpett at the age of six. What Dorothy's feelings were I cannot imagine: at any rate, she was soon unfaithful to me. One night, coming out rather late from prayers, I found her standing under the archway with a new companion. I passed her without even saying good night, and went up to bed with a sense of profound and unmitigated relief.

III

So, some tempestuous morn in early June,
    When the year's primal burst of bloom is o'er,
        Before the roses and the longest day –
    When garden-walks and all the grassy floor
        With blossoms red and white of fallen May
            And chestnut-flowers are strewn. . .

IT would be possible, I fancy, to compile a small anthology of English verse reflecting this same elegiac mood of frost-in-May and the ruins of an English Spring. It was a *genre* which, when I first started reading poetry, I found particularly sympathetic; hearing J. H. Badley read aloud Arnold's lines, on just such a stormy summer-morning, I felt that this was the kind of poetry I really liked: an evocation of country scenes accompanied by a sense of melancholy and regret.

So have I heard the cuckoo's parting cry,
　From the wet field, through the next garden-trees,
　Come with the volleying rain and tossing breeze:
The bloom is gone, and with the bloom go I!

Later, too, there was Housman, in similar strain:

The chestnut casts his flambeaux, and the flowers
　Stream from the hawthorn on the wind away,
The doors clap to, the pane is blind with showers.
　Pass me the can, lad; there's an end of May.

And that poem, too, of Wilfred Gibson, an ubiquitous anthology-piece, and the text for many a rhyme-sheet and poker-worked calendar, which I found very moving:

A bird among the rain-wet lilac sings –
But we, how shall we turn to little things
And listen to the birds and winds and streams
Made holy by their dreams,
Nor feel the heart-break in the heart of things?

I had begun, by this time, myself to write poetry; and I was acutely aware – or so I like to think – of the 'heartbreak in the heart of things'. It is a common enough symptom of puberty: an Anthology of Bedales Verse which I still possess is full of poems by children of twelve or thirteen about Eternity, fading flowers and unrequited love. A useful corrective, in my own case, was the discovery of T. S. Eliot, whom the English master referred to as 'Futurist'. Mr Eliot might well have demurred at being labelled as a disciple of Marinetti; but at that time – with *The Waste Land* fresh from the press – it was not generally realized that Alfred Prufrock was at heart a Royalist and an Anglo-Catholic. *The Waste Land* seemed extremely modern and revolutionary.

In my readings of poetry, I was apt to be rather uncritical; but in one respect, I outdid the most academic of textual critics in my pedantry. Inaccurate references to plants were liable to provoke me into a positively Housmanly cantankerousness.

And round green roots and yellowing stalks I see
Pale blue convolvulus in tendrils creep. . . .

Blue? Arnold, surely, had nodded . . . And in later editions *blue* is duly corrected to *pink*, for Arnold, unlike most English poets, was generally pretty accurate in his botany.

> I know these slopes; who knows them if not I? . . .
>   But many a dingle on the loved hillside,
>   With thorns once studded, old, white-blossom'd
>   trees,
>   Where thick the cowslips grew, and far descried
>   High tower'd the spikes of purple orchises,
>   Hath since our day put by
>   The coronals of that forgotten time. . .

Given the Oxfordshire background, it was tempting to speculate if some at least of the 'orchises', whose passing the poet laments, were *Orchis simia* or *Orchis militaris*. But Arnold's references to plants – and *Thyrsis* and *The Scholar Gypsy* are full of them – are nearly always pleasingly exact. For example:

> Some country-nook, where o'er thy unknown grave
> Tall grasses and white flowering nettles wave,
> Under a dark, red-fruited yew-tree's shade. . .

That is ecologically correct – and being so, for a botanist enhances the poem's effect. But turn from Arnold to Keats, for instance:

> I cannot see what flowers are at my feet,
>   Nor what soft incense hangs upon the boughs,
> But in embalmèd darkness guess each sweet . . .

And so on, finishing up with a vague reference to violets and eglantine. The lines might be quoted as typical of poet's botany. Shelley is the same, and most of the Romantics: where flowers are introduced, the poet tends to become vague, or to fall back on eglantine and roses, or else to plump for half-mythical but resounding names like amaranth and moly. Keats does indeed mention Wolfsbane as a poisonous plant, and may have meant *Aconitum napellus*, but it is highly doubtful.

Clare and Crabbe are justly famed, of course, for their flower-poetry; and Crabbe, at least, was a botanist, and seldom makes a mistake:

> Around the dwellings docks and wormwood rise;
> Here the strong mallow strikes her slimy root,

> Here the dull nightshade hangs her deadly fruit:
> On hills of dust the henbane's faded green
> And pencill'd flower of sickly scent is seen ⸳⸳⸳

Though even here I doubt the presence, on the Suffolk coast, of the Deadly Nightshade: I suspect that Crabbe meant the Black Nightshade, or possibly Bittersweet, neither of which is particularly deadly.

But if poets can claim their traditional licence, what are we to say of prose-writers? Most of them are worse than the poets, and with less excuse. Even the most self-consciously rural of novelists seem incapable of being factually accurate about flowers; what makes matters worse is their pretentiousness, their air of omniscience. No novelist would write so cocksurely about numismatics, for instance, or toxicology, without checking his statements; yet anyone can write nonsense about flowers and get away with it.

An exception was D. H. Lawrence; a genuine lover of flowers, he took the trouble to be accurate about them. Another, rather surprisingly, was Proust. He seldom describes flowers for their own sake, but how many of his similes and analogies are botanical, and how exact they are! Sometimes, indeed, he becomes almost too technical, as in the parallel which he draws between the Charlus-Jupien encounter (in *Sodome et Gomorrhe*) and the fertilization of the orchid belonging to Oriane de Guermantes. We are supposed to be a nation of flower-lovers; but as far as novel-writing goes, it has taken a Frenchman to tap the resources of botany.

The Elizabethans are popularly supposed to have been, as writers, particularly botanophil: but D. H. Lawrence, I think, summed the matter up when he called their imagery 'upholstered'. Their lilies and violets and gilly-flowers are seldom more than conventional decoration. Shakespeare seems to have had a genuine taste for flowers, however – and wild ones at that; moreover, he is often unusually explicit – though sometimes his nomenclature has given rise to confusion, as with the

> ⸳⸳⸳ long purples,
> That liberal shepherds give a grosser name,
> But our cold maids do Dead-men's fingers call them ⸳⸳⸳

Millais, in his picture of Ophelia, assumes that Shakespeare meant the Purple Loosestrife: but the Loosestrife was never called Dead-men's fingers, nor, for that matter, by any 'grosser name'. Dead-men's fingers, in fact, refers to one or other of the palmate-rooted orchises, and is also loosely used for *Orchis mascula*, one of the round-tubered species, all of which were given 'grosser names', not only by liberal shepherds, but by the early herbalists; the reason being that the twin tubers suggested a pair of testicles. (This seems to have accounted, too, for the ancient use of orchis-roots as an aphrodisiac – presumably on the principle of sympathetic magic. 'Satyrion' is mentioned by Petronius and Pliny, and under the name of Salep was still sold in this country up till the early nineteenth-century. It is still used in Turkey, and considered to have mildly stimulant properties.)

Some of the older references to flowers in literature raise the interesting problem of how much (or how little) the Flora of this country has changed in the last three or four hundred years. Accurate plant-records, of course, were almost unheard-of before the last century; and most theories about the British Flora, as it existed before that period, are the purest speculation. For example, Shakespeare mentions the Oxlip, as a familiar wild-flower. Now the Oxlip, today, is a rare and local plant, confined to a few districts in East Anglia. Presuming that Shakespeare meant by Oxlip the flower which now bears that name – and it is quite possible that he meant something else – the question arises: was the Oxlip, in Shakespeare's time, a common and widely-distributed plant, which has since become scarce? It is possible, of course, that Shakespeare merely used the name 'Oxlip' because he liked it; but this, with Shakespeare, is unusual. Some of the plants he mentions can still be found in the localities which he specifies – a classical example is the Samphire on the Dover cliffs. The supposition that the Oxlip was common in his day, and has since become rare; that this can happen, is proved by plenty of modern instances – including *Orchis militaris*.

IV

But my main occupation, during those last terms at Bedales, was writing 'novels'. I wrote at least half-a-dozen: some of them I still possess – closely-written, in thick, cloth-covered school exercise-books on both sides of the paper. In 1939, at the outbreak of War, I disinterred them from my old school playbox ... *Il faut, Nath-anaël, que tu brûles en toi tous les livres* ... Yes, I thought, it would have saved a lot of trouble if I had burnt them 'within myself', instead of allowing them to take this too, too solid form. *Quand aurons-nous brûlés tous les livres?* I thought, feeding the fire with yet another abortive adolescent masterpiece.

At the top of the box was my earliest 'novel': it was called (very suitably) *Clouds*, and must have been written when I was about fifteen. I turned the closely-written pages – the writing was formed and legible, almost without corrections. That fatal facility, I thought – I must have possessed it even then. The novel, needless to say, was about the country; 'plot' and character, indeed, were plainly the merest pegs on which to hang my rhapsodical descriptions of Spring in the Kentish woods. A rather dim young man called Ian lived near Canterbury: he was married, but his wife didn't like the country, or perhaps she merely didn't like him. In any case, Ian was very unhappy, and the 'story' consisted almost entirely of descriptions of his long, lonely walks through the countryside, interspersed with reflections upon God and War and the League of Nations – topics about which, in real life, my feelings at that time were singularly luke-warm.

But it wasn't the world of the novel itself that came back to me as I turned the pages, squatting on the floor by the playbox: what I chiefly remembered was sitting in the library at Bedales, the hot air from the heating apparatus wafting a smell of dust and muddy football boots among the high shelves, the autumnal trees dripping outside the windows, and a pianist in the neighbouring hall repeating over and over again the same passage from Rachmaninoff's Prelude in C sharp minor. The Prelude itself, hackneyed as it is, became evocative in after years of just this complex of feelings and sensations; the dusty indoor-warmth after football, the autumn dusk falling over the school-buildings, the dripping trees – and the warm, almost sexual feeling of release as my pen raced over the lined paper, turning out page after page of facile, middle-brow prose. It was at least, I suppose, a more rewarding occupation than passing notes to Dorothy.

There were several more 'novels', on similar lines, after this: then there came a complete break. *Shepherd's Hey* (which must have been my fifth or sixth 'novel') was prefaced by a quotation from Aldous Huxley. I had read *Crome Yellow* and *Antic Hay*, and a new world had opened for me. Worse still, I had discovered, at about the same time, the Nineties.

Both in my prose and in real life, I became henceforward 'a little weary', at the same time affecting a Gumbrilesque cynicism towards all the things which I had previously taken seriously. Up till this time I had continued to cling, rather half-heartedly, to Christian Science – or at least to a personal, rather heretical and pantheistic version of the Faith; Mrs Eddy, however, could not long survive the atmosphere of Mr Mercaptan's *dix-huitième* boudoir. *Shepherd's Hey* was nothing more or less than a Huxleyfied version of my daily life at school; my friends were portrayed without the least disguise; whole conversations went down almost verbatim. True, some of the characters – particularly myself – tended to speak the Huxley dialect: but after all, I was trying hard to speak it in real life. I wrote chapter after chapter with immense enjoyment: there seeemed no reason why the book should ever come to an end. A shameless exhibitionist, I showed the manuscript to my friends, who were all depicted in their worst lights: after all, I had been merciless enough to myself. With the fever of a convert at his first confession, I had described minutely my most intimate sexual preoccupations; what would have happened if a member of the staff had got hold of the book, I cannot imagine. While I wrote it, I identified myself so completely with the hero that I find it almost impossible to remember, nowadays, whether certain episodes really happened, or whether I invented them. But if Maurice, the hero, was based on myself, it is no exaggeration to say that myself came to be based largely on Maurice. Our development – Maurice's and mine – was a sort of race: sometimes I was ahead, sometimes Maurice. If I read Verlaine, Maurice had read him within the week; if Maurice was reading Joyce I was wrestling with *Ulysses* as soon as a copy could be obtained. On the whole I was honest: I didn't often allow Maurice's cultural activities to eclipse my own. It was more of an effort, though, to keep up with his emotional development; in his sexual life Maurice was as unenterprising and as much frustrated as I was myself; but there came a time when he threatened to put into action what had remained, for me, the most cerebral and inoperative of desires. Reluctantly, and with a sense of rather noble renunciation, I brought the book to a sudden and somewhat unsatisfactory conclusion.

But I had reckoned without Maurice: with the best intentions on my part, he simply refused – once having been set in motion – to lie down and die. Soon I had begun another novel about him; and in this, alas! wish-fulfilment had triumphed completely. But how I enjoyed writing it! The book was, I suppose, chiefly a kind of protest – begun in the previous 'novel' – against Bedales, and the depressing fact that I was still at school. I felt grown-up, and I was chafing at the restrictions of school-life, which I couldn't be bothered, now, even to satirize: I merely wanted to escape from it. Maurice was already at Oxford: and the fact that I hadn't caught up with him seemed a mere historical accident.

None the less, the life of the school made certain demands upon me: I became a prefect, which gave me a certain amount of authority (though far less than at a public school) and involved a fair number of duties. Moreover, though I might have decided to be Literary, my liking for botany persisted. It became, once again, a semi-secret and rather shameful passion: unworthy, as I considered, of an aesthete and a decadent ... The trips to Harting or Winchester continued, but coming back in the evening, sweating, happy and healthier than ever, I would retire to the Library and write: a new chapter of Maurice's saga, or perhaps a poem – probably a villanelle – about fading flowers and spiritual corruption, and how everything was unbearably sad, and Life was Futile.

It would be highly entertaining to myself – but not, alas! to anybody else – to follow the subsequent career of the unfortunate Maurice. But the later volumes of his saga were committed, perhaps wisely, to the flames ... It is sufficient to say that his behaviour-pattern conformed impeccably to type. Having been sent down from Oxford, he worked for a time (as might have been expected) in a publisher's office; frequented the bars and nightboxes of Bloomsbury and Montparnasse; paid visits to Trou-sur-Mer, and nearly (but not quite) became a Communist. Never altogether happy in Mr Mercaptan's boudoir, he could never, on the other hand, quite bring himself to follow in the footsteps of Alfred J. Prufrock along that *via media* which led, so consolingly (if somewhat painfully) out of the Waste Land ... Nor, like his creator, did he ever succeed in finding the Military Orchid. He died in 1939, murmuring passages from *The Hollow Men*, and regretting the *paradis perdu* of a vanished age: a good old-fashioned Futilitarian to the last.

PART THREE

The High Mountains of Clova

Now let's think what shall we throw
what
   do
     you
       think, a
bomb? No let me suggest a Commode
    CLERE PARSONS

I

Major Wilmott was *alakefak*: so much so, that it was difficult to get him to do any work at all.

'Anybody I ought to see this morning?' he would say, coming into the Clinic-tent at about half past ten. Fifty or sixty patients had been waiting outside since nine o'clock: their restive noises could be heard beyond the tent-flap – a subdued bourdon of whispering, scraps of swing, muttered curses, shuffling feet.

'You ought to see the patients in "A" tent,' I said.

The Major looked bored.

'How many's that?'

'About fifty.'

'H'm – yes. Well ... the fact is I'm really rather busy. I promised the Surgeon I'd go over and look at a case of his. And the Staff-sergeant's waiting for me to go through the monthly returns. Could you sort out the most – um – urgent ones, and I'll run through them?'

'Very good, Sir.'

I sorted out the case-cards as best I could, while the Major had a cup of tea with the Sister. The tea-drinking took rather a long time; another MO came in, and the Major seemed to have forgotten his patients entirely. At last I went to remind him – taking the cards of those I had weeded out as 'urgent'.

'H'm – yes. You know, I really ought to get over to the Surgical Division. I promised to be there by eleven.'

No doubt, I thought, there was another cup of tea waiting for him in the Surgical Sister's bunk.

'Really, you know,' he went on, 'I don't think I need see all this lot today. They're all on treatment, are they not?'

'Oh, yes, Sir, they're all on treatment.'

The Major looked at me, and his eyes twinkled.

'I always say that, in dermatology, there's a great deal to be said for leaving things to Nature. One shouldn't over-treat skin-conditions; let Nature take its course. H'm – what do you think, Edwards?' He turned to the other MO, a captain.

'Oh, I agree, Sir. Nothing like letting Nature take her course.'

'Er – well, yes. I think we might leave these over till tomorrow, don't you?'

As Clinic -orderly I was of course only too pleased: it meant an hour's less work, and I could go and help with the treatments.

'I think you ought to see Boughton,' I said.

'Boughton? Boughton?' The Major twinkled again. 'Ah, yes: how does it go?' And suddenly he began to sing:

'How beautiful they are –
The lordly ones
Te *tum*-titty *tum* –
In the hol-low hills ...'

'No, Sir,' I said, 'not Rutland Boughton – Private Boughton, that impetigo case with the high temperature.'

'Oh, yes, Boughton. Of course. Well, we'll see Boughton. Better send those other blokes away till tomorrow. *Tum*-titty *tum* – in the hollow hills.'

I sent the other blokes away: they were not unjustly rather annoyed.

'Cor, what sort of place is this?' they said. 'Don't you ever get no ——ing treatment? I'm not standing for this. I'll see my OC about this, I will.'

Then we saw Boughton.

'H'm yes. I think we'd better evacuate him. It's no good trying to treat a case of that kind up here in the blue. No facilities, no facilities. Fix it up with the Medical Wardmaster, will you?'

The Major was very keen on evacuating his patients; it saved no end of trouble.

Coming out of the tent, he hummed the *Faery Song* again.

'I'm afraid the Colonel takes a very poor view of me,' he remarked. 'I was trying over Brahms's *Sapphic Ode* at the Mess piano before breakfast this morning. I feel he took a very poor view of the whole proceeding. H'm, yes. A very poor *shufti* indeed

. . . Oh, by the way, one more thing: I wonder if you'd mind running down to the RE's Mess with a message for the Colonel? I'll give you a chitty – you needn't wait for a reply.'

I had a cup of tea while he wrote out the chitty. Then I walked down to the RE's Mess.

We were stationed near a small Italian colonial town, in the Cyrenaican green-belt. The hospital, formerly an Italian military one, lay on a slight hill: all around, the vast open countryside stretched away for miles; highly-cultivated, yet strangely desolate, a land half-reclaimed from the desert. To the north, a range of low, rocky hills broke up the landscape; but to southwards, the cornfields – already burnt golden by the hot March sun – seemed to roll away endlessly towards the heart of Africa. Disposed in regular patterns across their vast expanse, the square white farm-houses of the Italian colonists looked like toys.

The hospital itself was built round an enormous quadrangle of bare sand. The white, arcaded buildings had a certain Italianate grace, and the whole disposition of them suggested, nostalgically, some *piazza* in Southern Italy. In a British colony, I thought, the hospital would have been of red-brick and corrugated iron, and the whole place would have looked exactly like Aldershot.

Over the sandy quadrangle tiny sky-blue irises grew in profusion, springing nakedly from the dry, trodden soil. The March sun was almost hot enough for KD. Walking across the quadrangle, I tried to translate the fascist slogans which were painted on the walls of the buildings:

MEGLIO UN GIORNO DA LEONE CHE CENTO
ANNI DA PECORA.

I knew that one, of course. Then there was the one about machine-guns (wasn't it Marinetti's?) – something about the song of the *mitragliatrice* being the song of Life. And on every other wall, in enormous blue letters:

CREDERE, OBBEDIRE, COMBATTERE.

We were a VD Treatment Unit, attached to a General Hospital; but Major Wilmott had been prevailed upon to 'lend' half-a-dozen of his orderlies to the Skin Division, and to offer his own services in his capacity of Dermatologist. We were accommodated in two tents, with a Sister of the QAs to supervise. In practice, the

Sister's duties were confined to making tea; I dealt with the case-cards and the running of the Clinic, and helped with the treatments. It was a cushy job, and I enjoyed it.

Walking down to the R Es' Mess, I passed our own quarters: rows of billets which looked like a cross between stables and pigsties. They had been used formerly by Italian colonial troops, and were full of bugs. But between the two rows of billets was an avenue of mulberries and acacias, and the place looked clean and charming in the spring sunshine. Outside the Treatment-rooms, the VD patients squatted in the sun, waiting for their irrigations or injections; they looked browned-off. One of them, a Libyan Arab, was playing some kind of reed-instrument, which sounded oddly like bag-pipes. Along the paths and on the banks, grew a profusion of the Starry Clover – *Trifolium stellatum*, one of the rarest plants in the British Flora, confined, in Britain, to a patch of foreshore at Shoreham, in Sussex. It was pleasant, but rather shocking, to see it growing so abundantly in the middle of a VD hospital in Libya.

My friend Kurt Schlegel, an Austrian Jew enlisted in the British Army in Palestine, emerged from one of the Treatment-rooms as I passed. He seeemed excited.

'What balls-up then is this?' he exclaimed, without preliminary, in his fluent but very peculiar English. 'I write up all the twelve-forty-sevens for that bastard – PC double-plus, EC ——ing plus and every bloody thing, and give them to him, and he then say: No, Schlegel, I do not want that you write up my cards. I do them myself. So then, you bastard, I say, you ——ing do them yourself, isn't it?'

'I bet you didn't call him a bastard,' I said.

'No, in effect I did not. But for why should I his bloody cards write, and then like a child be treated?'

'Never mind. We're both on half-day today. Coming out for a walk?'

Kurt looked black.

'It is very well for you,' he muttered. 'You work on Skins. Very nice, very cushy.'

'I like Johnny Wilmott.'

'Yes, I think he is the true English gentleman, isn't it?'

'Except that he's Scotch.'

'He cares also a —— for his orderlies.'

'I expect that's because he's a gentleman.'

Kurt nodded.

'It is to expect,' he agreed. 'Where then do you now go?'

I told him where I now went, and left him.

The REs' Mess, when I arrived there, seemed deserted. I went into the hallway: the place had been a small country villa, the property perhaps of some richer colonist. There were polished tables and chairs in the hall, and the whole place looked oddly unmilitary. On one of the tables stood a bowl full of tall, pinkish flowers. I went to look at them: I looked again; at last I took one out of the bowl. Yes, there could be no doubt: the plant I held in my hand was the Military Orchid.

At that moment a woman emerged from the kitchen-quarters. Johnny Wilmott had warned me about her: she was Italian, but spoke a little French. I gave her the Major's note; then I asked her about the Orchid: did she know where it grew? She didn't. Who had found it? *M. le Colonel* had found it, she said. Was *M. le Colonel* in the mess, I inquired? At that moment I, a private, would have been quite prepared to beard the Colonel in his bedroom, or even in the lavatory, had he been there. But he was not. *Mi dispiace*, said the woman, *c'est dommage* ... But the Colonel wasn't there, and she had no idea where he had found the plant. *Nella campagna, dans la campagne*, no doubt. I asked if I might take a specimen. *Mais volontiers*, she replied.

I left her, and, bearing a fine specimen of the Military Orchid, walked back towards the hospital. I left the orchid in my billet, and returned to the Skin-tent. When the Major returned, I told him about my discovery. He was sympathetic, and promised to ask the Colonel of the RE unit where he had found it. I waited a few days, and then broached the subject again. The Major was vague: he hadn't had an opportunity ... The days passed, weeks passed. I lacked the courage to return to the RE Mess myself; and Johnny Wilmott no doubt felt that to approach a Colonel whom he scarcely knew, merely to oblige one of his orderlies who happened to be a botanist, was hardly befitting to a Major and a Specialist-Dermatologist.

Owing, therefore, to the exigencies of military etiquette, the Military Orchid had eluded me once again. I consoled myself, however, on a closer examination of the plant, by deciding that it was not, after all, the true Military. The divisions of the mid-lobe were too narrow: it was probably an 'intermediate' between *Orchis militaris* and *Orchis simia*. (When I returned to England the plant was identified as a variety *tridentata* of *Orchis militaris*.)

And shortly afterwards the Unit moved to Tripoli.

The Military Orchid might have eluded me once again. But Cyrenaica had its compensations. The North African flora is not unlike that of Southern Europe; and very much more 'European', of course, than that of South Africa. Botanizing round Cape Town, on the way out, I found the flora entirely bewildering: it was difficult to assign a particular plant to any Natural Order, much less to a species. But in Cyrenaica, the flowers were at least half-familiar; one could usually spot at a glance which Natural Order they belonged to. And in many cases they were plants which, in England, are exceedingly rare. Such as, for example, the wild Gladiolus, which in March grew in great drifts in the cornfields; or the Starry Clover, the commonest weed of the way-side banks. In the cornfields, too, there were the two *Adonises* – the scarlet one, an English rarity, and the yellow species, unknown in Britain. And everywhere grew the big, yellow Ranunculus, as large as a poppy, which, earlier in the year, had covered the desert round Tobruk. And in mid-winter, the meadows near the hospital had been starred with a small lily, bluish-purple and cold as Sirius, flickering like a weak spirit-flame among the drenched grasses.

After Alamein, the chase across the desert, the fall of Tripoli, the landings in Algeria, it began to seem that the War might one day be over: the 'end-of-term' was in sight, one would be going home for the holidays.

In Tripoli we had six weeks in transit, with nothing to do; if one could avoid the vigilance of the Staff-sergeant after breakfast, one could hitch-hike down to the beach and bathe. I spent a week-end, unofficially, with a friend of mine, a masseur at a Convalescent Depôt along the coast, on the way to Homs. He was a musician and a Catholic convert; in the afternoon he played the Ravel *Sonatine* on the piano in the Garrison Theatre, and in the evening, sitting on the sand beneath the tamarisks on the edge of the desert, he chanted the *Veni Sancte Spiritus* from the Sarum Gradual.

All this was, naturally, too good to last; the General Hospital to which we were attached 'borrowed' us for ward-duties. Casualties were streaming in from the Sicily landings; I was put on a Surgical-ward. I knew nothing about surgical cases. One of the Sisters, very upper-class and Miniverish, told me I was 'futile', which was probably quite true. Our patients were mostly head-injuries; they were nearly all unconscious, and wet their beds every half-hour or so. They muttered to themselves perpetually; but scarcely ever violently and obscenely as one might have expected. Mostly they murmured 'Oh dear, oh dear,' quite quietly, over and over again.

One of the patients was an enormous Basuto. He sat up in bed, supported in Fowler's position, helpless and silent, looking very sad, staring in front of him. Occasionally he smiled, but I never heard him utter a word. One afternoon an orderly came to take his temperature; he was sitting up, as always, silent and expressionless.

'Not got much to say for yourself, George, have you?' the orderly said, feeling for the patient's pulse. The black hand fell back heavily from his own as he lifted it. 'George' had been dead for some time.

II

Every day we expected to get a Movement Order: the Unit was waiting to go to Sicily. But the ADMS, so the office said, had made a balls-up; there were no VD units in Sicily, yet we could get no authority to move. In the torrid camp in off-duty hours, or on the wards, I dreamt perpetually of Sicily, trying to remember all I had ever heard about it. Empedocles on Etna, Proserpine at Enna, Aleister Crowley at Cefàlu, *L'Après-midi d'un faune*, D. H. Lawrence and his peasants, the ruins at Agrigentum, Magna Graecia and Pythagoras, Mrs Hurstpierpoint and her 'wild delicious scheme' of visiting Taormina – Sicily became for me a fantastic Land of Heart's Desire, a complex of arbitrary and incongruous images, in which the campaign then raging – the stream of casualties pouring into the hospital, the tales of malaria, *scirocco*, flies and bugs, syphilis, drought and starvation – had little or no part. *N'importe où, hors du monde* – I would have willingly gone anywhere to escape from Tripoli, from the Surgical Wards, the broiling August sun beating on our tents, the daily and unvaried ration of M. and V.

'So then, I start now to learn Italian, isn't it?' Kurt Schlegel announced. We procured, from the Hospital Library, a not very adequate Italian grammar, and began to study it.

'*Avete del vino?*' Kurt would say, adding with determination: 'When we come to Sicily, I get drunk, that is sure.'

But it was not till mid-September that our Movement Order did eventually arrive. I was down with sandfly-fever and nearly missed the boat. Fortunately we crossed in a Hospital Ship; leaning over the side, as the ship ploughed through the sun-dazzle of a late summer evening,

> 'Betwixt the Syrtes and soft Sicily,'

we watched for the first sight of the Promised Land. At length it emerged – a blue, hilly, irregular coastline; at the eastern extremity rose a mountain – conical, formal as a Fuji-yama painted on a fan, a child's naïve idea of a mountain: it was Mount Etna.

Nearer at hand, on the rising ground above the bay which we were entering, stood what appeared to be a Greek temple, severe and classical in the waning light as the Parthenon itself. Darkness had almost fallen when we docked. The quay-side seemed deserted. As we stepped on to the landing-stage, a small grey cat scuttled across to greet us. I realized suddenly that this was an Italian – or at least a Sicilian – cat: we were back, at last, in Europe.

We were to spend the night with a detachment of Marines. The trucks dropped us, after a rough ride, before an enormous, minatory façade which we recognized as that of the building which we had taken for some ruined temple. It was not, however, a temple, but an airship hangar. Inside it, in the darkness, the roof seemed as high as the sky itself; eating our M. and V., unrolling our blankets, visiting the improvised latrine, we might as well have been back in Tripoli, or in Palestine, or for that matter at Aldershot. My vision of Sicily had fizzled out – as such visions always do in the Army – into this squalid nocturnal process of 'settling-in' to a new billet.

In the morning, however, Sicily was revealed again: the bay of Augusta lay placid and sun-bathed below the hangar; on the horizon Etna had reappeared, an abstract vision of 'mountainousness', formal and serene. A soft, delicious warmth pervaded the morning; nobody seemed to have the least idea what we were to do, or where we were supposed to go. It was as though the soft Sicilian airs had infected us already – infected, indeed, the very mechanics of Army procedure, slowing down the tempo of movement, infusing the military machine itself with a kind of *dolce far niente*. The office said the ADMS had dropped another bollock: there ought to have been transport laid-on to take us to Catania.

Meanwhile, we moved out of the hangar and prepared to camp in a nearby field. It was almost certain we shouldn't get transport now till the next day – perhaps not for several days. We dropped our blanket-rolls under the olive-trees, hanging our mozzy-nets from their branches. Olive-orchards and fields stretched away towards the rising hills; here and there, farmhouses lay calmly, solidly, like natural features, an indispensable part of the picture's composition. The whole landscape seemed immensely pictorial; yet its 'picturesqueness' was no mere superficies of prettiness, an effect of light or ephemeral vegetation or the viewpoint of the observer, as a 'picturesque' scene would have been in England; here the pictorial effect was achieved by the bare architecture of the landscape which now, at the end of the summer, dried-up and flowerless, was perhaps less conventionally 'pretty' than at any other time of the year.

Compared with English landscapes, this first vision of Sicily was like a Cézanne compared with a fuzzy Victorian water-colour. I had seen the landscape of the Midi; but here, even more than in the landscapes which Cézanne himself had painted, I became aware of the architecture, the 'bare bones' of a natural scene. There was nothing 'soft', after all, I thought, about Sicily: it was a hard land – hard, but with an honesty, a primitive candour which concealed nothing.

Presently the landscape began to be peopled with figures. The first to appear was a small boy. Kurt and I decided to practise our Italian.

'*Avete del vino?*' we asked.

'*Mafeesh vino,*' he replied.

'So then, these bastards learn Arabic already,' exclaimed Kurt, with disgust.

Later on, a little pony-cart drove up laden with barrels. The cart was painted gaily with bright garlands and pictures of saints. The elderly peasant who drove it stopped and greeted us. Yes, we could buy some wine. Sixteen lire a litre. Or perhaps we would like to buy a barrel? No, at the moment we didn't need a barrel. We filled our water-bottles; I tasted the wine.

'It's the real thing,' I said to Kurt, as the cool, lovely stuff struck the back of my palate. It was full-bodied yet dry, like a burgundy, but with the salty tang that I remembered from Italian wines in England.

Soon the rest of the Unit had followed our example. We sat in the sun, drinking; and later, walking across the hills, found a farm-house with a table set out in front of it, under the trees. The *padrone* invited us to have a drink. We sat under the olives, drinking slowly, and practising painfully our phrases of Italian. In my brain, like an incantation, the words repeated themselves over and over again: 'I am back in Europe; I am in Sicily.'

By midday, when the rations were issued, the entire Unit was drunk. Not for a long time had bully-beef tasted so good as this did, washed down with the first Sicilian wine. Dinner, on this first morning back in Europe, was a kind of celebration. After it, we began to feel sleepy. Some of us unrolled our blankets. Suddenly three trucks appeared from nowhere, and pulled up on the edge of the field: they were our transport.

Somehow we got our kit aboard, and piled in after it; the driver must have been drunk too, for the drive was a nightmare. We were scheduled to pick up a train at a station on the way to Catania: the drivers attempted several short cuts, one of them over a partially-demolished bridge. The few members of the Unit who were comparatively sober said that it was the worst moment of their lives. Most of us, fortunately, were too drunk to notice.

We arrived, eventually, at Catania. Needless to say, nobody expected us, or had even heard of us. The ADMS, they said in the office, had made another balls-up. We should have gone to Syracuse, not to Catania at all.

Next day we went to Syracuse: we were to be attached, it seemed, to No. — General Hospital. This, we found, occupied a half-built lunatic asylum outside the town. There were over two hundred patients waiting for our arrival, they had been waiting for some weeks, it seemed. More were arriving all the time. At present they were being treated by a part-time Medical Officer and a couple of orderlies. There was no sanitation, very little water, and no accommodation. The office said the ADMS had bollocksed things up as usual.

It certainly looked like it.

Two days later we had opened up our hospital and started work. 'You'll go on "nights",' the Staff-Sergeant told me.

I went on nights by myself: there was nobody else to spare. Soon we had over four hundred patients. During the night there were temperatures to take, sulphonamide tablets to distribute, dressings to apply. It was also at night that most of the convoys arrived. These chiefly came from the mainland; sometimes they had been travelling for a week, and many of the patients had developed acute prostatitis or epididymitis as a result of delayed treatment. Often, when they arrived, there was nowhere to put them; on these occasions they lay down in the fields until tents could be erected and stretchers procured.

In the mornings, the sun rose behind Etna, waking the calm, classical landscape to another broiling day. I sat in the office tent, admitting the last of the night's convoy, eating grapes and drinking wine and water out of a rusty tin mug. After breakfast I walked down the dusty road towards Syracuse. Half-way down were the remains of a Greek theatre, and nearby, in a deep lane shadowed by lemons and oleanders, a wine-shop. The wine-shop was cool and cavernous, with barrels ranged round the walls; the *padrona*, who served behind the bar, was a massive, severe-looking matron like the Mother of the Gracchi. I sat in the wine-shop, looking out on the small garden full of ripening lemons; drinking my wine, and eating grapes. Later, I walked down to the Greek theatre, and sat on the ruined tiers, watching the lizards darting in and out among the Vervain and the Grape-hyacinths.

Then the rainy season began. The Hospital tents were flooded; sometimes they blew down. The patients increased, and our Unit decreased in inverse ratio, a section of it having left for the mainland. The advance-section, however, could find nowhere to open up: the nightly convoys continued to arrive, in increasing numbers, at Syracuse. The ADMS, they said in the office, had dropped another goolie.

*

After a month, I went on 'days'.

'I want this man to have hot sitz-baths four-hourly,' said the MO one morning.

'I'm sorry, Sir, there's no water. We've hardly enough for the ordinary treatments, and we have to boil that up on the Primus. We've no facilities for heating big quantities, even if we had enough water. The patients on tablets can't get enough, as it is. The office says the ADMS – '

'Yes, I see,' said the MO. He appeared to have been listening carefully to what I was saying. 'Well, the point is, I want this patient to have hot sitz-baths four-hourly, so you *will* see that he gets them, won't you?'

The work was hard, our conditions appalling; the MOs demanded impossibilities; half the Unit, moreover, was absent; yet the infection of the Sicilian *dolce far niente* persisted: a sense of balminess and easy gaiety pervaded our billets and even the hospital itself. We laughed immoderately at absurdities; and the discomforts of the place were outweighed by an imponderable and irrational happiness.

One day a singular patient was admitted: an elderly Chinaman in the Merchant Navy. He arrived with an enormous trolley, pushed by two Italians, laden with vast quantities of kit, including a bed. It is doubtful if he realized in the least why he was there; he knew not a word of English, but shuffled about the hospital, urinating in unsuitable places, apparently perfectly contented, and wearing upon his face a broad and placid smile.

Charlie Dacres, a Cockney, and a friend of mine and Kurt's, found him irresistibly amusing. This, apparently, the Chinaman (who became known, inevitably, as Who Flung Dung) took as a compliment, which he politely returned by offering to present Charlie with his bed. Charlie as politely refused it; they exchanged cigarettes and grinned and nodded blandly at each other with the greatest friendliness.

One day I went into the treatment-tent where Kurt was working. Surrounded by a crowd of other patients, he was trying to explain to Who Flung Dung that he must come for sulphonamide tablets every four hours, at eight o'clock, twelve o'clock, four o'clock, and so on. Black in the face with the effort, poor Kurt pointed to his watch, repeating over and over again to him the hours at which he must attend: the Chinaman stood there, entirely unconcerned, wearing as ever his bland, impenetrable smile, not understanding a word, but replying politely to each new attempt of Kurt's with the only syllable of English which he knew: 'Yiss ... yiss ... yiss ...' The more Kurt stormed, the more polite the Chinaman's smile became.

'So then,' Kurt threw at him, finally, his own command of English becoming impaired in the face of such blank incomprehension, 'or you come when I say, or you go and get stuffed, you bastard.'

I related the story to Charlie, who worked in the Irrigation Room. A mischievous light sprang into his eyes.

'Can't have Kurt ill-treating my old china,' he said. 'Oh, no. You just wait.'

For the rest of the day he kept watch, and at intervals of not more than a quarter of an hour, seized hold of Who Flung Dung and conducted him to the entrance of Kurt's tent, motioning him with unmistakable emphasis, to enter ... That evening, Kurt appeared in the billet which the three of us shared, looking more than usually exhausted.

'For what does that bastard Chinaman every ten minutes for ——ing treatment come?' he burst out. 'I tell him to come at eight, twelve, four and eight, and now he comes every ten ——ing minutes. If they admit bloody Chinamen, why do they not an interpreter ask? He comes and he nods and he smiles, and I think I go mad.'

'Have some *vino*,' suggested Charlie diplomatically, his face as innocently inexpressive as that of the Chinaman himself.

'So then, I get drunk,' Kurt declared, with determination, and thereupon emptied the bottle at a draught. Charlie and I went out to get some more; our laughter, freed from the restraint of Kurt's presence, was explosive and prolonged.

We had made friends with a peasant-family, and used to spend most of our evenings with them. The house lay back from the road, down a dusty lane bordered with prickly-pears: the children would see us coming down the lane and call *Buona sera*. We sat in the doorway of the house, in the dusk, eating almonds and drinking an excellent red wine from Floridia. Inside the door, the mother sat with her youngest child on her knee; the father sat nearby, at the table, on which the wine-bottle gleamed darkly in the light from a primitive lamp, consisting of a wick floating in olive-oil; the other children crouched in the doorway, in the dusk. They were the most beautiful people I had ever seen, and the most civilized.

For them, the process of living – on however low a scale, and of however limited a scope – remained an art. I knew, of course, that any of my comrades in the Unit – except perhaps Kurt – would have laughed at me for calling them 'civilized'; for the modern, popular sense of the word has little or no connection with its ancient meaning. Our peasant-friends had no lavatories, no wireless, probably their house was bug-ridden; their children would probably grow up illiterate; but their most trivial doings and sayings – a hand waved in greeting, the position in which the mother held her child, the manner, apologetic yet proud and dignified, in which they lamented their poor hospitality – these things revealed them, no less surely than his physical features reveal the Jew, as belonging to a race which deserved, more than most, to be called civilized rather than barbarian.

In mid-October the rains abated somewhat, and a kind of St Martin's Summer occurred. We walked over to bathe at Santa Panagia, a few miles along the coast from Syracuse, on the way to Augusta.

Santa Panagia is possibly not the most beautiful place in the world; but it would be hard, I felt, to find its rival. A small fishing village, built upon two spurs of rock, forming a small cove; rocky slopes rising to the higher ground behind it; and, to seaward, across the calm, enormous bay, the hilly lands beyond Augusta, and behind them, again, towering dimly into the hazy blue, yet preserving its august and formal outline, the immense cone of Mount Etna.

As one approached the village, the first thing one saw, immediately below, outlined against the bright blue waters of the cove, midway between the two rocky spurs, was the brand-new railway station: a square, bright-pink, 'modernistic' affair, very fascist, and doubtless a source of much pride to the inhabitants. That station ought to have spoilt Santa Panagia; but somehow it didn't. Planted in the midst of a village in Sussex or Somerset, it would have been frightful; but here, against this solid, classically-proportioned background, it seemed a mere joke, childish but inoffensive, like the balloon or bicycle which a modern painter such as Chirico or Rousseau le Douanier will introduce incongruously into an archaic or 'primitive' landscape.

We bathed in the cove, and afterwards sat on the rocks, drinking our wine and eating our bread and cheese. The rainy season had brought a kind of autumnal Spring: the paths above the village were fringed with emerald-green grass, and the stony slopes were carpeted with 'spring' flowers: tiny white narcissi, a species of squill, a miniature pink crocus an inch high, yellow ranunculi, grape-hyacinths. Walking back to the hospital, through the orchards which bounded the road, one expected to see the peaches and apricots in blossom; but all one saw – for it was autumn, after all – was the peasants gathering the olives and lemons.

When we returned to the hospital, it was to find that reinforcements had arrived: the office expected a Movement Order to rejoin the forward-section of the Unit. We made up our minds to re-visit Santa Panagia before we left. But the Movement Order arrived a day or two later, just as the office said it would. We never saw the little cove, with its crowded cottages and pink railway-station, again.

Our Movement Order took us to Taranto – by landing-craft. From there we moved to Bari, thence to Foggia. At Foggia the winter met us, and it was bitterly cold. The building requisitioned for our hospital had very few windows left intact; our billets had none. The billets had formerly been inhabited by the lay-sisters from a civilian hospital. On the walls hung oleographs of the Sacred Heart and St Anthony; in the cupboards, however, objects of a very un-nun-like character were discovered.

'So then, here you are,' exclaimed Kurt, in a triumphant outburst of anti-clericalism, 'even the nuns do not despise the love. I think,' he added reflectively, 'I think they are very sensible, isn't it?'

We were not long at Foggia: but long enough to get the hospital opened up, and working as smoothly as circumstances permitted. Then another Movement Order arrived.

'Can't understand it,' said the Corporal-clerk. 'The bloody place isn't on the map.'

'What's it called?' I asked.

He spelt out the letters, painfully. The name was quite

unfamiliar. 'Must be a code,' said the Corporal. 'Looks to me as if somebody's made another balls-up.'

'Probably,' I suggested, 'it's the ADMS.'

But for once ADMS had done nothing of the kind. The transport duly arrived, and we set off. The journey had a curious paranoid quality, like a story by Kafka. Nobody knew quite where we were going or why. Hour after hour the trucks lumbered on, further and further into the country. Gradually the land fell away around us, as we began to climb; soon we were up in the hills, coasting along narrow roads between rocky banks sprinkled thinly with snow. Late in the afternoon we arrived: a solitary building presented itself, among fields, on a hill. Across a valley, a village perched on another hill. All round the building was a sea of mud and half-melted snow. An inscription over the doorway announced that the place had been a *Scuola Agricola*, an Agricultural College.

'Cor, what a dump,' said Charlie Dacres.

'So then, chum, you've had it,' Kurt remarked, with a certain vindictive satisfaction.

'I wish I could have five minutes with that ADMS,' said the Corporal-clerk.

III

But by the time we had opened up the hospital once more and were settled into our billets, the place didn't seem so bad. It was at the southern extremity of the Abruzzi, in the Vastese region. On the first clear day after our arrival an enormous snow-covered mountain revealed itself to northward: it was the Maiella. From beyond its towering whiteness we could hear, when the wind was favourable, the distant thunder of the guns, bombarding Pescara.

The weather turned sunny and warm, and lasted for three weeks; then the winter returned. But on the intermittent fine days, the slow, furtive approach of spring revealed itself. I took to going for long walks: on my first outing, it was pleasing to find *Helleborus foetidus* growing in the hedges. Kurt and I and Charlie began to make friends with the peasants; they were cautious but friendly. We sat outside their houses, drinking wine, in the afternoon sun. It seemed hard to believe there was a war on.

'I think,' said Kurt, 'this will be a good place.'

Ringed with its low, soft-contoured hills, topped with remote villages, the country had an oddly static, formal air: it suggested, in this lenten weather, with the snow still streaking the hilltops and lingering under hedges, some emblematic vision of winter in an illuminated missal or Book of Hours. Superficially, the landscape resembled Northern Europe rather than Central Italy: the level tillage, the copses of young oaks, the cart-tracks fringed with thorn and bramble – even the Coltsfoot flowering in the waste patches – gave it an almost English air. Only when the eye encountered the changeless, classic olives, or the hill-top village with the snow-covered Maiella beyond, did the view suggest Italy.

Yet even in these weeks of almost unrelieved greyness and intermittent rain, the landscape never quite lost that lucid, sharp-edged quality peculiar to the South. Its 'northern' air was elusive, fleeting. These fields and woods declared themselves with too much frankness; they had none of that mysteriousness, that hint of the *au delà*, which lurks always in the English countryside, even in the Home Counties, and especially during the winter and early spring. Here, the grey skies, the snow, the dripping copses, existed, so to speak, in their own right: details merely, of the winter landscape. Turn the page, and the scene would change to Spring, another and equally formal vision (the Gothic comparison recurs) of the monkish chronicler.

As with the landscape, so with the figures: they recurred in each static, gilt-bordered version of the identical scene – actors in this country chronicle, employed in tasks suited to the season. Now, in March, in the copse of young oak-trees which clothed the slope by the village, the peasants – seen as blue and red blobs in the middle-distance, bright against the dun, neutral background – were occupied in chopping wood for fuel. Nearby, at the farmhouse door, a woman sat with bent, kerchiefed head, babe at breast, half-watching the scene before her; and our eyes, lighting upon her calm, immobile figure, demanded something which seemed unaccountably missing; the gilded, expensive nimbus about her bent head, the painter's pious collage upon this rural and naturalistic landscape.

*

It had snowed for a week: and suddenly the wind came soft and the brown and green patchwork of fields, the silver-grey olives were revealed again. The sun at midday was warm as an English May, the stream-side was miraculously fringed with white poly-anthus narcissi, their heavy scent evoking the atmosphere of English drawing-rooms. In the copse, white crocuses sprang like sudden stars, and among the undergrowth crimson anemones flickered like strontium-flames. Next day the snow returned, powdering with soft precision the fields and woods, formal and pictorial as the snow in a Victorian glass paperweight. The anemones, the narcissi were a freak, a vision of Spring in Winter; fleeting as the sudden, never-to-be-repeated lyric thrown off by some dull, time-serving pedant; a promise not to be fulfilled in this winter land, this never-turned page of the missal, lying open on the lectern, showing only Winter: the reader away at the Wars, perhaps dead by now.

Yet the slow invasion of Spring continued, becoming gradually more insistent: infecting the landscape like the advance of some recurrent fever. Violets succeeded the anemones in the copses, the thin, stripling oaks burst into sudden leaf overnight; and then, walking into the nearest copse after an interval of some days, I saw the first cyclamens; tongues of rosy flame straining upwards from the still-leafless ground, as though in celebration of some Plutonic pentecost. Soon the wood-floor was covered with them: mingled, here and there, with the blue Mountain Anemone, which used to grow in the gardens of our Kentish village. In the cornfields, the Gladiolus grew as it had grown in Cyrenaica; and on waste patches or in the young corn, the Grape-hyacinth spread its drifts of ultra-marine among the drooping yellow bells of the wild Tulip.

Here, as in Africa, the flowers were near enough to those of Northern Europe to strike a familiar note. In the woods, I had been watching some orchid-leaves. According to an Italian Flora, which I had unearthed in the *Scuola Agricola*, the Military ought to occur in these parts. The broad, unspotted leaves, abundant in the woods nearby, were promising; but the next few weeks revealed their secret: they were not, after all, the Military, but *Orchis purpurea*, the orchid which, on a June evening nearly thirty years before, nameless, then, and unrecognized, had been brought to me by Mr Bundock.

Another Orchid, however, grew nearby: so much smaller that I took it to be an *Ophrys*, the Bee, perhaps, or the Spider. It was later in flowering: I decided to keep my eye on it.

We were not hard-worked: patients came in in manageable quantities, and the two sections of the Unit were reunited. Major Wilmott was more *alakefak* than ever; we arranged our duty-times as it suited us.

Kurt, Charlie and myself spent much time with the peasants. We had treated some of them at the hospital, and they showed their gratitude by frequent offers of wine and eggs.

One house had aroused our curiosity for some time: it lay some little distance away across the fields, and for some reason we had never visited it. One day, however, just before Easter, we decided to investigate it.

'I think we find some good *vino*,' said Kurt.

We set off – Kurt, Charlie and myself. Half-an-hour's walk brought us to the house. It lay by itself at the side of a cart-track: similar to the other houses in the neighbourhood, but larger than most. A flight of steps led up the southern wall to an upper room; there was a small vineyard nearby, and a tall, conical haystack, which had been sliced into at need like a cake, and began to look top-heavy. With its white walls and rust-red pantiled roof, the house looked friendly and welcoming in the spring sunshine.

A small boy, playing in the yard, looked at us curiously. Presently he sidled up to us.

'*Sigarette? Cioccolata?*' he asked hopefully.

'We go to ask some *vino*,' said Kurt. '*Avete del vino?*' he asked.

'*Si, si,*' the boy answered with a charming smile.

We followed him round to the doorway on the other side. A woman appeared at the door: tall, broad-bosomed, brown-faced, dressed in nondescript clothes which had once been gaily-coloured, and still hung gracefully upon her straight, stalwart body. On her head was a bright-coloured kerchief.

'*Buon giorno,*' she said, with a curious, dramatic sweep of her arm: a stylized, almost operatic gesture of welcome, at once proud and humble, which seemed to imply that we were free to take possession, if we wished, of the entire farm, such as it was. She accompanied the movement with a broad, delightful smile, revealing two rows of strong, white teeth.

'*Dov'è il padrone, Signora, per cortesia?*' asked Kurt.

The *padrone* was working in the fields, she replied. '*Cosa vuole?*'

'*Se avete un mezzo-litre di vino . . .?*'

'*Si, si. S'accommodino,*' she exclaimed, and immediately pushed forward three little wooden chairs for us.

'In moment her husband works in the fields,' Kurt explained to Charlie, whose Italian was almost non-existent. 'But she gives us wine.'

We sat down, and presently the woman returned with a jug of wine and three glasses. I poured out the wine, and we all said '*Saluti.*' The woman watched us as we drank; so did the little boy, still on the look-out for chocolate.

'*E bùono?*' she asked.

'*Molto buono,*' we said.

It was true: the wine was a *vino nero* – dark, sour, potent, with a purplish glint when held to the light; much better than most of the local wines, which were light and watery, like alcoholic lemonade.

We sat in the sunshine, drinking it slowly, and talking a little to the woman. Kurt did most of the talking: he spoke ungrammatically, but with the confidence of a Central European. I was more shy, being English, and had to think up my phrases carefully. Charlie contented himself with saying '*molto buono*' and playing with the child.

Presently other children appeared, stealing up like shy birds whom the sight of us had driven away: another little boy, a girl of fifteen strikingly like her mother, and another, younger girl, perhaps eleven or twelve, blonde and uncannily beautiful.

We were introduced: the elder girl was called Assunta, the younger Graziella, the two boys Leonardo and Giovanni.

'*Quanti bambini?*' Kurt asked.

'*Cinque,*' the woman replied, holding up the five fingers of one hand; adding that one, the eldest son, was working with his father.

'She is beautiful,' Kurt remarked, of Graziella.

'Like a Botticelli,' I said.

'*Volete ancora?*' the woman asked.

'I think we drink some more,' Kurt said, with decision.

'Too bloody true we will,' said Charlie. 'Best *vino* I've had since we came to this place.'

Kurt asked the woman for more, explaining that we would pay for it.

'*Non fa niente,*' she assured us.

'We give her cigarettes,' Kurt suggested.

We pulled out our cases, and contributed ten each. Kurt handed them to the woman.

'*Per il padrone,*' he said.

'*Eh ... Lei è molto gentile,*' she said, with a half-protesting gesture, and hurried to bring more wine. This time she brought, in addition, three pieces of bread, some cheese, and some sprouts of fennel.

Did we like *finocchi*? she asked.

We said we liked it.

It was not good to drink without eating, she added apologetically.

We sat over the second jug of wine ,relaxed and happy in the warm sun. In front of the house, fields sloped down to a little wooded valley; beyond this, the country stretched away flatly to the low hills, capped by small villages. The brightly-coloured landscape had a curious quality of *naïveté* and innocence. Two cypresses, a few yards from the house, divided the picture abruptly into sections, like the divisions of a triptych. In the middle-distance, figures moved across the fields, hoeing, as though in a picture by Millet. Perhaps the *padrone* was among them.

Presently the beautiful child, Graziella, who had wandered off, reappeared, carrying a little bunch of flowers: grape-hyacinths, narcissi, and yellow tulips. These she presented to us, gravely smiling, then shyly backed away again.

'I've a feeling we're getting well in here,' Charlie said. 'What say we ask for some *parster shooter*?'

'She'd do it,' I said. 'Go on, Kurt. You ask her. Not today, though. I'm on at five o'clock, you know.'

'No, I don't ask. Always you want me to talk bloody Italian. You ask her yourself.'

Finally Kurt and I together approached the topic with as much delicacy as our Italian allowed.

'*E possibile mangiare qui, alla vostra casa?*' we began, and, antiphonally, pressed our point: *pasta asciutta*, perhaps a salad, some eggs. We were so tired of Army food, we explained: we wanted to eat well, *mangiare bene all' Italiana*.

The woman shrugged her shoulders. They had so little food, now, in Italy; the *tedeschi* had taken everything – cattle, poultry, wine, anything they could carry – *e niente pagato*. It was different in peace-time; but now, *in tempo di guerra* . . .

'Heavy going,' I said to Kurt. 'We'll have to use bribery. Jimmy'll give us a tin of bully out of the store, if we get him a bottle of *vino*.'

Kurt nodded, a glint coming into his eye.

'We make business,' he said.

At mention of *carne*, the *signora* obviously began to weaken. She would ask the *padrone*. I added that I would bring some clothes: I had some old civvy vests and pants in my kit which I never wore. The outlook began to seem more hopeful.

At that moment the *padrone* himself appeared, with his eldest son. The father was short, with a pleasant, sharp-featured face and beady-black eyes; he wore a battered trilby, and a brightly-coloured handkerchief round his neck. The son, about sixteen, was beautiful. If Graziella was Renaissance, Umberto was something archaic: a faun from a Greek vase-painting.

The father was presented with the cigarettes. He immediately called for more wine, and we all sat down again, inside this time. Charlie came in, and the atmosphere became distinctly festive. I wished I wasn't on duty at five: I began to feel rather drunk, and refused any more wine. The bare, whitewashed room was very clean; bunches of drying tomatoes hung from the ceiling-beams, and a few *salami*. In the open stone hearth a fire of olive-wood was blazing, and a vast cauldron hung over it, waiting for the *pasta*, which lay ready for cooking, in a floury pile, on the scrubbed wooden table.

The *padrone* was very friendly. He wanted to know all about the war: we were soldiers, we should know. We explained that we were medical orderlies, *croce rossa, non combattere*. He looked half-convinced. *Ieri sera molto boom-boom-boom*, he insisted: over there, beyond the mountains – pointing northwards. There was a big battle, we said: beyond Pescara, on the way to Bologna. We were lucky, he said, not to fight. Had we many *feriti* in our hospital? No, we only dealt with medical cases, we said, *ammalati*. Our hospital was in the *Scuola Agricola* across the fields. We tried to explain, in our faulty Italian, that we were a VD Unit.

Time was getting short, and after a discreet interval we

broached the subject of food again. Yes, certainly we must come, he said: next Sunday was Easter – *una grande festa*. It was also a special feast for the family – Leonardo, the second son, was to make his first communion. The cigarettes had done their work. We scraped up a few more for Umberto, and prepared to leave. This we were not allowed to do until we had drunk another glass of wine. We repeated, for the *padrone*'s benefit, our promises to the *signora*: we would bring a tin of bully, some old clothes, some chocolate for the *bambini*. Suddenly made bold by our success with her husband, the *signora* took me aside and half-whispered that if we could see our way to bring a *coperta* as well ...

'They want a blanket,' I said to Kurt.

'They've had it,' Kurt said. 'I don't go over the wall for two years, that's sure.'

'We've all those buckshee ones from Foggia,' I pointed out. 'They've no check on them.'

'I'm not mad,' said Kurt.

'Plenty of blankets,' said Charlie, who had been putting back a good deal of *vino* on the quiet. 'I'll bring her one.' He turned to the Signora. '*Si, si,*' he assured her, '*molto* blankets – what the ——ing hell are blankets?'

'She understands all right.'

'Certainly she does,' said Kurt. 'Don't you be worried.'

'*Io portare molto* – you know, blankets,' Charlie insisted. 'Compree?'

'*Si, si. Troppo gentile,*' the *signora* exclaimed, rewarding Charlie with one of her broad, maternal smiles. She was like a Demeter, an Earth-Goddess, I thought.

'See, she's taken a fancy to me,' Charlie said proudly. 'I told you we'd get well in.'

We promised to come at two o'clock on Easter Sunday, and with difficulty left the house. At the last minute, Assunta presented us each with a little bunch of violets, and Umberto, no doubt on instructions from the *padrone,* brought up a bottle of wine, which I stuffed into the front of my battle-dress. The family watched us out of sight. Looking back across the fields, we saw them standing in the doorway, waving. The house, with its two dark cypresses, stood out brilliantly against the sun-flooded landscape: it seemed like a symbol of happiness, a vision of the good life.

*

The problem was to get the blanket out of the billets without being seen.

'It is better if you take it at night,' Kurt advised.

'Is it ——' retorted Charlie. 'Looks too bloody suspicious. Much better to take it in daylight.'

'So then, Private Dacres, you go over the wall,' Kurt predicted with morbid relish. 'That is sure.'

'And you ——ing come with me, Private ——ing Schlegel, RAMC,' said Charlie with gusto. 'It's all right, mate, I wasn't born yesterday.'

We walked out of the billets just before two o'clock on Easter Sunday. Charlie had rolled up the blanket – one of a buckshee issue, unchecked, which we had acquired at Foggia – in a bundle, adequately disguised, to unsuspicious eyes, by several layers of dirty linen. Kurt also carried a bundle: he had compromised with his scruples sufficiently to part with a couple of KD shirts which weren't shown on his 1157. My own bundle, innocent enough to all appearances, contained the cast-off civvy underclothes which I'd bought in Cairo; in the front of my battledress was a tin of bully for which I had bargained with Jimmy James, the Ration Corporal.

We stepped jauntily out of the hospital entrance, looking rather consciously innocent, and walked straight into the Staff-sergeant.

'Where're you blokes off to?' he said.

My heart sank like a stone. Just our luck, I thought. If the Staff was in a bad mood, he might quite easily make things awkward. He flogged too much himself, as we all knew, to regard our bundles without suspicion.

'What's in all them ——ing bundles?' he asked.

I mentally decided to unroll my own first, if he pressed the point: there was nothing in mine he could pick on. I hoped he wouldn't ask to see Charlie's.

'We take our laundry to a farm,' Kurt explained.

'That's right,' Charlie agreed. 'The old *biancheria*, you know.'

The Staff grunted.

'Remember,' he said, 'if I find anyone in this Unit flogging stuff, I'm coming down heavy on them. Very heavy.'

'Ain't got —— all to flog,' Charlie said, nervousness making him cheeky.

The Staff gave him a nasty look.

'Is anyone on duty in this joint?' he asked. 'Who's in the Clinic, eh?'

'Smudge is relieving me,' Charlie said. 'It's my half-day.'

'Who's in the Lab?'

'Nobby does the Lab. in moment,' Kurt replied. 'He has two dark-grounds and one instillation, then finish.'

'What about the office?'

'Mac's there,' I said. 'He's on long-trot today.'

'Well, don't get too pissed. If I had my way I'd have those bloody *casas* all put out of bounds. You'd think this was a bloody rest-camp, instead of a pox-joint.'

We escaped.

'Miserable old sod,' Charlie muttered. 'Just 'cos he doesn't like *vino*.'

'He likes *finocchi*,' I said. 'We might bring him some.'

The day was brilliant and cloudless, hot but with a fresh breeze. We walked through a field breast-deep already with pink clover. In the little copse at the field's edge, nightingales were singing. In the meadow beyond the clover-field the stream-side was still fringed with white narcissi.

'It's a wonderful country,' Charlie said. 'Bloody wonderful. Garden-flowers growing wild, and all.'

Kurt and I laughed.

'Three months ago you were saying how bloody awful it was,' I reminded him.

'I didn't know it then.'

'So now you stay in Italy *dopo la guerra* and marry a nice Signorina, isn't it?' Kurt suggested.

'I might if I hadn't a wife and kids in Blighty,' Charlie agreed.

Our way led through the copse on the slope of a little valley, where I had been watching a colony of orchids. Today, after only a week's absence, I was amazed to find them in blossom: their pinkish tufted spikes were scattered over the copse, among the dwarf yellow genista and purple gromwell. I examined them; they were not, as I imagined, a species of *Ophrys*, but a particularly luxuriant form of *Orchis simia*, the Monkey Orchid: the very plant which, more than twenty years before, had arrived at St Ethelbert's in a brown-paper parcel and had been stuffed, unceremoniously, into a tooth-glass in the dormitory.

Now, as then, I felt impelled to suppress – or at least to modify – the pleasure which the sight of it gave me: not that Kurt and Charlie would have minded in the least, but one is apt to be self-conscious about such private enthusiasms, which one cannot share. The Italian Monkey, as a matter of fact, differed considerably from its English counterpart: it was more robust, with broader divisions of the lip. Still, it was undoubtedly *Orchis simia,* and to find it, on this Easter day, when we were on our way to a *festa,* when the whole countryside, indeed, seemed already to be flooded with a warm delightful sense of happiness – to find it thus had the effect of suddenly crystallizing my own contentment, like the final grain of some mineral which, dropped into the beaker, is enough to saturate the solution.

Growing among the other 'Monkeys' I observed one which was not yet in flower; much larger and more robust than the rest; it differed from them, also, in having a long, cylindrical spike. There seemed, I thought, little doubt that this, at last, was the true Military Orchid. A day or two more would decide the point; and meanwhile, after gathering some specimens of the Monkey, I rejoined the others.

We came out on to the track again, by a little row of houses. Some of the families were standing outside, wearing their best finery for Easter. They greeted us with smiles and welcoming gestures.

'*Buona Pasqua,*' they said; Christ might have risen, this very morning, for their special benefit: so happy did they seem. It was hard to believe there was a war on – not so far away either. Even as we passed the house, a muffled rumble came from over the mountains – away beyond the Maiella, white and austere on the horizon.

A family with whom we were friendly – we had treated the daughter for malaria – refused to let us pass without a glass of wine. Their neighbours followed suit. We were not allowed to go on till we had drunk a glass at each house in the row. When at last we arrived at the farmhouse where we were invited, we were, as Charlie said, 'Well away.'

We had been asked for two o'clock, but time in Italy is elastic, and dinner was far from being ready. The *signora* was busy with pots and pans; Assunta, the eldest daughter, was cutting up the *pasta* into long strips like tapeworms. The other children sat with the *padrone* just inside the door. At the hearth sat an ancient woman whom we had not met before: grey-haired, dressed in drab, ragged clothes, she looked like a benevolent witch. Introduced to us as *la nonna*, she croaked an unintelligible greeting, in dialect, and went on with her task of stoking the fire with olive-wood. Leonardo, who had taken his first communion that morning, was the hero of the occasion: with his face scrubbed, and wearing a little suit of snow-white linen, he looked cherubic and very self-important. With immense pride he showed us his *Ricordo della prima comunione* – a three-colour print showing an epicene Christ surrounded by very bourgeois-looking children, all with blond hair.

With many nods, gestures and whispered thanks (as though the entire Corps of Military Police lay in ambush round the house) the blanket, the bully and the underclothes were secreted in a back room. A two-litre flask of wine appeared as though by magic: this was not good wine, the *padrone* explained; later we would drink good wine, *del vino tanto buono.*

It was good enough for us. We had had no dinner, and must have already drunk nearly a litre apiece on the way. We distributed cigarettes to the *padrone* and Umberto, and chocolate to the children. Leonardo received six bars all to himself, and Giovanni, who resented his brother's hour of glory, burst into tears. He was consoled with half-a-glass of wine.

'Wish I'd been brought up like that,' said Charlie.

'It's all for a cock, these bloody Catholic *festas*,' said Kurt, who, being both Jew and Communist, objected to Easter on religious and political grounds.

'Ah, you miserable old bugger,' exclaimed Charlie, and, lifting Giovanni on to his knee, consoled him further with an extra piece of chocolate.

Presently the meal began: the steaming, fragrant tomato-juice was poured over the two enormous bowls of *pasta* and we sat down round the table.

'*Ancora, ancora,*' the *padrone* insisted, before we had finished our first platefuls. '*Oggi festa – mangiamo molto per Pasqua.*'

After the *pasta* there was chicken cooked with tomato and *peperoni*. This was followed by *salami* fried with eggs. Then came a dish of pork with young peas. Roast sparrows followed, and afterwards a salad. At about the *salami* stage, after several false alarms, the 'good' wine was produced: two bottles the size of magnums.

It was a Homeric meal. Kurt, who had been a student in Vienna before the war, quoted Homer very appropriately. but in German, which nobody understood. Charlie was trying to sing *Lilli Marlene* in Italian to Graziella, who sat on his knee. Umberto produced an ancient concertina and began to play it. Kurt, forgetting Homer, started to sing a very sad Austrian folksong. The *padrone*, for my benefit, kept up a running commentary on the proceedings, comparing the occasion unfavourably with Easters before the war.

'*Prima della guerra era bella, bellissima,*' he insisted. Today everyone was poor. '*E sempre la miseria.*' The Germans had taken everything. It could hardly be called a *festa* at all. He was ashamed: ashamed to offer such an Easter meal to his guests, and mortified, moreover, that Leonardo's first communion should be celebrated so wretchedly. '*Siamo poveri, poveri – noi contadini. Eh, la guerra – quando finirà?*'

I was not only extremely drunk by this time, but I had never eaten so much in my life. So far as I was concerned, Leonardo's first-communion party had been more than adequate.

Presently Umberto struck up a *tarantella,* the whole family, as though at a given signal, took the floor. We all paired off, indifferent as to sex, and bobbed and jigged in time to the music. Charlie insisted on taking *la nonna* for his partner; I danced with the *signora*. I found to my surprise that I was perfectly steady on my feet. Moreover, it seemed that I had been dancing the *tarantella* all my life. Gravely, wearing her calm Demeter-like smile, the *signora* advanced and retreated, hands on hips, bobbed and circled and bowed, all with a goddess-like dignity. Her brown face, beneath her coloured kerchief, was as calm as though she were at Mass; only a beatific happiness irradiated it, as though Christ indeed were risen. She seemed immensely aware, too, of her own personal fulfilment: she had given pleasure to her man, borne him healthy children and (more recently) cooked a dinner fit for those Gods whose Olympian peer she seemed.

The music became faster, the dancing less restrained. The *padrone* whirled about like a ballet-dancer; Giovanni, still taking a rather disgruntled view of the occasion, did a little dance by himself in the corner. Leonardo didn't dance at all: he stood at the doorway and watched the proceedings with the distant air of one who has, that very morning, eaten the body of Christ for the first time. The two girls, Assunta and Graziella, danced a little apart: separated, it seemed, from the rest of us by a mysterious barrier, a mutual understanding; it was as though they were priestesses, gravely celebrating the godhead of their mother. Umberto sat in a corner, with his concertina: an archaic, sculptured faun, younger and older than anybody else in the room.

At last we could bear it no longer, and staggered out into the late afternoon sun, to cool off. Charlie's face was scarlet, his battle-dress and shirt gaped open, showing a pink, damp expanse of skin. Kurt's hair had fallen over his square, heavy-browed face: he looked like Beethoven would have looked if he had ever got seriously drunk. I told him so.

'Ach, I could write great symphonies in a moment,' he declared. 'I am great *Musiker*. Too bloody true I am, you old sod.'

'You're a fat Austrian c——,' Charlie remarked happily.

'It is pity for you I am not, my friend,' Kurt replied.

Umberto came out, his concertina still slung over his shoulder. He took my hand.

'*Sei felice?*' he asked, his teeth flashing white in his brown face.

'*Sono felice,*' I said.

Beyond the twin cypresses the country lay flooded in the warm, slanting light. Away on the horizon, hill upon hill lay revealed in the evening radiance, each topped with its fairytale village or castle. In the oak-copse nearby, where the Monkey Orchid grew, a chorus of nightingales shouted. Graziella had run into the field, and was gathering a bunch of white narcissi.

'*Eh, la guerra. Quando finirà?*'

It was the *padrone*. He looked sadly across the fields. '*Siamo poveri, poveri,*' he added, as if to himself.

There was a war, they were poor, the landlords in Naples or Rome ground them underfoot, their children were uneducated, the priests were paid to keep them in ignorance . . . I knew it all: I had heard Kurt, the Communist, expound it all in Sicily – with conviction, with passion, and at length. Yet I knew also that with these people, on this Easter day, I had felt happier, I had felt a more genuine sense of the joy of life, than ever in my life before.

At last we prepared to leave. Farewells were protracted, and delayed by innumerable afterthoughts in the form of presents and souvenirs: a bottle of wine in case we were thirsty on the way, another for when we got home, one more because it was the 'good' wine, the special wine for Leonardo's first communion. A fourth bottle was added for some further, rather complicated, reason: perhaps it was to drink Leonardo's health tomorrow. A bundle of *finocchi* was produced for the Staff-sergeant, whose partiality for it we had mentioned. Pieces of Easter-cake were pressed upon us for our friends who had not been to the party. A *salami* was offered by the *signora* in case we were hungry in the night – we had had a poor meal after all, she said. Bunches of narcissi and violets could not be refused. Umberto even offered a loaf of bread, in case we should have none with which to eat the *salami*. A pot of some conserve made of pig's blood was proffered by *la nonna*, because a pig had been killed recently.

Our tunics bulging with bottles, our hands clutching *finocchi* and narcissi (and in my own case, a bunch of Monkey Orchids), we started out across the fields. Half-way, we were overtaken by Umberto with a dozen new-laid eggs. When at last we reached the hospital, and staggered across the yard in front of it, we observed the Staff standing before the entrance exactly where we had left him. He was accompanied by MacDowd, the Corporal-Clerk, and Smudger Smith. Their mouths opened, they stared. Then Smudger began to laugh; Mac began to laugh too. Only the Staff kept his countenance: he looked as black as thunder.

''Ere you are, Staff: 'ere's the mustard and ——ing cress for you,' Charlie bawled, and advanced towards the Staff-sergeant, proffered the bundle of *finocchi*. Unfortunately for the success of the gesture, he tripped over a stone and fell flat on his face: the bottle of wine secreted in his tunic smashed noisily, and spilt itself, like some sudden and appalling haemorrhage, over the gravel.

A quiver which might have been a smile flickered over the Staff's prim grey face.

'You'd better get straight into your ——ing billets and get to ——ing bed before the Old Man sees you,' he said.

In the billets that night I said to Kurt:

'You can say what you like, these people know how to enjoy themselves. They may be politically uneducated and downtrodden and priest-ridden and all the rest of it, but they know how to live.'

'Too bloody true,' said Charlie, who was finishing off the bottle of 'good' wine.

Kurt sat up in bed, looking more than ever like Beethoven after a night out.

'So then, have you forgotten?' he asked, with the ominous air of a minor prophet. 'You think they give you all that for nothing? You are ——ing stupid, both of you.'

' 'Course I'm stupid. Who wouldn't be after all that?' Charlie commented, and let a satisfied fart.

'Do you not then realize to what you owe this *festa*?' Kurt pursued.

'Well, what?'

'To *una coperta*, one blanket, GS, property of the ——ing British Army. To that you owe your bloody *festa*, isn't it?'

'Too bloody true,' Charlie agreed. 'But it was cheap at the price. Wasn't it?' he appealed to me.

'Yes, it was cheap at the price,' I said: thinking of the *signora* dancing like a goddess, the wine and the sunshine and the flowers, and, beyond the dark cypresses, beyond the copse loud with nightingales where I had found the Monkey Orchid, the sun-flooded country rolling away towards the distant hills.

IV

A few days later I returned to the copse to look at the plant which I believed to be the Military Orchid. It proved, after all, to be only a 'gigantic' form of *Orchis simia*: the lip divisions were too narrow, their colouring too pale for even the most wishfully-thinking botanist to think otherwise.

I sat in the copse, listening to the nightingales: realizing for the first time, too (for how often does one ever *see* a nightingale in England?) that Swinburne's 'brown bright nightingale' was an exact description. Around me, the pink spikes of the Monkey flaunted themselves bravely, with none of the coyness of their English counterparts, among the broom and purple gromwell. Other orchids lurked in the copse, too – the Lady, the Green Man, the Late Spider; a gathering of notabilities which, assembled here merely by the principles of Italian ecology, I could never have seen together, in England, except perhaps in Mr Bickersteth's wild-flower show at Bedales.

Across the little valley, by the farmhouse where we had gone on Easter Sunday, I could see, from where I sat, Leonardo and Giovanni playing round the doorway; and presently the *signora* herself emerged to spread out some snowy bundles of linen upon the bushes in the garden. She stood for a moment, framed between the two pillars of the cypresses, and, catching sight of me across the valley, waved her hand with a fine, sweeping gesture. Presently I would walk across the valley, and enter the cool, whitewashed kitchen; the *padrone* would be coming in from the fields, and we should drink some wine. I thought that, one day, I should like to come back and live here; or was the sense of happiness which permeated this countryside merely, as Kurt would insist, an illusion? Was one sentimentalizing one's impressions, like any tripper? It was possible; but I chose not to think so. I picked the 'gigantic' plant of the Monkey, and walked slowly across the valley towards the house.

'So then, we go,' announced Kurt when I arrived back at the hospital.

A signal had arrived; we were to close down the hospital, and be prepared to move off at forty-eight hours' notice.

'It's a bloody shame,' said Charlie. 'Just as we were getting well in, too.'

'Before we go we take another blanket to that *casa*,' Kurt suggested recklessly. 'Then they give us another *festa*, isn't it?'

It was some weeks before we finally departed. But at last, one brilliant, windless morning, the trucks arrived. We piled in; for most of us it was just another move. Leonardo and Giovanni had trotted across the fields to say good-bye. We gave them some chocolate, and some cigarettes for papa. At last the trucks moved off, down the white dusty road: past our farmhouse, past the little copse where I had found the orchids. The house was on a slight rise, and its red roof, flanked by the two cypresses, remained clearly visible for the first five miles of our journey: beckoning to us across the fields and wooded valleys with a promise of happiness which we must ignore, an invitation which we should never again have an opportunity to accept. All that remained, for myself, would be the brown, dried skeletons of the orchids which I had found in the copse: the Lady, the Late Spider and the Monkey; and, among the specimens of the latter that taller, robust plant which, before it was in flower, had so tantalizingly raised my hopes, and which, if I chose to base my identification upon Linnaeus, Bentham and Hooker or Colonel Mackenzie, might be considered to be the Military Orchid. It was, as a matter of fact, *Orchis simia*; an intermediate form which was almost worthy to be called *Orchis militaris*.

Almost, but not quite.

JOCELYN BROOKE

A MINE
OF SERPENTS

To
Mrs William Ford
of Bishopsbourne
'Much love, all burnt'

Contents

Author's Note

This book is not a 'sequel' to *The Military Orchid*, though a few of the same themes and characters recur in it. The two books should be considered rather as complementary – two sets of variations upon the same or similar thematic material. None of the characters is entirely fictitious; none, on the other hand, attempts to be a 'truthful' portrait; 'Hew Dallas', 'Basil Medlicott' (and, for that matter, the narrator himself) are all composite characters.

The account of my great-grandfather, Joseph Hewlett, in Part V, appeared in a somewhat extended form in *The Nineteenth Century and After*, to whose Editor my grateful acknowledgements are due. The quotations from poems by W. H. Auden and Clere Parsons are reprinted by permission of Messrs Faber and Faber.

J.B.

Some Truths seem almost Falsehoods and some Falsehoods almost Truths; Wherein Falsehood and Truth seem almost aequilibriously stated, and but a few grains of distinction to bear down the balance . . . Besides, many things are known, as some are seen, that is by Parallaxis, or at some distance from their true and proper beings, the superficial regard of things having a different aspect from their true and central Natures.

SIR THOMAS BROWNE: *Christian Morals.*

PART ONE

The Big Rocket

Le bal tournoie au fond du temps
J'ai tué le beau chef d'orchestre
Et je pèle pour mes amis
L'orange dont la saveur est
Un merveilleux feu d'artifice.

GUILLAUME APOLLINAIRE

I

THAT long, pale face – severe, disgruntled, consumed by a chronic anxiety – where had I seen it before? Its owner I judged to be in the late thirties: young for his age, in spite of his receding hair and a missing tooth or two. He wore a good suit beneath a very dirty Burberry; sitting in the bar on the Channel boat, he smoked cigarettes incessantly, and kept glancing, with an unnecessary frequency, at his wrist-watch. I had already characterized him, privately, as a type – the travelling English intellectual; but I had little faith in my own judgement, and should have been only slightly surprised if he had told me he was a film-star, a motor-salesman or a traveller in ladies' underwear.

So far, however, he had allowed me to retain my illusions. We were seated at neighbouring tables in the bar; but we were careful to avoid each other's glances. Once or twice, turning suddenly in his direction, I caught his eyes upon me; but their mild brown gaze shifted immediately as our glances crossed, and, after staring for a moment with an assumed interest at some point on my other side, he buried his face once more in his book.

The book was a Penguin: I looked at the title, half-hoping for some clue to the reader's personality. It was a novel by Graham Greene – non-committal, proving him neither a highbrow nor a low-brow. He sipped his brandy, flicked his cigarette ash on the floor, looked at his watch again: performing these actions, I fancied, with a progressive increase of self-consciousness, as though aware that I was watching him. It was almost certain that we were both catching the Paris train; and nearly inevitable that, sooner or later, we should speak to one another. But plainly he wished not to be the first to break the ice.

Had we really met before? Or did he conform, merely, to one of those privately evolved archetypes by which one classifies a new acquaintance? Most of us, I suppose, employ habitually some such principle of identification: equating each new face with one or another of a private gallery of masks. These type-*personae* remain constant – modelled from the faces of those who impressed us most in the formative years; and each fresh face, as we encounter it, is instantaneously classified according to a private scale of correspondences – just as the varietal form of some plant is assigned at a glance, by the botanist, to its type-species. Independent of sex, age or social condition, this unifying factor can breed some odd incongruities; in the face of the waiter at a Swiss hotel one recognizes the lineaments of one's spinster-aunt at Budleigh Salterton; the procuress at Marseilles may body forth the remembered countenance of a sergeant-major in the Army; but the type-face remains unmistakable, one of the half-dozen or so basic categories of one's social botanizing.

Timid yet arrogant, consumed by an incurable *Angst* (surely the true *maladie anglaise*), my travelling-companion continued to read, with a feverish concentration, his Penguin Graham Greene. I, meanwhile, surveying each in turn my private collection of archetypal masks, had at last run him to earth: his type-*persona* proved to be that of a housemaid who had been in my mother's service some twenty-five years before, and whose existence, up till this moment, I had almost entirely forgotten.

The discovery, when it came, proved disappointing; I had hoped for a less basic, a more exact identification. It was as though one were to discover, after a laborious study of Bentham and Hooker, that a plant belonged to the Natural Order *Ranunculaceae* – satisfactory up to a point, but there remained the harder task of identifying its correct genus and species. One's plant might, in fact, be anything from a delphinium to a buttercup ...

But that face, those eyes! They belonged, I felt sure, to somebody who had shared, in some past epoch, my own background. Oxford, London, Montparnasse, the Army? A series of odd, inconsequent images chased across my mind, like the images of a half-waking dream: a sprig of lilac floating in a cup of tea, a table with a checked cloth on a café-terrace, a picture by Braque of oysters and a guitar ... Some episode, some forgotten associative link, continued maddeningly to elude me: the recollection was, as it were, upon the tip of my tongue. Each time I looked at my fellow-traveller, I felt the same start of half-recognition: the sensation had the odd, hallucinatory quality of that moment when, turning the corner of a corridor in a strange hotel, one encounters suddenly, in a mirror, the unexpected and disquieting image of one's own face . . .

I amused myself by making a kind of clinical diagnosis of his personality. He was 'literary', I decided; probably he wrote himself. I judged him to be a bachelor, very likely with a small private income. Listening to his voice (as he ordered another drink) I identified it as certainly 'public-school' and probably Oxford. I could guess that at school he had hated games and been bad at maths. Possibly he was a Communist, but more probably an Anglo-Catholic; I was even prepared to wager that, during the War, he had had a cushy job in the Ministry of Information or the Air Force Intelligence Service. By a stretch of imagination, I could visualize him on horseback – but it was impossible, somehow, to believe that he had ever learnt to drive a car.

II

I was on my way to Italy; but it was a fact which, as yet, hadn't impinged upon my inward consciousness. I could, if I liked, verify it from documentary evidence – by looking at my ticket and my visa; the printed statements were incontrovertible; yet I still couldn't quite believe that I was really going to Italy.

I took out my ticket and looked at it again – *Dovra à Milano*. I turned to the freshly-stamped visa in my passport: *Buono per un soggiorno di quarantacinque giorni.* It was true, after all – thus I assured myself, rather as a flat-earther might accept, reluctantly, the fact of the world's rotundity: convinced, intellectually, by the scientific evidence, but remaining, for all that, emotionally a sceptic.

Anticipation, indulged to excess, is apt to result in an unforeseen overdraft on one's emotional capital. One is left, at the moment of realization – or sometimes earlier – a spiritual bankrupt. This was precisely what had now happened to myself. For weeks past, as the date of my departure drew nearer, the knowledge that I was really going to Italy came to seem less and less exciting, became more and more a mere tedious necessity to which, in a rash moment, I had committed myself. I had obtained my visa, I had bought my ticket and my travellers' cheques; there was no help for it now, I should have to go. But if something had happened to prevent me – illness, say, or an international crisis – I should not have been much disappointed; I should, indeed, have been almost relieved.

Yet a few months ago, when this trip to Italy was still a mere wishful-phantasy, unlikely (it seemed) ever to be realized – how much it had meant to me then!

I had left Italy as a soldier, nearly two years before: returning home to be demobbed, I had embarked upon the gradual and depressing process of settling into the old rut, in an England more drab and unaccommodating than even the worst reports from home had led me to believe. It was an England in which even the climate seemed to have worsened: the dreary, sunless summer of 1946 followed by the worst winter in living memory; the snow lingering on into April; the endless cold lying like a weight on the mind, nipping every crescent thought like a precocious seedling, imposing upon all one's actions the leaden burden of anxiety and an irrational guilt ... And all the time, in the hinterland of my consciousness, there remained the precious, the unalterable vision of Italy: an image of the Good Life, a *paradis perdu*.

True, I had seen Italy at its worst: a vanquished country, ruined by war. Moreover, I had seen it as a private soldier, constrained by Army discipline from entering into any genuine relationship with the land or the people. Yet even in these conditions I had fallen in love with it: like a fairy-tale princess disguised as a goose-girl, Italy had asserted her power over the heart of one who was destined (it seemed) to love her.

Distractingly, the sunlit image haunted that hopeless, rain-drenched summer, that interminable winter with its snow, its fuel-restrictions, its burst pipes and its gathering sense of impotence and moral defeat ... And my memories of those vanished years were at last synthesized, concentrated with the passage of time, into a vision of a particular place, a particular moment ...

The place was a farmhouse in the Abruzzi, the moment a spring evening when we had gone to drink wine with a peasant-family, friends of ours. We had sat in the open doorway, looking out across the calm, level landscape towards the castellated height of Monteodorisio; the *signora* sat at her spinning-wheel on the threshold, her husband lounged at the table periodically refilling our glasses with the dark *vino corto* from the big *fiasca* on the table; the children played some interminable, mysterious game, darting to and fro like swallows, in and out of the door, in the gathering dusk. It had rained in the afternoon, and, against a retreating bank of thunderous purple cloud, a rainbow spanned the level sunlit fields between the twin columns of the cypresses before the door.

That moment, that vision became for me a kind of yardstick against which I judged, in moods of heightened consciousness, my present discontent. That was the Good Life: the calm, ordered routine of country living, the relaxed hours after work, with the wine and the easy talking and the children playing in the twilight . . .

I wrote poems, I wrote stories about my friends in that remote, haunted region, inland from Vasto: the names of towns and villages echoed like incantations in my mind – Pollutri, Scerni, Casalbordino . . . One day I would go back there . . . But I scarcely believed in any such resolve; the place and the moment had become fused into a kind of private myth, gathering accretions from the nostalgic poems I had written; becoming, as the months and years passed, further and further removed from the reality: a Land of Lost Content which I could never revisit, since it had never, in fact, truly existed.

Yet now I was actually returning to Italy; I was in the train; my visa was valid for a *soggiorno di quarantacinque giorni*. The high, sweeping fields of the Pas de Calais drained away in the train's wake; tomorrow morning we should emerge from the Simplon into Italy, the Promised Land . . . But I was still – in spite of my passport, in spite of the hurrying French fields – I was still unable, in my heart of hearts, to believe that it was genuinely true.

III

My companion of the boat was, as I expected, on the train: he occupied, apparently a compartment not far from mine. On my way down to the restaurant-car, at tea-time, I passed him – standing irresolutely in the corridor, still smoking, still clutching (as though it were an amulet against intrusive strangers), his Penguin Graham Greene. Our eyes met for a second, we exchanged a polite half-smile of recognition; some minutes later he followed me along to the restaurant, taking a seat as far away from me as possible, and burying himself, once again, in his book.

Nothing could have been more off-putting than his behaviour; had I actively desired to make his acquaintance, I could only have done so by the most importunate breach of tact. His manner was about as encouraging as a barbed-wire fence. None the less, I was convinced that he was at least as interested in myself as I was in him; his curiosity warred with his timidity; over and over again I caught him glancing in my direction when he thought I wasn't looking.

I was certain, now, moreover, that we had met before: but the occasion, the shared background of our acquaintance remained, irritatingly, on the verge of memory. Beneath his young-middle-aged exterior there seemed to me to lurk something perennially youthful; his whole countenance retained the stigmata of a retarded adolescence. He belonged, for me, to an epoch upon which time had conferred a curious ambiguity; a period which, when I recalled it at all, seemed a blend of fact and fiction: real episodes overlaid with the atmosphere of some poem or oft-read novel, living personalities I had known equivocally mated with the characters of fiction ... This young man, I thought, might just as well, so far as I was concerned, be a character out of Proust: he was neither more nor less familiar to me than Saint Loup or Albertine – if anything, rather less.

I debated with myself whether, when the next opportunity occurred, I should break the ice. Was it, after all, worthwhile? He might prove to be a bore; and on a journey as long as this one, bores must be avoided at all costs ... At the same time, he had roused my curiosity; and I decided that, if the chance offered, I would find out who he was.

It was even less easy than I had supposed. At dinner that night he evaded me again: we passed one another in the corridor, once more exchanging a brief complicit smile of recognition. Thereafter, he remained closeted in his sleeper, not to emerge again till the next morning.

It was at breakfast between Lausanne and Montreux that I at last seized my opportunity. He had arrived in the restaurant-car before me; most of the seats were already taken; but there was a vacant one at his table.

'Do you mind if I sit here?' I said, and sat myself down without waiting for his reply.

His eyes flickered warily over me; he ducked his head, smiled, and then, absurdly, blushed scarlet. Mercifully the waiter arrived, and we ordered our coffee and *croissants* The lake slid past the windows, veiled with rain; the snow-flecked mountains of Haute Savoie gleamed and vanished and reappeared behind a smudgy curtain of mist.

'How far are you going?' I ventured.

He paused, as though the question required some thought.

'Oh well – actually, I'm going to Florence,' he said, with a rather secretive air; implying, it seemed, a host of possible destinations, among which he had chosen Florence for some mysterious reason which he was beginning, already, to regret.

'I'm going to Milan,' I said brightly, feeling myself, by contrast with his languorous indecision, unnaturally brisk and efficient. 'I'm going on to Florence later,' I added, hoping that he would not be too much alarmed at the news.

'Oh yes – well, I'm going on to Siena – and perhaps Spezia – it's all rather vague, at present,' he muttered, casting a regretful look at the Penguin which lay beside his plate. He had finished Graham Greene, I noticed, and was now reading *South Wind*; as a clinical sign this was promising – it confirmed, in part, my earlier diagnosis.

The coffee and the *croissants* arrived, and we lapsed into silence for a few minutes. But I wasn't going to let him down so lightly.

'Do you know Italy?' I asked him.

Yes, he knew Italy, he admitted; but there was something oddly shamefaced about the confession: it was as though he were admitting acquaintanceship with some lady of easy virtue.

A tedious rehearsing of place-names ensued: did he know the Abruzzi? He didn't. Did I know the Dolomites? I didn't. About

Naples we agreed in knowing little or nothing: I had passed through it on my way back, after the War ... A gleam of interest shone in his eyes.

'You were in the Army, were you?' he asked.

I admitted it, but tactfully by-passed the topic of National Service. The War, I felt, would get us nowhere: the image of him which haunted the back of my mind dated, I was convinced, from an earlier epoch.

For the next ten minutes we circled warily about each other's defences; one topic after another fell abandoned among the dregs of our coffee; conversation proceeded in a series of tangents. It was heavy going; if I was to make any headway, I should soon have to burn my boats. I racked my brains for some formula which, without being too baldly importunate, might serve to break down the barriers which our shared bourgeois upbringing had raised between us. Barriers between classes could prove often enough unscaleable; but they were nothing, I thought, to the barriers of mutual distrust which could alienate two members of the same caste.

The train had slowed down: we were passing through Montreux. Other passengers were waiting for our table; we should soon have to get up and return to the *wagons-lits*. My companion's hand was already grasping *South Wind* ...

I glanced out of the window; a shop-sign caught my eye: Rumpf, Aubort et Cie., Succursale. Immediately an extraordinary excitement possessed me: one of those sudden transports which demand, however unsuitably, to be instantly communicated. Had I never spoken to my companion before – had he been a Lapp or a Basuto or even a deaf-mute – I could still not have repressed the words which rose to my lips.

'Why, how extraordinary,' I exclaimed, 'there's Rumpf.'

My fellow-traveller looked at me in astonishment, as well he might.

'There's *what*?' he asked.

But I scarcely heard him. I was staring backwards, out of the window, at that magical name; transported suddenly into a remote, mythical past in which my companion could have no possible share ...

I was recalled at last, reluctantly, to the present, by the arrival of the waiter with our bill. Simultaneously, I observed that my fellow-traveller was still staring at me with undisguised astonishment. Quite unwittingly, I had at last succeeded in puncturing his protective shell. His gaunt, inhibited countenance was transfigured by a blatant curiosity.

'What in the name of goodness *has* happened?' he asked. 'Have you seen somebody you know?'

'Yes – I mean no,' I replied lucidly.

He continued to stare at me, his eyes widely open.

'Well *really*,' he murmured, shaking his head dubiously. 'Might one ask, in that case, who it was you *didn't* see?'

He deserved, I felt, an explanation.

I explained . . . As I did so, I witnessed a miracle. His timidity, his nervous, caste-conscious reticence, fell from him like a garment; his eyes brightened. He interrupted me; I interrupted him; we both spoke at once. Within a couple of minutes, we were chatting away like old friends. The other passengers waited for our table; we disregarded them . . .

What had happened? Merely that we had stumbled, by a hundred-to-one chance, upon a concealed tract of common territory; a shared aberration, a quirk of temperament which, but for the happy intervention of M. Rumpf, would almost certainly have remained unrecognized by us both. Without M. Rumpf, we might have talked for hours, for days perhaps, without having the least suspicion of the peculiar and improbable bond which united us.

This shared mania, this *amour qui n'ose pas dire son nom*, was none other than an incurable passion for . . . fireworks. We were, both of us, chronic pyrotechnomaniacs. We loved fireworks to the point of imbecility – fireworks of all kinds, from Brock's Benefit at the Crystal Palace to the humble half-crown's-worth in the back garden. It is not a common vice among adult males; its Freudian interpretation may well be sinister; but whatever the explanation, it tends to be – among its rare addicts – an absorbing (if often a somewhat frustrated) passion.

As to M. Rumpf – his miraculous intervention amounted to no more than the fact that he was a dealer in (among other things) *feux d'artifice*. Nearly a quarter of a century before, I had once bought some fireworks from his shop; a tenuous association – but it had been sufficient to make me, for the moment, a child again, and, as such, capable of that ill-considered outburst which had electrified my companion: 'There's Rumpf.'

It was, I thought (considering it in retrospect), a singularly idiotic remark.

By this time we were well past Territet, and speeding down the valley towards Bex. We left our table at last, and walked back along the swaying corridor towards the sleeping-car; discussing with an intricate and delightful technicality the respective merits of Messrs Pain and Messrs Brock; comparing notes upon the Crystal Palace, the Armistice Display of 1918, the displays at Wembley (they were by Pain's) in 1925. Both of us knew Messrs Brock's (pre-war) headquarters in Cheapside, and those of Messrs Pain's in St Mary Axe; and if my companion could brag that he had once helped Brock's men to set up a regatta-display at Bournemouth, I could reply with the more solid boast that I had given yearly displays, all by myself, at the village where we used to spend the summer; moreover, I had once written an article on fireworks for the *New Statesman* ...

The conversation, in fact, showed every sign of lasting, without interruption, as far as Milan.

IV

My discovery of Messrs Rumpf, Aubort et Cie. dated from 1924, in the spring of which year I had gone with my parents to Montreux for a holiday.

I was fifteen, and it was my first trip abroad. My young enthusiasm was still divided, at that time, into two parallel streams: botany and pyrotechny. Flowers and fireworks: with a few negligible infidelities in the shape of butterflies, white mice or tame grass-snakes, these twin passions had ruled my childhood.

But so far as fireworks were concerned my cult had already entered upon a period of decadence; not that I was, at heart, less enthusiastic; but the pressure of outward events had begun to make itself felt. I was fifteen: in another year or two I should be considered 'too old' for fireworks. Already my family deprecated my incurable passion; indeed, they had always deprecated it: their view being that fireworks were a 'waste of money'. At school, too, I had become a little self-conscious about my pyrotechnomania, and somewhat more secretive than formerly; the catalogues of Messrs

Brock, Pain or Wells would be hidden away in my play-box, and studied rather furtively, when nobody was about.

Botany, on the other hand, was apparently something one didn't – or at any rate needn't – grow out of; it could be, at a pinch, a respectable occupation for adults, though frowned on by athletes, and considered, on the whole, more suited to women than to men. Botany, moreover, was not a 'waste of money' – it cost, indeed, practically nothing: though on this very holiday in Switzerland I had persuaded my family to buy me Correvon's *Album des Orchidées d'Europe*, which cost twenty-five Swiss francs – an unprecedented outlay; but after all, it was better than spending it on fireworks.

Yes – I should be sixteen this year; I was due to take the School Certificate – a preliminary stepping-stone towards the distant, unimaginable goal of Oxford ... In three years I should be 'grown-up'! It was an alarming thought: alarming, though tinged with a pleasant, rather heroic excitement – like the prospect of a bathe on a chilly morning ... Plainly it was time I started to 'grow out of' fireworks. My brother advised me to start saving up to get a motor-bicycle – a suggestion of adulthood which I found flattering, though the prospect of actually possessing a motor-bike merely bored me. I didn't want a motor-bike; what I wanted, more particularly, at the moment, was a Horizontal Wheel with Mine and Roman Candles, or a Devil-among-the-Tailors, both of which I had seen pictures of in Messrs Brock's catalogue.

But the Silver Age of pyrotechny had, after all, set in; memories of an *Age d'Airain* haunted me; fireworks which I had bought years ago and alas! let off, were fringed with an inexpressible nostalgia. Others, which I had merely seen in shops but never been able to buy (for it would have been a 'waste of money') became for me the objects of a hopeless and unassuageable desire. They belonged, these memories, in almost every case, to the magical epoch of my earlier childhood, the years before I went to boarding-school. Ever since my first term at St Ethelbert's, I had been gradually elaborating this cult of the past; and in the collections of fireworks which I hoarded, through every winter, towards my annual summer display, I tried as far as possible to revivify the old nostalgic passion – a passion which existed in several modes, but which was usually typified by the memory of Messrs Pain's

Assorted Guinea Box, which I had seen and gloated over at Gamage's in 1918, just after the Armistice.

Needless to say, I never dared even to suggest that I might buy it. A whole guinea! My expenditure on fireworks seldom exceeded half a crown at a time. But the Guinea Box became a symbol of my ideal: on some distant day, when I was grown-up, perhaps, I would walk into Gamage's and buy just such another Guinea Box.

But *would* it be exactly the same? Messrs Pain's (and Messrs Brock's too, for that matter) were liable, from time to time, to alter the contents of their Assorted Boxes. Perhaps, when the great day came – the day when, as an emancipated being, I should be free to buy a Guinea Box – perhaps it would be something entirely different, something unrecognizable.

Meanwhile, I decided to collect, piece by piece, as many of the original items as I could. I remembered almost all of them: there was a portentous one called a Barrage Fire Curtain, for example, which alone cost four shillings; there was a Bouquet of Gerbs, a Triangle Wheel, a Golden Fountain and a Mine of Serpents . . . It was that Mine of Serpents, more than any of the rest, which really captured my imagination. The vast cylinder (at least it had seemed vast, in those early days) with its protruding fuse; the whole demonic and sinister machine decorated with its gilded and starry paper wrappings; the green, closely-printed label, instructing one to place the Mine on a flat surface, to 'light blue touch-paper and *retire immediately*' . . . Yes, it was the Mine of Serpents which gave the Guinea Box its peculiar and irresistible magic . . . One day I would possess one; I had already collected a Triangle Wheel, a Bouquet of Gerbs and a coloured Roman Candle . . . Meanwhile, the Mine of Serpents became for me a kind of Pandora's box, within whose august form lurked a whole resplendent brood of unimaginable joys or terrors.

At the Montreux period I was still, slowly and with loving care, reconstructing the Guinea Box. My last act, before leaving England, had been to lay out the treasured pieces, one by one, on a table; dwelling nostalgically upon their romantic lineaments, and calculating how much money was still needed to complete the original assortment.

My pyrotechny, indeed, had reached a stage of rather sterile Byzantinism. I clung more ferociously than ever to past memories

... Yet I was still capable, at times, of breaking-out; and one such infidelity to the Guinea Box occurred at Montreux.

We were passing the shop-windows of Messrs Rumpf, Aubort et Cie., and I noticed, affixed to the glass, among other advertisements, a poster bearing the magical words: FEUX D'ARTIFICE. I persuaded my mother to enter the shop; an assistant bounced forward.

'*Feux d'artifice?*' I said, trying to speak casually, but inwardly bubbling with excitement. To a botanist, the Swiss flora had been exciting enough – the fields of globe-flowers and narcissi, the oxlips and mezereon in the copses; now I was to be initiated into the mysteries, no less exciting, perhaps of Swiss fireworks.

'*Mais oui, Monsieur,*' murmured the assistant, beckoning me forward to a counter at the back of the shop. '*Voilà,*' he said, and handed me – a tube of tooth-paste.

Excitement had been bad for my accent; I explained, as well as I could, that *dentifrice* was not what I wanted. I wanted *feux d'artifice*. At last he understood; we were wafted up to an upper floor, and there at last were the *feux d'artifice* – recognizably related to their English counterparts, yet subtly different.

Just as I had observed that the Early Purple Orchid, notable in England for its blotched and spotted leaves, assumed, here in Switzerland, an immaculate purity of green, so now did I assess the differences between an English rocket and a Swiss one. It was called a *Fusée* to begin with; its 'cap' was broader, the conical tip blunter. The instructions, moreover, were written almost unintelligibly (to me) in French ...

I came away from the shop, at last, happily carrying a parcel which contained that foreign and outlandish *Fusée*, and a Maroon which had the deceptively innocent look of a ball of string. I would have liked to buy more; but after all, I had already bought Correvon's *Album des Orchidées*, and wasn't I perhaps getting rather 'grown-up' for fireworks?

Besides, they were such a Waste of Money.

V

Pyrotechnophils of round about my generation must have suffered, more than any of their forbears, from a frustration of their ruling passion; for during the two world wars fireworks were not only illegal, but practically unobtainable.

To have been a child, as I was, in World War I, and to have conceived a passion for fireworks was indeed unlucky. Many of my contemporaries must have avoided this particular misfortune, by virtue of sheer ignorance: for during a war it is quite possible to grow up without even knowing that fireworks exist. My own enlightenment was due to *Little Folks*.

At what period did that excellent children's magazine come to an untimely end? It was certainly still being published after the first War; after about 1920, however, I have no exact recollection of it. But during my earlier childhood it was my staple reading. I was lucky, too, in possessing a considerable collection of back-numbers; for my brother and sister, a decade or more older than I, had taken it regularly, and by the time I started to read, the collection had assumed imposing proportions.

Was *Little Folks* really so good as it seems in retrospect? Alas I shall never be able to decide; for in 1927, when we left our house at Sandgate, the pile of *Little Folks* was sent, with a cart-load of other 'unwanted' literature, to a local branch of the Girl Guides. 'Unwanted' – by my parents, possibly; but neither my sister nor myself have ever quite forgiven the sacrilege. I retain to this day an unfair and illogical prejudice against the Girl Guides.

Best of all, perhaps, were the Serial Stories: being the lucky possessor of all those back numbers, I could read them consecutively, without having to break off at the most exciting point and wait for next month's instalment . . .

Little Folks had, I think, the advantage of appealing to children in general, as opposed to the sectional interests represented by *Chums, The BOP, The Girl's Own Paper* and so on. There was something in *Little Folks* for everybody. Fairy tales – I remember an episodic serial which seemed to go on interminably: *Tales of Cuckoo Common*, all about gnomes, elves, leprechauns and such;

humour – a writer called Murray Fisher (reputed in some quarters, I believe, to be a woman, like Homer), who produced a
monthly story which seemed to me exquisitely funny; whimsy – I
recall a series of rather embarrassing tales called *Billy the Bird-
charmer*. And of course, school-stories: a boys' school-story and a
girls' one.

I seem to have preferred the girls' stories: at least, I have a
much clearer recollection of them. Girls, it seeemed to me, had
more fun: they played practical jokes in the dormitory and went
for botany-rambles, both of which activities seemed to me prefer-
able to the endless cricket and football which monopolized the
stories about boys' schools. In particular, there was a series called
The Scrapes of a Schoolgirl, with very dashing pen-and-ink illustrations, in the style of Phil May. The heroine, a fascinating girl,
bore the mysterious name of Ymmot; it was some time before I
realized, rather to my disappointment, that 'Ymmot' was merely
'Tommy' spelt backwards.

There were articles, too, of general interest; nature-notes, a
puzzle-corner; and a monthly article called 'The Editor's Den,'
written in a very matey, let-me-be-your-father style which I found
faintly objectionable. Even the advertisements – and *Little Folks*
carried what must have been a very profitable number – even the
advertisements fascinated me. Van Houten's Cocoa, Plasmon Oats,
Robinson's Patent Barley – they sounded delicious, particularly
the 'Patent' Barley.

But best of all, of course, was the Adventure Serial: always
thrilling, but more so than ever when I began to take *Little Folks*
myself, and had to wait a month for each new instalment. I remember one which must have appeared about the end of the first
War; *Lost Island* it was called, and for six whole months I came
under the spell of that romantic title.

The title, alas! nowadays is all I can remember; not a single
character or incident has remained with me. Yet I can remember
as if it were yesterday the thrill of opening the new number of
Little Folks, and settling down greedily to read the fresh instalment. At the head of the story, each month, was printed a line-
drawing showing, I think, a boy in a sailor's jersey scanning a
palm-fringed island upon the horizon; and the picture, combined
with the romantic-sounding title, set the mood for what followed.

The story has gone: but the mood remains – an alien, throbbing excitement, a sense of inhabiting a world of muscular, pugnacious heroes whom I adored, but whom I felt to be in some way alien and unapproachable. I never, I think, *identified* myself with those heroic and masterful beings; I was too acutely aware, perhaps, that I should never, in reality, be that sort of person. I was content to be a spectator, a fellow-traveller, a *voyeur*. My own native mental climate was represented, perhaps, rather by *Billy the Bird-charmer*, or the adventures of Ymmot; *Lost Island*, for me, was a true phantasy-world, an over-compensation for my natural timidity and introversion.

I evolved indeed, at a somewhat later date, an island of my own: a cloud-cuckoo-land based partly on *Lost Island*, partly on *Robinson Crusoe* and the stories of Ballantyne. Here I could play out my own heroic sagas to my heart's content – and without having to wait a month for the next instalment. I peopled it with heroes of my own choice – some fictitious, some real; boys at school, friends of my brother's. It was to remain with me, in part a legacy from *Little Folks*, long after that dusty pile of masterpieces had been despatched, irretrievably, to the Girl Guides.

Browsing, one day, through some of the older numbers, I came upon an article which I didn't remember to have seen before. I began, casually enough, to read it; and before I had got half-way, I was entirely captivated. The article, in fact, had sown the seeds of an absorbing and life-long passion.

Its title was 'All about Fireworks'; it described a visit to a firework factory and carried a rather dim photograph of one of Pain's Alexandra Palace displays, showing a set-piece of the King and Queen. The basic ingredients of firework-making were described: charcoal, sulphur, saltpetre, strontium nitrate, iron filings and so on. Rather sketchy indications followed of how to manufacture roman candles, squibs, catherine-wheels. No sooner had I finished the article, than I began to pester my family for further information; why had I never had any fireworks? Could I please get some as soon as possible? My family shook their heads, smiling at my *naïveté*. There was a War on, I was told; there were no fireworks to be had. I should have to wait till the War was over . . .

It was a crushing blow. The War, after all, had been going on (I was dimly aware) almost as long as I could remember; there seemed no particular reason why it should ever stop. The 'end of the War', at any rate, was an event as unreal and unimaginable to me as the end of the World ... I decided, forthwith, that if I couldn't get real fireworks, I would manufacture my own.

I read the article again, more carefully. Charcoal, sulphur, salt-petre ... Sulphur was easy; there was a tin of it in the medicine-cupboard, for my nurse was a great believer in brimstone-and-treacle as a 'spring' medicine. Charcoal, too, was available; I had been recently ordered by the dentist to clean my teeth with it. Saltpetre was more of a problem; doubtless it could be obtained, but I was too impatient to tolerate further delay. I mixed charcoal and sulphur in equal parts, and added a few toy-pistol 'caps', hoping that they would compensate, in part, for the lack of salt-petre. This mixture I enclosed in a paper tube, and hung on the nursery fireguard – one of those high, old-fashioned guards like wire cages, with a brass rim at the top. Tremulously, I applied a match to it; but alas! it was a case of *Hamlet* without the Prince of Denmark. Lacking the essential ingredient, my 'firework' smoul-dered sullenly for a few minutes, exhaling odours of the abyss; spat at me viciously, once or twice, as the 'caps' ignited; and then went out.

I don't know what I had expected: perhaps I had hoped that a gilded and argentine portrait of King George and Queen Mary would spring into sudden, fiery life on the wire guard ... At all events, my experiments ceased for the time being; partly, no doubt, owing to my own sense of failure, but chiefly because people objected to the smell.

I was promised, however, that when we went to our cottage in the country for the summer, I should be allowed to buy some saltpetre. Why the buying of saltpetre at Sandgate was thus out-lawed, I don't know; possibly my mother felt that, if I insisted upon blowing myself up, it would make less mess in the country.

The summer came at last; we arrived at the cottage; and I was allowed to pay a visit to Mr Barron, the chemist in the next vil-lage.

Mr Barron's shop was fascinating in itself, quite apart from the purpose of my visit; in the window, the two traditional jars of coloured water gleamed with a double splendour of crimson and emerald-green; the shop itself was poky, dark, and over-crowded, and one was assailed, as one entered it, by a complex, un-identifiable odour: the blended exhalation, no doubt, of those rows of heavily stoppered bottles which, with their gilded, mysterious labels, seemed capable of harbouring all the genii of the Arabian Nights.

Mr Barron, though bluff and good-humoured, and quite unlike one's conception of a professional wizard, was tinged himself, to some extent, with the magical atmosphere of his surroundings. He would attend to our wants in a rather solemn, mysterious manner, as though the dispensing of a bottle of Parrish's Food were invested with a kind of sacramental quality. When I asked him for saltpetre, charcoal and sulphur, he blew through his moustache, glared at me from his pale eyes for a full minute, and then exclaimed: 'Well I'm jiggered.' Had I asked him for dynamite or prussic acid, he could hardly have looked more overwhelmed.

Having recovered, however, from his first shock, he proved extremely obliging; putting up the chemicals I ordered in little pill-boxes (each carefully labelled), and himself proffering a few suggestions about the manufacture of fireworks ... He became, indeed, before long, a valued and fascinating friend; I haunted his shop with an increasing frequency, and was initiated into innumerable secrets of his trade. Sometimes, too, I would take him specimens of medicinal plants, in which he showed much interest – Deadly Nightshade, Henbane, Monkshood – and he would treat me to a lecture on the drugs derived from them.

Armed with the operative, the essential components, I embarked, once more, on the making of fireworks. This time, I was certainly more successful; more than once, in the slumberous hush of a summer afternoon, the village would be startled into wakefulness by an ear-splitting detonation, followed by the pervasive stench of gunpowder ... I was not ambitious; such complex 'pieces' as rockets and roman candles were beyond me – and perhaps would have taxed the resources of Mr Barron. I contented myself with Bengal Lights, Golden Fountains and an occasional big bang.

One day I was visiting my friends the Igglesdens, and talking, inevitably, of the subject uppermost in my mind. As though divinely inspired, Mrs Igglesden suddenly rose to her feet and began to search in the recesses of a tall, deep cupboard in the farmhouse kitchen. Presently she handed out a cardboard box with a gaily-coloured label on the lid. I looked at it: 'Brock's Crystal Palace Fireworks', I read. The words took my breath away; had the box contained the Crown Jewels, I could not have been more impressed; indeed, I should have probably been considerably less so.

Real fireworks! They had lain in the cupboard since before the War, said Mrs Igglesden; a present from some friend of the family, they had for some reason never been let off. There they had waited, neglected and forgotten, until this very moment.

As a matter of fact, they were rather small fry: penny squibs and catherine-wheels and golden rains. Haunted, a little later, by the ornate and costly splendours of the Guinea Box, I was to look back on Mrs Igglesden's humble collection with something like disdain. But at the moment of their discovery, I was thrilled beyond measure; after my poor home-made efforts, they had all the glamour of professionalism; I felt rather like a student from a provincial art-school visiting the Uffizi for the first time.

But alas! there was still a war on. For the first time I became genuinely, acutely conscious of the fact; I resented it bitterly, and developed a quite creditable hatred for Germany ... A discussion ensued, leading to a compromise: I couldn't let fireworks off after dark, 'because of the War'; but there would be no harm, surely, in letting them off in daylight ... To do so, however, would be wasteful; it was therefore decreed that the bulk of the box should be saved till After the War; but I was to be allowed to let off one or two fireworks, occasionally, as a special treat.

The first special treat was that very evening; I could hardly be expected, in my state of high excitement, to postpone it longer. I chose the biggest catherine-wheel the box contained; it was affixed, by a pin, to a post in the backyard – discreetly screened, from above, by the projecting eaves of the house, in case enemy aircraft should happen to be passing over at the time. Rather nervously, with a taper tied to a broom-handle, Mr Igglesden ignited the wheel; for at least half-a-minute nothing happened; perhaps, suggested somebody, the fireworks were damp, or had gone stale with disuse ... Suddenly there was a terrifying hiss; Mr Igglesden sprang back as though a cobra had struck him; and the wheel began furiously, in a cloud of impenetrable and malodorous smoke, to revolve.

A whirling vortex of smoke, a few sparks – that was all that was visible, in the late-afternoon sunlight. But it was a catherine-wheel, a real, genuine firework; I was satisfied, I wanted nothing more. I watched it in an ecstasy: it went on for quite a long time, and Mr Igglesden became nervous; less on account of possible German aircraft – though that was something to be considered – than because of the village policeman, who was known to be a stickler about the Defence of the Realm Act.

The catherine-wheel, however, whirled to its conclusion without interruption either from the Law or from enemy action. I begged for another – just one more. But the Igglesdens were adamant; it would be a shame to use them all up – there would be none left for After the War. Moreover, it was generally felt (if not explicitly expressed) that Mr Jackson, the policeman, though he might wink at a single catherine-wheel, was liable, if the display continued, to assert his authority.

VI

I continued to experiment, during that summer and the next, with chemicals obtained from Mr Barron; and on special occasions – a birthday, an Allied victory in France, or a Bank Holiday – I was allowed to let off an isolated squib or catherine-wheel from the Igglesdens' jealously-guarded hoard.

'After-the-War' came to seem more than ever an improbable if not a mythical millennium; I identified it, I think, with that other remote and unimaginable state of being 'Grown-up' ... One was perpetually being adjured to 'save'; economy was in the air, and present pleasures must always, it seemed, be postponed till some unspecified occasion in the post-war, grown-up future. Not only fireworks; money, too (in the form of avuncular tips and suchlike), disappeared invariably into a mysterious place called The Bank: an institution which I visualized as the steep, grassy verge of a river, haunted by water-rats and kingfishers. I submitted, having no redress; but my temperament was far from being of that prim, costive kind known to psychologists as the Anal Type; on the contrary I was by nature untidy and spendthrift, with (so far as I can remember) a perfectly adequate peristaltic action ... I had a shrewd suspicion, morever, that such postponed pleasures might prove, when the time came, disappointing; they were linked (I dimly felt) by a thousand intangible associations with the present moment; only here, now, and in these particular conditions of mood and opportunity, could I enjoy them to the full.

In this, alas! I was not mistaken. When the great day came for letting off the Igglesdens' box of fireworks, they had to a great extent lost their peculiar quality of magic; the occasion was enjoyable enough, but had nothing of that romantic, breathtaking splendour which it would have possessed (I was convinced) in that summer of nineteen-sixteen.

Nineteen-sixteen! For me, it was the first of the magic years; and the three following – nineteen-seventeen, eighteen and nineteen – were similarly coloured with their distinctive and peculiar atmospheres. The period corresponded, in my childhood, to a kind of Renaissance, an epoch of creative energy and high endeavour; the years before receded into a kind of Dark Age, the forgotten world of infancy; and the years after nineteen-nineteen seemed a decadence: stripped of the earlier magic, they were infected with the 'new commonness' of schooldays and dawning puberty.

Long years afterwards, at a period when I was making one of my several unsuccessful attempts to be a 'business-man', those magic years rose again to haunt me. I had entered my father's business (the experiment didn't last long) and my first job was to copy out a pile of invoices into a ledger. Consumed by a paralysing boredom, I found myself investing the rows of figures with a peculiar and incongruous life of their own. Nineteen-seventeen – nineteen-eighteen – nineteen-nineteen ... fortuitously encountered in the accounts of Messrs Brown, Gore and Welch, or Messrs Bass, Ratcliff, the dead, meaningless cyphers became suddenly fringed with romantic evocations; my task was suddenly lightened, the ledger became a kind of magic palimpsest in which I could trace, in detail, whole chapters of forgotten autobiography.

Nineteen-sixteen – perhaps it represented the figure for our annual account with Messrs Calvet of Bordeaux; but for me it evoked immediately the cliffs above Sandgate hung with a sapphire splendour of Viper's-bugloss; spring sunlight patching the sea with green and blue and gold between the thin mist of tamarisks; a world of seaside brilliance and gaiety, haunted by the crying of gulls and the moan of fog-horns far out in the hazy distance beyond Dungeness ...

Nineteen-seventeen, on the contrary, was tinged with the duller, heavier, more post-prandial tones of late summer on the Surrey heathlands. We had gone to stay at Camberley that year, to be near my brother, who was at Sandhurst; it was, apart from the annual migration to the cottage, my first experience of 'going away'. To cross the border from Kent into Surrey was in itself a thrill, corresponding, on a smaller scale, to the adult excitement of crossing a frontier into a foreign country.

Surrey, moreover, had for me certain special associations, concerned with flowers; I had learnt, from one of my botany-books, that the Lizard Orchid had occurred there; so had the Late Spider. If it lacked the high romantic qualities of (for instance) Breadalbane and Clova, Galway or the Hebrides – places which, as a botanist, I had learnt to invest with a particular magic – Surrey did, none the less, possess a certain aura of excitement. And, of course, the mere fact of 'going away' was itself a pleasure not to be disdained ...

I didn't find the Lizard Orchid at Camberley; I didn't really expect to – indeed, it seemed highly unlikely that I ever should find a plant of such legendary rarity. But Surrey was far from being a disappointment; for a young botanist who knew only the chalklands of East Kent, the heathy commons round Camberley abounded in pleasant surprises ... Bog Asphodel, Cross-leaved Heath, Whortleberry – these and many more I found for the first time, and identified, with considerable pride, from the plates in Edward Step's *Wayside and Woodland Blossoms*...

Down a side-road near the town, not far from the Barossa golf-links, was a patch of waste ground, which an adjoining notice-board identified as 'Crown Land'. This mysterious title, conferring upon the desolate patch an atmosphere of jewelled and hieratic splendour, puzzled me for a long time; but it didn't, on the whole, seem a bad description, for the flora of the area had a richness, a prodigality which might well have suggested royalty.

A group of cottages must have been demolished not so very long before, for one stumbled continually over piles of rubble and half-buried brick foundations; the flora, too, consisted largely of garden-flowers run wild – Valerian, Borage, Lupin – and included other, more ambiguous species, such as Moth Mullein or Orpine, which might by a stretch of imagination be classed as indigenous. I preferred, at any rate, to consider them so; and was thereby able to congratulate myself on the discovery of a number of 'rarities'.

A plant which had long haunted my imagination, partly because I had never found it, partly because of its spectacular, somewhat un-English magnificence, was the Purple Loosestrife. This I discovered in a marsh near Frimley; and my cup of happiness was full. Camberley seemed an earthly paradise – an illusion for which, alas! I can muster very little sympathy today.

So potent was the spell in those days, however, that when we returned to Sandgate at the end of the summer, I was inspired to write a book about my holiday-experiences. I actually succeeded in writing half a dozen chapters before my enthusiasm began to ebb; the style was based, I think, to some extent, upon that of J. G. Wood, author of *Common Objects of the Country*. I illustrated the 'book' with little watercolours of heather and pine-trees, and my father very obligingly offered to type each chapter as I wrote it, so that I was able to taste, for the first time, one of the authentic emotions of authorship: the thrill of seeing one's work in typescript.

I still possess those typewritten sheets; my 'book' must, I should think, be nearly unique: for who else (apart from Mr John Betjeman) has ever written in praise of Camberley, Blackwater and North Camp?

So nineteen-seventeen became coloured, in memory, by the rich, purpureal glow of heather and loosestrife; and the chance concatenation of those four figures, in an invoice, could evoke the prim tar-smelling roads shadowed by conifers, the angry red villas – Gairloch, Pendennis, Burnbrae – with their rhododendrons and monkey-puzzles; a country smelling of war, flushed, like the faces of its warrior-inhabitants, with the apoplectic puce-colour of the rosebay-willowherb.

By contrast, nineteen-eighteen acquired in retrospect an airy, windswept quality, tinged with the brackish, salty odour of Romney Marsh and the dunes about Camber. We spent the spring holidays at Rye, and the summer at Winchelsea; and for some reason, the cone-shaped town standing lonely in the marshes, the wide, windswept levels rejected by the sea, became for me a land of myth. I peopled it with heroes: legendary figures who would later be incorporated into the endless and many-peopled saga of Lost Island.

Chief among these were the cowboys. They were not, needless

to say, real cowboys, but the riders from Broncho Bill's Circus, which paid a visit to the town while we were there. They swaggered through the streets on their piebald horses, dressed in shaggy sheepskin trousers and slouch hats. Their romantic figures were repeated, with an exaggerated glamour, in the garish posters which blazed from every wall. My sole ambition was to be taken to the circus: I wanted it more than I had ever wanted anything before in my whole life – even fireworks. And I wasn't allowed to go. Circuses, I was told, were Dirty: I might Pick Up Something – fleas or worse. I would have willingly risked bubonic plague for the sake of seeing those cowboys; and had I passionately insisted, I might have been allowed to go. But I was afflicted with that innate perversity which invariably, on occasions when I really wanted something badly, caused me to understate my case. I was shy of revealing how much I wanted to see the circus; perhaps I felt that there was something not quite respectable in my enthusiasm. So I swallowed my misery, and pretended, as best I could, that I didn't really mind.

And indeed, I did recognize, dimly, that the cowboys represented something alien to myself, a world which, like the world of Lost Island and the other stories, I could never genuinely inhabit ... I consoled myself by beginning another book – this time about cowboys. I didn't get very far with it, for narrative was not my strong point; even in my reading, it wasn't the 'story' which held me so much as a private vision of the characters and of their way of life: a complex of images which probably had very little to do with the book, and which produced in me a secret, rather guilty excitement. My 'book' was soon abandoned; but, lying in bed at night, I elaborated a whole cowboy saga, in which a series of inconsequent episodes succeeded each other with an increasing bloodiness and violence ... Compared, indeed, with my own private conception of them, the real cowboys had I been allowed to go to the circus, would doubtless have proved a disappointment.

VII

At last the unimaginable, the impossible event occurred – that event which had haunted my whole childhood with its romantic promise of future delights: the War came to an end.

We were living, temporarily, in London at the time, in a furnished flat in Earl's Court. Two events which I had awaited impatiently for years had already occurred: I had been taken to the Zoo, and I had seen a balloon. (By 'balloon' I mean the old-fashioned spherical balloon, which one still saw over London in those days; though what purpose it served in a world of Zeppelins and Gothas, I cannot imagine.) But with the Armistice, my thoughts turned naturally to fireworks. And sure enough, within a few days, there was a Victory display (by Messrs Wells) in Hyde Park.

I was taken to see it, but the crowds were so vast that we couldn't get near enough to see much, except the rockets. The rockets, however, were enough for me: for what seemed hours I watched their serpentine trails cleaving, one after another, the winter darkness; waiting for the agonizing, orgasmic moment when, with a faint 'pop', they would discharge their freight of many-coloured fire.

'A-a-a-ah!' sighed the voice of the crowd, as the shower of stars or golden rain burst overhead ... I felt suddenly immensely older, almost adult: had I not, for years past, identified the end of the War with being 'grown-up'? And now the War was really over. Centuries seemed to separate me from the day when I had come upon that article in *Little Folks*; almost as remote seemed the single catherine-wheel let off furtively (for fear of Mr Jackson) in the Igglesdens' backyard ... The rockets continued to burst over my head in undiminished glory; a sense of immense fulfilment swept over me, as though I had been initiated into some tribal mystery ... At last, as a patriotic finale, a sheaf of rockets ascended simultaneously, and burst amid cheers into a blaze of red, white and blue.

The fireworks were over.

*

Not long after this, I was taken to Gamage's; I was to be allowed, as a special treat, to buy a white mouse.

The mouse was duly purchased – complete with a little wooden house containing a kind of treadmill for the occupant to exercise himself. We left the 'Zoo' department, and made our way through Hardware, Garden-tools and Sports Goods towards the exit. But in the 'Sports' section my eye was caught by a long counter on which was ranged a collection of unfamiliar shapes ... Unfamiliar, yet at the same time evocative, fraught with meaning ... I edged nearer to the counter; a row of large spindle-shaped objects, covered with brightly-patterned paper, had riveted my attention. I looked more closely; yes, there was no doubt about it: they were rockets. And by the side of them lay a box filled with other strange shapes, among which I recognized some which I remembered from the Igglesdens' war-time hoard – catherine-wheels, squibs, crackers.

The assistant bustled forward. Struck all of a maze, I could hardly speak coherently. I pointed to the rockets ... The assistant obligingly handed me one, remarking that they were four shillings each.

Four shillings! It was an unthinkable price. Dazed by the lust of possession, I was aware of grown-up heads being shaken, grown-up voices saying No. Not since the forbidden circus at Rye had I wanted anything so much as I wanted that rocket. I clutched it passionately to my breast: the bright glossy wrappings of scarlet and yellow, the funnel-shaped 'cap' with its conical top – forms and colours combined to make it infinitely desirable, the very archetype of all that I most wanted to possess.

But it was no use; four shillings was too much; and had I not just bought a mouse? I cursed the mouse; I wished all mice at the bottom of the sea ... Edging my way down the counter, I came upon another box, packed with an array of fireworks even more exciting than those I had already seen: Bouquet of Gerbs. Mount Vesuvius, Mine of Serpents ... It was the Guinea Box.

But if four-shilling rockets were out of the question, still more so were the wonders of the Guinea Box. The assistant, a good fellow at heart, admitted that he had a rocket at two shillings ... It was not so impressive as its larger fellows; but I seized upon it with joy, and was actually allowed to buy it. In addition, I chose a coloured Roman Candle, an Italian Streamer, and two crackers.

In the Underground, returning to Earl's Court – clutching my mouse, my fireworks, and the stick of the rocket – I was lost in a mystical ecstasy, a Nirvana of gratified desire. At last – after all those years of waiting – I possessed some Real Fireworks of my very own.

Other visits to Gamage's followed: at long intervals, certainly, and only by way of a very special treat. But by the time we left London in the spring I had managed to acquire quite a respectable collection.

I required, nowadays, no adjurations to 'save'; the fact that the fireworks were my Very Own was sufficient to induce in me just those qualities of prudence and economy which my family had tried, unsuccessfully, to instil into me at an earlier period. We were not to return to Sandgate till the autumn; instead, we were to go to the cottage for the whole summer. It was understood that some time during that summer (it was nineteen-nineteen) the official peace-celebrations would take place; the War was not really quite 'over', after all, and it would be only reasonable to save up the fireworks until it was.

My willingness thus to hoard my treasures was due largely to the fact that I was too much in love with them to bear the thought of their final dissolution. For hours together I would contemplate their strange and emotive forms, arranging them in a series of *natures mortes* upon the table; the rocket, the roman candle, the square canister of a 'Jack-in-the-box', the curious, serpentine arabesques of jumping crackers ... Their bright, garish wrappings carried a suggestion of gaiety and festivity; they recalled the tawdry splendours of a country fair or a circus ...

And indeed, they still do; or they did, as lately as before the last war. In future, perhaps, fireworks will become functional and austere in their outward trappings. But up till nineteen-thirty-nine they still preserved their air of conforming to some gay old tradition. The striped or starry patterning of their wrappings seemed to date, like the designs painted on swing-boats and roundabouts, from an earlier age. Are fireworks, like fairs and circuses, doomed to be liquidated in the Brave New World of the Atomic Age?

Of all those enchanted years which, in later days, would spring suddenly from ledger or invoice to haunt my mind with memories of happiness, nineteen-nineteen was the most heavily charged with magic.

For one thing, we spent the whole spring and summer at the cottage – an unprecedented delight; then there were the peace-celebrations, and the letting-off, at long last, of my own collection of fireworks and the pre-war hoard of the Igglesdens ... But more important, nineteen-nineteen was for me the end of an epoch; the next year I was to go to boarding-school. Henceforward, I should look back on that last summer of freedom as a kind of Golden Age; rather as elderly people nowadays look back on the Edwardian epoch – a peak-period of happiness and stability before the deluge.

I had brought with me from Gamage's not only the white mouse, but also a pet grass-snake; frequently I would electrify the village by walking down the street with the snake twined round my neck. For the rest, I spent my time – when I was not contemplating my hoard of fireworks – in hunting for orchids. The Bee, the Man, the Lady, the White Helleborine – these grew almost at my door; but the great rarities – the Military, the Lizard, the Epipogon – continued to elude me. They were as unattainable as the Mine of Serpents or the Barrage Fire Curtain – more so, indeed, for even if I had been allowed to draw every penny I possessed out of 'The Bank', it would not have enabled me to find the Military Orchid ...

I centred my hopes upon the Lizard. It had, after all, occurred in Kent quite recently; there seemed no reason why I shouldn't find it as well as anybody else.

For that summer-term, I attended a day-school in Folkestone, whither I went by train every morning, returning in the evening by the 4.36 from Shorncliffe. The dusty third-class carriages smelt mysteriously of hard-boiled eggs. Chugging back along the Elham Valley in the summer evenings, I was possessed by a tranquil, immeasurable happiness; the long evening stretched before me – a walk over the park to look for orchids; hunting for frogs in the Igglesdens' garden to feed the grass-snake; a further prolonged contemplation of my hoard of fireworks ...

Once a week I was allowed to spend threepence, at Shorncliffe Station, on a new issue of 'Books for the Bairns'. How much pleasure I obtained from those little pink paper-covered books, with their badly printed, double-columned pages, and their smudgy line-blocks by third-rate illustrators! Many of them were written specially for the series – coy and rather embarrassing little tales about gnomes and pixies. Others were abridged and watered-down classics, such as *Gulliver* or *Ali-baba*. I remembered reading *Undine* in this form: it left upon me an indelible impression, a sense of vast and terrible unhappiness associated with death by water in a landscape under flood. Reading quite recently, and for the first time, Fouqué's original, I was far less impressed: in retrospect, it was the anonymous abridgement in 'Books for the Bairns' which seemed, by contrast, the authentic masterpiece.

Two grammar-school boys travelled with me daily to Folkestone; they spoke with 'common' accents, and ignored me completely. I never made their acquaintance: I was too timid, too nervous of what seemed their uncouthness, their alien speech and manners. They, too, usually had something to read in the train; but not, like myself, 'Books for the Bairns', or *Little Folks*. The things they read were as alien to me as their personalities: *The Gem* and *The Magnet*, or twopenny thrillers. I knew that these were what 'common' boys habitually did read; but I myself was not allowed to buy them. They had, indeed, acquired for me a slight aura of evil; at the same time, they had the inadmissible charm of forbidden fruit, and I would have liked to read them if I could have done so on the sly, without being discovered.

One twopenny novelette in particular captured my imagination: one of the boys was absorbed in it, and his companion, who was without a book, was waiting impatiently for him to finish it. The brightly-printed cover showed two ferocious men, stripped to the waist, squared up for a fight.

'What's it about, then?' asked the bookless boy. 'Do them two blokes have a scrap?'

'That's right,' said his companion, his eyes glued to the page.

Would I dare ask them to lend it to me when they'd both finished it? I wouldn't. But the two blokes having a scrap were invested, thenceforward, with a romantic glamour: they continued to scrap with a bloody violence, in my imagination, long after I had lost sight of the book and its owners; they became, indeed, permanent inhabitants of my private fascist state – the crazy, pugnacious, paranoid universe of Lost Island.

At last the great moment arrived: the Peace-treaty was signed at Versailles, and a day was fixed for the celebrations. There were several false alarms: once, seeing some of the village children running down the street with Union Jacks, I immediately concluded that the moment had come, and had actually let off a roman candle before I could be persuaded that the War was not, after all, quite over yet.

But at last the day dawned: the day for which I had been waiting ever since I read that article in *Little Folks* ... By late afternoon, the fireworks were ready to let off. The display was to take place in the front-garden of our cottage; roman candles, golden fountains, Italian streamers were tied firmly to upright stakes; the Igglesdens' catherine-wheels were pinned to the fence. The two-shilling rocket from Gamage's was fixed ready for firing, slanted at a safe angle towards the open fields, lest it should fall on the thatched roof of the cottage next door. The village boys had collected a pile of wood and dumped it in the middle of the street, for a bonfire ... I could hardly wait for the evening to come; the hours after tea seemed interminable. At half past seven the grown-ups had dinner; they took an interminable time over it: I could almost fancy that they were doing so on purpose.

The village, meanwhile, was assembling in force: the Igglesdens, Mr Bundock, Miss Trumpett – even Mr Jackson the policeman, who stood at the side of the road glaring dourly at our preparations, aware, no doubt, that DORA was not officially rescinded, and only restrained from interfering by the fear of making himself unpopular ...

Presently it was decided, by the grown-ups, that it was time to begin; it was scarcely dark yet, but the crowd was becoming impatient. The display was to start with the Big Rocket: it was called that, though it could hardly be considered 'big' compared with those four-shilling giants I had seen at Gamage's ... My father approached it gingerly, with a lighted taper on the end of a stick. He lit the touch-paper: it smouldered sullenly for several minutes; and nothing happened.

I waited, in an agony of apprehension. What could have gone wrong? Could the rocket have got damp? Were we lighting it the right way? My father applied the taper again – but without result. We waited for several minutes longer; and still nothing happened.

Desolated by this ill-omened beginning, I prepared to let off the other fireworks. One after another, my hoarded treasures blazed and popped in the gathering dusk. Bengal lights cast their green or crimson enchantment upon the cottage-walls and the over-hanging hedge; roman candles flung their jewelled stars high into the twilit, bat-haunted air; crackers hissed and spat among the feet of the onlookers; catherine-wheels wove their bracelets of golden fire upon the garden-fence. Suddenly the bonfire in the road, liberally fed with paraffin, leapt into a sheet of flame. A cheer went up: squibs and crackers, concealed in the fire, leapt and cur-vetted in all directions. A catherine-wheel, escaped from its pin, went flying up the street like a meteor, narrowly missing the trousers of the Mr Jackson . . .

It was magnificent, but (I felt) it wasn't War – or more accu-rately, it wasn't Peace; not Peace as I had dreamed of it for so many years. As usual, I had overdrawn on my capital; I had no store of emotion left with which to meet the occasion. And already I felt a twinge of nostalgia, a backwash of regret for all those hard-won treasures which I had gloated over for so many months . . . They were all gone: the squibs and catherine-wheels which Mrs Igglesden had hoarded so jealously from before the War; all my own purchases from Gamage's – the Golden Fountain, the Jack-in-the-box, the Italian Streamer – there they lay, what remained of them, scattered over the street and garden: blackened, burned-out bits of cardboard, their brief moment of glory already half-forgotten.

But there was still, I suddenly remembered, the Big Rocket . . . I went to look at it. There it was; still unfired, still pointing skywards, its blunt-pointed head a symbol of undiminished potency . . . My father was persuaded to make another attempt. Patiently, he re-lit the taper, and held it beneath the base of the rocket. We waited. The crowd was dispersing, the bonfire almost out . . .

Suddenly there was a hissing roar of flame, so violent and so sudden that we leapt backwards incontinently among the flower-beds. Hardly realizing what had happened, I saw a trail of fire surge upwards into the violet dark. Spanning the valley, it slanted in a long, rainbow arc across the upward-sloping fields; plunged earth-wards, still blazing, over the level crest of Barham Downs; and there, no doubt, somewhere on those Druidic uplands, discharged its freight of coloured stars; burning itself out, invisibly, on the sheep-cropped turf, among the thyme and the Bee orchises . . .

The tears pricked my eyes; I was hard-put to it not to sob

audibly. I felt suddenly immensely tired. Coldly, I assessed the disaster; the rocket had been slanted, for safety, at too low an angle; I had feared something of the kind – but had allowed grown-up opinion to prevail.

'Well, that's that,' said my father, with some relief, and went indoors, where the rest of the family, and Miss Trumpett, were waiting for him to make a fourth at bridge.

The village boys were leaping, with shouts and laughter, over the embers of the bonfire. I didn't feel inclined to join them; instead, I crept unobtrusively up to bed, and, huddled between the cool sheets, cried myself to sleep.

VIII

The summer passed – that golden summer of nineteen-nineteen, with its retrospective flavour of *après-moi-le-déluge*. The fireworks were over; and I addressed myself, with a single-minded passion, to the quest of the Lizard Orchid.

I didn't find it; a year or two later it did turn up in the district – and was found by the Igglesdens; but by that time I was at boarding-school. For me, the Lizard remained romantically unattainable; I had no more hope of really finding it than I had of acquiring the Guinea Box, with its august and sinister inmate – the Mine of Serpents.

Next year I went to boarding-school – to St Ethelbert's. I continued to spend every penny of my pocket-money on fireworks. By the summer-holidays, I had collected enough for a first-rate display: a far more ambitious and varied affair than that of the previous year. In the year following, and the year after that, I gave further displays: they became a regular village function. I could look back upon that first, unambitious effort of nineteen-nineteen almost with disdain; yet, splendid as they were, these later displays seemed to me always, in some indefinable way, incomplete. At the back of my mind, lurked the romantic ideal of the Guinea Box; and somehow it was as an ideal which remained unattainable . . .

I bought a Mine of Serpents; but it was never quite as exciting as its august prototype . . . I bought other, less familiar pieces: Tourbillions, Devils-among-the-Tailors, Feux de Joie, Parachute rockets ... They were all very fine; the displays were a great success; but something was lacking.

No – the ideal Mine of Serpents, like the Lizard Orchid, eluded me. Even a Pain's four-shilling rocket, which eventually, in an extravagant moment, I acquired, could not revive the glamour of those multicoloured giants which I had seen at Gamage's ... No, not even the outlandish *Fusée* from Messrs Rumpf could give me back the lost world of my childhood.

I was fifteen – too old (or nearly too old) for fireworks. Nostalgia devoured me; nostalgia for that long golden summer of nineteen-nineteen: the hot mornings spent wandering over the Park in search of the Lizard Orchid, the daily journeys in the train to Folkestone, the long June evenings scented with new-mown hay and clamorous with late, broken-voiced cuckoos ...

But I enjoyed Montreux, none the less. We stayed in one of the big hotels on the lake; it was patronized entirely by English tourists, and in the dining-room in the evening one might have imagined oneself at Bournemouth or Budleigh Salterton. Not knowing these places myself, however, and filled with the exciting sense of being 'abroad', I accepted the ambience as genuinely 'Swiss' and was appropriately thrilled.

The gong would sound, and, after a few minutes discreet delay (lest they should appear greedy) the first guests would file in; many of them were old ladies – alone, in couples, or accompanied by virgin daughters or 'companions'. They had, most of them, spent the morning at the Kursaal, and the afternoon in their bedrooms, brewing tea in 'infusers'. They would nod kindly at me, and sit down at their tables, upon which reposed the inevitable cheerless bottle of Evian or Vichy.

The family at the next table to ours was rather exceptional: an elderly gentleman, his wife, a pretty daughter, and two young men; one of the men was the son, the other perhaps the daughter's *fiancé*. Our two families exchanged polite remarks. My brother quickly became friendly with the two young men, whom he accompanied to the Kursaal, or to dances at the Montreux Palace ... On one or two occasions they addressed a patronizing word or two to myself; but I shrank into my shell, sensing them to be my natural enemies.

They were thickset, muscular, aggressively healthy, with pink, scrubbed faces and small moustaches; they talked in short, sharp barks about polo and pig-sticking – for they were on their way home on leave from India. Consciously, I hated and feared them; yet secretly – and it was a secret which I could almost succeed in keeping from myself – secretly I admired and wanted to emulate them; knowing that they were all I would have liked to be, yet could never, by the laws of my physique and temperament, attain to in reality; fighters and athletes, like the heroes of Ballantyne or the cowboys at the circus; inhabitants of Lost Island.

Back in England, Montreux acquired the inevitable aura of romantic nostalgia; I began, the very next term at school, to write a book about it – just as I had written 'books', years before, about our trips to Camberley or Rye. But in this case, I was more ambitious: I set out to write a proper grown-up novel – and if length alone is any criterion, I nearly succeeded. The 'novel' must have run to forty or fifty thousand words; the narrative-element was decidedly weak, but the long descriptions of Montreux were better, and I was extremely proud of them.

As a full-blown novelist, I felt that I had taken a big step towards adulthood. It was time, no doubt, to put off childish things. There remained, however, my latest hoard of fireworks (including the ones from Messrs Rumpf); I had started collecting them more than a year ago – long before my *début* as a novelist. How much had happened in that year! I began to be aware of fundamental changes in myself – I felt that I had crossed a frontier, irrevocably and without hope of return. My hoard of fireworks was a survival from an earlier age; and as such, I invested them, more than ever before, with nostalgic sentiment.

At last, during the summer holidays at the cottage, I fixed a night for the display. The thought of letting off those hoarded symbols of the past was almost unbearable; the display, I dimly felt, would be a kind of *auto-da-fé*, a final exorcism of the spirit of my childhood.

The appointed night arrived; I was embarrassed, feeling adult and self-conscious. The Igglesdens were invited, but nobody else; this was not, I felt, an affair for public clamour and applause. One by one the cherished pieces were let off; the Barrage Fire Curtain was a disappointment – a mere shower of golden rain; even the Mine of Serpents failed to live up to its mysteriously exciting

name, or to the legend which I had built up around it – exploding
with the mildest of pops, and scattering the garden with a few
dispirited crackers and whizz-bangs. The four-shilling rocket ascended with a faultless precision, and discharged its cluster of
coloured stars; but it didn't – and none of its kind, I realized, ever
would – fulfil the promise of its heroic forerunner, that ill-fated
Icarus which, in nineteen-nineteen, had plunged to its disastrous
end on the windswept spaces of Barham Downs.

IX

Roaring through the Simplon, I glanced at my fellow-pyrotechno-
phil, who was sitting with me in my *wagon-lit*. Our conversation
had died down – the tunnel was too noisy. We had been talking
like life-long friends for the last hour; yet I realized that, apart
from our shared mania for fireworks, I still knew nothing whatever about him. Once again, looking at his gaunt, anxious face, a
memory hovered on the outskirts of my mind; but I couldn't local-
ize it, my companion remained for me someone I might once have
known – or perhaps merely a 'type'.

Once out of the tunnel, and we should be in Italy. The thing
was incontrovertible, a geographical fact. I tried to realize it; tried
to think of the Abruzzi, of that farmhouse with its door open
upon the sun-flooded countryside ... But it was no good; emotionally overdrawn, I was totally unable to re-create the cherished
vision.

The train roared on, like a rocket through the night, bearing
with it my hoard of nostalgic anticipation; soon the potent, swift
trajectory would reach its climacteric, discharging, in its moment
of fulfilment, the promised vision of happiness ... Unless, of
course, it misfired. Why should I suppose, after all, that my vision
was anything more than a subjective phantasy?

Switzerland had been dull and rainy; Montreux had looked as
'English' as usual. It was too much to hope that Italy would really
live up to its reputation – that, once past this mountain barrier, we
should emerge into southern sunshine ...

Yet this was precisely what did happen. Plunging with a roar
and a clatter out of the darkness, we were dazzled as though by a

Danäean shower; a cloudless, sapphire sky was stretched above the mountains; pink and white Italian houses smiled their welcome. Italy received us, once again, with her age-old gestures of hospitality.

At Domodossola, after the customs formalities, we stepped out upon the platform into sunshine which seemed to us, in our thick tweeds, as hot as a Turkish bath. The warm, operatic voices of Italians sounded in our ears. Trolleys appeared, laden with oranges, fresh rolls and straw-covered flasks of Chianti ... My heart made a sudden motion of recognition; for the first time for weeks past I grasped fully the stupendous fact that my trip to Italy was no mere figment of the intellect, but a physical reality.

We bought wine and oranges and returned to the train. The landscape began to unfold, to become every minute more indisputably Italian ... Lake Maggiore was like a tourist poster; the first cypresses and olives printed their classic shapes upon the flying landscape; groups of labourers, stripped to the waist, waved their brown arms at us, flashed us their brilliant smiles ...

My companion and I spoke little, dazed by the clamorous impressions which assaulted, with an ever-increasing violence, our prim English sensibilities. Presently we went along to the luncheon-car.

In France, the food had been austere: soup, a slice of spam, a single vegetable. Here, for our first meal in Italy, we were confronted by a banquet: an enormous plate of *pasta*, a '*bifstecca*', cheese, fruit, unlimited bread, and wine for the price of English beer. Our stomachs, conditioned by years of English feeding, threatened to rebel ... My companion, looking slightly green, refused the *pasta*, asked for *acqua minerale* ... Less cautious, I refused nothing; devouring my *pasta* and my steak, and taking great draughts of Chianti: aware, with a renewed conviction of truth, as the cool, lovely wine struck my palate, that I was really back in Italy.

'You know,' I said at last, made bold by Chianti, 'I can't help thinking that we've met before somewhere.'

My companion looked up at me, cautiously.

'I daresay,' he admitted vaguely. 'In London, probably, don't you think?'

He was being as evasive as ever; yet I had a curious impression that he remembered more than I did.

'It might have been London,' I agreed. 'Or possibly,' I added, flinging my bolt at hazard, 'possibly Oxford?'

He shot me a guarded glance.

'Oh well – yes, perhaps it was.'

'When were you up?' I asked.

'Let me see – it must have been about 1926 — it's so *long* ago, isn't it . . .?'

His voice trailed off, timid and embarrassed.

'I went up in '27,' I continued, mercilessly.

'Oh yes . . . How funny,' he murmured.

'Well, that's where we must have met. I felt sure I'd seen you somewhere. I was at Worcester.'

'Oh yes . . .' He suddenly gave a little giggle. '*I* was at a place called *Wadham*, actually.'

Here coffee arrived, and provided an interruption – a welcome one, I suspected, so far as he was concerned. I attempted to renew the topic, but he wasn't having any.

'Do you know,' he suddenly remarked, with a deceptively casual air, 'I've so often wondered – why is it that one always buys fireworks from ironmongers and bicycle shops?'

We speculated for some time about this singular anomaly; concluding, finally, that it was not really any funnier than buying stamps at a tobacconist's in France.

It was evident that my companion didn't want to talk about Oxford. Nor, for that matter, did I. I was satisfied to have 'placed' him, satisfied to have laid that ghost which had wandered, homeless, in my memory . . . Yet the ghost wasn't, after all, completely laid; for I could remember no details. Oxford, in my memory, had become a blur, in which I could hardly distinguish a single face which I remembered.

But what, after all, did it matter? It was highly unlikely that I should ever see him again; I didn't even particularly want to. He was going on to Florence; I was leaving the train at Milan. Like a wandering comet, he had crossed my orbit – for the second time; it was hardly to be expected that he would cross it again.

Yet, before we reached Milan, a lingering vestige of curiosity made me write down my name and address on a scrap of paper and give it to him. At the same time, I handed him my pencil, and another piece of paper. He could hardly refuse such a direct challenge, I thought.

'We may run into one another in Florence,' I said, airily. 'If not, we might meet in London sometime.'

'Oh yes – it would be awfully nice,' he said, vaguely, scribbling something on the bit of paper I had given him.

He handed it to me, and I glanced at it curiously. H. D. Dallas – and an address in Buckinghamshire. The name did ring a bell; but the bell had no echo; its chime fell flatly on the surface of my mind. Dallas, H. D. Dallas – no, it meant nothing; or almost nothing.

We were at Milan; I shoved the paper into my note-case, and began to take down my luggage. My companion, with a vague smile and a wave of the hand, wandered off to his own compartment. From the platform, I looked back once at the standing train: but Mr Dallas was not to be seen. I wasn't surprised; for it had been obvious that he wasn't particularly keen on prolonging the acquaintance.

PART TWO

The Watertower

Now joy's cartographer I trace
My acres of gay and wellbeing's land
O my summer be Proust and Sisley and
With me in the dead season, pastoral days
CLERE PARSONS

I

From the village, the watertower was invisible: hidden from our sight by the high chalky plateau of Barham Downs. But on many of our walks (since most of these took us on to higher ground, above the valley) we would, sooner or later, at one point or another, catch a glimpse of the tower: its peaked white summit gleaming above the trees which surrounded it. Perhaps we had wandered further than usual through Gorsley Wood, and, unsure of the way (for the wood was large and the paths innumerable and confusing), had at last come to the wood's fringe; we would gaze out anxiously through the thinning trees to see exactly where we were; and there, on the north-eastern horizon, like a beacon to guide us, we would recognize the tower, and know that we were, after all, within twenty-minutes' walk of the village.

It was a landmark, and also a limit: bounding, in that north-easterly direction, the familiar zone covered by our afternoon walks. We never went far beyond the tower: the wood at the back of it, which we called (rather inaccurately) 'Waterworks Wood', was good for primroses and bluebells, and once or twice a year, in the spring, we would make the expedition. It was one of our longest walks: to get there and back in an afternoon was considered something of a feat, and the whole outing had a faint tinge of adventure.

It was not, in fact, a very heroic undertaking: 'Waterworks Wood' was hardly two miles from the village; but the way was all uphill, and for my own nurse and Alec's, pushing mailcarts laden with all the materials for a picnic, it must have seemed quite far enough.

Alec Bell lived at the big, Queen Anne manor-house in the park which fringed the village. My family knew Colonel and Mrs Bell, and our respective nannies had struck up a corresponding friendship. Nurse Collier was a plump, brown-faced, commonsensical woman with a pleasant little chuckle and a fund of proverbial wisdom; she was a typical nanny, and had been employed one felt, only by the best families. Sometimes we would go to tea at the big house, or at the dower-house where, at one period, the family preferred to live. I was impressed by the grandeur of Alec's surroundings: he had a day-nursery *and* a night-nursery, and Nurse Collier had a nursemaid 'under' her. There was a very large and (for those days) a very modern gramophone; a great many different kinds of cake for tea; and innumerable toys – far more than I had imagined it possible for one child to possess.

I didn't envy Alec the grandeur, and didn't, I think, covet many of his possessions: an exception was a book on natural history with very fine engravings of animals. I had a passion for bats and snakes, both of which were extensively illustrated; and at Alec's tea-parties, I was with difficulty dragged away from my fascinated contemplation of the Great Fruit-eating Bat or the Puff-adder. The Puff-adder I particularly loved; that thick body half-embedded in the sand, that blunt triangular head slightly raised, ready to strike – like de Lautréamont before his octopus, I was thrilled by a sense of romantic evil.

But these tea-parties happened comparatively rarely; far more often we went for picnics – laden, like a party of explorers, with our numerous baskets of provisions: sandwiches, enamel cups, Thermos flasks. Sometimes, especially when the weather was hot, we went no further than one of the two parks which bounded the village: encamping under the bee-haunted lime-trees whose lower branches were nibbled by pasturing cattle, to a dead level, like the formal trees in a Noah's ark. But when the weather seemed settled, and not too warm, we would go further afield: to Ben Hill, which we called Teazel Wood, or to Gorsley; sometimes penetrating to the mysterious territory beyond the woods towards Pett Bottom, which was known locally as California.

In the Gorsley direction, the limit of our journeying was Langham Park: an isolated farm which, like the watertower, marked, for me, one of the verges of the known world. Mr Adams, the farmer, had a milk-round, and would drive into the village of a morning: an emissary from another land, the remote, mysterious border-country beyond Gorsley Wood.

Ben Hill, or Teazel Wood, a kind of *côté de Méséglise*, was a 'short' walk; instead of climbing the long hill to the station, we left the village by a narrow, tree-muffled lane, skirting the beech-plantation where, a few years later, I discovered the Fly Orchid and the White Helleborine. We traversed the corner of one of the parks and crossed an iron railway bridge, beyond which the line curved away mysteriously between chalk embankments towards Elham and Lyminge. Across the line, Apps's farm lay in its hollow, grey and damp-looking and slightly sinister: dogs barked fiercely in the farm-yard, and nobody ever seemed to be about. Once we saw a fox dart through one of the farm-gates; we never went too near the farm, because of the dogs. Beyond the bridge – our heels clanked hollowly as we crossed it; we were rather frighteningly aware of walking over an abyss – a grassy path continued between high, untrimmed hedges towards the woods. Teazel Wood was hardly more than a copse; a narrow strip running steeply uphill. It was famous for its bluebells; beyond it lay the deeper woodlands, seldom visited: once we found a dead badger there, lying across the footpath.

Teazel Wood, though small, was just large enough to possess the authentic atmosphere of a 'wood'. Though narrow, it straggled on for a considerable distance: one never felt very far from the fields on either side, but one never, on the other hand, knew quite how far the wood extended over the hillside. The upper part became dense, the paths narrowed; we had our tea in a clearing, and then turned back and went home the same way. Once we did penetrate to the furthest boundary: coming at last to a hurdle, overlooking an unfamiliar field, which sloped away gently into a valley ... Our eyes travelled adventurously over the valley, searching for something familiar: and there, sure enough, overtopping the dark crest of pine-trees, beyond Barham Downs, was the white peak of the watertower.

The valley was our own valley, after all; we were seeing it, merely, from an unusual aspect. Even the unknown field proved to be the upper part of Mr Apps's pasture-land, which fringed the railway. The grown-ups insisted that it was so, and I was forced to believe them: but to me it still seemed a 'different' field, with a secret of its own.

There was no mystery about the way to the watertower. On the days when we undertook the great expedition, we started off up the lane, beneath an arching avenue of beeches, towards the main Dover road. The lane was known, after about 1914, as Boring Lane: not because it was particularly tedious, but because of the extraordinary phenomenon which, at about this time appeared at the top of it, where the lane joined the main road. The Boring had risen suddenly, portentous and sinister, in the corner of the field known as Forty Acres: a chimney which belched a volcanic plume of smoke, a group of sheds, and an exciting contraption of wheels and pulleys. Occasionally one caught a glimpse of strange, black-faced men entering or leaving it. They didn't belong to the village, and were generally held to be dubious characters.

It was the pioneer-period of Kent coal: in a few more years, it was commonly predicted, East Kent would become Black Country. It never did; the few collieries which were developed remained localized, remote and (unless one lived near them) unsuspected. Our own Boring was shortly disused: bryony and Traveller's Joy festooned the rusting headgear, the chimney smoked no longer. After a year or two, the sheds and chimney were removed, and the ground levelled.

The Boring disappeared: but the name remained. Further afield, however – in the remote lands beyond the watertower – other 'Borings' remained permanently: Snowdon, Tilmanstone, Betteshanger. We were not concerned with them – they didn't belong to 'our' country; only occasionally, from the higher places of Barham Downs, would one glimpse a far-off chimney, its plume of smoke hanging like a pennant, dimly discernible in the mysterious distance.

Passing the Boring, we crossed the road and walked on up a chalky lane which wound away over Barham Downs. Here there was always a wind: it rustled faintly but insistently across the uneven downland, and sang its high, remote song in the telegraph wires. The wires stretched away into unimaginable distances, between their black posts which seemed to flower, at their summits, into corymbs of small white buds ... Sometimes on summer days, the wind's song was the faintest of humming: a low, perpetual bourdon, like the held chords in the introductory passage of *Brigg Fair*; a haunting undertone beneath the treble *motifs* of lark's song and plover's cry. On gusty days in April, or when the first gales of Autumn began, one detected a less placid, a wilder note – a bardic rhapsody of successive, violent statements, abrupt as the lashes of a whip: the opening of the third movement of Ireland's Sonata for 'cello and piano.

The downs themselves, after the tree-muffled, post-prandial atmosphere of the village, had a quality of wildness: the wide, uneven plateau of chalk stretching away towards Dover, punctuated by the diminishing telegraph-poles. Larks sang perpetually in the high emptiness of the sky, and peewits circled, plaintively crying, above the further ploughland. The downs were partly cultivated, partly aboriginal chalk, clothed with the tufted tawgrass and, in August, with the delicate, waxen-pink Squinancy-wort (which had inspired a rather coy little poem by Edward Carpenter, whose bearded but crypto-Uranian talent my father much admired). At this time, the uncultivated tracts had just been laid out as a golf-course; little red pennants fluttered gaily in the perpetual wind, and the earthworks and tumuli which, on these Druidic heights, had once perhaps witnessed a bloodier kind of ceremony, now provided bunkers for the Saturday amusement of Canterbury business-men.

Sometimes, as we crossed the downs, an angry voice would shout 'Fore!', and I would duck my head, having an ingrained horror of round objects which flew violently through the air ... I was prejudiced, indeed – and at an even earlier age than this – against balls in any form. In infancy, when kind aunts presented me with them – woolly or painted or rubber ones, it made no difference – I would be overcome by an intense and painful embarrassment. For myself to be observed in possession of a ball was, I felt convinced, a circumstance so unnatural that it could only be a matter of laughter among the grown-ups. Shamefacedly, I would immediately conceal the ball in the most convenient place: in my pram or in my bed, or, if I happened not to be in either, behind my back.

This highly un-British prejudice was to last my lifetime: at school, my horror of football was only excelled by my passionate loathing for cricket. Balls, for me, had a horribly fluid, unstable quality: they never kept still, they had no firm base on which to rest, they rolled and slithered perpetually, they were unseizable and remote as the idea of God. (Years later, I found highly sympathetic one of Kapp's drawings in a little book called *Minims*: the drawing was called 'God', and showed – just a circle.) At cricket I was so hopelessly bad that, to my relief, I was usually, when fielding, placed at long-stop or some such remote and comparatively irresponsible position. Here I could watch from a safe distance the other players (who seemed to be enjoying themselves, in their own mysterious way), or preferably do a little furtive botanizing in the long grass at the edge of the pitch. Cricket and football were, for me, as meaningless and unreal as the world of *Beowulf*: an endless, boring saga in which people's motives remained, so far as I was concerned, impenetrably obscure.

> Nu is se raed gelang
> Eft oet the anum. Eard git ne const,
> Frecne stowe, thaer thu findan miht
> Felasinnigne secq: sec gif thu dyrre![1]

'Over!' the master-in-charge would call, just as I had spotted a Green-winged Orchid in the grass fringe: or 'Go for it! Chase it! Wake up, Brooke!' and the hard, red orb would fly past me, speeding away into the long grasses. 'You must be more keen!' they said. 'Brace up! Put your back into it!'

I did my best, but without any conviction; flinging the ball back (underhand, like a muff) to the wicket-keeper.

> As yet you know not the haunt where you may cope
> With the paramount evil ...

Wake up, run for it, *felasinnigne secq*: the heroic saga-world was not for me, and I knew it; why was I born with a different face?

Over the crest of the downs, we suddenly came in sight of our objective: the tower greeted us, remote still, but at least visible. We could see, too, the last part of our way – a white, chalky track winding up to the very edge of the wood.

The road dipped down to Coldharbour Farm, then rose again. To the left, another road swung away towards Bekesbourne and

---

1 Once again our hope
Rests with you to upbear:
As yet you know not the haunt where you may cope
With the paramount evil: seek if you dare!
                              Gavin Bone's translation.
                              (Blackwell, 1945.)

the remote country beyond. In this country of hills, there was never what could properly be called a 'view': one reached the summit of one hill, only to be confronted by another. Somewhere, one felt, one would come one day upon the focal centre of this land: see it stretched out around one, the familiar hills and valleys falling into position, making a completed pattern. But this never happened: the gentle hills rose in their long undulations and sank again, the dark crest of woodland masked the further valley; one was perpetually enclosed, there was always something 'just beyond' which one could never reach.

The watertower, as it happened, was built on the highest point in the countryside; and as we approached it, on fine days, we would begin to look for what was, in this landscape, the nearest approach to a 'view'. Over to the north-east, beyond Bekesbourne, beyond Wingham and Chislet, the country swept away, gently and unemphatically, in a long slope towards the sea. It was said that on a very clear day you could actually see Pegwell Bay. Perhaps you could: but one could never be sure. A faint gleam on the horizon might have been sea, or merely a sunlit bank of cloud; a streak of more solid whiteness might have been cliffs, but could equally well have been some chalky outcrop further inland. Pegwell Bay remained remote and mysterious, never really revealing itself: a mirage trembling on the verge of reality.

But by now we were approaching the tower itself: the mail-carts creaked and lumbered up the chalky track, and we could see the brick arches, which supported the water-tank, above the dark pine trees. The track ran for a few hundred yards along the wood's fringe, then plunged into it, ending a quarter of a mile further on at the house of Mrs James; we never approached near enough, in those days, to see the house: I took its existence on trust, and invested it – lying as it did, isolated beyond the frontier-station of the tower – with a rather sinister quality. (Years later, I penetrated to the very gate of the house, and my suspicion seemed confirmed: for it proved to be a small, grey-stone early Victorian building, fronted by a grove of dark shiny evergreens, and surrounded by woodland: reminding me of the steel engraving which formed the frontispiece to my copy of *Wuthering Heights*.)

By the time we reached the wood's fringe, the tower had disappeared. It had, in fact, an extraordinary capacity for thus suddenly disappearing and reappearing; from miles away, on the other side of the valley, it could be seen, at one moment, shining out clearly above the woodland; and a few seconds later, it would have entirely vanished, masked suddenly by an intervening tree, or by some higher reach of Barham Downs.

As we approached it, skirting the outermost fringe of the wood, I could feel creeping over me the rather sinister feeling which its proximity always evoked. Partly it was the wood itself: seldom visited, incompletely explored, it was not as other woods. It existed on the frontier of the known world; moreover, it was to some extent enemy territory, for it didn't belong to Colonel Bell. In Colonel Bell's woods, on the other side of the valley, we could brave the keepers with impunity; but here the keeper was our natural enemy. He was a big, red-faced man, and would appear suddenly, as though from nowhere, at the end of a ride, or at the corner of one of the narrow, winding paths; armed with a gun, and followed by a large setter who growled at us threateningly ... Often we picnicked and primrosed in the wood for hours without meeting the keeper: but the threat was always there, and instinctively we kept close together and spoke in low voices.

Once beneath the trees, the tower was upon us almost before we realized it. It stood in a little clearing on the edge of the path, surrounded by a spiky iron fence, and exhaled a peculiar atmosphere, as one approached it, of inviolability. There was a little gate, always kept locked, in the fence: people could and presumably sometimes did enter that holy ground; but not just ordinary people – only those specially-privileged persons whom Nurse Collier referred to as 'officials'. No official, however, was ever visible on our visits to the tower; perhaps they only came at night.

So potent was this atmosphere of exclusion, that we were not allowed, Alec and I, even to touch the surrounding fence; perhaps our nannies had a vague fear that it might be charged with electricity. We could only stand on the path and gaze across the forbidden territory – weed-grown and untidy – to where the fabulous bulk of the tower reared itself skyward.

It was an extraordinary structure: not 'functional' at all, as one might have expected, but built with the solidity, the pretentious respectability, of a stockbroker's villa in Surrey. (Even the group of pine-trees which surrounded it gave an added touch of suburbanity; the rest of the wood was mainly oak and hazel.) Four columns of brick-work, converging at their summits, formed four corresponding arches: the tower had the look of an arcade or a viaduct folded in upon itself to form a quadrilateral. The brickwork was solid and expensive-looking, and one expected to see at its base, instead of the jungle of nettles and willow-herb, neat beds of lobelias and calceolarias. But above the four conjoined arches, the suburban impression ended abruptly; for, instead of a red roof and gables, the tower bore upon its summit the vast, rectangular tank, painted white, and bearing the inscription:

MARGATE CORPORATION DISTRICT WATERWORKS
1903

Margate was miles away in the Isle of Thanet; what were its waterworks doing here? The mystery seemed, as we gazed up at that portentous tank, entirely insoluble. The tower loomed over us: vast, sinister and inexplicable, guarding its secret.

For it had a secret; and the secret was perpetually, it seemed, on the tip of my tongue – something I once knew but couldn't remember, like a forgotten tune or the name of a book. The tower was fringed with a special atmosphere unlike anything else; one would never reach its secret by comparison with other things, for it was unique. It was not, taken as a whole, *like* anything: the brick towers were like a house, but the white rectangular summit was like nothing so much as a vast, an elephantine lavatory tank; one expected almost to see a chain hanging from it with a porcelain handle on the end, so that one could 'pull the plug'. This impression was intensified by the peculiar noises which sometimes emanated from the interior: muffled clankings and gurglings such as one often heard in the wc at home.

The tower was disturbing, as I now see, largely by reason of its incongruity: Lautréamont's sewing-machine-on-a-dissecting-table was not more calculated to *épater le bourgeois* than this enormous lavatory-tank resting on top of a folded-up viaduct. I was not exactly frightened of the tower: indeed, I was rather fond of it. But my affection was tempered by a certain awe, a sense of some unknown potency residing within that august form. I felt about it, in fact, very much as I felt about my own father, whom on the whole I liked, but whose several attributes could be individually frightening: at about this time, for instance, he wore a rather bushy blond moustache, for which I had lately conceived a profound and irrational terror.

Once the tower was reached, we turned down one of the paths, on the other side of the track, to a clearing where the primroses were particularly abundant. Birds must have sung there: but in memory 'Waterworks Wood' seems to have been wrapped in a tomb-like silence – probably for no better reason than because we spoke in whispers, for fear of the keeper.

Here among the primroses, the tower was once more out of sight. Wandering on through the wood, however, we would suddenly glimpse it again: its august and minatory outline appearing momentarily in the vista of a ride . . . One late afternoon in April I had my first private encounter with the tower; I had wandered away from the others, through the hazel-thickets, in search of purple orchises. They grew scattered among the bluebells at intervals of a few yards: the biggest and best were always just a little further on. The late sunlight slanted through the thickets, creating an oddly illusory atmosphere: things appeared to be what they were not – a flint-boulder looked like a couched animal, an enamelled milk-can, dropped by some workman, took on the contours of a human skull. The bluebells themselves, in this hallucinatory radiance, had a purplish tinge, so that I ran hither and thither fruitlessly, thinking they were orchids.

The grown-ups were calling already from the clearing: it was getting late. But I must just get that tall, resplendent orchid a few yards further on . . . Another orchid and another lured me forward. Suddenly the bushes thinned, and I reached a path – but not a path I knew. I emerged and looked round me, and with a start of astonishment saw, at the end of the path, only twenty yards away, and presenting to me (owing to the new angle from which I was viewing it), an aspect of itself which I had never seen before – the brick arcades and the white peaked summit of the watertower.

Because I had never seen it from just that position, and because I was alone with it, the tower seemed, more than ever, to be offering me some extraordinary and desirable secret . . . If only I could grasp it! I stood and stared at the white tank for several minutes; encircling the base of it, above the brick-work, was a little gallery, with an iron fence round it – used, no doubt, by the 'officials' on their secret visits to the tower. A zig-zag iron ladder led down from this gallery, to the ground. Perhaps if I waited long enough I should see one of those mysterious visitors cross the little clearing within the fence, and climb the ladder . . . But I couldn't wait: the voices calling from beyond the thicket were becoming impatient and rather angry ... I turned away, and hurried back through the close-growing hazels. The sunlight was fading, the bluebells were blurred into a vague, uniform greyness; the milk-can was just a milk-can, the stone an ordinary stone.

II

At this time – early in the first War – one of my great excitements was to watch for airships. Aeroplanes were already a fairly common sight: but an airship was a rarity. I possessed one of the first posters showing the various types of British and enemy air-craft; and the airships, in particular, I invested with a kind of totemistic quality: they were like sacred tribal animals, strange leviathans possessing, like the watertower, a mysterious and indefinably potency of their own.

Like animals, indeed, they were reputed to have regular habits: the best time to watch for them was apparently in the late evening, at which hour, it was said, they could often be seen 'on their way home'. So sometimes, for a treat, I was allowed to go up to Barham Downs after my usual bed-time: having, of course, had an 'extra' rest in the afternoon.

For hours, it seemed, we watched with strained eyes the north-easterly horizon, whence the airships were expected to appear. By too-long staring at the bright, empty sky, I induced in myself a kind of hallucinatory state: I began to see, not only airships, but a whole menagerie of aerial monsters ... Sometimes we walked up the narrow road over the crest of the downs: and my heart would give a jump as I saw a gleam of white appearing over the distant trees. At last! But it was no airship, only the tank of the water-tower gleaming in the last rays of the sun.

One spring evening, returning from one of our expeditions to 'Waterworks Wood', I began to yawn, and to feel abnormally, unpleasantly tired. Alec skipped from one side of the road to another, as alert and lively as usual: he squealed with excitement as a weasel ran across the road; a little further on he found a dead frog, crushed flat like a pressed flower by a passing cart-wheel.

Normally I should have been extremely interested; but this evening the frog seemed merely a dead frog, nothing more; even the weasel could not arouse my flagging interest.

The grown-ups began to notice my preoccupied air, my dragging steps.

'He's tired,' they said, and, *sotto voce*, added the humiliating words: 'He's not very strong.'

Tears stung my eyes, my mind swooned into an ecstasy of self-pity. The westering sunlight falling across the downland seemed, all of a sudden, unbearably sad. I hated Alec for being so obviously not tired; nobody said of *him* that he 'wasn't strong'. Perhaps I should soon die, like Judy in *Seven Little Australians* – she had died, I remembered, at sunset: it seemed to me a profoundly appropriate time of day to die.

I was put into the mailcart and pushed the rest of the way home; but I began to feel worse instead of better; and I realized, at last, that I was beginning to feel genuinely and unmistakably ill.

The word, once admitted to consciousness, tolled like a tocsin through my mind. I was terrified of illness; for me it meant one thing only – vomiting. This had only happened to me once or twice since babyhood; but the sensation of retching was, for me, the ultimate horror. And now, coming down 'Boring' Lane, I began to recognise the familiar sensations: the 'full' feeling in the stomach, the sense that my throat was about to turn inside out. I laboured under the curious delusion that I had once vomited up the bulb of a large electric-torch: I had been 'taken poorly', as they said, during the night, and either the torch had really slipped into the bowl, or had been placed suggestively near it. Now, once again, I was haunted by the horrible image of a torch thrusting its way up my gullet ...

I suffered in silent misery; above my head, the grown-ups kept up a cheerful, a positively sprightly conversation. The last sunlight faded in a glory of red and gold behind the beeches – just as it had in *Seven Little Australians*. I tried vainly to believe that I was only, as they said, 'a little over-tired'; I refused to admit, with absolute finality, that I was really Ill.

But reality triumphed at last. I managed to hold out till we reached home, and were safely in the bedroom. Then I made no further attempt to deceive either myself or anybody else.

It was nothing very serious – a tummy upset which the doctor diagnosed as a 'touch of colitis'. But I vomited frequently for two or three days; and the doctor's diagnosis haunted me alarmingly: I fancied the word was 'killitis', and had no doubt that I should die. Owing to the 'k' and the 'itis', the dread word evoked also the image of a triangular purple kite, such as I had once possessed, straining at its string.

I was 'ill' only for a few days, but in retrospect it always seemed weeks. I was given albumen water to drink, after my bouts of vomiting; and the insipid stuff became inseparably associated with the delicious relief which followed each attack, acquiring thereby a flavour which seemed to me positively ambrosial.

At last I was better; I was taken to the window to look at a rainbow: I had never seen a rainbow before, and felt that it had appeared at this moment solely to compensate me for being ill. A gramophone in the next-door cottage played the Toreador's Song from *Carmen*: and to this day, I cannot hear the tune without recalling the burst of sunlight after rain, the rainbow itself, and the insipid taste of albumen water.

I was better: but one never recovers entirely from any illness, slight or serious. An attack of 'flu, a mere cold in the head even, takes something from one inexorably, something which is never paid back. One may succeed in forgetting one's illness entirely: but the loss of sensibility, the enforced withdrawl from life, is none the less a little death. A fraction of oneself – infinitesimal, but measurable – has gone for good. It is Death by instalments – the instalments may be minute, but, slowly and mercilessly, they add up towards the final reckoning.

Illness in childhood – like most childish misfortunes – is more acutely experienced than ever in after life; the instalments paid out are greater. The developing capacity to reason, if it doesn't diminish one's liabilities, at least enables one to dodge a payment or two; or perhaps only to imagine that one has dodged it – which amounts to the same thing.

I, personally, was rather lucky in the matter of childish illnesses: colds, bilious attacks, mild bouts of 'flu – they didn't take a very heavy toll. But I feared illness more than I feared anything else, and I still do. Exterior dangers – being bombed or run-over – at least give one a sporting chance: even the supernatural can be evaded by the simple process of disbelieving in it. But illness – the insidious assault from within, the revolt of body against mind – against illness one has no chance. One may begin by refusing to believe in it; but unless one is a Christian Scientist, one can't keep it up for long.

I wasn't often 'ill' as a child; but on the other hand, I suffered from that mysterious and indefinable defect of being 'not very strong'. This involved, after my minor attacks of 'flu and so on, long periods of convalescence and being 'taken care of'. These I found delightful: I wasn't 'ill' but I enjoyed all the privileges of illness.

It was during one of these periods that I started reading Shakespeare.

My mother had been to a sale in Folkestone, and had 'picked up', as part of a 'lot' which doubtless contained other and more desirable objects, a three-volume edition of Shakespeare and a microscope. These were given to me; and proved to be the most exciting presents I had ever received.

The microscope was a small, low-powered affair: but quite good enough to magnify a fly's wing or a grain of pollen to miraculous proportions. I spent many absorbed hours with it: but it was the Shakespeare that was to become for me, in due course, the more rewarding of my mother's two purchases.

I opened the volume of tragedies first, and was enthralled by the very first page.

How many autobiographers have thus described their first introduction to the pleasures of literature! The sensitive child wandering among dust-grimed folios in the library; the volume of Keats (or even Milton, incredible though this must seem), 'selected at random'; and then the instantaneous recognition of a life's mission: the 'magic' of the language 'grips' him, he determines in that crucial moment to be a poet ... (Often enough he does, indeed, become one; and may even qualify, in time, for the more dazzling honour of writing middles for the weeklies, or scholarly articles on eighteenth-century poetasters for the *Cornhill*.)

My own experience was rather different; I did indeed open the volume of tragedies and was quite genuinely enthralled: not by the text, however, but by the illustrations.

These consisted of 'engravings on wood, from designs by Kenny

Meadows'. The text was edited, 'with a memoir', by Barry Corn-
wall, and was interspersed with 'annotations and introductory
remarks on the plays, by many distinguished writers' who preferred, however, to remain anonymous. The fat, royal octavo
volumes were bound in chocolate-brown cloth with thin leather
backs, and were published by Robert Tyas, 8 Paternoster Row, in
1843.

I opened the book at *Macbeth*; and at the opening of Act I was
held entranced by the three-quarter-page engraving which start-
lingly preluded the play ... A vast scaly serpent lay coiled, apparently, upon a cloud; within its coils, as though in a nest, sat the
three witches, raising their 'choppy fingers' skyward; their
hatchet-faces, with protruding teeth and cavalry-moustaches,
peering from nun-like hoods. Perched insecurely on the serpent's
flank, sat Paddock and Grimalkin, the latter clutching at the sli-
thery surface with claws prehensile and elongated as the talons of
an eagle. Above this unconventional family-group impended a
dark and thunderous cloud behind which, evidently, some vast
and nameless monster was concealed: enormous bat's wings protruded from the swirls of vapour, and two muscular hands, grasping daggers, menaced the cloaked heads of the witches below. The
face of the monster was concealed: but upon the dark centre of the
cloud was inscribed, in black-letter script, the word MACBETH.

Lying in bed, lapped in the delicious passivity of convalescence,
I was in a state to appreciate with an almost too-acute sus-
ceptibility the art of Mr Kenny Meadows. I realized that, without
knowing his work, I had long been one of his predestined admirers
... Snakes, bats, witches, corpses dripping with blood – here was
all the horrific imagery of the 'Romantic Agony' in its later stages;
the demonology of a Hieronymus Bosch transposed into terms of
Gustave Moreau, with side-glances at Mrs Radcliffe and Monk
Lewis ... I realized that it was the vestigial hint of this quality
which had so endeared to me the engravings of bats and puff-
adders in Alec Bell's natural history book. Fascinated, I turned the
pages: horned and semi-human incubi clutched, with eagle talons,
at the stomachs of their slumbering victims; serpents with the
heads of women writhed in fantastic copulations; blood dripped
from jewelled daggers; an asp with a human death's-head
wriggled from a glass phial held in a skinny hand ... Thunder and
lightning, in this dark and murderous world, seemed incessant;

and in every engraving, even the most innocent, some evil symbol – a skull or a serpent – lurked in the background; incubi lay concealed in the boudoir, nude muscular ravishers crept unseen upon unsuspecting virgins; on the first page of *Romeo and Juliet*, a tiny human skeleton, bearing an arrow, clambered like some noxious insect from the corrupt heart of a rose ...

I wonder if the surrealists ever discovered Kenny Meadows; if not, I can certainly recommend him to the survivors of the cult. Not even Max Ernst, in his Victorian *collages*, has succeeded more admirably in producing an effect of horrific incongruity.

My pleasure in the engravings was mingled with surprise: I had only read 'Lamb's Tales', and was inclined to think of Shakespeare as a rather milk-and-water, almost a goody-goody writer – like *Pilgrim Street* or *Jessica's First Prayer*. Plainly he was something quite different; far from being goody-goody, he seemed to me, by this time, to belong rather to the class of literature which I was 'not allowed to read'. I detected, I think, even then, the signs and symptoms of something which children seem often able to recognize without in the least understanding: a preoccupation with physical sexuality, plus (in this case) a strong element of sadism.

Kenny Meadows, in fact, was a crypto-pornographer; he kept adroitly on the side of 'niceness', but the insistence on buttocks and breasts, the juxtaposition of hirsute, half-human monsters and early-Victorian damsels, perpetually betrayed him. Had I acquired his engravings in any other form, I should almost certainly not have been allowed to enjoy them; but fortunately they formed part of 'Shakespeare', and were, therefore, apparently considered blameless.

Sated temporarily with Gothic horrors, I began, hopefully, to read the text. *Macbeth* started promisingly with witches; at the very moment, moreover, that I began the first lines, a genuine clap of thunder burst, with an almost too-obliging appropriateness, overhead ... Much of the play I skipped, naturally enough; but I did go through it to the end, and, helped out by the frequent oases of the engravings, which decorated (for Kenny Meadows was nothing if not prolific) almost every page, I persuaded myself that I was enjoying it. Parts, of course, I did genuinely enjoy: any child would be thrilled by the witch-scenes and the murders. The Scottish names, the feeling of a world remote and 'prehistoric', thrilled me too; and the desolate, thunderous horror of such outbursts as

'Glamis hath murdered sleep!' and 'Macbeth shall sleep no more!' haunted my mind with an obsessive potency long after I had finished the play. The very name 'Macbeth' came to have a romantic and almost an onomatopoeic quality: the sharp, crackling 'Mac' followed by the muffled reverberation of 'beth' seemed appropriately to suggest the noise of some remote and menacing storm.

My next choice was *Lear*, and I found it heavier going. But Kenny Meadows helped me through: Lear, white-gowned and bearded, like a Druid at an eisteddfod, shaking his fist at the thunder; Goneril and Regan shown symbolically as bat-winged harpies with serpents' tails; Lear again, 'crowned with rank fumiter' . . . It was not quite so exciting as *Macbeth*; but the blinding of Gloucester, Edgar's ravings as Tom O'Bedlam, and the 'gentleman with a bloody knife' seemed to me almost up to the standard of Kenny Meadows; besides, I was interested, as a botanist, in the bits about flowers.

'Fumiter' was recognizable as fumitory; 'harlocks' I assumed to be charlock; samphire I recognized with a thrill of delight: I had found it myself, only the year before, on the foreshore at Seabrook. 'Dost thou know Dover?' asks Lear. I did; and felt the thrill of the suburban theatre-goer who finds that Miss Dodie Smith's new play is actually about a family at Ruislip – 'just like *us*, my dear.'

It was windy March weather when I read *Lear*, and I was still convalescent after 'flu: the play came to be associated, ever afterwards, with the first daffodils, the chestnut-buds bursting along the Undercliff, the first, warm, melancholy spring days. But it was the Dover passages which, for me, gave the play its character. Dover acquired for me, on our subsequent visits there, a special literary quality; it was 'in' Shakespeare, and seemed to me to have thereby gained an added reality: I began to notice it, consciously, for the first time, like a native of Dorset who has just started to read Hardy.

We lived at Sandgate; our visits to Dover were infrequent; when they occurred, they had (even before I read *Lear*) a special kind of excitingness. The only other town of comparable size which I knew well was Folkestone; Dover, only eight miles away, seemed to me to belong to a different world. I was prepared by hearsay for this 'difference': Dover was considered 'dirty', 'sordid'

– one didn't go there unless one had to. Other, more sinister rumours attached to it, too: 'things' had happened there which were spoken of in whispers – 'nasty' things. This element of 'nastiness', I gathered, emanated chiefly from the Dover Hippodrome, a small music-hall which I invested with goodness knows what horrific glamour. I didn't know what a music-hall was, but I suspected it to be connected in some way with girls – the kind of girls whom my family referred to as 'fast', whatever that might mean. (One or two of my sister's acquaintances were thus stigmatized by my mother: I observed them carefully for signs of this reprehensible motility; but they seemed to me very much like other girls, though somewhat nicer than most.)

The very word 'Hippodrome' had, for me, a faintly immoral flavour: I connected it with hips, which apparently were not quite nice. My brother had bought a gramophone record of a song called 'Florrie the Flapper', which had a passing reference to this wicked if indispensable part of the body; he was not allowed, after the first time, to play it in my presence . . . Then one day I heard the maids whispering about a girl who had recently been found dead under the cliffs; she had been employed, it seemed, at the Dover Hippodrome . . . So much I heard: the rest of the story was related in whispers, punctuated by exclamations of shocked disapproval. Visualizing some horrific disembowelling *à la* Kenny Meadows, I begged for details: but I was only told that they 'weren't fit for a child's ears'. Not unnaturally, this increased my curiosity a hundredfold; and by judicious eavesdropping I did at last overhear, uttered in an appalled whisper, the horrifying words: *rotten with disease.*

I wasn't much the wiser; but the images evoked by the phrase did tend to confirm the Gothic vision of Dover which I had evolved for myself by reading *King Lear*. Any woman we passed in Dover who could be identified, in my estimation, as 'fast', seemed thereafter to be a combination of Regan or Goneril and the girl-from-the-hippodrome. (I could hardly have been aware, at the time, that the name of Lear's eldest daughter did, in fact, by a faint verbal echo, justify in part my rather tenuous association.) Similarly, any old man with a white beard, whining outside a pub, was Lear himself.

Even without these romantic associations, however, I should have detected the 'difference' between Dover and Folkestone. Folkestone (apart from the old town round the fishmarket, where we seldom went), was impeccably 'nice': the buildings were newer, the streets cleaner, and the people one saw shopping or walking along the Leas were, most of them, recognizably the same sort of people as my own family. In Dover, it was all quite different: the houses were old and rather ramshackle, the streets were grubby, and nearly all the people were of the class which I was accustomed to hear spoken of as 'common'. They had loud, alien voices, and strange gestures; the women's clothes seemed shabby, many of the men wore cloth caps and mufflers.

This strangeness frightened me rather, but I found it, none the less, exciting. I was thrilled, too, by the trams which clanked and rumbled down the narrow streets, their long antennae striking forth blue sparks from the overhead wires. And from beneath East Cliff, one peered up at an astonishing series of 'houses' built into the solid chalk: some of them had brick walls and even windows, just like real houses; some were mere tunnels and hatchways leading into the interior of this mysterious, subterranean 'town'. How far, I wondered, did this underground world extend? Perhaps, I conjectured, it went on as far as our own village, ten miles inland; perhaps the 'Boring' itself, in Forty Acres field, was an extra outlet for the inhabitants ...

I was to learn, before long, that these troglodytic 'houses' were the relics of fortifications, built during the Napoleonic wars; they had nothing to do, after all, with the inland collieries at Bettes-hanger and Snowdown, or, for that matter, with our own temporary 'Boring'. But I was haunted for years, and still am at times, by the sense of a great subterranean town extending from Dover, inland under Lydden and Coldred and Sibertswold, towards Barham Downs and the remoter country beyond the watertower.

III

In spring and summer, coming back from our walks in the late afternoon, I used to be tortured by the fear that there might be 'people to tea'. If there were, I was liable to be seized upon and made to say 'how-do-you-do'. I possessed even less social aplomb than most 'difficult' children: the prospect of being faced with a crowd of unknown grown-ups (or even children for that matter), terrified me out of my wits. I still suffer, at times, from the same fear: and one of my nightmares is that, by some extra-ordinary concatenation of circumstances, I may one day have to be received at Buckingham Palace. An unlikely contingency, to say the least, it is the adult equivalent, for me, of my mother's tea-parties.

As often as I could – if I detected, in the garden, the fluttering of ladies' dresses, or white flannel trousers (for the cottage lawn was just big enough for badminton, though not for tennis) – I ran away and hid myself: as often as not in the Igglesdens' garden. The Igglesdens had an immense orchard of nut-trees: it was prac-tically a wood, though so familiar, its bounds so well-defined, that it lacked the element of fear and mystery which, in a 'real' wood, would have prevented me wandering for long there alone. The Igglesdens' wood, moreover, had a fascinating flora: half-wild, half-cultivated. In early spring, the ground was covered with great drifts of snowdrops: later came daffodils, and later still, in May, carpets of ramsons, the starry-flowered wild garlic. Other more coy denizens were the Turk's-cap Lily and the blue Mountain Anemone, both considered 'doubtful natives' in the floras, and almost certainly not truly wild in the Igglesdens' orchard. But I preferred to think them indigenous. Truly native, however, was an orchid – *Epipactis latifolia* – of which a single plant turned up one summer: I had only found it once before, and was immensely excited.

One April evening when there were 'people to tea' I had es-caped from the visitors, and was wandering by myself through the high, sun-pierced thickets of hazel. It was a Sunday, and the church-bells were ringing for evensong; three placid notes leisurely and interminably repeated: tum-*tum*-ty, tum-*tum*-ty, tum-*tum* . . . The bells were in need of repair, and the third note was so faint that one could hardly hear it at this distance: shrill, uncertain, slightly cracked, it had, none the less, a curiously pro-longed echo, which was 'held', like a dotted minim, above the subsequent repetitions of the other two beats, producing an effect of some vague, remote descant, faintly discordant, as though the traditional 'tune' of the bells had been re-set by some modern composer.

The westering sun poured its sheaves of gold through the

hazels; the notes of the bell seemed a kind of thickened, concentrated essence of the light, exuding in drops of a darker, richer tone from the very core of the evening. A cuckoo began to call, too, its iterated note cutting across the song of the bell with an effect of increased 'modernity', as though the composer had redrafted his score, 'thickening' the orchestration, and adding an atonal element in the manner of Schönberg or Webern ...

I wandered to the limits of the garden, to where it was bounded by the bottom of 'Boring' Lane. The orchard was separated from the road by a narrow stream and an oak fence; the stream was a tributary of the Nailbourne or 'woe-water' which flowed through the village in spring: rising irregularly every few years, and supposed, by its appearance, to herald disaster. It seemed, in those days, to rise more often than not: they were the years of the first War, so perhaps the legend seemed more than usually plausible ... On this particular evening the stream was flowing turbulently between its banks; and on the banks themselves and above them, on the higher ground, stretching away under the trees as far as I could see, their cups still wide-open to receive the later sunlight, was a golden carpet of celandines.

In the quiet, sunlit orchard, their sudden splendour took me unawares: I had seen them often enough before, but never in such prodigal quantities, never at this precise moment when the last sunlight fell full upon their innumerable stars, burnishing their gold to an infinitely richer brilliance. The cuckoo called across the held note of the bell: the sunlight glanced on the brown, chuckling stream: the golden, sonorous evening seemed timeless, eternal. I felt suddenly inclined to cry: it was too much, the moment was making some vast, intolerable demand upon me which I knew I couldn't satisfy. To escape its importunity, I began to gather a bunch of celandines: pretending that this was just an 'ordinary' evening, and that I was doing something quite casually which I might equally well do at any other time ...

As I picked the flowers, the light began to fade: the sun was dipping behind the great chestnuts beside the church. The celandines were rapidly closing their petals; when I had picked a bunch, they looked curiously drab and inglorious. I returned to the house, leaving my flowers in the porch: I would collect them when I went home.

An hour later I went to look for them: they had gone. Mr

Igglesden had thought they were 'rubbish', and thrown them in the dust-bin. I burst into passionate tears, an outburst so unreasonable, so out of proportion to its cause, that Mrs Igglesden concluded that I must be ill. It wasn't as if the celandines were 'rare': there were plenty more of them. I could go and pick some more now, if I liked ... Nobody 'understood'; I could hardly have specified, even to myself, the reason for my tears. But I continued to cry with a desolate unhappiness until, at last, exhausted and almost unable to speak, I was escorted home.

On the days when I couldn't escape, and was made to go and say how-do-you-do to the visitors, I would be led, like a victim to the sacrifice, towards the tea-table spread under the plum-trees, where enormous aunts or cousins loomed in a semicircle, like figures of some terrifying myth. They all seemed immensely old, and reminded me vaguely of the picture of the Graiae in the 'Told to the Children' edition of Kingsley's *Heroes*. 'Lend me thy tooth, Sister, that I may bite him ...' My Aunt Ada or Aunt Gertie did not, in fact, show any signs of wanting to devour me; though Aunt May Hewlett, on one occasion, did give some colour to my phantasies by seizing hold of me and (painlessly) pretending to take a mouthful out of the back of my neck ... I protested, with some vigour; offended, Aunt May said that *her* little boys simply loved having their necks bitten. (At a later date, when I met her offspring, I not unnaturally expected them to be rather peculiar; little boys who *liked* being bitten must, I felt, be in some way extraordinary; but – rather to my disappointment – they proved to be perfectly normal.

Sometimes Cousin Howe would be present too, and his wife, Cousin Lucy. Howe Hewlett was a portentous figure: an evangelical parson with an immense white beard and huge hands with horny, spatulate fingers. Everything about him was enormous: even when he gave my parents a present, he chose a vast, an outlandishly outsize edition of Webster's dictionary, almost a yard wide ... I think he disliked me; Cousin Lucy certainly disapproved of my upbringing, and said so in no uncertain terms. Once she gave me a picture-book which, naturally, at bed-time, I took upstairs with me. For reasons which I have never fathomed, this action was in some way 'naughty'; what tenet in Cousin Lucy's extraordinary system of ethics specifically forbade the taking of books upstairs, I cannot imagine. But I was sternly rebuked, and the book remained, in future, below stairs.

Often Miss Trumpett had come to tea: resplendent in crimson or scarlet, like some extraordinary macaw. She terrified me, but I was also half in love with her. She was at least familiar: other visitors, strangers, held for me the terror of the unknown. Mrs Sabatini, Mrs Noblett, Mrs de Lacy Bacon ... their very names were alarming. Mrs de Lacy Bacon – a vision of rashers swathed in lace; Mrs Noblett – she seemed to be covered with curious protuberances. 'So this is the *baby?*' they would say, when I was introduced. My brother and sister were a decade older than myself: it was an eternal humiliation to me.

'Visitors' were divided, by me, into two classes: friends and relations of my mother and father, and friends of my brother and sister. My parents' visitors all seemed to me incredibly ancient: they were remote as gods, and as unapproachable. The friends of my brother and sister, being younger – though still immeasurably older than myself – occupied a kind of no-man's-land between Godhead and mortality: they were less than divine, but more than mortal. Unlike my parents' friends, these demi-gods could consort, to a limited extent, with mere mortals like myself. It was, indeed, a rather unsatisfactory kind of intercourse: the half-godly ones had the whip-hand every time, and could dispense or withdraw favours as they chose. But they did possess certain human characteristics: one of which (an important one for me) was that they could be fallen in love with.

And fall in love with them I did: distantly, secretly (I would have died rather than reveal my passion), but none the less wholeheartedly.

Hertha de Lacy Bacon (whose mother was one of the Olympians) endeared herself to me for life by doing for me a beautiful drawing of a Bee Orchid. I treasured the drawing – the gift of a half-goddess – for years. It was seldom, though, that such tangible contacts were established ... Usually, I was no more than an enthralled observer of the rites and ceremonies with which these heroes and heroines of myth occupied their time: badminton, bathing (when we were at Sandgate), golf (on Barham Downs: I was careful to keep at a safe distance), listening to the gramophone; and, of course, talking.

Their talk was interminable and, because I couldn't understand half of it, fascinating. The conversation of my sister's friends, in particular, had an esoteric and magical quality which thrilled me. Often they would speak in low voices, sometimes in whispers: there were quick, complicit glances, bursts of incomprehensible laughter ... What was their talk about? What were the jokes that amused them? I tried my best to overhear; but when I did succeed in doing so, I was seldom much the wiser. Sometimes, overhearing some remark which had provoked screams of laughter, I would hypnotize myself into believing that I, too, thought it extraordinarily funny. I would repeat it to myself in private, not understanding it in the least, but thinking how exquisitely witty it must be. Once, unable to keep such a gem of wit to myself, I repeated it to my mother: she gave me an odd look, didn't laugh at all, and told me not to be rude. After this, I noticed that my sister's friends became all at once much more difficult to overhear ...

Elspeth, Violet, Hertha, Dolly – they sprawled their big, athletic bodies on deckchairs in the sunlight, talking; the more daring of them smoked cigarettes – which was still considered a little 'fast' by the Olympians (Cousin Howe and Mrs Sabatini), sitting aloof beneath the plum-trees' shade ... I was thrilled and exasperated by the sense of a world beyond my ken: the innumerable jokes and allusions belonging to a shared past, a community of age, experience and upbringing. They had nearly all been at the same school: Miss Pinecoffin's rather 'advanced' and very strenuous establishment at Sandgate, Gaudeamus, where I myself was soon to go to the Kindergarten. Hockey and high ideals and high-jinks in the dormitory – it all sounded fascinating, like the stories in *Little Folks*; but it remained for me, as did the totemistic world of ball-games, an insoluble and provoking mystery.

This sense of a communal past which I hadn't shared became, in later years, inseparably associated with the secretive, clannish world of my sister's school-friends; and after a time, the association became concentrated in and almost confined to Dolly Matheson. I don't know that she was any more typical than the others: a jolly girl, given to frequent bursts of laughter, she does not, in retrospect, seem specially memorable. But to this day, if I find myself in some society to which I am a stranger, where the conversation turns on a common past which I have not shared, my sense of being alien, my irritation at private jokes which mean nothing to

me, find vent in the silent, laconic exclamation: 'Dolly Matheson!'
And I see, for an instant, with perfect clarity, the chubby face, the
athletic body, and the complicit smile at some mystery which I
shall never be able to solve ...

My brother's friends shared equally a common fund of memories: but they were less secretive, less given to giggling in corners
over jokes which were, perhaps, a little 'fast' ... Could men be
'fast' as well as women? I wasn't sure; it seemed to be chiefly a
feminine quality, but perhaps all men were fast by nature, anyway,
and accepted as such. They seemed, at any rate (I thought), to take
life more easily, they didn't seem to mind whether people disapproved of them or not.

My brother's friends were mostly at Sandhurst, or about to be;
some of them were already in the Army. Sometimes they appeared
in uniform, sometimes in tennis-flannels: they all seemed very
large, with loud voices and big moustaches, and they smelt of
tobacco and Anzora. They talked interminably about games: I
was rather bored, but quite contented so long as they only talked.
When they were actually playing, I kept well out of the way, for
fear of balls.

Heroic inhabitants of a world to which I knew I should never
rightfully belong (the world of Ballantyne and *Lost Island*), they
squatted on the grass playing a portable gramophone and smoking
pipes or what they called, rather deprecatingly, 'gaspers'. I was
faintly shocked because they wore their tennis-shirts open at the
neck: extremely prudish myself, I would never have thought of
doing such a thing; though once or twice I unbuttoned my own
shirt, in private, before the glass, to see what it looked like.

They talked a lot, too, about 'shows'. I realized they meant
theatres, and as I had at that time a devouring passion for the
stage, I felt a certain sympathy ... But I had only been to *Peter
Pan* and a performance of *Twelfth Night*; the 'shows' attended by
my brother's friends (and my sister's too, for that matter) were
quite different. They had names like *Bubbly, Tonight's the Night,
Razzle-Dazzle*; they appeared to consist largely of music, and my
brother bought gramophone records of them. These were mostly
two-sided, labelled 'Selection I' and 'Selection II' respectively, so
that I conceived of a musical comedy or *revue* as being arbitrarily
divided into two parts, each with its own special atmosphere.

I was not allowed to go to these 'shows'; nobody, indeed, ever suggested such a thing. I knew very little about them, except from the fragments of talk which I managed to overhear: one had some 'ripping girls' in it, another had a Scottish scene, others had marvellous tunes or (in one or two cases) very 'low' jokes. Like the Dover Hippodrome, these 'shows' had a faint flavour of wickedness: especially the kind called *revues*. I studied attentively the posters of the Pleasure Gardens Theatre, Folkestone, hoping to wrest from them some inkling of what a *revue* really was. All I could gather, once again, was that it was something to do with girls – and particularly girls who wore very few clothes.

I possessed a model theatre, in which I used to give performances to my family on Sunday evenings. After studying the posters with more care than usual, and storing up a few quotations I had managed to overhear, I decided to 'produce' a *revue* called *Razzle-Dazzle*. All went well till I introduced upon the stage a woman with a pram and a baby and, like player and prompter combined, delivered the appropriate lines. I cannot remember the joke; I have a feeling that it alluded to babies; in any case, my production was banned there and then, and subsequent ones, I was told, must be confined to *Peter Pan* or *A Midsummer-night's Dream*.

Naturally I developed a passion for *revue*: it lasted well into my adult life. Directly (at the age of sixteen or so) the opportunity occurred to go to a real one, I went. Goodness knows what glamorous immoralities I expected; I was bitterly disappointed, anyway. But I wouldn't admit it; perhaps this wasn't the right kind of *revue* ... I tried again – and again; for years I couldn't bring myself to lose hope. But at last I gave it up. Evidently, I thought, *revues* weren't what they had been in my childhood: a fond illusion which I still vaguely cherish.

Rupert Cockayne, Basil Medlicott, Jack Fearnside-Speed, Neville Penlington – heroic friends of my brother, sprawling on the lawn and listening to records of *Tonight's the Night*: how many of them are still living, after two wars? I loved them and hated them – hated them because I felt inferior, because I was 'not very strong' and couldn't play games; loved them remotely and respectfully, knowing them to be demi-gods. I imagined, too easily, that I was being laughed at; my brother's friends were really very kind, and hardly laughed at me at all, but I still had a nasty feeling that they might be doing so behind my back.

Basil Medlicott, big and stalwart, with an enormous black moustache, was already in the Army. He laughed less than the others; he was quieter altogether. My hero-worship, for a time, became concentrated upon him: I particularly admired, for some esoteric reason, his white flannel trousers. I can remember nothing about them, now, which made them different from any other white flannel trousers; yet they must have possessed some mystical virtue which distinguished them from the ordinary article. I admired them so much that (as is the way with lovers), I had to talk about them, sooner or later: and confessed my infatuation to my nurse, who told me not to be silly.

My libido, as it happened, was soon diverted into other channels ... When we returned to Sandgate, the girls of Gaudeamus gave a performance of *A Midsummer-night's Dream*, to which, for a treat, I was taken. I fell hopelessly in love with the girl who took the part of Puck. Her name was Alison Vyse; her blonde hair was bobbed – a novelty in those days – and she played Puck with verve and distinction. My passion was a singularly hopeless one, for she was a year or two older than I, and, by the time I began to attend the Kindergarten, was of an age to be quite unapproachable. However, she formed the centre of my amorous phantasies for a long time; I invented, in due course, a 'wild' Alison Vyse, which (had she but known it), was a compliment of the first order. I preferred wild flowers and wild animals to tame ones; therefore, if I liked anybody, it seemed natural that, in my wishful phantasies, I should evolve an undomesticated variant. The Undercliff was already peopled, for me, with 'wild' airmen, who nested in the bracken, and were partly covered with hair, like fauns. There was at one time a wild Basil Medlicott; and now Alison joined the indigenous fauna: hopping about on rabbit's paws, her blonde bob flapping seductively among the tamarisks and conifers under the cliff. For a time I even kept her in a cage and fed her on Plasmon oats, which I had seen advertised in *Little Folks*: it seemed to me to be the sort of food she would probably like. (Later, she came to stay for a time with my family – an experience which, alas! was to prove disillusioning.)

At Sandgate, badminton was replaced by bathing; our garden descended in terraces to a semi-private beach, and my brother and sister and their friends bathed frequently and with gusto. I would watch them from afar off, as they ran down the steps with shrill screams and laughter – '*Wouldn't* Myra love it!' '*Do* you remember that time at Seabrook?' – always those echoes of some unknown, exciting past which I hadn't shared ... The girls wore voluminous costumes, covering their arms and almost all of their legs; the men's attire was scarcely less prudish – curious garments like combinations, patterned with gay stripes.

I was encouraged – even, on occasion, compelled – to bathe; but the water terrified me. I would as soon have plunged into a fire as into those hostile, icy breakers ... I was frightened; but my prejudice against bathing was occasioned quite as much by *pudeur* as by fear. I had a rooted objection to undressing in public; that other people could do so struck me as shocking, though I secretly admired my brother's friends for being so shameless, so nonchalantly 'fast' ... I watched the bathers from the terrace above the beach: shouting, laughing, splashing each other in the shallows. I envied them: but only as a mortal may envy demi-gods – not with any real hope of ever having a share in their fabulous existences.

My own existence was divided sharply into two contrasting modes, distinct as the cleavage in music between major and minor; two worlds which seemed so different that, when the transition occurred from one to the other, I could fancy that a corresponding change occurred in myself.

These two distinct modes of thinking and feeling were symbolized by our life at Sandgate (our 'real' home) and our sojourns in the 'country', at the cottage in the Elham Valley. Between these two ways of life the opposition was complete and irreconcilable. Even geographically the barrier was clearly marked; the 'country' lay, remotely, beyond the line of chalk-hills at the back of Folkestone. We penetrated, on our walks, to the extreme verge – climbing Caesar's Camp or Sugarloaf to hunt for the Bee Orchid or the Spider; but we never crossed the frontier. When the time did come, at last, in spring or early summer, to go to the 'country', we took the little local train from Shorncliffe Station; or sometimes we would go, more excitingly, by car: actually penetrating the mysterious barrier of the hills, driving through Swingfield and Denton and along the high plateau of Barham Downs, until at last we would see, gleaming above the far woodlands, the white, familiar peak of the watertower.

Yet it was possible, on special occasions, without going by train or crossing the frontier of the hills, to take a sort of magical short cut into that Land of Lost Content. At Seabrook, between Sandgate and Hythe, a turning called Horn Street led off the main coast-road, under a railway-bridge. The branch-line was disused; the bridge was plastered with ancient, rusty tin placards, advertising Virol and Veno's 'Lightning' Cough-cure. Once under this bridge, one could imagine oneself, already, in the 'country'; fields and hedges bordered the road; sheep cropped the pasture; a stream gurgled with a country-noise beyond the hedge. And if one walked on for half a mile, and turned up a lane to the left, one actually came to real woods.

Pericar Woods they were called, rather oddly. Primroses and bluebells grew in them, undoubtedly – also wild foxgloves, which were rather rare in the district, and supplied, usually, the official reason for our expedition; yet I could never feel that Pericar Woods were quite genuine. Without the train or the car, without the sense of crossing the frontiers of Caesar's Camp or Sugarloaf, I couldn't convince myself that I was in the 'real' country.

None the less, Pericar Woods were a good substitute for the genuine article. They lay on a steep hillside: at the top of the hill was Shorncliffe Camp, and in the still, June afternoons, as we gathered our foxgloves, we could hear the far-off crying of bugles. Sometimes we would meet soldiers, about whom I felt rather as I did about the inhabitants of the 'Boring': they were an alien, rather inimical race, given (if the grown-ups were to be believed), to almost perpetual 'drinking', and to other things which were only hinted at in whispers. I decided that I would be a soldier when I grew up; I would have died rather than mention the fact – my publicly-admitted ambition was to be a bus-conductor – but I cherished the idea in secret. I don't think I really quite believed in it myself: but I derived a peculiar thrill from imagining myself dressed in the rough khaki uniform (with a leather belt), and living in the remote and rather sinister territory beyond Pericar Woods.

I

I was a hero-worshipper in spite of myself: I didn't want to be, but I was drawn into one passionate admiration after another, whether I liked it or not. This totally one-sided love-life of mine was an inviolably private affair: it remained even, at times, almost concealed from myself – I didn't approve of it, and would sometimes refuse to admit its existence. This ambivalence bred in me a not-so-unusual impulse to 'take-it-out-of' the people I loved; to injure, humiliate, or in some other way 'do the dirty' on them. Only, of course, in phantasy: in real life, I remained as polite and self-effacing as ever. But Basil Medlicott, and after him Alison Vyse, were 'punished' by being kept in a cage.

I had few friends of my own age: I was painfully shy, and my dislike of ball-games didn't help to induce a spirit of mateyness. I tended, instead, to form 'friendships' with adults and preferably on paper: I developed a taste for 'pen-friends'.

My earliest pen-friend was, or should have been, Pimpo, the clown, of Sanger's Circus, to whom I wrote an enthusiastic fan-letter at the age of four. Unfortunately, the letter was returned by the Post Office as 'insufficiently addressed'.

I was luckier, however, with Mr Hesse.

Mr Hesse was a taxidermist in Dover; I had been, for some time now, collecting a 'Museum' of butterflies, fossils, stuffed animals and so on. When I found some dead stoat or barn-owl, I was allowed to send it to Mr Hesse, who stuffed it, and mounted it on a little platform with realistic appendages – twigs or grass – appropriate to its habitat. I had never seen Mr Hesse; I was not to meet him for years. But a curious and voluminous correspondence sprang up between us: he wrote me long letters, in his crabbed handwriting, about anything and everything – animals and plants, his own family, aeroplanes, the war, fretwork, gardening. I replied at even greater length: I told him about everything I did, and illustrated my letters with little vignettes in the style of Kenny Meadows – pierced hearts, daggers dripping with blood, serpents with bats' wings. The correspondence lasted for several years, uninterruptedly. Then, one summer, when we were at the cottage,

Mr Hesse was at long last invited over to tea. He came: an elderly, tubby little man with a bald head and steel-rimmed spectacles. I was not exactly disappointed: I had never imagined Mr Hesse to be of the race of heroes. But somehow, after that, my letters to him became less frequent, and finally stopped altogether. The impact of his physical presence had destroyed some delicate adjustment: I would have preferred our relationship to remain purely epistolary. To this day there are certain people whom I prefer to write to rather than meet; it is a weakness, I suppose, of the 'literary' temperament.

No doubt I invested Mr Hesse with a certain added glamour owing to the fact that he lived at Dover. The town remained for me a thrilling, slightly sinister place, and our infrequent visits there continued to be fraught with a special kind of excitement.

I was shown the Grand Shaft – that mysterious spiral staircase built through the sheer cliff, leading up to the Barracks: it seemed to be (we never ascended it) yet another entrance to that vast subterranean town which I imagined stretching inland towards the 'Boring' and the watertower.

Then there was a mysterious creature called 'the dredger' which lived in the harbour; all day it grunted and snorted and roared somewhere out in the dazzle of sunlight: monstrous and invisible, it seemed to me a kind of tutelary spirit, a totem-beast guarding the town.

There was, too, the 'twelve o'clock gun', which exploded, up at the Castle, punctually at midday, its thunderous roar echoing with a terrifying, a more-than-Shakespearian reverberation along the beetling cliffs ...

The gun, the dredger, the 'town' inside the cliffs: Dover was full of romance, a fit background for heroes such as my brother's friends, many of whom were stationed there ... The gun and the dredger remained for me mysteries which I scarcely dared – or even wanted – to try and penetrate; but I had read some article about mining and the invention of the Davy Lamp, and I began to have some inkling of the real meaning of the 'borings' in the surrounding country.

Walking up to 'Waterworks Wood', I would be haunted by the feeling that, hundreds of feet below, lived a dark, alien race, their naked bodies crouched in narrow, pitch-black corridors where the 'Davy Lamps' gleamed like glow-worms, and canaries hung in cages to give warning of the deadly firedamp ... They seemed to me, this underground tribe, to represent all that was dark, dangerous and inadmissible; and I was possessed by a fear that, on one of our longer walks, they would emerge in force, black-faced and naked from their caverns, and carry us off with our primroses, like so many Proserpinas at Enna, into the infernal regions below Snowdown and Womenswold ...

One afternoon we set out for 'Waterworks Wood'; we were going primrosing, and it must have been, I think, Easter-time, for Nurse Collier was heard to murmur that she only hoped the woods wouldn't be full of 'bank-holiday people'. This outcast race was known to infest, at certain seasons, Mrs James's woods, and even – despite the increased vigilance of the keepers – Colonel Bell's. I had seen them myself once or twice: they were usually very fat, they roared with inexplicable laughter when they saw us, and wherever they went left a litter of paper-bags, as though they were engaged in a perpetual paper-chase.

We walked up the hill, and skirted the first part of the wood. As we neared the watertower, we could hear voices – a most unusual occurrence. Rather cautiously, we continued on our way; and at last reached the fenced enclosure ...

The sight that met our eyes was fantastic and, to me, shocking in the extreme. The august, inviolate mass of the watertower was alive with human figures: they clambered up the zig-zag iron ladder, they clung like monkeys to the railing round the tank; some had mounted to the gallery itself. The enclosure itself was full of them. They wore black clothes, most of them, and cloth-caps; their shirts were open at the neck, and their faces all seemed exactly the same: smooth, round, bright-red, with enormous mouths full of very white teeth. They laughed and chattered in some extraordinary dialect of which we could understand not a single word; some of them pointed at us, and roared with laughter.

With one accord, we turned away and hurried back by the way we had come: out into the blessed sunlight again, away from the enveloping trees, down towards Coldharbour.

'Just what I was afraid,' I heard Nurse Collier muttering. 'Those miners ... it wouldn't do to stay, not with *them* about. They'd been drinking, too – you could see.'

So they had been miners: the watertower, no doubt, was one of their outlets from the Plutonic kingdom below the woods ... I looked back, furtively, once or twice, to make sure that the black, red-faced figures were not following us. But all I saw was the white cap of the tower, floating serenely as ever above the dark crests of the pines.

PART THREE

Bouquet of Gerbs

bring on your fireworks, which are a mixed
splendor of piston and of pistil; very well
provided an instant may be fixed
so that it will not rub, like any other pastel.

E. E. CUMMINGS

I

My friend Imogen Grahame was one of those people who make one feel that one was born (as the saying goes) a couple of double whiskies below par. Bursting with a demonic energy, she had welcomed me in Florence as though I were her long-lost brother instead of a mere acquaintance.

I had arrived at midnight, but for Florentines, in summer, the day can scarcely be said to have begun before ten o'clock at the very earliest.

'First thing tomorrow I'll take you round,' said Imogen, with an air of chafing somewhat at the delay; for two pins, I felt, she would have taken me round there and then – at midnight, and after an eight-hour train-journey from Milan, sitting on my suitcase in the corridor.

'First of all,' she continued, 'we'll see about cashing your traveller's cheques. I'll take you to my friend Donnini – he's frightfully well in on the *Mercato Nero*, and he ought to give you not less than two thousand five hundred.'

'The official rate's nine hundred, isn't it?' I queried.

'My *dear*, nobody takes the slightest notice of that – the least anyone ever gets is two thousand ... Then you'll have to go to the *questura* and get your *carta di soggiorno* – I'll fix that up in no time: I know old Marelli at the *questura* – I did him a good turn once, and he's never forgotten ... Then you'd better book your sleeper for the return journey – you have to book at least a month ahead, or you can't be sure of getting one ... I know the head-man at Cook's, old Settembrini – he's an old friend of mine ... Then, if you like, I'll take you round the Pitti ... We might lunch at *Zi' Rosa* if you can afford it ... And in the afternoon, I thought we'd go up to Fiesole and have a nice long walk. You look quite pale – I expect you need some sun, coming from England.'

That was last night; now we were sitting, at seven in the evening, over a vermouth on one of the café-terraces in the Piazza della Repubblica. Imogen had been as good as her word – better, indeed; I had been 'taken round' till my legs ached and my head swam. Signor Donnini had given me two thousand four hundred to the pound – 'Not bad,' said Imogen, 'but I could have got you three thousand a week ago'; old Marelli at the *questura* had been excessively obliging; so had Signor Settembrini at Cooks; we had lunched at *Zi' Rosa* off a Neapolitan *pizza*; and had had a nice long walk at Fiesole.

'If you're not too tired,' said Imogen, 'we might stroll up to San Miniato and look at the view.'

I said I thought I'd leave San Miniato till another day.

Imogen had lived in Italy, almost uninterruptedly, for nearly fifteen years. The Italian entry into the War had hardly discommoded her at all: she spoke Italian like a native, and had passed as one.

'It was only when the Jerries started to take over, after the Armistice, that things got a bit difficult,' she said.

The Jerries had interned her, but this was quite a bearable misfortune.

'I lived in a nice little villa up in the hills,' she said. 'Lots of food, and a charming peasant family to look after me. I thoroughly enjoyed it. There was a very nice young Oberleutnant used to come and see me occasionally – I very nearly promised to marry him, only I don't in the least want to be a German, especially nowadays. A British passport does still mean something, though not as much as it did.'

Then the British arrived: that was when her troubles had really started. The Germans had always been 'correct'; but the English, said Imogen, were just damned rude.

'They shut me up in a cell, just as if I'd been a prostitute,' she said. 'By the time they let me go, I just *hated* the English – the whole lot of them. I got so that I couldn't bear the sight of all those grinning faces and those pink knees.'

Suddenly she burst out laughing.

'Did I tell you how I was nearly raped by two Canadians? I didn't? Well, I was: they got me up against a wall – two great hulking brutes, they were, too. I didn't want to let them know I was English, you see – there was a company of CMPs just round the corner ... Well, when things really got a bit desperate, I just let them have it – in English, and the only sort of English they understood, what's more. You should have seen them! They just turned and scuttled like rabbits. How I laughed!'

Nothing, she said, would make her go back to England now if she could avoid it.

'I was back there last summer, you know: my dear, it was awful. Was the climate always so frightful, or is it that I've forgotten? It dripped and dripped and it dripped, and the grass grew taller and taller, and it was just like being in a hot-house at Kew, only with the heating turned off.'

I said I thought the summer of nineteen-forty-six had been a bit worse than usual.

'But then the people – all hopelessly depressed and rude and bad-tempered ... Why *do* they put up with that silly government? Why don't they have a revolution – or just ignore all the regulations, like the Italians do? Honestly, d'you know, everyone in England struck me as half-baked – half-alive, if you see what I mean. They just seemed to have given way ... I suppose it's the climate, really.'

I said I thought it probably was. From where I was sitting, I could just see the top of Giotto's *campanile* rising above the neighbouring roofs: its pink marble, catching the slanting, golden sunlight, looked like a stick of Brighton Rock.

'And then the way they take such a high moral line over everything,' continued Imogen. 'It's all very right and proper, I daresay, but where does it get you? They go all moral over such silly things – things which aren't a matter of morals at all, but just common sense. And they're so shocked at the Black Market, and yet not one of them'll refuse an extra half-pound of butter or sugar if it's offered to them.'

'I expect it's just our puritanism coming out, as usual,' I said.

'You're telling me. Well, I may be living in a fool's paradise – but do you blame me?'

A fool's paradise ... Perhaps it was, I thought, looking round the café terrace, the *piazza* with its car-park full of expensive cars, the leisurely crowds drifting between the cafés; probably it was a fool's paradise; but I certainly didn't blame Imogen for living in it.

'Well,' she went on, 'I've lived on my wits for fifteen years, so I don't know what's to stop me now. By the way,' she added, with apparent inconsequence, 'I've started learning Russian.'

'What on earth are you doing that for?' I asked.

'Why, for the next war, of course, And did I tell you I'd just become a Catholic?'

'No, have you?'

'Oh yes. My dear, it was the funnist thing you've ever heard – I must tell you.'

I ordered another vermouth, and settled down to listen to the story of Imogen's conversion.

The sun was off the *campanile* now. A delicious coolness descended with the twilight. As the dusk deepened, a host of lights leapt into being; the cafés blazed with them, the tall buildings were bright with Neon signs. The square was more crowded now. Everybody – men as well as women – seemed smartly dressed; more so than any crowd I had seen since before the war. I felt ashamed of my shabby tweed coat and flannels ... And they seemed happy, too, these people; happy and gay. After Piccadilly Circus, it seemed unbelievable. Yet Italy had lost the War; Italy – I had read it over and over again in the highbrow weeklies at home – Italy was on the verge of bankruptcy, inflation, starvation ... I watched the beggars circulating between the tables, the boys selling Swiss and American cigarettes, the Black Market moneychangers: 'You wanta shange sterlina, Swiss francs?' A fool's paradise? Possibly; but it was none of my business ... I raised my glass, and drank a silent toast: to Italy, perhaps, or merely to myself, and the fact that I was here.

'... And I was dressed as a bride, you know,' Imogen was saying, 'and they poured about half-a-pint of oil over my head. So messy – and with oil at a thousand lire the *chilo*, too ... My special priest said it was quite the grandest conversion he'd ever seen.'

Presently I suggested having dinner; it was early by Italian standards – only just after eight o'clock – but I hadn't yet accustomed myself to the enormous gulf which, in Italy, separates the two main meals. We made for a restaurant in one of the sidestreets near the Duomo. The entrance was unpretentious: a bead-curtain, flanked by two bay-trees in tubs. Over the doorway was painted the single word *trattoria*, in unobtrusive lettering; Italian restaurants, if they are any good, do not bother to advertise themselves too obviously. In the window were displayed a lobster, some *funghi* and a basket of strawberries.

Just inside the entrance was the *mescita di vino* – a cool, cavernous alcove lined with rows of straw-covered flasks; the restaurant itself was through an archway: a long, low-ceilinged room, plain and undecorated, but spotlessly clean. Two rows of tables flanked the walls, spread with gay pink-checked cloths, and ready laid with napkins, glasses, knives and forks. The whole place had a business-like, utilitarian air; yet there was about it, also, an indefinable air of elegance and *savoir-vivre*. It was a place to eat, but a place, too, where eating was given its proper status as one of the civilized arts; to have a meal here, one felt, would be an aesthetic, not merely a gastronomic experience.

We were early, and the restaurant was still half-empty. The proprietress served us herself; her manner betokened an unassailable professional pride, modified by an infinite desire to please.

'I don't know about you, but I'm jolly hungry,' said Imogen.

We began with an *antipasto* – slices of *salame*, and delicious curled fragments of smoked ham; *tagliatelli* followed – vast, steaming platefuls, generously laced with a sauce of tomato and *peperoni*; then came *calamai* – small cuttlefish fried in oil and served with a green vegetable; after this a salad of crisp young lettuces; and finally strawberries, swimming in bowls of red wine. To drink, there was a red Tuscan wine, light yet potent, with a quality reminiscent of a *vin rosé*.

Throughout the meal, Imogen kept up a perpetual flow of anecdote and gossip – much of it concerned with the English occupation. There was the story of the English chaplain and the Contessa; the tale of the Town-major and the Neapolitan prostitute; and a highly dubious anecdote about a couple of Guards officers, which led in its turn to the story of the goose . . .

'The Guards were a scream,' said Imogen. 'We asked about half a dozen of the officers to a party – Luisa and I. Luisa scarcely knew a word of English – she was just starting to learn it. Well, they arrived; we'd asked some very nice girls as well, but of course *they* didn't speak English either, and the Guards hadn't two words of Italian between them. The poor mutts stood in a bunch round the fire, looking too pathetic for words. I did *my* best, and Luisa tried out the bit of English she knew, but my God, it was heavy going. They all seemed to have bright pink faces and ginger moustaches, and honestly I couldn't tell half the time which was which. Poor Luisa had a terrible time; she told me afterwards that almost the only word they uttered was "Er" – they began every sentence with it, she said, and never seemed to be able to get any further. She actually went out, there and then, and looked it up in a dictionary, but of course she couldn't find it . . .'

Imogen took a deep draught of wine, and gave a reminiscent laugh.

'Well,' she continued, 'I suddenly remembered that we'd got a goose outside in the kitchen – the *contadini* had sent it up from Luisa's country place, and it was to be killed the next day. So I thought perhaps *that* might break the ice, if nothing else would; so out I went to the kitchen, and came back with the goose under my arm. I just flung the door open, and let go of the goose – right in the middle of the Guardsmen. My dear, you *should* have seen their faces! The wretched goose got in a regular panic – I didn't blame it either – and went flapping and squawking all over the place. And the Guards all stood there like statues, with their mouths wide open, wondering what the hell they were meant to do. So finally I said "Why don't some of you catch it?" and then they all sprang to attention and went careering round the room trying to seize hold of it . . . Well, by that time, everyone was laughing so much that the Guards began to laugh too, and Luisa brought in some drinks, and after that the party was a raging success, and the Guards got as tight as owls and had to be taken away in a truck at four in the morning.'

By now the restaurant had filled up. A warm, tingling, all-embracing happiness possessed me – a sense of almost mystical beatitude; not for years had I eaten such a dinner, or drunk such wine . . . I ordered coffee and cognac, and looked about me at our fellow-diners.

They were nearly all, I judged, of the small-bourgeois class, with a sprinkling of professional or business-men: clerks or shopkeepers with their families, young men with their girls, and in one corner a large and ebullient family who were evidently celebrating a betrothal or a wedding . . . Nearly all the girls were remarkably pretty; all, without exception, well dressed. How did they do it? How, in a country on the verge of bankruptcy and anarchy – and I had, of course, the *New Statesman*'s word for this – how could this façade of elegance and civilized living be maintained?

I asked Imogen.

'These people you see in here,' she said, 'are the successful rack-eteers. If they weren't, they couldn't afford to come here. This whole country's run on gangster-lines at the moment ... But the point is, these people really have the *will* to recover. It's an indi-vidual thing – every man for himself. There's a thing called a government, which makes regulations, fixes prices and so on; but no one takes the slightest notice. In any case, the government's in the racket too, up to its neck ... Everyone's intriguing and rack-eteering and doing the next man down the whole time – and of course they love it, it's their very blood. They've always been the same – look at the Renaissance. If the country was in a state of tip-top prosperity, they'd still be at it; there'd always be endless rackets and *camorras* and *imbroglios*. You can't stop 'em. As things are, at the moment, it's the only way they can exist ... Being British, you'll think it's all very immoral, but the fact is it does *work*, up to a point. It's a case of the weakest going to the wall – there's plenty of poverty, of course; but then, there always was, especially in the south.'

'There's poverty in England, too, for that matter,' I said.

'Of course there is. But the point about England is that your standard of living's so high; you all want to be bourgeois. Why, any farm-hand in England has to have his wireless and his piano and his pictures and his wool-mats ... The peasant here is satisfied if he's got a bed to sleep in and enough to eat. That's why the peasants are the richest class here at the moment. The worst off are the middle-class and the professional people: prices are high and getting higher, and wages don't keep pace. The shops are full of stuff, but no one can afford to buy it, except tourists with ster-ling or Swiss francs ... I'm damned if I can see where it's going to end. Probably the War'll come before things get much worse: that's what everyone expects, anyway. And meanwhile, they just don't worry.'

In which, I pointed out, they were unlike the English.

'You're telling me,' said Imogen. 'The English never stop worrying – it's just a national disease. I suppose they always did, but they've got worse lately – I noticed that when I was back there last year. Out here, they're different: they just say *"Così è la vita*," and go off and have a drink and hope things'll be better tomorrow.' Imogen emptied her glass and gave a sudden laugh. 'And the odd part of it is,' she added, 'that things often *are* better.'

Lapped in my state of rosy contentment, I could well believe it. Presently the *signora* brought our bill; by current rates of exchange, our dinner had cost us the equivalent of less than six shillings each.

Later, over another drink in the Piazza della Repubblica, I remembered that Imogen's family had lived at Oxford when I was up twenty years before; Imogen and I, moreover, were approximately of the same age.

'Do you remember anyone at Oxford called Dallas?' I suddenly asked her.

'Hew Dallas? Good Lord, I should jolly well think I do. He was at Wadham, wasn't he?'

'*Hew* Dallas!' I echoed. The missing christian name – with its unusual spelling – flashed across the gulf of the years, illuminating with a sudden, unequivocal brilliance the dim figure of my travelling-companion. Something in my brain clicked abruptly into place; the imperfect image, evoked by that scribbled surname at Milan, was suddenly rounded and complete.

'Why, of course I remember him,' Imogen was saying. 'What's happened to him nowadays? Have you seen him?'

'I met him in the train.'

'How frightfully funny. What's he doing, do you know?'

'I don't know.'

'I suppose you talked Oxford all the time.'

'We scarcely mentioned it.'

'Well, what did you talk about?'

'We talked about fireworks.'

'*Fireworks?* How extraordinary. Is he still as much of an aesthete as ever?'

'No. I should hardly say so.'

'Why, it only seems like yesterday – he was the man who fought that duel at Merton, wasn't he? And he brought out some paper, too – it was banned by the proctors. And he gave a frightfully drunken party in Beaumont Street ... It's awfully funny you should run into *him*, of all people.'

It was funny, I agreed, that I should run into Hew Dallas – in a *wagon-lit*, twenty years older and scarcely recognizable, in this year of grace nineteen-forty-seven ...

II

Hew Dallas must have been in his second year when I went up to Worcester. He had already become a legend; there were innumerable stories about him – most of them, no doubt, apocryphal. Like all mythical hero-figures, he took upon himself many of the attributes of his forerunners; anecdotes which had been current in Oxford for half a century were linked with his name and took on a new lease of life.

There was a story, for instance, of how, when dining one night at the George, he had been heard to remark in a resonant voice which carried from one end of the room to the other: 'Yes, it's delicious – but don't you think it has just the *slightest* flavour of babies' brains?'

The story was quoted *ad nauseam* – though few of the people who repeated it seemed aware that Hew had borrowed the remark, without acknowledgement, from Baudelaire.

He was reputed, on his first arrival at Oxford, to have driven from the station to his college in a pony-trap drawn by two llamas; he was supposed to sleep with a revolver under his pillow; he had threatened to horsewhip the Senior Proctor; he had celebrated the Black Mass in the public lavatory at Carfax ... These were but a few of the (probably) apocryphal legends which became attached to his name. The famous affair of the duel, however, had a firmer basis in fact; Robin McQueen of Christchurch, so Hew alleged, had accused him of having improper relations with a woman-writer of mature age, celebrated for her asyntactical prose, who had come from Paris to lecture to the Poetry Society ... The very next morning, one of Hew's friends 'waited upon' Mr McQueen in the time-honoured manner. A rendezvous was appointed; Hew arrived in good time, attired in a frock-coat and top-hat; Robin McQueen, not to be outdone, appeared a few moments later, magnificent in *quattrocento* doublet and hose and an enormous blond wig. Fortunately – or unfortunately – the proctors had wind of the affair, and arrived just in time to put a stop to it.

Authentic, too, was the story of the OUDS smoker, in which Hew had appeared as Yasmin in a skit on Flecker's *Hassan*. Sylph-like in his Persian costume, he had brought down the house; on the second night, the stage was banked with roses presented by his admirers ... So much was perfectly true; but the rumour that a young man at Keble had actually sent him a telegram proposing marriage, was probably a legendary accretion ...

'My dear, have you met Hew Dallas?' one would be asked at parties. '*Quite* the most amusing man.' For me, he remained for a long time a legend: doubtless I attributed to him a good deal more glamour than he really possessed. The later 'twenties at Oxford was a period of decadence; the great figures of the post-war epoch had gone down long ago; real honest-to-God aesthetes were becoming rather rare. It was the turn of the tide – already Spender and Auden were contributing to *Oxford Poetry*; in another few years, the full tide of Marxism would have swept away the last tremulous survivors of the Mauve Epoch.

Meanwhile, however, the old two-party system still survived; one was either a hearty or an aesthete. I was only too anxious to throw in my lot with the unpopular party; but alas! they were, even the longest-haired, the most determinedly Oscar-ish of them, faintly disappointing ... Where was the glamour of *The Green Carnation*, of *Sinister Street* even? True, there were parties: in College, out of College, at Thame, at the Beetle and Wedge ... They lacked, however, the authentic note of diabolism, the perfervid *chichi* of an earlier epoch. Aestheticism, as and when it occurred, amounted to little more than the wearing of grey suède shoes and a nodding acquaintance with *Corydon* and *Du Côté de Chez Swann* ...

Against such a subdued background, the legend of Hew Dallas acquired a disproportionate lustre. One week a drawing of him appeared in the *Isis* – one of a series entitled 'Seen at the George'. It showed an immensely tall, serpentine young man with a grave Roman profile and a lock of hair falling across his forehead. The caption read, discreetly, 'Mr H–w D–ll–s'. I recognized the face: I had seen it myself at the George, and in the 'Super' at morning-coffee time ... Encountered in the flesh, however, it hadn't really made much impression on me.

Amongst other things, he was a poet.

'You ought to look at his stuff,' said Clere Parsons, who was editing *Oxford Poetry* that year. 'I think he's one of the best people writing at the moment . . . though that man MacNeice at Merton seems rather promising . . .'

I read his poems in the *Oxford Outlook*: one was entitled 'Bouquet of Gerbs', which I naturally found sympathetic. Another was called 'Cheiropompholyx,' which sounded like a character from *Tamburlaine*, but turned out, when I looked it up in the dictionary, to be a skin-disease . . . The poems showed all the fashionable influences – Eliot, Cummings, Cocteau; yet a curiously personal note sometimes emerged, a timid note of ninetyish nostalgia struggling through the modish mannerisms. I detected an odd ambivalence in his work – a kind of Warlock-Heseltine cleavage between the hard-boiled cynic *de nos jours* and the 'Nineties' young man born out of his time . . .

Clere showed me also the manuscript of a story of his, written entirely in words of one syllable. For some reason, the first sentence lingered in my mind for years afterwards, though I could probably not have remembered who had written it: 'To Mant the room did not seem strange . . .'

He was reputed to be 'living his novel' – a vast work, like Proust's, in a dozen volumes; he hadn't started writing it yet; but it was understood that he was basing his life upon it, and had so far lived through the first two volumes . . .

In my second term, a new magazine appeared. It was announced with a great fanfaronade: sandwichmen patrolled the streets with bright yellow posters on which was printed:

LIBIDO
Not a Medicine but a magazine

I managed to secure a copy: a big octavo pamphlet with a bright yellow cover, upon which appeared an abstract woodcut of remotely phallic design . . .

Libido was edited by Hew Dallas and somebody who called himself Kiril Vanx. It was fortunate that I bought it when I did; for the very same day, the remaining copies were swooped upon by the proctors and suppressed.

I wondered why: *Libido* contained nothing very seditious or very shocking – apart from a libellous remark or two about Robin McQueen . . . About half of it was monopolized by what purported to be the first instalment of a work-in-progress; it was generally supposed to be by Hew himself. Written in a jerky, unpunctuated prose, in the manner of Joyce, the fragment was possibly his first attempt to transcribe the *roman vécu* of which we had heard so much . . .

I went to a party that night in Wellington Square. The banning of *Libido* had created a mild sensation.

'Nigel says he's certain to be sent down – the Dean told him so himself.'

'My dear, what can you expect of *Wadham*?'

'The Senior Proctor said the most *loathsome* things at the interview.'

'*Such* a wicked old man! I'm positive he wears *stays*, too.'

'He said to Hew: "This is not realism, Mr Dallas – it's filth." '

'Hew's drunk at the George – the Ershams were trying to get rid of him when I left. He had a napkin over his head and said he was Queen Victoria.'

'Sixty years a queen, dear . . . *I* heard that he'd sent copies to Gertie Stein and Sylvia Beach *and* Aleister Crowley.'

'I adored the remark about Robin, did you see?'

'Yes – here it is: "Mr Robin McQueen wishes to correct the rumour that he craves abjectly for Houbigant parfum, and is devastatingly revolted by Coty . . ." My dear, *won't* Robin be in a tantrum?'

'There'll probably be another duel . . .'

'The verse was rather indifferent.'

'So derivative.'

'Who's Kiril Vanx?'

'My dear, that's the queerest part – nobody knows.'

'*Queer* is the operative word . . .'

Hew was not sent down; but he had had, it seemed, a narrow escape. For some weeks, nothing was heard of him. He had retired, people said, into his phantasy-life . . .

Suddenly, one bitterly cold afternoon, he appeared upon the tow-path, protected from the weather by a vast crimson carriage umbrella. He trotted up and down for an hour, keeping more or less abreast of the crews; waving his umbrella at them madly, and inquiring, in his resonant, high-pitched voice, why they didn't bump? He had come specially, he said, and in *such* weather, to see these big strong men bumping each other, and not a bump had he seen the whole afternoon . . .

That night, somewhere in the neighbourhood of BNC, he was ruthlessly debagged by the rowing-men . . . Later in the evening he appeared at the George in a magnificent kilt and sporran; nobody knew where he had managed to acquire them. When asked the reason for his peculiar garb, he replied: 'Those beastly boys have stolen my lovely new trousers.' Whereupon (it was reported), he ordered a bottle of Clicquot and burst into tears.

A host of other stories about him continued to be circulated; there was the classic one, for instance, about the speech which his landlady had delivered to him after a party in his rooms. Perhaps it really was Hew's landlady; or possibly it was somebody else's. At all events, the anecdote went to swell the gathering *corpus* of legend which attached itself to him. From frequent repetition, the landlady's words acquired a lapidary perfection of phrasing, accent and cadence:

'Now, Mr Dallas,' she was reputed to have said, 'I *don't* mind them toughs from Trinity, what smashes me furni-tewer; I don't mind them Balliol boys, what breaks me Ming vawses; but what I 'ates and abhors is them *Magg-dalen* men, what makes a lava-*tory* of me front gardin.'

III

That summer at Oxford left with me chiefly a memory of rain: warm summer rain falling gently upon the lilacs in the gardens, upon the lake at Worcester, upon Christchurch meadows. Was it really an unusually wet season? Probably not; but the rain, when it occurred, suited my mood, and by association became imprinted on my memory.

Predominantly, it was a mood of despondency and frustration: a damp and cloudy sense of melancholy which I found rather enjoyable. I felt myself a victim of circumstances – though exactly on what circumstances I laid the blame I cannot remember. My temperament, perhaps . . . I saw myself – particularly when I was tight, which happened rather frequently – as a *poète maudit*, a kind of *vierge folle* deriving from Verlaine. *Pauvre Lélian!* I was consumed with self-pity, and at the same time, with a scientific, a positively Proustian detachment, I applied myself to a minute and painstaking study of what I thought of as my 'spiritual corruption'. To observe this fascinating process in operation was my chief – almost my only – pleasure. Lying on my bed, after a party, I would analyse my behaviour during the evening – and not only during that particular evening, but at other times as well. Fascinated, I perceived that every word and gesture, and (which was worse) every idea that passed through my mind, was bogus and derivative; my life, private and public, was a series of poses. I posed to other people; I posed – perhaps rather more convincingly – to myself.

And somewhere at the back of it all was a real person ... But where? How could one identify that core of reality among the *personae* of my own fabrication? Only by evoking my childhood could I achieve any conviction of my own reality; and even my childhood had been sentimentalized, overlaid with the emotional tone of the poems I had written, confused inextricably with an artificial private mythology ...

The truth was, I was weighed down by the burden of an adulthood which I felt subconsciously to be profoundly alien and incongruous ... Occasionally, I would walk out towards Godstow or Iffley and botanize; for a few hours I was happy. But soon the compulsion to resume my adult pose would reassert itself, and I would return in time for a cocktail party or dinner at the George.

And in the previous autumn, I had sometimes found myself stopping in front of the shops which sold fireworks; fascinated, as always, by those *natures mortes* of rockets, roman candles and gerbs; yet unwilling to admit my fascination, remembering that I was, after all, 'grown-up',

In the summer, in the rain-wet evenings, the gramophones on the river brayed out the tunes of the moment: *Rain, The Man I Love, A Room with a View.* For me, they had already – after only a few weeks – acquired a quality of intolerable nostalgia. My sense of the past had somehow so telescoped itself, that some episode of a month ago or less could seem as poignantly symbolic of my 'Lost Content' as the scenes of my childhood.

Whenever I was in London, I went to the Cochran *revue* at the

Pavilion – *This Year of Grace*. It had only been running since the spring; yet already, for me, my first visit had become steeped in the magic of the Past. *A Room with a View, Dance Little Lady* – the tunes, when I heard them on the river, in the damp June evenings, brought tears to my eyes. Every day, every hour that passed, was taking me further from my Lost Paradise, nearer and nearer to what harsh and intolerable encounter with reality?

But at Oxford, in that summer-term, it was not difficult to postpone the day of reckoning – or at any rate, the idea of it. Even the fact that I was due to take Law Prelim at the end of the term wasn't allowed seriously to interfere with my main preoccupation – the clinical observation and analysis of my own spiritual degeneration. I wished only that my 'corruption' was less 'spiritual' and more earthy; but Vice, though much discussed, seemed to be little practised, and my efforts in that direction (apart from alcohol) were markedly unsuccessful. Party conversation hovered, perpetually, about the more 'amusing' aberrations, but, like a conversation in a Firbank novel, seldom relinquished its tone of polite detachment. Our whole code of manners, indeed, aspired to a condition of complete artificiality; Firbank, Wilde and the early Huxley were our models, even if we hadn't yet read them ...

I hadn't been to a lecture for months; I could as easily have translated the Rig-Veda as construed a passage from Justinian; but the certainty of failing in my Prelim merely provided me with an extra thrill, an additional excuse for posing to myself as a misunderstood and persecuted *poète maudit*.

It was at this time and in this mood that I became acquainted, at last, with Hew Dallas.

It seems incomprehensible that I had not met him, to speak to, before; we frequented the same parties, the same cafés, the same friends; yet Hew had remained for me a legend, a kind of dumping-ground for my illusions about what a contemporary Oxford aesthete ought to be. And indeed, when I finally did get to know him, our acquaintance was so short and (while it lasted) so blurred by a perpetual haze of alcohol, that it was really not to be wondered at that, twenty years later, I should hardly recognize him. He remained for me, while I knew him – and he continued to remain afterwards – a kind of legend.

I met him at a party; he had read some of my poems, and, flatteringly, told me that he admired them.

'You know Clere Parsons, don't you?' he asked me. 'I adored that poem of his about the commode.'

His tall, emaciated figure was encased – somehow, one felt, rather unsuitably – in a very smart dove-grey suit with a double-breasted waistcoat. Yet he just failed, in spite of it, to look 'smart'; the collar of his silk shirt was askew, the mauve shantung tie was badly tied and crumpled; his grey suède shoes needed the wire-brush. His whole personality gave an impression of indecision, a perpetual struggle between conflicting elements. It was as though he were trying to encase himself in some mould which didn't quite fit him.

He asked me to tea the next day to his rooms in Beaumont Street; he was very tight when he issued the invitation, but I decided to take him at his word and go.

I went; a slightly sinister man-servant received me at the door with the information that 'Mr Dallas was in his bed'. I said I had come to tea, and was reluctantly shown into Hew's sitting-room and told to wait.

I wandered curiously round the room; it exhaled precisely the same air of indecision as his social personality. Efforts towards a certain smartness and luxury – multi-coloured cushions, expensive hangings – were countered by a hopeless untidiness and even by traces of positive squalor: dirty glasses left on the mantel, an old cocoa-tin used as an ash-tray ... Masses of flowers were every-where – delphiniums, irises, mauve sweet peas; but most of them were slightly faded, and the water was stale in the vases. Over the fireplace hung a Matisse reproduction; on the mantel, among countless invitation cards, stood a Chinese ginger-jar, from which depended a magnificent and many-flowered orchid. On another wall hung what was probably a Braque and possibly an original. In one corner stood a piano. On the music-rest was a piece of music: a prelude by Sciabin, I think. I noticed the indication printed over the opening bar: '*Lent, vague et indécis.*' Was its appropriateness, I wondered, quite unintentional?

On the shelves were all the books one would have expected: *Antic Hay, South Wind, The Green Hat, Ulysses, Time and West-ern Man, The Decline of the West.* There was a new novel pub-lished in Switzerland – *Pool Reflection,* by Kenneth Macpherson;

there was Proust – up to and including *La Prisonnière* – in the original French; there was Lawrence, almost complete; odd volumes of Gide, Cocteau and Apollinaire; and first editions of *Valmouth, Vainglory* and *The Flower beneath the Foot*. A centre table was littered with a bewildering collection of magazines, ranging from *transition* through the *Criterion* and *London Mercury,* to *Vogue,* the *New Yorker* and (even) the *Tatler* and *Bystander.*

Presently my host made his appearance: in pyjamas and a resplendent dressing-gown. He blinked at me vaguely.

'I'm terribly sorry – I'm afraid I don't remember – did I——'

'You asked me to tea,' I said.

His long, willowy body wriggled in an agony of embarrassment.

'How perfectly frightful,' he murmured. 'I'll order some tea at *once* – unless you'd rather have a drink?'

I said I thought some tea would be nice. He rang the bell, the sinister man-servant reappeared, and tea was ordered. Hew had thrown himself into an armchair, and was twisting and untwisting his legs with a nervous restlessness. Presently he got up, and began to pull one book after another from the shelves.

'You've read *this,* of course? And Cocteau – oh my dear, you must read him – so amusing. I saw *Parade* in Paris last year. Music by Satie. Do you know Satie? Extraordinary – he was writing just like Debussy and Ravel before they were born. I'll play you his *Gnossiennes,* and you'll see ... He was the Mayor of Arceuil, too, which I think is *rather* grand, don't you? How's Clere? There's somebody called *Spender* at Univ. – they tell me he's a *Socialist*! Isn't it fantastic? Oh yes, and this – I've been reading the mystics, you know – I love the title so, *The Cloud of Unknowing* ... I must play you my records of the Solesmes choir singing plainchant – it's the *only* music worth listening to, except Satie and Poulenc ... You know *Les Biches*? So naughty! Marie Laurencin did the *décor* ... You haven't read Firbank? Oh my dear you *must* – Beardsley in prose, but *much* better ... Have some tea.'

While we had our tea (Earl Grey, with lemon) he played the records of the Solesmes choir.

'I'll probably become a Catholic quite soon,' Hew announced, as though it were a question, merely, of buying a book or a new gramophone record.

'Surely you won't really?' I protested. 'You couldn't honestly believe all that nonsense.' My crude Bedalian scepticism had received a shock.

'Why not?' Hew demanded. 'It's quite as plausible as Freud, and far more amusing.'

As he talked, he became more and more at ease; his affectations dropped from him; his genuine enthusiasms bubbled to the surface ... I was charmed; the legend which I had woven about him was being realized; at the same time, I found that I liked him personally – a factor I hadn't reckoned with.

Presently he left the room for a few minutes, to get dressed: he was going out later, he said. While he was away, I made another tour of his bookshelves; and this time lighted upon something which seemed wholly incongruous. It was Alan Brock's *Pyrotechny* ... Coyly concealed in a corner, it had previously escaped my notice. I remembered Hew's poem, 'Bouquet of Gerbs', in the *Outlook*. So he liked fireworks!

He returned, a moment later, to find the book in my hand. The secret was out; we were, both of us, as we soon discovered, secret and passionate addicts ... The subsequent conversation was a curious contrast to what had gone before; I was delighted; I had hardly enjoyed myself so much since I had been up ...

Soon, however, several of his other friends dropped in; drinks were produced; the plainchant records were put away, and the deep-chested bellow of Sophie Tucker filled the room.

Hew became tight with an astonishing rapidity. After a couple of drinks, he was giving an imitation of Mistinguett; two more, and he was showing us how Nijinsky danced the *Faune* before the censorship intervened ... He chattered and clowned without a moment's respite; one had the curious impression that he was playing against time; it was as though he lived under the shadow of some imminent disaster which might be fatal and would almost certainly, in any case, interrupt his performance.

Presently, we all set out, through the warm, rainy evening, for the George bar; Hew insisted on carrying a bunch of delphiniums – to present, he said, to Mrs Ersham.

After dinner, there was a party at the House; I have a dim memory of Hew being restrained, with difficulty, from giving a repeat performance of his Nijinsky act – in Peckwater, this time, and without a stitch of clothing. Finally he invited the whole party to lunch at the George the next day; I heard afterwards that he was actually there at the appointed time, waiting to receive his guests; but none of them turned up.

IV

The term wore on towards its end; party followed party; I attended my schools and spent my time in the examination hall writing a series of defiant and exclamatory poems in the style of Guillaume Apollinaire. Hew gave a famous tea-party at which the tea was laced with Cointreau; in each cup floated a sprig of lilac. As the guests arrived, they were each handed a lemon at the door; those who were not in the know, stood about with a puzzled air, handling their lemons awkwardly, and wondering what one was supposed to do with them ... The whisper circulated, in due course, that they were just meant to be stroked: 'The *texture*, my dear – so delicious.'

A young man called Phipps, from Teddy Hall, who had almost certainly not been invited, wrote this party up for the *Isis*. The affair nearly led to another duel; Hew, however, prudently contented himself with calling upon the unhappy Mr Phipps in the *rôle* of Kiril Vanx (who had been none other than his own *alter ego*), and demanding an apology. In a false beard, a tousled and greasy wig borrowed from the OUDS, and carrying a most convincing-looking horsewhip, he apparently succeeded in reducing Mr Phipps to a state of submission ...

One afternoon Hew called on me, surprisingly, after lunch, and invited me to go on the river. We hired a punt, and paddled it out beyond the town, mooring it at length under a tree at the edge of a buttercup field.

The day was dull and thunderous; the buttercups gleamed with a tarnished brightness; on the heavy air was borne the grating whine of distant gramophones: songs from *This Year of Grace* or *Hit the Deck*, or the strident, gin-soaked caterwaul of Mistinguett singing *Il m'a vue nue*.

'I'm going to Paris in the Vac.,' Hew remarked. 'You simply *must* come too.'

This, as it happened, was just what I had decided to do. It

would be my first visit; and Paris, at the moment, represented for
me the sum-total of all my desires.

'I'll show you round,' said Hew. 'We'll go to the *Grand Ecart*
and *Chez ma belle-soeur,* and they tell me there's a terribly amusing exposition in the Rue de la Victoire.'

Presently he went to sleep; I was drowsy myself – we had both
been late the night before. Asleep, he looked astonishingly young;
his face had the smoothness and innocence of a little boy's . . . Was
this, I wondered, his secret? Was he a kind of inverted Dorian
Gray, whose truthful 'portrait' was that of a small boy, fond of
books and fireworks, inclined to show off, but fundamentally innocent? The public Hew Dallas – the aesthete with his reputed taste
for Black Magic and peculiar vices – was he, after all, a fake?

Half an hour later, he woke up.

'I'm sorry, you know, that you're going down,' he remarked, as
though continuing a conversation which his sleep had barely interrupted.

I was almost certain to be rusticated after my schools; probably
I wouldn't come up again; we had discussed it all the night before.

'I shan't be very sorry,' I said. 'I'll get some job.' I hadn't the
vaguest idea what sort of job it would be: but to have made the
resolution was comforting, and gave me a delusive sense of coming
to grips with what I called 'reality'.

'It's a pity, though – I've so few friends up here—' Hew continued.

'I should have thought you had more friends than almost anybody,' I interrupted.

'Would you? I've practically none, as it happens . . . Oh, if you
only *knew*—!' Suddenly he gritted his teeth and flicked his fingers
in a gesture of exasperation. 'I suppose you think I'm happy – I
suppose you think I *like* all this trolling around and being amusing. Well, I assure you you're mistaken . . . You say you're going to
get a job: but what job? What sort of job's *worth* getting? And
anyway, people like you don't get nice, tidy jobs and settle down
and marry – it isn't in you; at least I should hope it's not' . . . Again
he gritted his teeth: he looked curiously young still – a little boy
over-indulged and exacerbated. 'I tell you I *won't* tie myself up to
some bloody job – not in a London office, anyway. I'd rather join
the Army, or even the Church.'

I laughed.

'I can't exactly see you doing either,' I said.

'Oh, I'll have to do something – I'm not rich, you know.' He paused, then added, meditatively: 'I have a feeling that I may do something rather surprising before I'm much older.'

We paddled slowly back. The sun had come out, slanting in a flood of misty gold across the meadows. The evening had a certain elegiac quality; I felt slightly sentimental, as though a phase of my life had come to an end. In two days time I should go down; then Paris, and then – but I preferred not to think any further ahead.

I left Hew at his roms; he waved his hand vaguely at me, and disappeared through the doorway.

I never met him in Oxford again.

I went to Paris. I tried not to be disappointed: the best specific against disillusion, I found, was Pernod, which one could at least pretend was absinthe; and in the romantic haze which it engendered, one could almost imagine oneself back in the Paris of Verlaine and Rimbaud, of Swann and Odette.

One night a familiar, willowy figure undulated towards me in the Dôme. It was Hew.

'My dear, how heavenly,' he exclaimed. 'Have you had dinner? Good, then you can come with me to *Chez ma belle soeur*. I'm told it's the end, my dear, the absolute *end*.'

Chez ma belle-soeur was said to be somewhere in or near the Rue Caulaincourt. We took a taxi; but the taximan couldn't find the place. On inquiry in the neighbourhood, it turned out to have been closed down a week before.

'Oh *dear*,' lamented Hew, nearly in tears. 'I'm always *just* too late for all the best things in life.'

The taximan proffered suggestions.

'*Vous désirez un cabaret amusant, Messieurs?*' he asked.

We were both fairly tight; we decided to risk it. The taxi drove for what seemed miles, pulling up at last in a dark and sinister street on the Left Bank. Too tight to notice details, we paid off the taxi, and entered the house the man had indicated.

It all looked very dull and normal. A robust and highly respectable-looking woman received us.

'*Attendez un moment, Messieurs,*' she said.

We waited.

'This seems a very dreary place,' said Hew. 'Do you think we've come to the wrong house after all?'

Presently the woman returned and ushered us along a passage. She threw open a door.

'*Entrez, Messieurs,*' she blithely exclaimed.

We entered. The room was furnished as a salon; it was devastatingly cosy and middle-class. In the centre stood a group of personable young women, waiting to receive us; they might, but for one particular, have been the Vicar's daughters welcoming us to a homey evening at the manse. The only aspect of the scene which contradicted this impression was that all the young ladies were stark naked.

Hew took one look, gave a stifled scream, and bolted; I was left to deal with the outraged *patronne*.

It cost me a hundred francs. When I finally escaped, and followed Hew out into the street, he had entirely disappeared.

It must have been over a year later that I met him again. It was in London: the occasion was perhaps boat-race night or rugger night, for I had fallen in with some Oxford people, and we went to the Alhambra.

Oxford had become for me, by this time, as remote and mythical as my childhood; as for Hew Dallas, he had reverted to his original status of a romantic legend. Suddenly, in the circle bar at the Alhambra, the familiar figure surged towards me.

'What *can* you be doing here?' he exclaimed.

He was as tight as usual, and could talk about nothing but Toulon, where he had recently spent a holiday. He accompanied us, becoming progressively tighter, to the Criterion brasserie and to the Blue Lantern in Ham Yard. There we lost him. I inquired of one of my companions, who had known him at Oxford, what he was doing now.

'Oh, he's living down in the country with his mother, I believe, trying to write.'

So his fate, after all (I thought) had been an undistinguished one. Almost all my past acquaintances were living down in the country with their mothers, trying to write ... Indeed, I was doing the same (at intervals) myself.

I didn't see him again. Rumours of his doings continued to circulate for a year or two; his legend died hard. After a time, however, I heard no more of him. Perhaps he was dead; more probably he had 'settled down' in some family business or on the stock-exchange. My slight curiosity about him diminished and soon wore itself out. In a few more years I had almost forgotten his existence.

V

Imogen had been in Rome for a week; during her absence, I had established myself at a *pensione* in the hills above Fiesole, whither, the day after her return, I invited her to lunch.

After lunch, we climbed to the top of the nearest hill. It was a steep and rather a high hill; a stony track wound upward through the *macchia* – the uncultivated wilderness of the hill country, brilliant now with broom and cistus. Half-way up I began to pant and sweat; I wasn't in good condition – a week of rich and plentiful food after years of English austerity had upset my stomach. Imogen, however, strode ahead with the lusty energy of a peasant.

'Of course, the Italians all think I'm mad,' she said. 'They never think of going for a proper walk ... I once brought Luisa's two girls up here: they wore the most ridiculous high-heeled shoes and, of course, their very best frocks. Every time they saw a lizard, they screamed; and finally they sat down and refused to go any further. No wonder they all suffer from anaemia.'

The path became steeper, running now through an open, grassy stretch covered with drifts of wild crimson gladiolus.

'There's a cross at the top of this hill,' said Imogen. 'If you climb right up to it, you get a hundred days' indulgence – it just shows how Italians loathe exercise. If you climb up the plinth and kiss the cross itself, you get two hundred ... I don't think I shall bother to kiss it though, myself, considering I've only just been received. I ought to be in a state of grace. But it may come in useful later, when I've got a few new sins on my conscience.'

We reached the cross at last: an ugly skeleton of iron-work, perched upon a high stone plinth. Before us, the immense classic landscape rolled away into an infinity of blue hills; a landscape vast yet manageable, its wildness tamed into submission by uncounted centuries of human mastery. Scattered over the nearer hillsides, the farmhouses seemed moulded from the very texture of the land; solid yet elegant, unobtrusive but (it seemed) proudly conscious of their function. Anywhere but in Tuscany (I thought) these houses would have either obtruded themselves too self-consciously, or else (as in parts of England) merged themselves with too shamefaced a reticence into their surroundings ... Here, the balance of Man and Nature was exact and harmonious.

Imogen had thrown herself down upon the thyme-starred turf, and lay with her eyes closed against the sun, sucking a grass-stem. The sun was hot, but a fresh wind blew from the north. Over the valley from Fiesole came a faint jangle of bells.

Presently Imogen sat up, throwing back her dark mass of hair, and lit a cigarette.

'It's a lovely place,' she commented; adding, with a spurt of laughter: 'I must say it seems an easy way of getting a hundred days taken off one's term of Purgatory ... If only I had time to come up here every day, I'd probably go straight to heaven when I died ... By the way,' she broke off suddenly, 'I thought you were going over to the Abruzzi?'

'Yes,' I said, after some hesitation, 'I suppose I'll have to, sooner or later.'

But I said it, as I quite realized, with a curious lack of conviction. Ever since my arrival, the half-mythical vision which had haunted me for so long – that vision in pursuit of which I had come half-way across Europe – had begun to recede, had lost already some of its reality, and threatened now to dissolve into the stuff of pure legend. Like the foot of the rainbow, the nearer I approached to it, the further off it seemed ... That farmhouse in the Vastese, with the door open upon the sunlit landscape; the woman spinning upon the threshold; Monteodorisio, a gilded, fairy-tale castle gleaming on its hilltop, between the columns of the cypresses ... The vision still haunted me; but it had become like a memory of childhood happiness, something unattainable and never to be renewed.

Italy, moreover, had imposed its traditional spell of *dolce far niente*. It was so pleasant, after all, at Fiesole; there was so much to see and do in Florence ... I had been to Cook's, to CIT (the Italian travel agency), and made inquiries. The Abruzzi? Signor Settembrini at Cook's, the girl at CIT, stared at me in bewilderment; they shrugged their shoulders; they smiled rather pityingly

... For what reason did I want to go to the Abruzzi? I had been there in the War, I said; it was a beautiful country. Beautiful? The Abruzzi? '*Ma*——' they exclaimed, pitying this *pazzo inglese*. It was a *brutto paese*, the Abruzzi – primitive, without works of Art, without sanitation ...

Since I insisted, however, maps and time-tables were produced. '*E un viaggio molto difficile,*' said the girl at CIT.

'Ver', ver', difficult, very much train-journey,' said Signor Settembrini.

The trouble really was the Apennines.

At school, drawing maps of Italy, I remembered pencilling in that defiant and uninterrupted barrier; a long, shaded fishbone extending from the Alps right down to Calabria. It was rather fun; Italy, altogether, so far as geography lessons went, was rather fun. It was 'easy'; an easy shape, (a booted leg kicking the football of Sicily), and with few rivers to remember apart from the Po (which evoked, usually, a rude giggle); even the exports and imports were fairly simple; and down the middle of the 'leg', that long, furry caterpillar of mountains ...

But Italy, alas! was less easy in fact than it had been in 'geography'; it was less easy, too, in peace-time than it had been in the War, for, in the Army, one could always hitch-hike. Nowadays, if I really wished to visit this *brutto paese* (Signor Settembrini spoke of it as a Cockney might speak of Wigan or Peebles), I should have to go first up to Bologna, then take a train down the coast to Ortona or Vasto ... It was not a comfortable train; it was not a fast train; it would take at least twenty-four hours, perhaps more; if I were at the station two hours before it started, I might just possibly get a seat, but it was highly doubtful. When I arrived at Vasto, I *might* find that there was a local bus-service, serving the inland villages. On the other hand, there might be no bus at all. *Chi lo sa?*

Alternatively, I could go down to Naples – I could, if I liked, fly there – and from Naples there *might* be some kind of bus plying across the mountains to the other coast; but who could say? Signor Settembrini couldn't, for one.

I decided to postpone it. After all, Tuscany was delightful. Besides, my stomach had been misbehaving; in the Abruzzi there were few doctors and still fewer hospitals. Visions of dysentery or malaria assailed me: lacking quinine or sulphaguanadine, I might

get really ill, or even die ... No, for the time being I would stay at
Fiesole.

Yet at intervals, hauntingly, the vision would recur, and I would
resolve to set off the very next day. I realized that the travel
difficulties, the fear of illness, were mere alibis, the habitual evas-
ions of a congenitally lazy and stay-at-home disposition ... I
would start the next day; but the next day it rained, or I remembered that I had a date ... How real, after all, was my vision?
Wasn't I remembering the nostalgic poems and stories I had written about it, rather than the place, the moment themselves? Similarly, at school or at Oxford, I had written poems and 'novels'
about my childhood, thereby distorting the pristine reality till
memory and invention became inextricably merged ...

'Perhaps it would be wiser,' said Imogen, 'to keep your illusions.
It's certainly a frightful journey, and if you aren't feeling too
fit ...'

Imogen's words were consoling; they calmed my conscience,
gave a renewed plausibility to my alibis ...

'By the way,' she said suddenly. 'I forgot to tell you ... You
remember we were talking about Hew Dallas before I went away?
Well, when I was in Rome, I met Nigel Mainprice – he was up at
Balliol about your time: you must remember him – he's got some
job with the British Council out here ... Well, I asked him if he'd
ever heard what had happened to Hew Dallas; and he said that
the last he'd heard was that he had gone into the Church ... That
was before the War, of course.'

'The Church!' I exclaimed. 'Nigel must have made a mistake.
Why, it's absolutely incredible ... At any rate, he must have left it
now – he was dressed in ordinary mufti in the train.'

'Oh well, English priests do dress more or less how they like,' said
Imogen. 'He's probably on holiday, and finds it convenient ...
Anglicans are so funny, aren't they? They think of God as a kind of
glorified Lord Chancellor who belongs to the same Club ...'

'All the same,' I repeated, 'I can't really believe it.'

Imogen was going away again in two days time, this time to
Venice. Her friend Luisa had a cousin there, a Contessa, who
wanted somebody to take charge of her daughters while she went

to visit her mother at Torino. The job would include giving the daughters lessons in English and French.

'She's very rich,' said Imogen, 'and she'll pay well. Pity I've got to go just now, when you're in Florence ... But I can't afford to turn down good jobs like that – it's the only way I can afford to live in my fool's paradise ... I'm a sort of Universal Aunt out here, you know ... You must write and tell me how you find the Abruzzi – and if you run into Hew Dallas again, do ask him if he's *really* a clergyman ... From what *I* remember of him, I should think he'd probably been unfrocked.'

VI

Fool's paradise? Yes, I thought, sitting on the café-terrace in Fiesole, probably it was. As an English tourist, here for a few weeks, who was I to affirm or deny it? Yet I was here, none the less, to write about the country; my publisher wanted a survey of its 'economic and political life' ... A professional journalist, I felt, might well have blenched at such a task; and I wasn't even a journalist.

It was with some such vague consciousness of my mission that, on the previous evening, I had approached an elderly labourer in a wine-shop. He was reading *Pomeriggio*, the Florentine evening paper. What, I asked, did he think of the present Government?

He looked at me contemptuously, and spat.

'*Non c'è governo,*' he said.

There was no government; none, at any rate, he went on, which demanded serious notice on the part of the working-man. There was some *camorra* in Rome, doubtless, which made a lot of stupid regulations; but one ignored them. When prices once more came within reach of a poor man's wages, then perhaps one would interest oneself a little in politics; meanwhile, it was more important that Giuseppe's wife's brother, in the country, was willing to supply enough *pasta* for the family in return for a weekly consignment of *Nazionale* cigarettes ...

Where did he get the cigarettes? Ah, that was another story. The stepson of Elena's Aunt Pozzi worked in a Bar-Tabacchi; the girl he was betrothed to was very fond of sweets – ah, but passionately fond of them: it was not healthy to love sweets so much. But what would you? The child grew up in the war, when there was no sugar; she lacked strength, she was anaemic. Very well; one made a little *imbroglio* with Uncle Maurilio at the *pasticceria* – not so easy this, but one knew certain facts about Uncle Maurilio about which it would please him if one kept silent. One obtained the sweets; Aunt Pozzi's stepson, in return, supplied the cigarettes and Giuseppe's wife's brother supplied the *pasta . . . Ecco!*

Sitting on the café-terrace, I looked across the *piazza* at the crowds waiting for the trolley-bus to Florence; it was a Sunday evening, and the Florentine trippers were going home.

I had been here early in 1945, with my friend Kurt Schlegel; we had had a week's leave in Florence, and had hitch-hiked up to Fiesole to look at the view. It had been bitterly cold, with snow covering the hills and the *tramontana* freezing one's bones at every corner. The cafés and restaurants had been closed, and most of the shops as well; the village had seemed desolate and ruined beyond hope of recovery. Now, two years later, the shops were full of goods, the cafés doing a roaring trade; trolley-buses disgorged, on a Sunday, their loads of trippers – all well-dressed, all apparently contented and gay. It was very deceptive, of course: I thought, once again, of Aunt Pozzi's stepson and Giuseppe's wife's brother. I thought, also, of the *New Statesman* . . . Yet was it possible that some force was operating here which Marx and all the other economists had left out of their calculations? Was it possible that the individuals comprising this conquered and bankrupt nation might, in time, re-establish their traditional way of life, in spite of corrupt government and in defiance of economic law?

I looked at the gay checked table-cloths fluttering beneath the trees; at the elegant shapes of the Chianti flasks in the *fiaschetteria*; at the pot of herbs – fresh, green and appetizing – on a neighbouring window-sill. I watched the gestures of two men engaged in an argument; a woman posed with unselfconscious grace at one of the tables; a brown-skinned boy, supple-limbed, with a face from a Greek medallion, who was scrabbling for cigarette ends in the gutter. Faces, forms and gestures spoke to me of a way of life which was inherently harmonious; a life which no doubt had its roots in corruption, but which could still blossom into an indigenous and untainted beauty.

I thought of England: the drabness, the incivility, the lack of any natural or imposed elegance. Nowadays, of course, we had a cast-iron alibi; what do you expect, with things as they are? Don't you know there's a War (or a Peace) on? Yet pre-war England hadn't really been more elegant or more civil; only more prosperous. We had merely exchanged a *nouveau-riche* vulgarity for a new-poor dinginess. Was our obsession with moral rectitude, our conviction of our ethical mission, really sufficient compensation for our total lack of beauty and of *savoir-vivre*?

The trolley-bus (it was the last one of the evening) suddenly rounded the corner of the square, and the crowd surged about it like wasps round a jampot. Wasps? Tigers at feeding time would be a better comparison. Pushing, jostling, fighting, the packed phalanx of men and women surged into the bus. Nine-tenths of them obviously wouldn't get a seat; yet they pushed and fought just the same – from long-ingrained habit, from pugnacity, or merely, perhaps, for the fun of it. I saw a woman, arriving late, seize hold of a young man at the edge of the crowd, and push him firmly (and far from gently) out of her way ... The crowd had seemed big enough to fill at least three trolley-buses; yet all that were left, when the bus moved off, were two or three old men (one of them crippled) and a mother with a baby-in-arms. These, with gestures of resignation, set off slowly and painfully down the hill. They had missed the last bus, and would have to walk the five kilometres into Florence.

I wondered, for the hundredth time, why it was that Italians, once brought within range of a bus or a train, invariably become transmogrified, by some Circean enchantment, into a pack of ravening beasts. I liked Italians, on the whole; but a trip on the *filobus* to Florence was enough to make me loathe the entire nation with an implacable hatred. Why must they do it? What atavistic memory of flights or migrations could make a penny bus-ride, for an Italian, into such a drama of Life or Death?

Once again I thought of England. An English crowd would have automatically formed a queue, and waited with an abject patience for the conductor to give the signal; they would then have filed slowly, in an orderly manner, on to the bus. Almost certainly the nursing-mother and the old men would have been placed in front of the queue and helped aboard. More than

two-thirds of the crowd would have undoubtedly missed the last
bus ...

There was, I felt, a moral to be drawn somewhere; but it was
hard to say what it was, or in whose favour it would operate.

I walked up the hill, and turned into the *mescita di vino* where I
had met my politician of the night before. He was not there tonight; the single table by the counter was occupied by two men
who looked like peasants. I ordered a glass of Chianti. One of the
peasants rose to his feet, and pointed to his stool.

'*S'accommodino, Signore,*' he said.

I refused politely, and offered him a glass of wine. He looked
genuinely surprised and rather embarrassed. No, no, he protested.
I insisted. He in his turn insisted that I take his stool. A polite
argument ensued; finally the *padrone* produced another stool, and
I sat down.

'*E inglese, Lei?*' my friend inquired. Was it true, he asked, that
it was always foggy in England? And that we drank tea with our
meals, instead of wine? It must be bad for our stomachs, he said,
but all the same, we were rich – that was something.

I explained that it was often foggy in England but not always;
agreed that we certainly drank too much tea; but we weren't, I
said, rich any more.

I had arranged to have supper late, and felt hungry. I ordered a
piece of bread and some *salame* and another glass of wine. The
wine-shop was cavernous and gloomy, with barrels ranged round
the walls; in the brown gloom, the wine in the carafes glowed with
a purpureal splendour. I ate my *salame*, and took a drink of wine;
the salty, vinous, peppery flavour of the sausage seemed the very
taste of Italy. The pepper made the cool wine prick my throat
pleasantly as it went down.

'*E buono?*' asked my friend, with genuine interest.

Yes, it was very good, I said. He gave a satisfied smile, pleased
that I was enjoying myself.

I sat for a few minutes longer, then left the wine-shop and
started to walk up the hill. Before I had gone five hundred yards, I
remembered that I had not paid. I hurried back.

The *padrone* was entirely unconcerned.

'*Non fa niente,*' he said. There was plenty of time to pay;

tomorrow would do equally well. My peasant-friend insisted that I should have another glass – with him, this time.

I said I'd had enough.

'No, no,' he insisted. Such wine as this – and it was good wine – did one no harm; it would never give anyone a headache.

I accepted another glass.

VII

I had spent the day in Florence looking at the Masaccios in the Carmine and the Fra Angelicos at San Marco. In the afternoon, I had bathed in the Arno, from the dam which spans the river below the Ponte alla Carraia. Now I was sitting, relaxed and contented, on the terrace of the *Giubbe Rosse* in the Piazza della Repubblica, sipping the evening vermouth.

I was hungry, but kept postponing the moment when I should walk round to my favourite *trattoria* for dinner. In a desultory way, I began to plan the meal in mind . . . It was odd, I thought, how in Italy the mere prospect of one's next meal took on this quality of an aesthetic pleasure, consciously and acutely savoured. The idea of dinner in half-an-hour's time was coloured with all the romance and excitement of a rendezvous with a pretty girl . . . Was it, I wondered – this gastronomic romanticism – an over-compensation for some emotional frustration, or a mere symptom of middle age? Both, possibly; but in any case, it didn't operate in England. For in England, our puritanism extends even to the stomach; there is something 'not quite nice' about good food. 'It's bad manners to *talk* about food, dear' – of all our tribal taboos, instilled in childhood, none has taken deeper root than this. Like Roman Catholicism or the continental Sunday, good food has become – or perhaps it always was – alien to our national temperament.

In the gathering dusk, the gaily-dressed crowds moved leisurely along the pavements; the neon signs leapt one by one into fluorescent brilliance: *Radio Marelli, Dentifricia Biemme*. A Black Market boy leaned over my table: 'You wanta shange Swiss francs, English pound?' A woman in rags carrying a month-old baby whined for alms: '*Signore* ... *fame* ... *la miseria* ... *soldi, per piacere* ...' Less obsequious, far more confident, a plump, smiling nun followed in her wake, proffering a bag bulging, already, with ten-litre notes ...

I paid for my vermouth, and walked away across the bright, clamorous square.

After dinner, I strolled without purpose through the streets, jostled perpetually by the crowds which thronged the narrow pavements. Italy, I thought, had solved the traffic problem in the simplest, most obvious way – by doing nothing whatever about it. I thought of Canterbury or Gloucester: the policemen, the traffic-lights, the eternal blocks; here in Florence, with its maze of narrow streets, the problem was exactly equivalent. But there were no lights, very few policemen and no traffic-blocks. Everybody walked in the middle of the road; the pavements, in any case, were too narrow to be used with comfort. Cars nosed their way tolerantly among the crowds; I had never yet seen a street-accident in Florence. Similarly, with the wineshops open all day and most of the night, I had never yet seen a drunken Italian ...

I found myself, at last, in the Piazza della Signoria. The square, top-heavy tower of the Palazzo Vecchio rose grimly against the stars; below, the great bearded Neptune, '*il Biancone*', straddled his aggressive, flood-lit nudity above his team of horses: a father-imago in the grand manner.

On the steps of the Loggia de' Lanzi beneath Giambologna's Rape of the Sabines, sat a British soldier, a private, in khaki-drill uniform. British soldiers were a rare sight, nowadays, in Florence, where the remnant of Allied troops was all American; this one must have come on leave here from somewhere up north.

I glanced at him, incuriously, as I passed; then stopped, and looked more closely. Was I dreaming? Was I mad? The soldier looked up, met my eyes, and rose to his feet with a rather embarrassed smile.

It was Hew Dallas.

'Well, if you don't believe me, I can prove it,' said Hew, after we had ordered coffee in the neighbouring café. He produced a battered AB 64 Part I and pushed it across the table. I looked at the first page: 72409798 Dvr Dallas, H. D. There it was in black and white: I could doubt the fact no longer.

'Well I'm damned,' was all I could say.

He had joined up in the War, he told me, and now he had signed on as a regular.

'But why?' I asked blankly.

He opened his eyes widely, shrugged his shoulders.

'It supplies,' he said, 'a framework to one's life.'

'But surely – ' I protested. 'You know,' I went on, feeling at a complete loss, 'I remembered you afterwards – it all came back to me. We used to know each other quite well.'

'Oh yes,' he agreed, vaguely. 'I remembered it all, directly I saw you . . . But I'm not particularly keen, you see, on reviving that particular phase of my past . . .' Suddenly he gave a giggle. 'It's rather a Proustian situation, isn't it?'

It was indeed – and in a sense which he didn't, perhaps, quite intend. Once again, as when I first saw him on the boat, I had a curious impression that he was a character from a novel read long ago, rather than a real person whom I had once known . . . The air of legend hung about him as always; I wondered if he was still 'living' the great Proustian work of which the first instalment had appeared in *Libido*, back in 1928.

He hadn't, he explained, worn uniform on the journey because, after all, he was on leave; a private soldier, moreover, was liable to be frowned upon in a *wagon-lit*. Also, his KD uniform didn't officially belong to him; he had scrounged it in North Africa at the end of the War.

'I thought it would be seasonable, though, out here,' he remarked.

He was stationed in England at the moment; getting leave to Italy had been a bit of a wangle – it was all very irregular.

'But I pulled all *sorts* of wires,' he said.

'What's your job?' I asked him.

'Oh, I'm just a driver . . . I drive Colonels and things about in staff-cars. I'm *very* friendly with some of them . . . My *particular* Colonel is a perfect dear – really *molto simpatico*.'

'I met someone who met Nigel Mainprice in Rome,' I said. 'Nigel told her you were a parson. Of course I roared with laughter.'

'Oh well – he's a bit out of date with his information, you know . . .'

'You *were* in the Church, then?'

'Oh yes, for a while . . . I left it in 1938.'

'Why?' I asked bluntly: aware that it was the most monumentally tactless remark of my career.

'Oh, there wasn't enough scope, somehow . . . I quarrelled with the Bishop. He was so Low-church you could hardly see his head above the ground . . . Then I thought I'd try the Army.'

'And you're happy in it?'

He shrugged his shoulders.

'It's a kind of lay-monasticism, I suppose . . . All the advantages and none of the drawbacks. I have lots of fun, really.'

The uniform reduced him, as it does most people, to a kind of basic essence of himself. I saw a tall, thin young man on the verge of middle age; not very exceptional in any way, though he hardly looked like a regular soldier. If I hadn't known him, I should have put him down, probably, as an Army clerk, or an RAMC orderly. Once again, as when I had first seen him on the boat, something in the cast of his features reminded me of the housemaid we had had in my childhood.

Presently he said he had a date, and got up to go. He was leaving for England the next day.

'I forgot to tell you,' he said. 'I went to Siena, and they had some simply *marvellous* fireworks – I did so wish you'd been there . . . Well, *ciao* – it's been nice seeing you.'

He smiled and waved his hand with the old vague gesture, and made off across the square. I watched him as he undulated away up the Via Calzaiuoli – Driver Dallas, RASC, ex-clergyman, ex-aesthete, amateur of pyrotechny, an Oxford legend of the 'twenties. Futile, charming, with his odd air of inhabiting some half-forgotten novel rather than the world of cold reality – I wondered how he had managed to survive at all into this harsh, inimical age; and as I watched him disappearing into the dazzle of the street-lights, I had a curious impression that it was no corporeal being to whom I had just bidden farewell, but a kind of ghost: a character in an unwritten Proustian novel, the projection of a self-created personal myth.

PART FOUR

Nanny Defeated

I see an important decision made on a lake,
An illness, a beard, Arabia found in a bed,
    Nanny defeated, Money.

W. H. AUDEN

I

Steep roads, a tunnel through the downs are the approaches;
A ruined pharos overlooks a constructed bay;
The sea-front is almost elegant; all this show
Has, somewhere inland, a vague and dirty root:
    Nothing is made in this town. . .

Next slide, please . . .

It is Mr Auden lecturing to the sixth-form: very intelligent, very clever, but one always feels that, at heart, he's just an ordinary chap like the rest of us. Highbrow, you know, but human: he likes Byron and Beatrix Potter, and doesn't mind roughing it when necessary – look at that trip of his to Iceland . . .

And filled with the tears of the beaten, or calm with fame,
The eyes of the returning thank the historical cliffs:
'The heart has at last ceased to lie, the clock to accuse;
    In the shadow under the yew, at the children's party
        Everything will be explained. . . .'

Had the 'heart ceased to lie'? I looked up at the 'historical cliffs': still honeycombed with their caves and tunnels and windowed 'houses', mysterious as ever; 'somewhere inland' was the 'vague and dirty root' – the subterranean town beneath the water-tower.

My family had left Sandgate, when my father retired in 1927, and gone to live at Blackheath, but my brother, after leaving the Army, had gone into the family business at Folkestone, and I often came down to stay with him. My life now, after the brief interlude of Oxford, was in London; Nanny was defeated; under the yew-tree everything had been explained; but nostalgia drew me back to this haunted coast, I would walk to the end of the Folkestone Leas and look down at our old house beneath the cliffs, now occupied by strangers. And I returned, again and again, with the old sense of crossing a frontier into an alien land, to Dover.

Dirty as ever, friendly and proletarian, with a faint aura of mysterious wickedness lingering about the Hippodrome – it had changed little in the intervening years. The 'ruined pharos', the Saxon church, the 'almost-elegant' sea-front, greeted me like the archetypal images of myth; I felt at home in this town.

On the cliff tops, the great grim barracks impended heavily upon the narrow streets; the trams still clattered and jangled, at this date, along their worn-out tracks (they were soon to be re-placed, regrettably, by buses). Along Snargate Street, by the Grand Shaft, the little shops and cafés, fringing the docks, had an almost continental air:

> Within these breakwaters English is spoken:
> without
> Is the immense, improbable atlas. . .

But Europe didn't seem so 'improbable' after all, here among the Italian cafés, the tattooists' shops, the pubs full of sailors; it might have been a small port anywhere in the world.

I was obsessed, at that time, by an *esthétisme des ports*: I loved the poetry of departures, my favourite poem was Mallarmé's *Brise marine*:

> *Mais ô mon coeur, entends le chant des matelots!*

I shared, too, belatedly and at second-hand, the circus-and-*bal-musette* aestheticism of Cocteau, Satie and Apollinaire; I visited the Rue de Lappe, and Charlie Brown's in the West India Dock Road; and I went, over and over again, to René Clair's *Sous les Toits de Paris* . . .

I went, also, at long last, to the Dover Hippodrome, that mythi-cal Temple of Shame in Snargate Street, haunted by the ghosts of Goneril and the girl-under-the-cliff. It was a bitter disap-pointment: blamelessly respectable, the haunt of Dover shop-keepers on Saturday nights – the petty-bourgeois ambience only enlivened by a few Wodehousian subalterns going gay in the bar. Where was the wickedness of yesteryear? The twice-nightly *revues* were third-rate: a lumpy and prudishly-attired chorus, a Scotch comedian, jokes about kippers – the world of Donald McGill's postcards ... Better value was the 'Artists' Bar' at the back, which was open to the public; the chorus-girls came down between their turns to have a port-and-lemon. There was a public urinal under the stage: visiting this one night, my brother and I were startled by a sudden bang, a blaze of light overhead, and the sudden descent, almost on top of us, of an enormous Chinaman, in the full regalia of a mandarin ... Aghast at this celestial visitation, we jumped aside just in time, and, feebly regaining our senses, found ourselves apologizing to Prince Sun Yat Sen, the illusionist, who was not unnaturally annoyed at being detected in his famous disappearing act.

My taste for 'low-life' drew me more than ever to Dover: I invested it, as usual, with more glamour than it really possessed. I liked the pubs full of sailors and soldiers –

> Soldiers who swarm in the pubs in their pretty clothes,
> As fresh and silly as girls from a high-class academy. . .

I felt, obscurely, that they were more 'real' than my own friends: I was, in fact, beginning to feel that inward pressure of the environment which sooner or later drives most adolescents into some form of escape or revolt. I was in a mood to be 'converted', but lacked the ability to be sufficiently serious for long enough at a time. Catholicism I found preposterous, and the opposed theology of Communism not only preposterous, but boring into the bargain; besides, I was too bad at maths ever to understand the Labour theory of value ...

I was sustained by the ambition to write (on some far-distant day) a vast Proustian masterpiece. It was to cover my whole life and the lives of everybody I knew; nothing was to be left out – the most intimate bodily functions would be described, of course, in unprecedented detail; the book would be, among other things, a complete anatomy of the sexual life ...

The trouble was, though, that I could never bring myself to begin writing the first chapter. The book remained a mere state of mind, an attitude to life, a defence-mechanism with which I could keep reality at bay ... Walking the streets, drinking sherry at a party, trying to read Rimbaud on the lawn at Blackheath, I would experience a sudden breath-taking conviction of my mission: the details of my surroundings were suddenly bathed in a gilded, romantic haze: the sunlight glinting on a roof, a line of Rimbaud, a tree-top against the sky, some face at a party signalling back a mutual flash of desire across the crowded room ... Everything, the whole of experience seemed absorbed in that single moment of vision. What did anything else matter? I had had my vision – so I assured myself, echoing Lily Briscoe in *To the Lighthouse*. *J'ai seul la clef de cette parade sauvage* ... At parties, when I felt bored or neglected, I found it consoling to repeat to myself such reassuring phrases. I felt myself a kind of Faustus, intoxicated by my initiation into the ultimate mysteries. I possessed all the required formulae: all I had to do now was to put them into practice ...

I suppose most of my friends felt much the same way: I know that in my own case it was an enormous and comprehensive gesture of overcompensation: it made up to me for me all my feelings of inferiority, all my amorous frustrations, the whole unformulated, complex unhappiness of adolescence. The magical vision spanned, like some rainbow-bridge, the appalling chasm between the Real and the Ideal: the fact that it was, like a rainbow, insubstantial, didn't really matter – I was not, after all, in any particular hurry to cross it; not just yet ...

At times, indeed, I would feel a little uneasy ... There might come a period, I thought, when this vision of a future masterpiece would fail to satisfy me; I should have to begin the unthinkable task of actually writing it. The thought was frightening; for I had learnt, by this time, the primary lesson of adolescence: that one can, by too long anticipation, overdraw on one's emotional capital ... I had learnt the lesson; but, being a natural spendthrift, it was a long time before I began to profit by it.

> The vows, the tears, the slight emotional signals
> Are here eternal and unremarkable gestures,
> Like ploughing or soldiers' songs. . .

I listened to the soldiers singing in the pubs – the Prince Regent, the Robin Hood, the Invicta – and lived my Proustian novel. At Dover, more than anywhere, the past leapt at me with the authentic, sudden purity of the madeleine-dipped-in-tea ... One day my brother and I were invited to lunch by some friends of his at the barracks: afterwards we walked down to the town by the

Grand Shaft, that extraordinary staircase through the cliff which used to seem to me so mysterious. There wasn't much mystery about it; but it was, I discovered, a monument – perhaps the most ponderous ever devised – to the caste-system. For there were *two* stairways: one for officers, another for NCOs and men. How much money and ingenuity, I thought, must have been expended, in order that a second-lieutenant should not pass a sergeant on the stairs.

One night my brother, my friend Eric and myself were sitting over drinks in the bar of the Grand Hotel; it was nearly closing time. Suddenly a large, burly man entered the bar: in mufti, but obviously an officer. He greeted my brother, who introduced us.

'You remember Basil Medlicott, don't you?' he said.

I was tight enough, I suppose, for my *id* to elude the censor, for I replied:

'Yes, I once used to keep you in a cage.'

It was the kind of private joke one enjoys making at a certain stage of intoxication. Basil looked not at all surprised.

'Really?' he said, fixing me with a pair of piercing black eyes. 'I didn't know I'd ever been kept by anybody – I'm delighted to hear it. I hope,' he added, 'the cage was a gilded one?'

Then he bought us all drinks: large ones. He exuded a rather alarming heartiness, calling us all 'old boy' and even (which pleased me by its period flavour) 'old bean'. I was rather bored; looking at him, I tried to think myself back to the days when he had seemed a hero. There was nothing very heroic about him now; his age was hard to guess – he had that dateless look which some men acquire in middle age; he might have been anything between thirty-five and fifty. He still wore a dark cavalry-moustache; his greying hair was cropped like a convict's; his clothes were just such as one would expect – an ancient but well-cut sports-coat, with leather patches on the sleeves, a paisley-patterned tie, a green pork-pie hat.

'I remember *you*,' he told me. 'You said once you wanted to go to some show at the Pleasure Gardens – I'd promised myself I'd take you, but something or other happened . . .'

My heart missed a beat: Heaven, after all, had lain about me in my infancy, without my ever suspecting it . . .

He asked us all to lunch in the Mess next day. On the way home, my brother talked ramblingly about him: 'My *oldest* friend

'... I haven't seen him for ages. He's really a most *remarkable* person.' I didn't think he was remarkable and said so: my brother, however, insisted. Basil had once been an Army boxing champion; he had had a very important job in Intelligence, during the war; he had a brother – or a brother-in-law – in the House of Commons; he was very rich himself; and so on.

I retorted, finally, that all this didn't really add up to anything very remarkable.

'He seems just Wodehouse to me,' said Eric.

'He really is a *most* extraordinary person,' my brother repeated.

I was to have, though I didn't know it, ample opportunity to judge: but to this day I cannot quite decide whether my brother or myself was nearer the truth. Was Basil really an 'extraordinary' person, or was he just a bore?

II

When we arrived at the mess the next morning, Basil was as hearty and un-extraordinary as ever. But looking round the book-shelves in his room, while we drank sherry, I had my first surprise. There were all the things one would expect to find: regimental histories, text-books on infantry-training and so on; among them, however, I came upon *A Shropshire Lad*, a volume of Yeats and *An Ideal Husband*. These were promising, I thought, but non-committal. A moment later, to my complete astonishment, I came on *Swann's Way*.

This was too odd to pass without comment.

'Do you read Proust?' I asked him.

Basil looked bored.

'He's rather heavy-going, isn't he?' he replied, and changed the subject.

The remark was what one might have expected: but it still seemed to me none the less astonishing that he should even have heard of Proust, much less possessed him.

After lunch we returned to his rooms and he talked. It was my first experience of hearing Basil talk: I was to hear the per-formance repeated often enough in the future, but this first speci-men must have been, I think, fairly representative. It did, at any rate, I am quite certain, fix for all time the precise attitude which I was always to assume when listening to him. I began by being respectfully attentive; gradually my attention wandered, though I retained my respectful air; soon I found even this becoming difficult. My eyes began to stray; I yawned; I tried to change the subject; finally, I surrendered, reassumed as best I could an expression of modified interest, and settled down to listen.

And still Basil went on talking.

He spoke slowly, in a manner which one might expect from a rather pompous professional writer: one was acutely aware of paragraphs and punctuation, and one could almost see, as he delivered himself of some ironic phrase, the inverted commas between which he carefully enclosed it ... His talk was so entirely 'out of character' with his appearance that I didn't know how to 'take him'; he was by no means, as Eric had said, merely 'Wodehouse'; but I found it easier to say what he was not than to decide, precisely, in what his positive qualities consisted.

I found also, half an hour afterwards, that it was almost impossible to remember what he had been talking about. At a later date, by frequent repetition, I was to learn most of his customary topics by heart, and could predict almost exactly the words he would use; but on this first occasion my mind, when I tried to remember, was an almost complete blank. All I could recall was being treated at one point to a lengthy analysis of the 'Protocols of Zion', in the truth of which, I gathered, Basil more than half believed.

'I think,' said Eric, when we were alone, 'the man's a prolix bore.'

I felt inclined to agree; yet I couldn't be quite sure ... I *had* been bored, it was true, after the first ten minutes; but then that might have been my own fault. I was, I knew, too easily bored; the very act of listening to a sustained exposition made me yawn. I was quite prepared to believe that Basil's talk had been, as my brother declared it was, 'frightfully interesting'. I felt, somehow, that it *ought* to have been ... I was slightly prejudiced in his favour: perhaps on account of those white flannel trousers, or by the fact that he had once, fifteen or sixteen years before, nearly taken me to a 'show'.

A few days later we met Basil in Folkstone: he asked us to lunch at the Metropole, and afterwards we bathed at Seabrook.

I enjoyed the afternoon; Basil's interminable talk seemed, on this occasion, less ponderous: perhaps he was feeling particularly light-hearted. I began to think that he was not a bore after all.

Even Eric had to admit that the afternoon had been amusing; he too perhaps wanted, as I did, to believe that Basil was something rather extraordinary; for only by so believing could we excuse ourselves for the time wasted in his company.

Eric and I had to return to London that evening; to our surprise, Basil offered to drive us up; we could hardly refuse without seeming boorish; and in the late afternoon we set off.

The drive was terrifying: Basil broke every rule of the road, and laughed heartlessly at our timidity. He boasted that he had never had an accident ... Arrived in London, he insisted on giving us drinks at the Trocadero Long Bar. He had changed, before we started, into a suit – a rather surprising suit; it was smart, as I should have expected, but for Basil it seemed, somehow, the wrong kind of smartness. Tight-waisted, tight-wristed, it made him look like an actor; or would have done so, if it was possible for Basil to look like anything of the sort. He wore with it a very expensive tie and a black hat.

In the Long Bar he was immediately surrounded by a group of bronzed, hearty men of about his own age: it was quite a reunion – some of them, he said, he hadn't seen for ten years. The Long Bar, in those days, was frequented incongruously by two distinct coteries: hearty Empire-builders back from Nigeria or the Malay States, and the younger, less-successful kind of actor. Genteel and faintly epicene, these latter watched speculatively our party from a discreet distance; I felt that I should probably prefer their company: Basil's friends were quite overwhelmingly hearty.

Eric and I exchanged glances.

'How the Empire bores me,' he remarked *sotto voce*. I agreed; we decided to escape. But this proved not only difficult but finally impossible. We were led away, cordoned by the Empire-builders, to Oddenino's, then to the Cavour. I had been introduced by Basil as the 'young brother of his oldest friend', and the rather tenuous relationship conferred upon me, apparently, a kind of honorary membership of this imperial fraternity. Indeed, when we went later to the Senior and afterwards to the In and Out, I began to feel quite imperial myself, and could almost fancy that I was sprouting a moustache.

Somewhere we must have had dinner, but where or with whom remained afterwards a blank. Later, we found ourselves in the Fitzroy, where Basil was a *succès-fou*; he was assumed (perhaps rightly), to be the richest person present, and he lived up nobly to this bubble-reputation, standing drinks all round and putting innumerable pennies in the mechanical piano.

We finished the evening at the Kinde Dragon, where Douglas Byng sang *Sex-appeal Sarah* and *Rome was a riot in my time*. The Empire-builders had left us by now; and after the cabaret, Basil began to talk. He talked and he talked: an interminable monologue which we were far too tired (and tight) to interrupt. We could only, helplessly, try to appear as though we were listening.

It was on this occasion that we first heard the story of Basil's brother-in-law; it was long, complicated and almost incredibly tedious. Basil was involved, for some reason, in endless litigation with his relative about some putative misappropriation of property. Viewed through the distorting-mirror of Basil's highly-prejudiced account of him, this brother-in-law appeared to be a monster of every conceivable villainy; there was no crime, no recondite vice even, which Basil didn't sooner or later impute to him. He was guilty, it seemed, of embezzlement, house-breaking, arson, assaults upon minors, and (in his house in Half-Moon Street) of what Basil referred to, with an ironic relish, as 'nameless orgies'.

'Why are they nameless?' Eric woke up sufficiently to inquire.

Obligingly, Basil proceeded to give them names: in detail and at length. The story went on and on; it became involved, obscurely, with Basil's 'Intelligence' job in the Middle East ...

At last we escaped; Eric and I were staying in Chelsea, and we walked back, exhausted, through the empty streets.

'Quite fun, but oh, what a bore,' Eric remarked.

It had been quite fun; I decided, rather dubiously, that I really had enjoyed the evening; but there had been about it, all the time, an uncomfortable sense of compulsion. It was as though we had been under orders to enjoy ourselves; and since Basil had done all the paying, we had had no alternative but to do so.

Thereafter I met Basil frequently: whenever he was in London he rang me up, and refused to take no for an answer. It was difficult, indeed, to say no to the offer of a good dinner and innumerable free drinks; I had about a pound a week of my own to spend on amusement, and it was worth my while, in the circumstances, to put up with a few hours of Basil's conversation.

Or so it seemed; by the end of the evening I usually began to feel doubtful.

I soon discovered two more peculiarities of his temperament: he was fantastically snobbish, and had a passion for conspiracy.

I often played with the idea of doing a little unofficial research into Basil's family-tree; but I lacked the energy for it. According to him, he was related to nearly all the leading families in the country: he would draw little diagrams on table-cloths to show us exactly why he was entitled to call himself a second-cousin twice removed of Lord So-and-So. Like many snobs, he affected a certain half-ironic disdain for his own distinguished connections.

'Un*for*tunately, you see,' he would say, the ironic inflections audibly underlined and italicized, 'Unfortunately, I happen to be connected *rather* intimately with the Earl of Cliffhaven (on his mother's side), so that I do feel it a *certain* affront to my family pride when I see his daughter disgustingly – in fact paralytically – drunk in a place which' (it happened to be the Blue Lantern) 'I can only describe as a House of Ill-fame.'

Basil's taste for conspiracy was, I came to the conclusion, an occupational disease. 'Intelligence' had got under his skin: it was an incurable infection.

He found conspirators everywhere.

'You see that man there?' he would mutter, in the Long Bar, indicating discreetly some inoffensive person drinking Worthington at the counter. 'You *may* not be aware of it, but he *happens* to be one of the most dangerous men in London. I know for a fact that he's not *only* one of the Kremlin's most highly-paid *agents provocateurs*, but that he's *also* in the pay of three different armament firms. He has *also*, I may say – ' Basil added this casually, as though it were a mere fleabite ' – he has *also* been convicted no less than *four* times' – here Basil's voice implied a whole compositor's stock of inverted commas – 'for the *abominable* crime of sodomy.'

Eric, who had been looking rather carefully at this monster of iniquity, suddenly burst out laughing:

'Why, it's Rupert Levin, who used to write leaderettes for the *Star*. He's utterly dull and harmless, and lives at Brentwood.'

Basil was not in the least put out.

'That,' he said calmly, 'is what *you* think.'

It was easy to dismiss Basil's 'inside knowledge', as well as his county connections, as merely bogus. They had, often enough, it was true, a bogus air, and his heavily ironic mode of putting them across didn't make them seem any more credible. I was prepared to write off most of his stories as so much blarney; but there remained a residue to which I had to give the benefit of the doubt ...

He could, at times, be very circumstantial about his relationships with the aristocracy; and once or twice I happened to discover that the dark hints which he had dropped about such-and-such a person were substantially justified ... It seemed probable that upon a slender basis of fact, he was building an immense superstructure of phantasy, in which, possibly, he partly believed himself. But it was impossible to tell, in any particular case, where fact ended and fiction began; and I don't believe that Basil himself, in ninety-nine cases out of a hundred could tell either.

I wasn't interested in politics, and when Basil became political, I found it more difficult than usual to attend to his interminable monologues. His views on politics were, as one would have expected, coloured by his mania for conspiracy. He had a fund of disobliging stories about every single member of the Cabinet; half of them were in the pay of one foreign power or another; so-and-so's recent departure on some industrial 'Mission' to Rumania was a mere cloak for private negotiations with a well-known international crook; Basil himself had first-hand information about somebody else's visit to Kemal Ataturk ...

'*Don't* look behind you,' Basil would suddenly hiss, in tones which (to quote Firbank) would have piqued a stronger character than Mrs Lot's, 'don't look *now* – but that man at the next table, I happen to know, has just arrived here from Berlin for the *express* purpose of negotiating with Sir Oswald Mosley ...'

As to Basil's own political views, it was easier to say what they were not than to make any more positive judgement. Indeed, this applied not only to Basil's politics, but to his whole character. One could sum him up in negatives; but his positive qualities remained oddly unseizable. I had felt this at our first (adult) encounter; I continued to feel it for as long as I knew him.

As a soldier, he often declared, he had 'no politics'; but this didn't prevent him from talking about them. One gathered – in so far as one gathered anything definite at all – that he was anti-Socialist, anti-League of Nations and anti-Russian; he was also, by temperament, inclined to anti-Semitism. He would refer, with infinite relish, to some prominent Jew as 'that ineffable Semite', and he took a special pleasure in attributing to Jews all those 'nameless' vices of which, habitually, he accused everybody he didn't like.

By implication, one gathered that he admired Mussolini and, even more so, Hitler, who had not yet, at that date, come to power ... His admiration for Germany, indeed, was one of the few positive qualities about Basil which emerged. He knew Berlin well, and sometimes entertained us with his stories of its night-life.

'Of course, in those days,' he would add (and we gathered that he meant two or three years ago), 'it was *much* more amusing. And *more*over,' he added, 'I was rich beyond the *dreams* of avarice.'

This was one of his favourite phrases; he could never say of anybody that he was merely rich: it was always 'rich beyond the *dreams* of avarice' – with a long, ironic pause on 'dreams', accompanied by an equivocal, rather naughty twinkle of the eyes, as though these 'dreams' were fraught, for him, with the most unmentionable, the most 'nameless' of associations.

Basil often insisted that he was not rich nowadays. But he seemed to have plenty of money, and we assumed his 'poverty' to be merely relative. Occasionally he would declare that he was 'reduced to the *extremes* of intelligence', and would drink (and stand) nothing but halves of bitter; at other times, he would announce that he was rich ('beyond the *dreams*', etc.) and take us to the Carlton or the Berkeley.

I decided that Basil was a 'character', and as such worth cultivating: I had to excuse, in some way, my economic semi-dependence upon him. He bored me; but rather than sit at home, I would accept his hospitality and listen to his talk ... Then, suddenly without warning, he disappeared; I didn't see him for months.

'What's happened to that crashing bore with the moustache you used to go around with?' people would ask.

I had to confess ignorance.

Then, one day, he turned up again in the Long Bar. I was with somebody else, and introduced him:

'Captain Medlicott.'

'Thank you for the courtesy-title,' said Basil, 'but in case you don't know' – he leaned forward and lowered his voice to a conspiratorial whisper – 'in *case* you don't know, I happen to have resigned my commission in His Majesty's Army.'

Had Basil just succeeded in escaping from a penitentiary, he couldn't have invested the circumstance with more sinister significance. Probably he had left the Army for the most ordinary reasons; but it would have been quite in keeping with Basil's character to make a mystery of it.

'*One* day,' he promised, 'I shall tell you the *whole* story.'

He never did; but one was encouraged to infer some vast and Machiavellian conspiracy.

Basil settled in London; and it soon became almost impossible to escape him. The only place I really felt safe was the Oxford and Cambridge Club, which was (according to his own account) one of the few clubs to which Basil didn't belong; though it was noteworthy that he very seldom invited anybody to these clubs of his, except (and that only occasionally) to the In and Out . . . I didn't, however, choose to slumber away my evenings among bishops and judges just for the sake of avoiding Basil. Hopefully, I would sally forth – to whatever bar or club I happened to be frequenting at the moment – and there, sure enough, I would find Basil.

It was my own fault, of course, for going to the sort of places I did – which happened to be the very places frequented by Basil. But there it was; Basil became a sort of inescapable fatality, an Ancient Mariner perpetually keeping me from the wedding feast.

He became, in fact, a nuisance. Over and over again I found myself missing some desirable introduction or rendezvous merely because I had reluctantly become involved, for the evening, with Basil. Sometimes I would be meeting so-and-so at some bar or other; our plans for the evening were made; we met; and then

Basil would appear, stand us drinks, and (for this was what it amounted to) buy up our company for the rest of the evening.

He seemed to have few real friends: the bronzed, moustached hearties, when they occurred (and their appearances were irregular), were little more than drinking-partners. I discovered that Basil was extraordinarily lonely. He was a bachelor; and his contacts with his vaguely defined (if aristrocratic) family seemed few and far between. (I never, so long as I knew him, met a single one of Basil's relations.)

He seemed, since he had left the Army, in some curious way diminished; he had lost some of his old confidence and *panache*; and the bitter-drinking occasions became more and more frequent ... 'Ungratefully, when they occurred, I would make some flimsy excuse and leave him; Basil, I felt, was just bearable at Boulestin's or the Kinde Dragon, but to have to endure his company undiluted, for a whole abstemious evening in some dull bar, was another matter altogether.

I continued, however, to meet him fairly regularly; I told myself that it was pity for his loneliness, but chiefly, I think, it was the mere inability to avoid him. Partly, also, it was a sense of guilt: on several occasions, he had made me small loans – a pound or two at a time: the whole amount wasn't much more than five pounds. But five pounds for me was a big sum; I was chronically broke, and week after week I put off paying it back. Basil said nothing: but on our beer-drinking evenings, when he complained of his 'indigence', I felt a pin-pricking uneasiness, and hoped he had forgotten how much I owed him.

If leaving the Army had shortened the stature of Basil's personality, it had also made him more difficult to explain. In the old days, when people asked who he was, one could say: 'Oh, he's just a queer Army officer,' and leave it at that. But Basil, nowadays, though remaining impenetrably queer, was no longer an officer. I began to be somewhat embarrassed by his incongruity. He never seemed quite to fit in: among Army people he had the air of an actor playing (rather badly) a 'military' *rôle*; among real actors, or in Fitzrovia, his hearty, 'Wodehouse' side became overwhelmingly apparent. Was he, I wondered, aware of this? I could fancy, sometimes, that he rather enjoyed being incongruous; it gave him, perhaps, a spurious sense of his own importance.

Difficult to 'explain' to others, he remained, well though I now knew him, something of a mystery to myself. Was he, at bottom, just a 'stupid' soldier with intellectual pretensions? Or was he something more? I found him impossible to analyse; I liked to be able to 'label' people, and Basil, alone among my friends, obstinately refused to fit into any category.

Nor was the 'mystery' attaching to him confined, nowadays, to his personality: it extended to his background. He had lately, I gathered, acquired a peculiarly vague and intangible sort of 'job'; but he never talked about it, and if directly questioned would become evasive. I never found out exactly what it was; perhaps I wasn't sufficiently interested to make any very serious effort. I was snobbishly bored by people's 'jobs' unless they happened to write, paint or compose; all the rest I lumped together as 'business' – including Basil's.

On at least one occasion I actually went to his 'office': two rooms on the fourth floor in a street off Long Acre. The name of the firm was painted on the glass panel of the door; but for the life of me I can't remember what it was. I have an impression that it was something very vague and comprehensive like 'Pan-European Distributors Ltd' or 'International Exports Ltd' . . . What Basil did there I had no idea; and cared less.

I found that an idea was growing up, among those of my friends who knew him, that Basil's activities were in some way rather sinister. He began to be looked upon as a 'Mystery Man': perhaps he was engaged on some secret-service job, or perhaps he was himself what he was so fond of accusing other people of being: an 'agent' for some foreign power. Perhaps 'Pan-European Distributors Ltd' (or whatever it was called) was a mere cloak for some revolutionary organization . . .

The myth grew at last to fantastic proportions; the trouble was, everybody had a different version of it. People began to find Basil less boring; they would listen with increased attention when he hinted at conspiracies in high places. One version of the legend declared that Basil was no more than a plain, ordinary crook. I denied this, whenever possible; all the same, I was half-inclined to believe it myself. It was a kind of wishful thinking; I should have rather liked Basil to be a crook – or at any rate a 'secret agent'; it would have been a further reason for cultivating him. I needed some such reason to explain my 'friendship' with him; moreover, I should have been quite pleased on my own account, for I still wanted, in my heart of hearts, to be able, as I had in childhood, to regard Basil as a 'hero'.

II

For a long time I didn't know where Basil lived. He would speak vaguely of his 'digs', but never mentioned the address. I quite imagined that he had, if not a house of his own, at least a luxurious flat. At last, one night when the bars and clubs had closed down and we hadn't succeeded in being invited to (or gate-crashing) a late party, he invited me back to his 'place'.

It proved to be a rather small bed-sitting-room in West Kensington.

Seeing my surprise, Basil launched himself into a long explanation: the room was just a *pied-à-terre*; soon he would take a proper flat. He was, he explained further, '*ineffably* indigent' at the moment; soon, however, he would be 'rich beyond the dreams of avarice': proceedings against the mysterious brother-in-law were once again in full swing, and he expected soon, as he said, to be in a position to claim his 'rightful patrimony'.

Meanwhile, his background seemed curiously incongruous. Basil was a big man, and the small room cramped him; it was almost, I felt, pathetic. On the shelves were the books I remembered from Dover – *Company Training, A Shropshire Lad, Swann's Way* ... Once he had revealed the secret of his 'place', he invited me back there frequently – usually in the small hours, after a party. There he would sit, wedged between the table and the wardrobe, drinking Pale Ale and playing the portable gramophone with a soft needle, and a dirty shirt stuffed into the horn. Mostly he played records of Douglas Byng or Ronald Frankau; but once surprised me by putting on *L'Après-midi d'un Faune*.

He was becoming, I thought, curiously subdued; he drank less, and even talked less; and though he wore the same suits – tight-waisted, rather 'actor-ish' – he began to look very slightly shabby. Sometimes he would be positively gloomy; and then, suddenly, he would resume all his old, bumptious gaiety.

Symptomatic of his return to cheerfulness was, as often as not, some new gloss upon the never-ending story of his Aunt Lizzie.

Basil's Aunt Lizzie had long been a legend; she was, undoubtedly, Basil's most successful 'turn'. I always had a certain proprietary feeling about Basil, and I was pleased when, at a party, he showed up to advantage. Aunt Lizzie could always be relied on to raise a laugh, and whenever possible I would encourage him to relate her peculiar saga.

Whether Basil ever really had an Aunt Lizzie I don't know; I am inclined to think she was the purest invention. Certainly even the least fantastic of Basil's stories about her must have been mythical. In his narration, he displayed considerable art: beginning with the fairly plausible and leading up gradually to the completely incredible. I would often watch him 'doing' his Aunt Lizzie turn for the benefit of some new acquaintance, or somebody, at least, who hadn't heard it before. Basil proceeded cautiously, carefully observing his audience to see how much it could 'take': at the first signs of incredulity, he would soft-pedal his phantasy down to a more or less 'realistic' level; then, gradually, with the most casual manner in the world, and with much circumstantial detail, he would proceed to relate some new enormity more fabulous than any that had gone before . . .

Aunt Lizzie was for Basil a kind of busman's holiday. She was a parody of all those other stories, only slightly less fantastic, which Basil related quite seriously, and expected people to believe. Perhaps he believed them himself; but Aunt Lizzie was a conscious outlet for his mythopoeic faculty: her exploits bubbled out of him in an inexhaustible stream: he scarcely ever repeated himself.

Aunt Lizzie, naturally, was 'rich beyond the dreams of avarice'; her present age was ninety-two; in her young days she had been a member of the royal harem at Constantinople; later, in Edwardian times, she had been the mistress ('but only for a week') of a Very Important Person, from whom she had contracted what Basil referred to pompously as 'a certain ignominious Neisserian infection'. She had afterwards been a leading suffragette, and had written to the Prime Minister a letter beginning 'You abominable old bastard'; she had also chained herself to the Albert Memorial, and, when forcibly dislodged, had bitten a policeman in the neck. Having at last achieved her object, she stood for Parliament herself, and electrified her constituents by appearing at a meeting in a bathing-costume – in order, as she explained, to discourage prudishness among the working classes, and thereby to raise the falling birth-rate ...

And so the story would go on: gathering momentum gradually until Basil approached the climax. The climax was always the same: Basil would pause, shake his head and say: 'Yes, she's an admirable woman: a dutiful wife, a valuable public servant an ornament to society. It's unfortunate – *most* unfortunate – that she has just one failing ...'

'And what's that?' the audience would gasp.

Basil would pause again, a sinister glint coming into his eyes; then lean forward, and in sepulchral tones guaranteed to curdle the blood of his listeners, would mutter:

'She devours her young.'

For some weeks Basil was away: part of the time, apparently, was spent in Berlin. When I saw him again, he seemed more than ever diminished; there was now a definitely seedy air about him, his drinking was reduced to a minimum, he fed at the cheapest restaurants. His tales of Aunt Lizzie became rarer and rarer and when he could be persuaded to give a new instalment, the portentous lady seemed, like her nephew, to have lost some of her vitality.

One night I persuaded Basil to come to a party to which I had been invited. The hostess was a woman called Renée – either I never knew, or have forgotten, her surname. She must have been well off; yet she tended to frequent Fitzrovia and the cheaper night-clubs, though there was nothing innately 'Bohemian' about her at all.

Her parties – staged in a large, rambling flat in Earls Court – enjoyed a certain temporary celebrity. Renée was anything but selective: she welcomed anybody, and provided her big, bleak rooms were crowded, she didn't seem to mind in the least who filled them. There was always plenty to drink; she herself drank like a fish, and, but for a tendency to remove her clothes at unsuitable moments, held her liquor like a man.

Tonight's party began badly: at midnight, the flat was still half-empty. The handful of 'regulars', whom one always found there, were ginning-up while the going was good. A gramophone rather depressingly discoursed songs by Yvonne Georges and Lucienne Boyer. Renée wandered round disconsolately, lamenting that she couldn't think where all the boys had got to.

'Eddie was bringing a whole crowd on from the Lantern,' said somebody hopefully.

'I saw Hew Dallas, and he promised to come along with Nigel.'

'I *know* Bertie was coming – '

'My dear, he was *stinking* – I saw him at the Fitzroy.'

'Nina's bound to turn up. She had some frightful BM creature in tow – '

'Darling Nina, I think she's heaven.'

'How boring everyone is.'

Presently the rooms began to fill, but not, for the most part, with the people whom Renée had invited.

'Beverley 'phoned me and said he was *terribly* sorry but he couldn't make it.'

'Eddie got involved with some negress . . .'

'Derek and Douglas said they'd try and get round later – '

'Elizabeth's in bed with a guardsman – she rang up to tell me.'

A young man from the British Museum turned up with two inarticulate Burmese: one was called Ba Om, the other U Maw. A rather famous black crooner appeared, partly consoling Renée for the defection of other half-celebrities. People began to dance, and the party, after a poor beginning, began to get going.

I felt rather boringly sober for the first hour or so, and this made me critical; I stood near the door, feeling detached and Byronically superior, waiting for somebody amusing to turn up. As for Basil, he sat by himself on a sofa, sipping a small glass of beer, looking extremely bored and speaking to nobody. He aroused a certain amount of curiosity; there were whispered speculations in corners, hostile or hopeful according to the varying temperaments of the speakers:

'Who's that sinister creature on the sofa?' 'Who's that cup of tea with the moustache?' 'My dear, *yours* rather than mine.' 'I was always eclectic' . . .

The Fitzroy contingent arrived, noisy, thirsty and demonstrative, like a troupe of not-very-clever performing animals. They had roped in a very drunk Guards officer and a West African Negro, a law-student, both of whom proved extremely popular at first, though on more intimate acquaintance they turned out (so people said) to be somewhat less than adequate . . .

Posted near the bar, I helped myself to drink after drink and began to feel a warmer, more receptive mood stealing over me. I still felt detached, but my detachment was tinged with a vague, inclusive benevolence: I saw the dancing couples through a romantic haze. The whole party became an episode in my future *magnum opus* a chapter out of one of the later volumes, equivalent to *Sodome et Gomorrhe* in the Proustian canon ... Once having invested the party with this specious glamour, I began, quietly, to enjoy myself; I saw myself as the detached, analytic observer, a merciless critic of society, a spectator of the *Untergang des Abendlandes*. The girls were all potential Albertines, the men Saint Loups ... There was so-and-so, whom I wanted to meet; there was somebody else with whom (so I believed) I was in love: but I remained where I was, enjoying the sense of being a martyr to my art; to go and talk to people would break the spell ... The truth was, of course, that I was far too timid: I needed a few more drinks before my societal instincts became operative.

I helped myself to more whisky.

After a time I noticed that Basil had disappeared. He couldn't have gone home, for I had been standing near the door all the time, and must have seen him ... The party was becoming perceptibly wilder. Couples began to detach themselves from the dancing crowd and retire to the bedrooms. Perhaps Basil had found a soul-mate, I thought; but it seemed highly improbable. Suddenly, in a lull between gramophone-records, there was an ear-splitting explosion. Everyone jumped; several screamed; Fitzrovia twittered.

The noise had come from one of the further rooms; suddenly apprehensive, I followed Renée down the corridor. I was convinced, quite unreasonably, that the noise had something to do with Basil ... Renée flung open the door of a small bedroom: there, on the narrow bed, Basil lay with his body limp and distorted. His face was dead-white; a trickle of redness smeared his chin. One hand dangled over the side of the bed; and below the lifeless fingers, on the carpet, lay a small revolver.

For a moment Renée stood at the door, perfectly silent. Then she began to giggle. Horrified, I turned to her.

'What – ' I began, and, to my complete astonishment, she burst out laughing. I felt suddenly sick: it was going to be no joke having a hysteric on my hands as well as a corpse ...

Then I followed my hostess's pointing finger. On the bedside table stood a bottle of red ink and a tin of talcum powder. A last-minute carelessness had ruined Basil's gesture: for all his habitual mystery-mongering, he had proved, in practice, a bad criminal.

The revolver-shot, at any rate, had been perfectly genuine: he had fired it out of the window. His 'act' had not been planned in advance: he always, he told me, carried a revolver nowadays.

'Frequenting as I do,' he added, 'the company of certain rather *unscrupulous* persons, I feel *more* than justified in so doing.'

Renée, fortunately, had been too tight to protest, with any force, against Basil's attempt at *Grand Guignol*. The party continued much as before: I returned with Basil to his bed-sitting-room, and finished the night with Pale Ale, and Douglas Byng records on the muffled gramophone.

Basil seemed not in the least put-out at the failure of his gesture: probably he had not expected much from it, anyway. No doubt he realized, too, that had he shot himself in good earnest, scarcely anybody at Renée's party would have cared a hoot – apart from the incidental inconvenience.

Basil once again disappeared for several weeks. And then, incredibly, I saw in *The Times* one morning the announcement of his engagement:

'The enagement is announced between Captain Basil R. Medlicott, the Royal –shire Regiment, only son of the late Mr and Mrs Richard Medlicott, of Letcombe Regis, Berkshire, and Marjorie ("Micky") Morrogh-Baker, eldest daughter of the late Colonel Edward Poulton-Entwhistle, CMG, BSO, JP, and of Mrs Edward Poulton-Entwhistle, of Greenways, Betchworth, Surrey.'

Had the Pope himself publicly relinquished the practice of celibacy, I couldn't have been more astonished. Not the very faintest hint had Basil let fall about the approaching change in his life. I read the announcement over and over again, trying to persuade myself that it was another Basil Medlicott. But there were his initials, there was his regiment, in cold print.

I hoped, for his sake, that Mrs ('Micky') Morrogh-Baker was a wealthy widow; I had felt rather sorry, lately, for Basil's increasing seediness, and I flatly disbelieved (as perhaps he himself did by now) in the 'patrimony' which he hoped to wrest from the iniquitous and orgiastic brother-in-law.

At last Basil turned up again. He had regained all his old bluff, soldierly confidence; he was wearing a new suit, and seemed to have plenty of money. His 'Wodehouse' side was uppermost: he called me 'old boy' and remained, till the end of the evening, breezily evasive about his marriage. Back in West Kensington, however, he became more confidential.

'Micky,' it seemed, was a delightful woman: he had known her for years, Dick Morrogh-Baker had been one of his brother officers. She was rich – 'beyond the *dreams* of avarice,' said Basil with an immense satisfaction. 'A circumstance,' he added with juicy relish, 'which will no doubt provide a salutary shock for a certain intransigent and in every way regrettable relative of mine' – by whom, of course, he meant his famous brother-in-law.

Yes, 'Micky' seemed in every way a desirable match. I was pleased that Basil had done so well for himself.

'There's just *one* circumstance, however, which I regard with some *slight* regret,' Basil confessed, lowering his voice to the familiar conspiratorial tone.

'What's that?' I asked, rather alarmed, and half-expecting to hear that his future wife 'devoured her young'.

'I'm extraordinarily fond of her,' Basil went on, 'but of course it *is* a circumstance for some regret – and *one*, moreover, which is in certain quarters – that the lady *happens* to be nearly twenty years my senior.'

IV

At about this time I began to be convinced that I was suffering from some obscure, insidious illness. It began with the vaguest of symptoms: a mere feeling of never being 'quite well'. Minor upsets became magnified, for me, into threats of worse to follow. I had had a job in a publisher's office, till recently, but had given it up. Increased leisure, gave me time to brood; I began to feel worse – with slight pains in the back and sides, headaches and a quickened pulse. My temperature in the evening went up to 99, sometimes higher. I couldn't taste a cigarette properly, and I was 'off my food'.

I sat in the garden at Blackheath feeling ill and frightened. The more anxious I became, the worse I felt: it was the usual vicious circle. I tried to write, but for almost the first time in my life I found myself incapable of putting pen to paper. My Proustian *magnum opus* seemed more remote than ever ... Probably I should die, leaving it unwritten. Winter came, and my depression increased. Blackheath seemed shrouded, perpetually, in fog; it was bitterly cold; I longed with an obsessive passion for the sun. If only I could get abroad, to the South ...

I went to the doctor; I went to several doctors: they all agreed that there was nothing much wrong, but that there was, indubitably, something not quite right. About what this 'something' was they seemed totally unable to agree ... One put it down to the liver; another to a faulty appendix; yet another spoke darkly but inconclusively of *Bacillus coli*. (I thought of the 'killitis' of my childhood, and shivered: remembering the Toreador's Song, the burst of sunlight after rain, the taste of albumen water.) None of my doctors advised any definite treatment: one recommended a light diet, the other told me to eat all I could; one forbade alcohol, another allowed it. I was advised to lead a strenuous life with plenty of exercise; to rest daily after lunch and go to bed early; to take calomel and mag. sulph.; to avoid all purgatives whatsoever.

This very vagueness on the doctors' part fed my anxiety: I would have welcomed with relief a definite, uncompromising illness, however grave or unpleasant. But I continued merely to feel 'not quite well'.

I remembered, with a sinking heart, the sinister, grown-up whispers of my childhood: 'He's not very strong ... he needs a lot of rest ...' Was I really suffering from some deep constitutional weakness?

I was not. What I was suffering from, more than anything else, was retarded adolescence. I had failed to adapt myself to any settled way of life: I was unattached, I belonged nowhere. A succession of jobs – with booksellers or publishers – which I had obtained owing to prolonged parental pressure, had been the merest pretence: I only wanted to 'write'. Now that I was at home, I was perfectly free to do so; but I wasn't 'well' enough ... Caught up in one vicious circle after another, I felt stealing upon me a kind of mental paralysis. I could analyse my state with a Proustian detachment; but I was incapable of doing anything about it.

Since about the age of seventeen I had regarded myself, with considerable satisfaction, as a sort of *poète maudit*; I was under a curse, I was an outcaste; only by subjecting myself to my fate could I hope ultimately to conquer. One day I would write a book: but this, I felt, could only be achieved by suffering. I duly suffered; though I preferred to do so, if possible, in 'amusing' surroundings ...

I read biographies of Verlaine and Rimbaud with avidity. I should have liked to pack my bag and leave, that very day, for Abyssinia ... But I couldn't have raised the fare, anyway; besides, I didn't feel 'well' enough ... I contemplated a series of noble gestures: I would join the Army, become a tramp, a Communist, a farm-labourer ... Needless to say, I did none of these things. Instead, I re-read Proust: feeling ill, and half-aware, all the time that my 'illness' was a mere alibi, a bolt-hole from a world where I was unhappy, badly adapted, frustrated.

Finally it was decided, by my long-suffering family, that I should go into the family business at Folkestone. It was hardly Abyssinia; but it did, for a time, jerk me out of my conviction that I was 'ill'. I decided to turn hearty, bought a checked cloth cap, and even tried (unsuccessfully) to grow a moustache. I took up riding again; I went for long walks, dosed myself with hypophosphites, and read the Coles's book on economics. After a few months of this hardening régime I really began to feel better. But the improvement in my health was accompanied by no corresponding increase in my business-ability. It was no good – I loathed 'business', and I always should. I was given the usual jobs appropriate to one 'starting from the bottom' – sorting invoices, entering up ledgers. I worked at first with an almost excessive conscientiousness; bored as I was, I felt obscurely that I was coming to grips with 'reality'. Like Rimbaud, I had been cursed, ever since I 'grew up', with an obsessive desire *'s'évader de la réalité'*. Here, at any rate, surrounded by ledgers and the invoices of Messrs Brown, Gore & Welch, Messrs Bass, Ratcliffe and the rest, I felt, for a time, all the exhilaration of a psychological adventure: I had crossed the frontier, I was Beyond the Pleasure-Principle.

But I had taken, as it happened, a return-ticket . . .

I was not allowed, for long, to work undisturbed at my ledgers; I was encouraged to 'have a look round', go down to the cellars, ask questions; I was supposed, after all, to be 'learning the business'. Initiative, ambition, 'common sense' – these were the qualities which I was expected to display; and they were, alas! the very qualities with which my fairy-godmother, at my christening, must have entirely forgotten to equip me . . .

I failed signally to develop these virtues; instead, when I began to feel better, I took to visiting Dover.

Nowadays, more than ever, Dover seemed an alien land, a town beyond the frontier. I was fixed, at last, it seemed, in a permanent ambience: the Edwardian pomposity of middle-class Folkstone. Dover provided an outlet: in the soldiers' pubs, or down by the docks, I felt at home again. My craving for the sun persisted; and at Dover I could at least watch the afternoon boat

lève l'ancre pour une exotique nature.

Drab, dirty, easy-going, friendly – the town huddled familiarly under the cliffs, the barracks and the castle impending grimly upon it from above. I was happier here than anywhere; I didn't in the least regret my exile from London – from the parties, the pub-crawls, the dingy, fog-bound gaiety. I wondered, occasionally, what had happened to the people I knew; Basil, for one, had passed out of my life completely; he had not written since his marriage, and I didn't even know where he was living.

Then, one Saturday evening, without warning, and just as I was leaving my lodgings to catch the Dover bus, Basil turned up. He drove up to the door in a large, expensive car; but he still wore the old clothes I remembered from his Army days: the leather-patched coat, the pork-pie hat.

'Come on, get in – we're going to Dover,' he said. 'Where's your brother?'

My brother was in London for the week-end. Without further words, Basil opened the car-door, I got in, and we started off.

'I thought we might eat out of doors,' he said, as we roared up the Dover hill. 'I've got some food.'

It was a late-summer evening, and fine. We parked the car in a side-road on top of the cliffs, and carried Basil's provisions to the edge of a chalk-pit, overlooking the town. Basil must have brought the food from London: crab-sandwiches, half a lobster and a terrine of *foie gras*. There were also two bottles of hock.

We sat on the edge of the chalk-pit and ate and drank. For some reason I felt oddly embarrassed by Basil; there was something altogether unnatural about his manner, he seemed pent-up, and had a peculiar air of urgency, as though some rendezvous of vast importance awaited him. The picnic was a hustled, pass-overish affair: I was scarcely allowed to finish my share of the sandwiches, or to drink my wine. When the bottles were empty, Basil threw them over the chalk-pit with rather a vindictive air, as though he hoped some enemy were lurking below.

'Come on,' he said.

'What's the hurry?' I asked. 'Are we meeting somebody?'

'Lots of people, probably, old boy.'

We drove on, into Dover, and went to a pub in the market square. It was twilight by now, the lights were coming out, and the streets were taking on that brief, hallucinatory beauty which even the dingiest seaside town can assume on a fine summer evening. The castle on the hill sprang into flood-lit brilliance; the pavements were crowded with soldiers and holidaymakers.

Once inside a pub, Basil's curious, taut manner began to relax. He kept up a gusty, rather evasive conversation: he was living down in Surrey, he said, with his wife – a nice little place. No, he didn't get up to London much nowadays. He was off to Germany tomorrow – that was what had brought him down. Was he going alone? I asked, surprised. Yes, his wife didn't care for travelling; besides, he was going on business. Had he still the same job? Basil looked vague, and said something rather silly about all jobs being alike.

I wanted to say: 'But surely you don't need to work any more.' A sudden sense that it would not be quite tactful kept me silent.

Basil had, as it turned out, made no arrangements for the evening; the hustle over food, the impression he had given of having some all-important engagement, seemed to have been mere 'nerves'. I had never seen Basil drink so much or so quickly. The evening rapidly became riotous. We went to pub after pub, collecting as we went a number of chance acquaintances, mostly soldiers or sailors, all of whom piled into the car. Basil stood drinks all round over and over again: nobody else was allowed to spend a penny. Two of the soldiers who had tacked on to us had to get out to the country somewhere – they were in Camp. Basil offered to take them back; and at half past ten we started off. Basil, as usual, drove with a terrifying disregard of traffic-regulations. The soldiers were vague about their route; we circled round Adisham and Bekesbourne for a long time before we found the Camp. At last we dropped them, and turned back.

'Have you the very remotest idea where we are?' Basil inquired at last. 'Because I haven't, I assure you.'

I had not been taking much note of our direction. But suddenly the edge of a copse, the angle of a road were familiar.

'Why,' I exclaimed, 'we're just near the watertower.'

'All right, let's go and look at it,' said Basil blithely. Perhaps he thought that, once at the tower, I should be able to find the way; perhaps he noticed the sudden excitement in my voice.

We turned up the narrow, chalky road towards the wood, and in less than a minute the head-lights were glaring on the dark, late-summer foliage of the hazel thickets.

'You can't get any further,' I said, and Basil turned the car, backing into a side-path opposite the tower. As he did so, the lights streamed across the fenced enclosure overgrown with rosebay and nettles, and lit with a vague, spectral radiance the brick arches, the zig-zag iron ladder. The arches curved dimly upwards into the gloom: the top of the tower was invisible. A night-bird squawked discordantly; moths fluttered in the stream of light; somewhere far away, in the remote country beyond the tower, a dog barked, and at some farm nearer at hand, Coldharbour probably, the first cocks began to crow.

We reached Folkestone eventually; and Basil suddenly realized that he had forgotten to book a room at a hotel. Fortunately, I had a fairly comfortable sofa in my sitting-room, and on this he agreed to sleep.

It was nearly two o'clock before we got to bed. But at six I was rudely awakened by Basil, fully dressed, with a towel over his shoulder.

'Come and bathe,' he said.

'I'm damned if I will,' I protested.

'Come on,' he repeated, in orderly-room tones.

Reluctantly I dressed and followed him to the car. It was a grey, rather chilly morning. We drove to Seabrook, and undressed below the ruined sea-wall. Not a soul was in sight: the houses beyond the foreshore, the coast-guard station, the cafés, seemed utterly deserted, as though the inhabitants had fled before the threat of battle or pestilence. A lonely bugle sounded reveillé up at the Camp; seagulls circled with remote, desolate cries above the shingle tract by the canal; the sea lapped gently upon the shore.

Basil had stripped off his clothes and was in the sea almost before I had started to take my coat off. He swam out with a kind of despairing violence, as though crocodiles were pursuing him. Watching his head bobbing further and further out I had a curious feeling that he really was being pursued and was trying desperately to escape . . .

He came out at last, shivering, his big boxer's body pocked with gooseflesh. He was, I noticed, beginning to run to fat . . . Driving up to the town, he was oddly silent: once again he seemed, as he had seemed on the previous night, pent-up, preoccupied by some secret which he couldn't or wouldn't divulge.

Once or twice a week I went riding: hacking out, by myself, along the coast road to Seabrook, then turning inland up the road called Horn Street which, in my childhood, had been our shortcut to the 'country'. It had not changed: the transition from seascape to landscape was as abrupt as ever; the little brook still gurgled under the hedge, sheep coughed in the pasture.

I rode through Pericar Woods, forcing my horse up the steep, narrow paths between the stinging whip-lashes of the hazels. At the top of the wood was Dibgate, a high barren plateau of open pasture, in shape like an inverted saucer, its sides sloping abruptly into the surrounding levels of plough and meadow-land. Across the fields one could see the grim red buildings of Shorncliffe Camp, and hear the crying of bugles; faint, sad calls which seemed to be carrying on an intermittent, mysterious dialogue with the wailing fog-horns far out in the channel.

Cantering round Dibgate on cold, grey winter afternoons, I had an odd sense of being isolated in some ambiguous territory between two worlds: as in my childhood, it didn't seem the 'real' country – that only began beyond the hills which stretched, an impassable barrier, along the northern sky-line. Yet the high, empty plateau was remote from the town and the sea: a frontier-land, inhabited only by soldiers.

Sometimes I encountered these frontier-tribes: parties of troops in training, out on a cross-country run. In shorts and singlets, they plodded heavily across the rough fields, their naked limbs stained purple by the shrewd east wind, their red faces set in an expression of dull, stoic endurance. They seemed some curious variant of the human species – *Homo sapiens* var. *militaris* – indigenous, like the Military Orchid, only in a few isolated, calcareous districts off the beaten track ... Remote and alien, they passed me by without greeting, no flicker of human emotion betraying itself in their coarse, meaty faces. Watching them, I felt a stranger from another world: barred implacably from any friendly contact with these denizens of an alien country.

v

I heard no more of Basil for a whole year. This surprised me: for the fact that he had bothered to look me up on his way through Folkestone seemed to herald a renewal of our acquaintance. I returned once or twice to his old haunts in London; but I never saw him. Rather to my own surprise, I was quite sorry: Basil, I suppose, had become to some extent a habit with me.

Not long after his visit to me, I ran into one of the soldiers to whom we had given a lift.

'Who was that bloke what drove us around, then?' he asked.

I said he was just a bloke – I didn't know very much about him.

'He told *me* he was on his way to see Hitler,' the soldier declared. 'Queer sort of bloke, but he was free with his cash.'

At last, at the end of a year, I received a letter from Basil. Its arrival surprised me considerably: Basil was never a great letter-writer – not to me, anyway. The letter itself was curiously vague and pointless; he wrote from the United Service Club – there was no other address; reading through the rather pedestrian inquiries about my health and so on, I found, at last, that the sting was in the tail.

'You may recall,' wrote Basil, 'that at one time or another, I have been privileged to offer you, on an exiguous scale, a certain amount of pecuniary assistance. As, by my own folly, I have lately been reduced once more to the *extremes* of indigence, I should take it very kindly if you could see your way to refunding the above-mentioned loans. The total amount owing, I venture to remind you, is £5 7s. 6d.'

There followed a little list, with dates of the exact amounts of every loan he had ever made me – 'Sept. 4th, 1931: £1 10s. od.,' and so on.

For a few moments I really thought Basil must have gone mad, and felt rather alarmed. Then, reading the letter again, I burst out laughing; it was so exactly like Basil – I could hear his voice in every phrase: at least, in the final operative paragraph. Was the whole thing a joke? No: there was no mistaking those last sentences – he really wanted the money, and the need had stung him into a fantastic overstatement of his case. I recognized all the old, malicious irony with which, on countless occasions, I had heard him attack others; now, for a change, it was directed against myself.

I was astonished at the appended list of his loans to me: I had not thought Basil capable of such accuracy. The more I looked at the letter, the more it irritated me: why ever couldn't he say quite plainly that I owed him five pounds odd and that he wanted it? Right, I thought: if he chooses to be pompous and stupid, he can damned well wait for his money. I didn't answer the letter.

It was a convenient course for me to take, as it happened; for I was more broke than usual. (I told myself, of course, that it was a matter of dignity.)

After a fortnight the second letter arrived.

'Having received no reply to my last letter, I at first concluded that you had left your present residence, or that you had fallen ill. I hear, however, on unimpeachable authority' – (I could hear Basil's voice, heavily ironic, in the ponderous phrase) – 'that you are still domiciled at the same address. I am therefore surprised that you have not replied before this to a request with which, believe me, only dire necessity' – (here again Basil was audible) – 'has constrained me to discommode you.'

A re-statement followed (again with dates) of the amounts owing.

Once again I didn't answer.

Within a week a third letter arrived.

'Since you choose, apparently, to neglect entirely the responsibilities and commitments of a gentleman, I must regretfully inform you that, unless I receive your cheque for the amount stated below before the 15th instant, I shall be compelled to take legal proceedings forthwith.'

This time, I thought, there could be no doubt of it: Basil had gone mad. I wrote to Eric, who I knew had seen Basil fairly recently, and asked him what was up.

'Haven't you heard?' wrote Eric in reply. 'The Basilisk is separated from his wife – nobody knows quite why, but we gather that she's found out some of his habits which, it appears, she didn't suspect before she married him. Unfortunately, all the money's settled on her, and she's got poor B. on a string: perhaps, during his pre-marital ardours (?) he may have overlooked this dismal fact. At any rate, B. is poor beyond the dreams of indigence (it's rumoured that she makes him an allowance of five pounds a week or less), and is therefore quarrelling madly with all his old friends, such as yourself, over all the half-crowns he's ever lent them. He's been rampaging round all the old haunts lately, and threatens to embark on orgies of litigation in the near future.'

I was still broke; I decided to take the risk, and wait for Basil's next move. I wondered how I could ever have been 'friends' with anyone capable of such behaviour: in retrospect, Basil seemed a pure, undiluted bore, with no redeeming features, and I bitterly resented, not only the time I had wasted in his company, but my sentimental impulses to make him into a private hero-myth.

As I half-expected, I soon received another letter – not from a solicitor, but again from Basil. This time he took a rather different tone.

'I am much disappointed, naturally, that you have replied to none of my previous letters, including the last, which, I may say, in consideration for my friendship with yourself and your brother, I much regretted having to write. In fact, as I have no wish to be hard upon you, I have postponed taking the legal action with which I was impelled, by the harshest necessity, to threaten you, and I would hereby suggest, in order to make things easier for you, that you send me, on account, as much as you can at present afford of the total amount, leaving the balance until such time as you are able to pay it.'

A postscript added:

'I am more than sorry that our former friendly relationship should have reached such a pass. I hoped, at our last meeting, a year ago, that you would recall your small debt to me, without my reminding you. Since, however, you have preferred to forget your obligations, I have had no alternative but to take the law into my own hands.'

I was not only still very broke, but increasingly irritated with Basil's fantastic goings-on. I decided to let him wait another week or two. Finally a letter arrived of no less than twelve pages: such a letter as I had not imagined anybody outside an asylum, let alone Basil, capable of writing. Much of it was sheer vituperation: over and over again I recognized accusations which, in the old days, I had heard him make, half-jokingly, half in earnest, against his brother-in-law or others with whom he had quarrelled. I was accused of every conceivable crime, every vice and aberration catalogued by psychologists; I lacked the instincts of a gentleman; I was a sponger, a parasite, an intellectual snob, a dipsomaniac, a moral degenerate, and probably destined to a degrading death from General Paralysis of the Insane.

I waited another month, and, as no more letters arrived, sent him a cheque. A receipt (with a twopenny stamp) came by return of post.

My odd, uneasy relationship with Basil had, I supposed, at last come to an end; I certainly hoped, devoutly, that I should never see him again. I realized that I had (or so it seemed, at least) 'grown out of' Basil; he had perhaps supplied, at one time, something that was necessary to me: but the necessity, I felt, no longer existed. It was a pity that we should have parted unamicably: but the fault, I considered, lay entirely with Basil.

Initiative, ambition, 'common sense' – I should never possess these attributes; they had been left out of my composition ... My hold upon the 'Reality-principle' became relaxed and insecure. For a few more months I stayed at Folkestone: feeling ill again, wanting to write but unable to make the effort. Then, at my own request, I left the firm.

The reoccupation of the Ruhr, Hitler's Blood-purge, the war with Abyssinia – the 'crisis' age was beginning; hitherto I had managed to preserve a twentyish aloofness about politics, but one could hardly ignore Hitler. My health became worse: all the old symptoms returned, I felt myself gradually spiralling downwards, day by day, into a chronic hypochondria. As always, I could analyse, to some extent, the process of my own disintegration; but I was impotent to check it. Events in Europe became oddly intermingled with my own state of health; my personal anxiety echoed the mass-dread which was beginning to afflict the whole country. The new poets seemed to confirm my own feeling: Auden, MacNeice, Charles Madge seemed obsessed with illness and the threat of war. Auden could write of 'England, this country where nobody is well', and the phrase haunted my mind like a faint, unpleasant smell. *The Orators* was, indeed, in the strictest sense a prophetic book: over and over again, in the next ten years, one was to recognize the tactics of the 'Enemy', the gradual demoralization, the war of nerves; even the landscapes of Auden's poetry – ruined farms, untilled fields, rusting machinery – became factually familiar.

Yeats died, Housman died, Kipling died; death was in the air. 'The King is sinking rapidly' – Sir John Reith's sepulchral tones seemed to usher out a tribal Scapegoat, the Dying God. My own father died; the whole background of my life, which for so long had seemed immutable, was rapidly disintegrating; the Gods were dying – an epoch was drawing to its close.

My vague ill-health persisted: I would have welcomed the outbreak of war, as I would have welcomed the onset of some acute, definite malady: I longed – as many people longed at that time – for some violent purgation of the crisis-ridden atmosphere . . . The air seemed thick with portents: the Abdication, the burning of the Crystal Palace. War was the ultimate horror: but secretly – almost unknown to myself – I waited for it with an excited, half-pleasurable anticipation . . .

I had long decided that when war really came I would join up instantly; I had no real convictions about pacifism and, though it was fashionable to laugh at Rupert Brooke ('Swimmers into cleanness leaping') I realized that I should feel, though for rather different reasons, much the same sense of release. I felt, in fact, about the Army, much as I had felt, in early adolescence, about sex: it was something difficult, rather disgusting and ultimately inevitable, which I dreaded yet longed to experience. Soldiers, too, were linked in some way with my childhood-heroes – the people I feared and secretly adored.

Meanwhile, the sense of personal crisis became ever more firmly linked with outward events. My sensibilities became curiously dulled: it was as though I were living inside a glass bell, aware of the outside world, but cut off from all sensuous apprehension of it. People moved and spoke, the sunlight shone on the garden-trees, I read poetry and new novels: but nothing seemed quite real, I apprehended the world remotely, caged in my transparent but impermeable envelope.

Finally I escaped: genuinely ill at last, I went to Switzerland, and the following summer to Cassis.

Leaving England was like escaping from a prison; perhaps, for certain kinds of people, it always is. I caught the boat at Dover; for me, the town had always been a frontier-station, a way of escape – in childhood, and again during my time at Folkestone. Now once again the dingy Victorian houses, the Castle, the 'station built on the sea', welcomed me with the promise of happiness; but this time it was Dover itself to which I was bidding good-bye.

VI

It was while I was at Cassis that I received Eric's letter.

'Do you see the English papers? If so, you'll have heard about the Basilisk. If you don't (believe it or not) the B. is up for trial, charged with selling "information of national importance" to a foreign power: guess which. The *News of the World* splashed him last Sunday: lots of juicy bits about his visits to Berlin, and all the night-boxes he frequented. There doesn't seem much real evidence though: all that emerges, so far, is that he seems to have been highly indiscreet. I should guess, myself, that for once somebody has taken his "mystery-man" pose at the foot of the letter – he always rather asked for it, didn't he?'

I read the letter over lunch at the Restaurant du Port: *moules-en brochette, bouillabaisse*, and a bottle of white wine from the vineyards of Colonel Teed, up the hill. In such an ambience, Basil seemed a long way away . . . I wasn't much surprised at the news; it was what one might have expected from Basil, with his passion for conspiracy. The fact that he had really *done* something, instead of merely tediously talking about it, gave me a certain brief, peculiar pleasure: it justified, to some extent, my old tendency to make Basil into a hero. Not that he had done anything very heroic: but at least it gave some substance to his eternal mystery-mongering, which I had always thought bogus. As a spy, Basil had attained at last, I thought, a certain dignity.

Other letters from Eric followed: the trial was dragging on, but undramatically. The papers printed it on the back pages, now, among the sports news; it was no longer a front-page sensation. The *Continental Daily Mail* had a *résumé* of the whole case, and an unsuitable photograph of Basil, in shorts, dating from his boxing days. The story made rather dull reading: I hardly bothered to finish it.

I didn't hear the result of the trial till I returned to England. Then I learnt that Basil had been acquitted, owing to lack of evidence. It seemed that Eric had probably been right: Basil had been highly indiscreet, and overdone his mystery-stunt. He had frequented suspicious people and places, and was mildly censured in the summing-up: the real culprit turned out to be a Major in the Artillery, with whom Basil had been fairly intimate, and whom he had accompanied to Berlin.

Back in England, I went to live for a time in the village of my childhood: our old nurse had a cottage there. I started to write again, and felt better; but the sense of an epoch drawing to a close persisted. War appeared so inevitable, that the facile optimism of most of the people one knew seemed scarcely credible. I waited as patiently as I could for the day of initiation; loathing the prospect, yet oddly excited: much as an inhibited adolescent might look forward to his first 'experience' with a woman.

At Woodville, by Lydden, outside Dover, I found the Stinking Hellebore: I had seen it in Switzerland, but had never before found it in England. It was a bright, windless morning in March when I made the discovery: the plant grew in a beech plantation sloping up over the downs towards Coldred, Sibertswold and the colliery country. There, beneath the silvery boles of the beeches, the big rosettes of iron-dark foliage lay scattered over the brown floor of last year's leaves; and from each tuft of leafage, rose the panicles of drooping, pale-green blossoms: the expanded flowers fringed with dull, cloudy purple, the unopened buds like the blunt heads of puff-adders poised to strike . . .

I had searched for the plant in childhood and never found it: to discover it now, though it gave me pleasure, filled me also with a certain melancholy. I ought, I felt, to have found it before: like most things in life, it had occurred at the wrong time. Desire and opportunity seldom coincide; once I had wanted to be a bus-conductor; there was nothing, now, to prevent me from applying for a job on the East Kent bus-service; but the prospect had ceased to be attractive. August and austerely beautiful, the pale flowers of the Hellebore rose above their dark, rusty leaves; the Germans had entered Prague; the harsh, inimical future impinged more sharply, every day, upon the present. A cloud crept up from over the hill, beyond Coldred, and covered the sun.

A landscape which had haunted me for years: high, remote chalk-hills, with hanging beechwoods, scattered here and there with cromlechs or monoliths. On Barham Downs, or in the country round Dover, I would impose my private vision on the real landscape, peopling it with the heroes of myth. In the verse of Yeats or Housman, in certain passages of Delius or John Ireland, I would detect the same quality: a kind of remote, nostalgic awareness of some legendary past – Celtic myth, the Druidic mysteries. Reading *King Lear* in childhood had perhaps sown in me the seeds of my obsession: they had germinated slowly, irregularly, but their roots had gone deep.

Intermittently, over a long period, I read books about Celtic myths and customs, or treatises (highly speculative) about the Druids. I learnt that there was no reason whatever to suppose (as most people do) that Stonehenge or any other megalithic structures were associated with the Druids: it was all guess-work. Most of the traditions about Druidism were no older than the Middle Ages, and had probably been established, without a shadow of justification, by such historiographers as Geoffrey of Monmouth. Knowledge of the Druids reduced itself to an infinitesimal residue of contemporary references: a few short, ambiguous passages in Caesar, Pliny or Tacitus.

I was vaguely disappointed; but the debunking of the druids

didn't much affect my own mythopoeic vision of my favourite landscapes. A vague, Wordsworthian awareness of

> old, unhappy, far-off things
> And battles long ago

was all that I needed as a basis for my myth-making. Certain features of a landscape – a yew tree outlined against the pale radiance of a February sunset, the 'inscape' of dark glossy ivy beneath bare beeches – could become impregnated with an extraordinary 'magical' significance.

I had embarked upon a full-length monograph on the British *Orchidaceae*: at that time (the Munich period) it seemed almost an act of defiance – fiddling while Rome burnt. I had no illusions about the fire: but I preferred to wait till the fire-brigade was officially called out.

I roamed the countryside looking for orchids; it was a return-to-the-womb, with a vengeance – but the intra-uterine sojourn would too evidently be short; I was in no hurry to undergo the trauma of rebirth – it was coming quite soon enough, whether I wanted it or not.

I stayed at Dover: in one of those Victorian houses under the East Cliff, where

> the cry of the gulls at dawn is sad like work ⁙ ⁙ ⁙

(As it happened, Messrs Auden and Isherwood had recently stayed there too: '*they* was a pair of scamps, if you like', the landlady alleged.)

Orchis ustulata was still to be found on the cliff-tops, just as it was in Anne Pratt's day; inland, the Lady Orchid haunted the copses, its pink-and-brown spikes towering like elegantly-dressed women above the Herb Paris and Dog's-mercury. Rumour had it that the Military Orchid itself had occurred near Deal, just along the coast ... I searched for it with a recurrent hope: traversing that remote countryside with its scattered 'borings' where soldiers, nowadays, seemed engaged on perpetual manoeuvres. The soldiers were there: but the Military Orchid remained, as it probably always would remain, unfound.

One day, with another botanist, I walked up to Three Barrows Down, a beech plantation on a hill-top, near Snowdown Colliery.

We were in search of an orchid – a rare one: perhaps this was the only place in the whole of England where it could be found.

I had been there before: isolated on its hill, reached by a narrow track impassable to cars, the spot was always deserted. Today, however, as we reached the top of the hill, we found the wood surrounded by soldiers. It was a hot day in August: they were in shirt-sleeve order, and sat about in groups under the hedge, sweating. As we passed they grinned at us, and we could catch crude bursts of laughter, snatches of talk; their voices, raw and demonic, fell oddly on the sunlit summer silence: it was like the sudden whiff of beer and stale sweat from a public-bar.

The three barrows lay diagonally across the plantation: once this had been open downland; today, tall beeches sprang from the tombs, their roots imprisoning more firmly, year after year, the warrior-bones below. Outside the wood, the troops had fallen-in again: words of command rang out sharply through the trees. The living soldiers marched away; only the dead remained.

'It ought to be about here,' my friend remarked.

And there it was: the little green Helleborine, modest and insignificant, waving gently in the breeze which blew perpetually through these upland beeches. Its flowers were not open: they never would open, for the Helleborine had long ago solved the sexual problem for itself by becoming self-fertile. Not only did the flowers not open, but the thin, papery lip withered in the bud, the rostellum was evanescent. The Helleborine seemed to have given up the unequal struggle: it was a case of floral introversion, an evolutionary retrogression to the auto-erotic phase.

We left the wood: the soldiers had moved off, but the heavy August air seemed infected with the very smell of war. Beyond the dark summer woods, the colliery-chimney rose like the smoking fuse of some firework: a Mine of Serpents at whose vast subterranean potency one could only guess. On the path at the wood's fringe, near the barrows, I had discovered a spot where the ground under one's feet rang curiously hollow; and I could imagine, as I had imagined long years ago, that dark kingdom beneath the sunlit downland, the black-faced naked men swarming in their airless labyrinth. The still afternoon seemed heavy with menace: were these dark men of the underworld about to rise up and overwhelm us?

We came out, at last, on to higher ground: and saw, above the distant woods, the white cap of the watertower. Remote, mysterious, it flashed its sudden signal across the sunburned fields: but the message was one which I had never been, perhaps never should be, able to decode . . .

One day, in London, I walked casually into a bar, and, as I ordered a drink, met the eyes of a heavily-built middle-aged man, clean-shaven and running to fat. I looked at him: a gleam of recognition flickered in his eyes.

It was Basil Medlicott.

Basil, in his time, had provided me with several surprises; but I had never been so taken aback as I was on this occasion. I had to think hard for several seconds before I recognized him: when I did, I was so shocked that I could hardly return his greeting coherently.

'So you've returned, have you,' he accosted me, 'to your vomit?'

The voice, at least, was unchanged: he spoke with all the old irony, to which was added, now a tinge of personal malice.

'How are you, Basil?' I said, in no particular tone. I still felt rather ill-disposed towards him, on account of that five pounds.

'I'm glad to see you looking better,' he said. 'I was really afraid, last time I saw you, that you were doomed to an early grave.'

The inverted commas were as audible as ever. Basil hadn't really changed at all: except (and I realized that this was what had really shocked me) that he had shaved off his moustache.

Afterwards, looking at him more attentively, I noticed other details: he was shabbier, definitely; his cuffs were frayed, his tie crumpled; his shoes, even, were not very clean. His teeth had begun to decay, too; and his hair was thinner.

A tacit agreement established itself immediately between us: the topics of (1) our quarrel over the five pounds and (2) his recent 'scandal' were barred. We conversed with a vapid conventionality for ten minutes, then parted.

A week or two later I met him again; once more we talked pointlessly but amicably over a drink: if there was war, Basil said, he would get back to the Army – he was still on some kind of reserve, apparently.

'But I don't think the necessity will arise,' he added, with his old air of having 'inside knowledge'.

'What, you don't think there's going to be war? Of course there will be,' I retorted.

Curiosity made me rather tactless: I asked him if he was still living apart from his wife. He said he was: and evasively changed the subject.

Later, on the same evening, I met him again. He was drunk: more obviously so than I had ever seen him. He began to talk about his 'case': I had rather expected him to do so sooner or later.

The story, as he gave it, was indistinguishable from all his other stories: a complex and interminable analysis of one 'conspiracy' after another. I gathered, dimly, that Stalin himself had been particularly anxious to establish Basil's guilt; the course of the Spanish War had hinged on it almost entirely; as for Chamberlain, his week-ends at Chequers had been constantly interrupted, it seemed, by the *affaire* Medlicott; Mrs Simpson had been obscurely involved; the Pope himself had referred, obliquely, to the affair in an encyclical . . .

If either Basil or myself had been sober, I might have been ruder than I was; as it happened, I had drunk just enough to make me tolerant. I laughed; I laughed loudly and for a long time. And to his eternal credit, Basil began to laugh too. Our laughter was a kind of mutual purge: the dreary, crisis-ridden years fell away, he became the Basil I had met at Dover, the Army officer who was a friend of my brother. He became, almost, the Basil whom I had hero-worshipped as a child: almost, but not (for I had certain reservations) quite.

After this, a curious renewal of friendship took place between us: our tacit agreement not to talk about the past – having been once, rewardingly, broken – was resumed. The distant past of my childhood was excepted: Basil seemed to have developed a romantic nostalgia for the first War, and would talk about it, if allowed, for hours at a time. Plainly he was longing for another war, whether or not he believed it was coming.

Only once did he ever revert to the affair of the five pounds: referring to it, in passing, and with an ironically malicious glint of the eye, as 'a certain *contretemps* which at one time, I regret to say, marred our friendship.'

It occurred to me, at last, to ask him what he was doing: and to my astonishment – but I was used to Basil's surprises by this time – he told me that he was on the Stock Exchange.

'In a rather minor capacity, of course, at present,' he qualified. (I could have guessed as much from his appearance, though I didn't say so.) 'But,' he added, 'I hope before long to be rich beyond the *dreams* of avarice.'

At midday on 3 September 1939 Lady Miniver (it is kinder to call her that) drove down the village street in a large car, shouting: 'Take cover! Take cover! The warning's gone! There's an air-raid!'

There wasn't, and nobody did. I went along to the pub to get some beer and cigarettes.

'So there's a war on, is there?' said Mr Peacock, the landlord.

Mr Iggledsen said:

'This War, it's going to upset everybody.'

'What *I* want to know,' said Jim Hawkes, 'is what's going to win the 2.30.'

'Them hops up at Spantons' ain't no bloody good this year, say what you like,' said John Quested. He paused for a moment, swallowed half a pint of mild, and added: 'Nor his apples ain't neither.'

I went home and finished writing a paper, for the *Journal of Botany* on the distribution of *Orchis simia* in Great Britain.

At four o'clock in the afternoon there was a knock at the door. I went to open it. There, in his old tweeds and his pork-pie hat and his Paisley tie, stood Basil. He carried an Army gas-mask slung over his shoulder.

'Hullo,' he said. 'Thought I'd look you up. I'm stationed at Dover.'

He looked fitter and more confident than he had looked for years. I noticed, too, that he had begun to grow his moustache again.

Tea on the lawn: 'It'll be over by Christmas,' said Basil. 'I know Germany fairly well, you know, and I'm certain they didn't want this war.'

Later he told me that he was reconciled with his wife. We walked up over the park: Basil had to catch a bus back to Dover. While we waited for it, we sat on the edge of the dip, near the roadside, known as 'Old England's Hole'. Local legend asserted that the Britons had entrenched themselves here in some last, desperate stand against the advancing Romans. The place today seemed curiously depressing: overgrown with ash and elder and dark clumps of Deadly Nightshade. Somebody had dumped a pile of empty tins under an ash-tree, and someone else had apparently used the place, quite recently, as a lavatory.

'Well,' said Basil, rising, 'I suppose this is where we say an affectionate but, I regret to add, a *long* farewell.' His voice had the old irony: his eyes glinted with a malicious appreciation of his own absurdity.

I walked with him down to the road. Perhaps I should never see him again. Did I really mind? He was hardly one of my best friends; he never had been. He wasn't even a romantic spy: I retained no vestige of faith in Basil's self-engendered myth. Yet something did remain: something – a faint tug at the heart – made itself felt as I took his hand to say good-bye. I had a fleeting vision of people sitting on a lawn, a glimpse of white flannel trousers ...

The bus arrived. Basil climbed on to it. Just as it began to move, he leaned out of the window and said:

'I'm sorry I never took you to that show.'

PART FIVE

Lost Island

Mon coeur, mon coeur, ne retrouveras-tu
que dans la mort cet immense amour
pour ceux que tu n'as pas connus
en ces tendres et défunts jours?

FRANCIS JAMMES

I

'Lady Winsleigh raised her head, and her eyes met his with a dark expression of the uttermost anger. "Spy!" she hissed between her teeth – then, without further word or gesture, she swept haughtily away into her dressing-room, which adjoined the boudoir ...'

It was a morning of thundery rain, and I had taken refuge in the Libreria Internazionale in the Via Tornabuoni. Here, at the back of the shop, I had discovered an unsuspected treasure-trove: shelf upon shelf of late-Victorian and Edwardian novels, in the Tauchnitz edition. Most of the authors weren't even names to me; we know far more, nowadays, about the minor writers of, say the eighteenth century than about those of forty years ago. Who, for instance, were Hamilton Aïdé, Lizzie Alldridge, Baroness de Bury? Popular novelists in their time, presumably, or they wouldn't have got into Tauchnitz ... It was a sad lookout, I thought, for the Priestleys and Charles Morgans of our own day.

I lighted, with relief, upon Marie Corelli. The authoress of *Thelma*, I thought (opening the book in the middle), had this much in common with Kafka, Sartre or Mauriac: plenty of people (including myself) took her for granted without having read a word of her books.

For me, her name exhaled the very odour of late-Victorian *chic*; one thought of plush, palms, mimosa and 'queenly' women with plenty of *embonpoint*. I associated her, vaguely, with the smart and slightly dubious Miss Trumpett who, in my childhood, used to come to tea at our country cottage. Marie Corelli, I suppose, was one of the most triumphant successes in the history of the novel. Why? I decided to buy *Thelma* and find out.

I read about half of it that very morning, sitting in a café. But my question was still largely unanswered. *Thelma* bore the sub-title: 'A Society Novel'. It was full of queenly figures sweeping out of boudoirs, costly napery, swan-like necks, immaculate evening-dress and so on. There was plenty of sex dished-up in the under-the-counter fashion of the period ... But it didn't seem any better, judged by its own standards, than a host of other 'Society novels' of the same date. It might, indeed, have supplied a certain amount of wish-fulfilment for servant-girls; doubtless it had: but Marie Corelli achieved more than this: she was taken perfectly seriously by the middle-brow library public, and more than half-seriously by the highbrows themselves.

Had she not written (from amid the palms and plush of Wampach's Hotel, Folkestone) to Millais, the painter of *Bubbles*, to protest against the use of this masterpiece as a soap-advertisement? Without success, as it happened; but Millais had at least written her a serious and considered reply. Marie Corelli, undoubtedly, was a force to be reckoned with in the aesthetic world of 1885.

Again, why? For it is, surely, rather as though Mr Augustus John should cross swords, on a purely aesthetic issue, with (say) Miss Denise Robins. The mystery remains, so far as I am concerned, a mystery; but once again, it suggests an unhappy prognosis for the future of *Sparkenbroke* or *Angel Pavement*.

It is probably salutary, for a writer, to take an occasional course of downright, honest-to-God Badness. Not the luke-warm, competent badness of the average twopenny-library standard; but the real thing, the wild, uninhibited, baroque badness of somebody like Marie Corelli.

I had recently, as it happened, taken a course of badness myself: badness of an earlier period than Miss Corelli's, and of a flavour more subdued; but badness, none the less – hopeless and irreclaimable.

All through my adult life, I had been haunted by a large black box which, carefully locked, was kept in one of my father's cupboards. It contained letters, manuscripts and various documents belonging to my great-grandfather, Joseph Hewlett, author of *Peter Priggins* and a number of other 'humorous' novels. There was a suitcase, too, containing the novels themselves – grubby, drab-looking three-deckers of the forties and fifties. I had often thought of 'doing something about' Hewlett – writing an article about him, or even a small monograph. It was partly an affair of family piety; but it would be fun, too, to 'revive' Hewlett, perhaps to establish a cult for him. Other people had been forgotten and then revivified – Trollope, for instance. Why not Hewlett?

Besides, from what little I knew of him, there was something rather sympathetic about my great-grandfather. He had been a writer; he had gone (like myself) to Worcester; he was (like the *Flopsy Bunnies*) 'very improvident and cheerful' – always an attractive combination; he had a weakness, moreover (like myself, again) for what his friend Thomas Hood referred to discreetly as 'potations'.

Why not 'revive' him?

The answer, alas! came all too promptly. I had not spent ten minutes on *Peter Priggins* before I realized that it couldn't be done. Poor Hewlett was no forgotten, neglected Trollope; he was just downright Bad.

One of his closest friends was Tom Hood; and *Peter Priggins*, I found, exhibited on a lower plane all the qualities in which Hood excelled – the qualities of the English comic tradition in its decadence. There were echoes (distant ones) of Sterne, and (less distant) of Surtees; puns abounded, but puns far worse than Hood's. For the rest, an irritating facetiousness prevailed, a boguslyhearty goodfellowship sprinkled with Latin tags – the Muscular Christian getting matey in the smoking-room.

I turned from *Peter Priggins* to the box of letters and manuscripts. Letters from Hood, Harrison Ainsworth, R. H. ('Ingoldsby') Barham; letters from publishers and editors – Colburn, Bentley, Theodore Hook. From the dingy background of Grub Street in the 'thirties and 'forties, the figure of Hewlett gradually emerged – shadowy, incomplete, but with a genuine character of his own ...

He was born, according to his own account, in the Tottenham Court Road on 30 April 1800. He was educated at Charterhouse – whence, however, at the age of eighteen, he was expelled; for what reason is not recorded. In 1819 he went up to Worcester; took his degree in 1822; and in 1824 married a cousin and, almost in the same breath, entered Holy Orders. Four years later he was appointed to the Headmastership of the Grammar School at Abingdon.

But Hewlett was not fitted for a career of pedagogy – he was too 'improvident' by half, and too fond, no doubt, of 'potations'. Moreover, his wife proved to be at once overfertile and totally incompetent as a housewife. 'She was unable,' remarks an anonymous obituarist, 'from want of tact in management, to keep his house in order.' To make up for this, she achieved the remarkable feat of producing seventeen children in eighteen years.

The family struggled along at Abingdon for eleven years, becoming steadily more improvident but not, one imagines, more cheerful ... In a brave effort to eke out his pedagogue's salary, Hewlett began to write; but success was slow in coming, and meanwhile things were getting worse. In 1840, he resigned his appointment, and was presented to the living of Letcombe Regis.

Here he prospered better; as a country parson, he found more time to write. Soon Colburn and Bentley began to publish his stories and articles; he became acquainted with Theodore Hook, and formed a fast friendship with Hood. But his health now began to fail; he was afflicted by attacks of 'muco-gastritis', about which Hood wrote to him, as usual, in a vein of rather flippant sympathy: 'Dreadful is that enforced temperance which forbids the animal spirits – mine are apt to get sometimes far below proof ...' Later, he adds that he himself has taken to drinking punch – which was not much consolation to poor Hewlett.

In 1842, the Hewlett family removed to Little Stambridge, in Essex. The move was in every respect disastrous. The village was situated in the middle of a snipe-bog; the population was ravaged by ague; there was not even a rectory to live in – a fact that the Bishop had apparently overlooked; Hewlett was compelled to build a cottage at his own expense ... Two years later his wife died. With a renewed ardour born of desperation, he continued to write. His output was astonishing: he must have written at least half-a-dozen full-length novels in half as many years, besides sketching-out others and producing, in addition, an unending flow of articles for *Bentley's Miscellany, The New Monthly Magazine* and the rest. Would Mr Colburn be prepared to buy the copyright of an historical novel (unwritten) about Cardinal Wolsey? Could Mr Bentley be persuaded to consider 'a novel about life in Wales'?

Negotiations with Grub Street were interminable and exasperating. Things would have been much easier if Hewlett could have got to London more frequently; Hood plied him with invitations – to parties, to dinners, to meet R. H. Barham, or young Mr Dickens; Hewlett's own novels were enjoying a mild success, and his friends wanted him there to celebrate. But he was ill; his children, one after another, sickened of the ague; he was busy on the novel about 'life in Wales'; the coach-fare was beyond his means. Everything conspired to prevent the trip to London ... He scarcely had time even to answer his letters:

'This will be the third letter I have addressed to you without receiving an answer,' complains Bentley, who had reluctantly bought for £250 the copyright of his (still unwritten) novel about Cardinal Wolsey ...

Things went from bad to worse. Hewlett had always published anonymously, for fear of his Bishop's disapproval; now Colburn, by some oversight, had let the cat out of the bag, and the Bishop was alarmed to discover that the author of those racy and frivolous novels about Oxford was none other than the Rector of Little Stambridge ...

In 1845 Hood died; it was a crushing blow for Hewlett. His wife was dead; eight of his seventeen children had followed her – victims, in most cases, of the lethal climate of Little Stambridge. And now his best friend had been taken from him as well ...

'Another winter here,' he wrote, 'if I should live to see it, will, I am convinced, kill me; but how to avoid it?'

How indeed? Still desperately poor, chronically ill, and with nine children to support, he struggled on: articles poured from his pen, he began the novel about Wolsey, made copious notes for half-a-dozen others, including the one about life in Wales ... He refused to give in; but Little Stambridge, with its malarious snipe-bogs, was too much for him. His parish-clerk died; even his dog succumbed to the miasma: 'The faithful companion of my walking hours died this morning of an inflamed throat, of precisely the same nature as that from which his master is still suffering ... Who is to be the next victim?'

The next victim was Mrs Smith, his housekeeper, who died on 3 January 1847.

Hewlett surrendered at last. 'I cannot work with my pen,' he wrote. 'Imagination is swamped by realities, fiction falls before truth.'

Before the end of the month he was dead himself.

It is obvious, from his novels, bad as they are, that Hewlett suffered, all his adult life, from an incurable nostalgia for Oxford. Doubtless Worcester, with its austere eighteenth-century quad. and its swan-haunted lake, became for him a symbol of past happiness: the greatest – perhaps the only – happiness he had ever known. Had he been able to win a fellowship, he might have been happier: the scholarly life, with its mild conviviality, would have suited him. Instead, it was his fate to become a popular novelist and the father of a large family: two activities for which he was eminently unsuited.

My researches, after all, had told me little enough about him: he loved writing (however badly); he loved wine; he looked backward nostalgically to better days, and lived in a state of constant anxiety about the future ... Charming, pleasure-loving, rather futile – a kind of Hew Dallas of his age, perhaps – his restless ghost still haunts, for me, the streets of Abingdon and the quiet gardens of Worcester; the shabby, unhappy ghost of a bad writer who, given more favourable conditions, might perhaps have succeeded in writing a good book. But the conditions never materialized; neither, alas! did the book. *Peter Priggins* remains a mere 'curiosity', a rare item in collections of Victoriana.

Yet Hewlett, in his time, had his admirers ...

'The other day,' writes Hood to Hewlett, 'Miss Lamb (Elia's sister) was here, an excellent old creature, with as much masculine sense as womanly feeling – she is mad occasionally, but in her lucid intervals enjoys as much intellect as many who have their wits all the year round. Well, she highly praised some paper in the Magazine[1] which she said had caused her to shed tears, and on my inquiry, turned out to be your story ...'

II

At Fiesole, the crimson gladioli in the cornfields had given place to poppies and blue cornflowers. Fields of sainfoin stained the hillsides with patches of dusky pink; and here and there, at the

[1] Probably *Hood's Magazine*, to which Hewlett contributed.

borders of fields and copses, the tall blue irises unfurled their resplendent banners; heraldic flowers, flaunting the brave insignia of Florence and the Medicis.

Beneath the grey haze of the olives, the poppies lay in drifts of arterial scarlet; in the copses, the crickets had begun their arid, interminable scraping, and the cuckoo changed his tune. Summer broke over the land with a harsh, uncompromising violence; my time was getting short, and I began to be haunted, again, by the vision of that cloud-cuckoo-land beyond the Apennines: the remote blue hills of Scerni and Pollutri, the archaic song of the reapers in the breast-high corn, the women spinning in the doorways . . .

I would book a ticket that very day; there was no time to be lost; only ten days remained of my holiday . . . But I remembered suddenly that today was a *festa*: the travel-agencies would be closed; I should have to leave it till tomorrow . . .

I walked up the stony track which wound its way through the *macchia* far up into the hills. The sun blazed mercilessly down from the hot, cobalt sky. The morning seemed immensely silent, with a quality of timeless desolation: it was the 'pious morn', fixed in a classic, sunlit eternity, of Keats's *Grecian Urn*:

> . . . and not a soul to tell
> Why thou art desolate, can e'er return.

Further up the path, among the broom and cistus, a company of Italian soldiers was engaged upon some unexacting, leisurely manoeuvre. Their grey-green uniforms merged in the undergrowth, they lay immobile as lizards beneath the chequered shade. Their presence, suddenly detected, came as a slight shock; I had almost passed them unawares, when a flickering eyelid, a finger shifting its grip on a gun-barrel, betrayed them. I was suddenly disquietingly aware of being surrounded; from weed-grown hollows, from beneath tufts of honeysuckle, one brown face after another stared out at me, intently, as I passed. They seemed the indigenous fauna of this Tuscan countryside: shy, watchful creatures, not dangerous, but none the less faintly inimical; goat-footed, possibly, and covered, below the navel, with thick, matted hair . . . One of them grinned at me as I passed: a sudden flash of white teeth in a patch of brown shade.

I passed on, coming out on the higher ground; a grassy, bushy slope swept down to a valley, with a farmhouse, like some natural outcrop of the soil, perched on a level promontory half-way down. I walked down the narrow track, between massy bowers of honeysuckle. Suddenly my eye was caught by a tall slender plant: a curious bearded spike of purplish-green blossom, standing up boldly above the tussock grasses. I looked more closely; and, with an extraordinary spasm of excitement, recognized it for what it was.

It was the Lizard Orchid: that legendary flower, most celebrated of English 'rarities', which I had sought for, year after year, on the Kentish chalk-lands – but without success. Once I had seen it; it had been found at last, by my old nurse, in 1924, and had been sent to me at Bedales, where I had proudly exhibited it in Mr Bickersteth's 'show' in the Biology Lab. But I had never seen it growing. And here, raising its fantastic head among the grasses, rooted and autochthonous as any other Tuscan weed – here was the half-mythical object of all my years of fruitless search; here was the dream made flesh at last, the myth incarnate.

I searched among the bushes, and other spikes revealed themselves. Once detected, they seemed, like the soldiers, to be ubiquitous; once again, I was surrounded: but this time by presences which offered themselves, rooted and without power to resist, to my desires.

I picked a spike; to *pick* a Lizard Orchid – the action had about it something unholy, something rather blasphemous ... I picked several more; examining with a wondering delight the long, slender lips, two inches long, cleft at the tip like serpents' tongues, unfurling themselves in delicate spirals from the opening buds.

Walking over the parklands of the Elham Valley, in those remote, magical summers of childhood – nineteen-eighteen, nineteen-nineteen – how often had I darted forward, my eye caught by some tall, upright plant, convinced that at last I had found what I sought! But alas! it proved always to be a *trompe d'oeil* – a slender hawthorn sapling, or a grey-budded spike of mullein. But here, on this Tuscan hillside, nearly thirty years later, it was no hawthorn or mullein that raised its august form among the grasses; it was, beyond any possibility of doubt, *Himantoglossum hircinum*, the Lizard Orchid.

Even as I looked at it, I found myself, quite unconsciously, humming a tune which for a quarter of a century had almost certainly never entered my head. It was a tune from one of those *revues* of the first world war whose forbidden glories had haunted my childhood; one of those 'shows' which my brother or Basil Medlicott had described for me so vividly, but which I had never been allowed to go to . . .

I had gone, instead, to *Peter Pan*; but the tunes from *Bubbly* – that was the name of this particular 'show' – had never quite lost for me their aura of romance. Whistled by my brother and his friends – those semi-divine inhabitants of Lost Island – they were the tunes of heroes, the musical equivalent of all that I regarded, at that time, as admirable, heroic and (for myself) hopelessly unattainable. Walking over the Kentish hills, in 1918, alert for those serpent-tongued and bearded spikes which never revealed themselves, I had hummed to myself the tunes from *Bubbly*. And now, on this Tuscan hillside in 1947, I found myself humming them again; impregnated with their hoarded associations – visions of heroes, of sunbaked chalkhills, of mysterious and thrilling 'improprieties' – they seemed to me as beautiful as Mozart. They were not; but in such matters, one's critical faculty is apt to let one down.

And after all, I had found the Lizard Orchid.

Only the sense of smell, perhaps, is more evocative of the past than those sudden-heard melodies which leap upon us, without warning, from a café band, a wireless set, or the lips of an errand-boy . . . They can, of course, make their assault from within, as well as from without: no errand-boy, no wireless even, could today have restored to me the forgotten tunes from *Bubbly* . . .

Next day I went to Florence; and journeying down in the packed *filobus*, my mind was haunted again by a tune – not *Bubbly* this time, but Solveig's Song from *Peer Gynt* . . . I was on my way to inquire, once again, how I could get across to the Abruzzi; I would go to the American Express, this time – they were said to be more efficient and more obliging than Cook's . . . But in the bus I was not thinking, particularly, of the American Express, or of the Abruzzi; I was thinking, in fact, of nothing at all. The notices and advertisements impinged vaguely on my consciousness: Vermut alla Crema Pini; Leggete *La Nazione*; Non parlare al guidatore . . . The Pini Vermouth advertisement had a picture of a grinning red devil, which I found obscurely irritating . . . It is just such banal and trivial details which, alas! we remember from a foreign journey; months hence, when I had forgotten, very probably, the Masaccio frescoes, or the Capella degli Spagnoli, I should remember the little Pini devil; for, unlike the Chapel or the frescoes (which I had viewed with a conscious effort) the vermouth-imp had insinuated himself, almost unnoticed, during my frequent trips on the *filobus*, into the deepest recesses of my subconscious; and once there, he would be exceedingly difficult to dislodge.

I became aware, once again, that I was still half-consciously humming Solveig's Song to myself; and the sudden, conscious recognition of the fact, brought me to a stop . . . I was transported, instantly, to the Abruzzi; it was the early spring of 1944, and I was walking, with my friend Kurt Schlegel, down a winding track through the hills towards the valley of the Sinello. It was a grey, wintry afternoon; streaks of snow lingered on the hillsides; but under the leafless hedges, the scented white narcissi were already showing among the dead drenched grasses. It was a silent, rather melancholy walk; we were both rather preoccupied. As he walked, Kurt sang to himself: a tuneless drone, repeated over and over again, which I at length recognized as Solveig's Song. I began to hum it myself: it seemed, somehow, appropriate to the grey, northern-seeming landscape . . .

Weeks later, I went the same way again, by myself; and walking down the track, I found myself whistling the melody from the slow movement of Grieg's Piano Concerto . . . Thereafter – for we often walked that way during the next few months – the path down to the Sinello was haunted, even in the heat of midsummer, by a cool Nordic ghost . . . Sometimes it was Solveig's Song; sometimes the Concerto, or *Im Frühling*, or Anitra's dance.

'I think,' said Kurt, 'that Grieg perhaps was once living in this place, isn't it?'

Today, three years later, I was on my way to book a ticket for Vasto; my mind was occupied by nothing more relevant to my purpose than an advertisement for vermouth; yet secretly, insidiously, a part of myself had stolen back already, across the years, to that afternoon walk with Kurt Schlegel; and I found myself humming, once again, the song which had haunted that ultramontane and desolate landscape.

At the American Express office in the Via Tornabuoni, I was received by a very civil young Italian, who spoke English with a broad American accent.

'The Abruzzi?' he grinned. 'Why, I guess that's a queer place to go.'

'Yes, I know,' I said resignedly. 'But I want to go there, all the same. Can you tell me the best way of getting to Vasto?'

He produced a very large and efficient-looking map of Southern Italy.

'Vasto?' he asked, wrinkling his brow. 'I don't seem to know that place ...'

'Somewhere here,' I said, running my finger down the Adriatic coast. I knew approximately where it was – just above the bulge that sticks out at the top of Apulia. I looked more closely – there was Termoli, there was Ortona, clearly marked; but not Vasto.

The young man ran his finger a little further down.

'Do you mean Vieste?' he asked helpfully.

'No, Vasto – V–a–s–t–o. It *must* be on the map – it's quite a good-sized little town.'

'Well, it doesn't mark it,' he said

And it didn't. Vasto wasn't on the map. Yet I had seen it, I felt sure, on other maps ... Or had I? Perhaps – a disturbing thought struck me – perhaps I had invented the name in some story I had written about the War. I *had* invented names, certainly. But Vasto? Suddenly I remembered something. Gabriele Rossetti, father of Dante Gabriel, was born there; he was even, I fancied, commemorated by a *piazza* named after him ... I tried to explain this to the young man; but he had never heard of Rossetti ... I began to wonder, rather wildly, if I had invented the whole Pre-raphaelite Brotherhood ...

The young man was very patient. On the assumption that Vasto was roughly where I said it was (though he was plainly sceptical), he worked out the itinerary. It was the same old story; I should either have to go up to Bologna or down to Naples; both journeys were long and somewhat hazardous. The best way probably would be to fly to Naples ... But my money was running short, and I couldn't afford trips by air. I thanked the young man and left him: wondering, still, if Vasto were a myth, and, supposing it were not, whether I had, in reality, ever been there.

III

In the afternoon, I went down to bathe in the Arno. In the town, a sudden heat-wave had made an inferno of the narrow streets; but here, on the dam, a fresh breeze blew up river, tempering the blazing sun with a Nordic coolness.

I lay on the flat, sun-baked top of the dam, and watched the girls and children paddling from the muddy strand below. Serious bathing was only possible from the dam itself: it was scattered, this afternoon, with young men and boys, roasting themselves like lizards in the first summer heat. A young man I knew ran past me, pursued by another; overtaken, he came to grips with his pursuer, and they began to wrestle; their muscular bodies heaving and straining as though in some ecstatic sculpture of Giambologna.

Presently the one I knew broke away, and turned to me with a grin.

'*Come va?*' he saluted me.

His name was Guido; he was a clerk, and came to bathe in the *siesta* time; I had met him here a few days before. At first, he had taken me for an American – probably a rich one; he wanted to know all about America: one day, when he had saved up enough, he was going there . . . I had explained that I was English, and not at all rich; but at this he had become more friendly than ever, and had insisted that I go to dinner one night, with his Aunt and Uncle, with whom he lived. Himself, he came from the Abruzzi, he was full of local patriotism, and was delighted to hear that I thought of going there.

'So you are still here?' he smiled. 'I thought perhaps you had gone away, without saying *addio*.'

'No,' I said, 'I'm still here.'

'*Va bene.* Then you can come to dinner tonight. It will not be a special dinner, you understand – just what we usually eat. The prices are terrible, it is difficult to eat well nowadays . . . But I shall go home before I return to work, and tell *la Zia* that you are coming.'

Knowing my Italians, I realized perfectly well that Guido intended to give me a vast and succulent meal such as *la Zia* would probably only prepare once in a blue moon. I didn't see why she should be put to the trouble, and I tried to get out of it.

But Guido would take no refusal.

'You are coming – that is certain. *E sicurissimo* . . . Do you like red or white wine?'

'I like red, but really – '

'*Va bene,* so do I. It is better for the stomach. Come at eight o'clock – no, half past eight, because I like to shave when I get home, before the *pranzo*. Come when you like – we shall be pleased to see you any time. You are my friend, I am very glad to have an English friend. *Sono carini, gli inglesi.*'

He began to do hand-turns along the top of the dam; finally he lost his balance, and went in with a splash. He rose with a burst of laughter, tossing back his black hair.

'Do you like *prosciutto?*' he asked, climbing out again.

I said yes, I did: forgetting for the moment about tonight's dinner.

'Good. Then we shall eat *prosciutto* tonight.'

Smoked ham was expensive, I knew; I wished I had sounded less enthusiastic.

'Listen,' he said suddenly. 'When do you go to the Abruzzi?'

I said I had more or less given up the idea; it was too far, my time was getting short, I was broke.

'Did you go to the American Express as I told you?'

Yes, I had been to the American Express. But I couldn't afford the fare.

'Wait – if you go partly by bus it is cheap. You go first to Bologna – '

In spite of my protests, he insisted on planning the journey for me all over again. He overruled all my objections firmly, one after another. What was twenty-four hours in a train, he asked contemptuously? Why, he had once travelled all the way from Messina to Milan; to go from Florence to Ortona was a mere nothing . . .

To a native, I thought, no doubt it *was* a mere nothing; where travelling was concerned, Italians possessed a quality of heroic endurance which, as soldiers, they conspicuously lacked.

'And think – is it not worth it? When you get there you will think so – *é sicurissimo*. I have planned it all; you will go and stay with my people – my father is dead, but my mother is there and my elder brother and my two sisters. They will be good to you because of me. You will eat well and drink well – our wine is famous in the province of Chieti ... Tonight I shall write a letter and arrange everything; my brother Umberto shall meet you at Ortona with the *carrozza*.'

I assured him again that I really had decided not to go; and even as I spoke, I felt tempted to change my mind – to make the journey at all costs.

'Ah, it is a good country,' Guido went on. 'The people are good, too. Listen: would you like to meet the most beautiful girl in the world? Good: then I shall introduce you to her. I shall write to her brother tonight ... I have only met her once, you understand – at a wedding-party; but she was the most beautiful girl I have ever seen ...'

She was seventeen, very dark, very slim, with a profile like some picture in the Pitti – he couldn't remember the painter, but there was a reproduction of it hanging in the *gabinetto* at his Uncle's house. I should look at it tonight ... The girl was the daughter of a notary in Casalbordino. Perhaps I would marry her, and then I should come and live in Italy, in Florence perhaps, and we would all be the greatest friends. He would be so proud, he said, to have an English friend, and it would be better still if I was *sposato* to an Italian girl. He would write to the brother that very night ...

It was useless to protest. I fell silent, allowing Guido to arrange my future for me as best suited him. I was to have at least a dozen children; I was to become a Catholic; I must buy a villa at Viareggio, or, if I liked, further south, at Amalfi ... I closed my eyes, and nearly slept. Offended, Guido leapt up without warning and pushed me into the river. I climbed out, and returned the compliment.

'And when you are married to the notary's daughter,' he continued, as though nothing had occurred to interrupt him, 'I shall be godfather to all your *bambini, non è vero?*'

At dinner that night with Guido's relations it was taken for granted that I was leaving for the Abruzzi the very next morning. It was assumed, moreover, scarcely less definitely, that once there, I should marry the notary's daughter. The picture in the Pitti – a Perugino–was removed from its home in the lavatory and handed round ...

The dinner itself was enough to sap anybody's resolution. I had scarcely ever eaten so much in my life. *Prosciutto, pasta*, calf's liver fried with sage, salad, cheese, fruit ... *La Zia* apologized profusely because there was no coffee. It was impossible to get the sugar for it, she said.

I left them at last, and on my way home at midnight – I was putting up for the night in Florence – I turned into a wineshop for a drink. After such a dinner, it was useless to go to bed for at least a couple of hours.

I sat near the doorway, drinking my wine, and looking out at the still-crowded pavements; watching the faces of the girls and young men as they strolled past, and every now and then glimpsing some face whose uncanny beauty caught at my heart with a wild, nostalgic pain ... Was I really taking the bus to Bologna tomorrow afternoon? During dinner and the hours which followed it, I had agreed to the project, merely to avoid argument; and little by little I had almost begun to believe in it myself ...

But I knew, after all, that I wouldn't go. As Imogen had said, it was better to keep one's illusions; and no illusions could be expected to survive that journey ... Besides, I was broke.

Once more the vision recurred of those low, soft-contoured hills, and the little valleys dropping down to the Sinello ... I recalled the wild, haunted remoteness of that land; the men like sculpture, the women like princesses in a mediaeval tapestry. I remembered the farmhouse with the open door – the firm, still centre of my shifting vision ... Was it, in fact, a vision of reality? Or had I invented it, as I must have seemed, to the young man at the American Express, to have invented Vasto? Was my vision of that land nothing, after all, but a projection of my own nostalgia for something I could never possess: a romantic Lost Island inhabited by the heroes of a private myth?

IV

It was my last night. They were giving *Bohème* in the Boboli Gardens, and I had booked tickets for Guido and myself. It was a special treat for him: he was very excited. He deserved his treat, I thought, after that dinner ...

The opera was supposed to begin at 9.30; as usual, in Italy, it didn't begin till 10.30. But the setting made such *longueurs* more tolerable than usual. The stage was set in a frame of dark, towering ilexes, among which the flood-lit statuary shone forth with a dramatic intensity. Fountains played in a tempered, cloudy moonlight; fireflies danced among the thickets. Only in Italy, where *lo spettacolo* is the very breath of life, could stage-management have scored such a triumph.

We waited, without impatience –

> Au calme clair de lune triste et beau,
> Qui fait rêver les oiseaux dans les arbres
> Et sangloter d'extase les jets d'eau,
> Les grands jets d'eau sveltes parmi les marbres.

At last the opera began. The performance wasn't anything outstanding; but we were in a mood to be tolerant. After the first act, there was an interval of three-quarters of an hour. We had a drink at the open-air bar behind the 'auditorium'. The 'house' was packed out: there wasn't a vacant seat.

'It is only since the War we have this *spettacolo* here,' said Guido. 'Before the War, you see, the garden belonged to the King.'

Presently we made our way back, and the second act began – the Café Scene. The Musetta knew how to act, and the comic passages went with a swing. Soon it was over, and we strolled to the bar for another drink.

'You know,' said Guido, 'you ought to have gone to the Abruzzi ...'

Even as he spoke, a series of deafening explosions burst upon our ears. Conditioned by six years of war, I ducked my head; it was exactly as though a heavy ack-ack barrage had started up. Then I saw that the crowd was staring skywards; I looked up too – just in time to see a fan-shaped burst of silver fire dropping in a dazzling rain above the trees.

'*Fuochi d'artificio!*' exclaimed Guido.

The third act of the opera was due to begin; but nobody thought of going back while the fireworks were on; besides, it would be impossible to sing through the incessant popping and banging. The opera would have to wait.

Just as in Hyde Park in 1918, we were too far away to see anything but the shells and rockets; but these, by themselves, were of a splendour such as I had never seen before – not even at the grandest Crystal Palace displays. The rockets rose in immense flights, fanning out across the sky like some dazzling aurora borealis; the shells blossomed into an endless and fantastic series of metamorphoses: showers of stars exploding into other stars, writhing congeries of serpents bursting in sudden magnesium brilliance, showers of silver and gold changing to rubies and emeralds ...

There was no post-war austerity, I thought, about Italian fireworks; or if there was, what must they have been before the War? There was an extravagance, a total lack of inhibition about this display which took one's breath away. By contrast, the best English fireworks I could remember seemed banal and unimaginative – infected by our native puritanism, our distaste for the extravagant gesture.

'*Bellissima!*' exclaimed Guido. He was as excited as any child of ten. He clapped his hands; he banged me between the shoulder-blades; he seized my hand in his, and squeezed it in a bear-like grip ... The rest of the crowd were hardly less demonstrative. I remembered the crowds at the Crystal Palace; remembered the well-bred boredom of the grown-ups who had taken me there ... It was not 'done', in England, to like fireworks after the age of puberty.

The rockets soared, the shells burst with a *crescendo* of magnificence; I wished, suddenly, that Hew Dallas were here to see them ... I regretted, too, that we couldn't see what was going on beyond the trees; between the bursts of aerial activity, we could see the reflected glare of Bengal lights, and hear the popping of roman candles; a loud bang followed by an interminable rattle of minor explosions was perhaps some unimaginably splendid Italian equivalent of the Mine of Serpents – that august and haunting image of the unattainable which I had looked at so longingly, with such a passion of concupiscence, at Gamage's, in 1918 ...

The finale was approaching: a kind of Lisztian *cadenza* of iridescent fire played itself out against the violet depths of the sky. At length, an unprecedented clamour of bangs burst forth behind the trees; a score or so of trailing yellow stars soared zenithwards; and burst at last into such brilliant and far-flung glories that the previous flights were as nothing. Golden and silver rain poured earthwards in a dozen immense cataracts; glaring magnesium fires floated like suns in mid-air; serpents whirled and whistled over the tree-tops; a whole Aladdin's cave of rubies and sapphires spilled itself above the heads of the crowd ... The brief incredible splendour flamed like lightning down the far corridors of my memory – leaping backwards across the years, lighting with an instant's glory one darkened shrine after another; fixing itself, at last, upon a single image, the remote, archaic progenitor of all the rest: a small boy crouched motionless, his whole body taut with a fascinated concentration, over a tattered copy of *Little Folks.*

The fireworks were over; and after a further brief interval, the opera began again.

It was nearly two o'clock before we left the gardens. We walked back, unhurriedly, across the Ponte Santa Trinità, up the Via Tornabuoni. Guido left me by the Duomo.

'I shall come to the station at eight o'clock to say *addio,*' he promised. 'It is a great pity that you have not gone to stay with my people ... I shall write to them just the same, and tell them you will come next year. I shall write also to the son of the notary at Casalbordino ... *A rivederci,* then – *a domani alle otto.*'

He was gone; and I began to walk back through the warm, still-lighted streets towards the hotel.

Guido was at the station, as he had promised, to see me off.

'You will come back next year and stay with my people,' were his parting words.

The train moved out of the station into the brilliant morning. Would I come back next year, I wondered? Once in the train, the pull of England had reasserted itself; Italy, already, was receding. Houses, fields, orchards swept past; the mountains rose dimly on the skyline: somewhere beyond those remote heights lay a land to which I had once wanted to return – a lost land of heroes, in which I could no longer quite believe ...

At Domodossola, we heard that there was a railway strike in France. Nobody took much notice; international expresses, we thought, would not be affected by such local upsets.

As it happened, we were wrong. At Vallorbe, at one o'clock in the morning, we were brusquely awoken. It was necessary to descend; the train went no further.

We descended; we were herded through the Swiss Customs and

the French Customs; we were penned for an hour in a waiting-room with the door locked. It was as though war had been declared, and we were refugees fleeing from the wrath to come ... There was a train, we learnt at last, going as far as Dijon; we were at liberty to travel on it – third-class.

At six in the morning we reached Dijon; it was raining. The train had apparently changed its mind since we left Vallorbe: it would now go on as far as Paris.

We arrived in Paris at half past ten; it was cloudy and chilly. There were no trains to Calais; there was no food to be bought at the station; nobody from Cook's was there to supply information; it was next to impossible even to get a taxi.

'*C'est la grève*,' said a gendarme unhelpfully.

A British officer on the train thought that possibly the Army might do something – lay on a truck to Calais, perhaps. He would ring up the transport people ...

He did so; yes, said the Army, there were two trucks laid on for Calais; but they were for military personnel only ... Some of the women of the party showed signs of hysteria. One, who had travelled from Palermo with a two-year-old child, alleged that she was the widow of a British officer, and therefore ought to count as 'military personnel'.

Sitting on the pavement outside the station, among our stacked luggage, we consumed what remained of our sandwiches. There was a rumour that buses were running to Calais; but people had already been queueing for them, we heard, since daybreak. We should have to go to the British Consul; but how were we to get there, with all our luggage? The *consigne* at the station was shut; it was nearly impossible to get a taxi ...

About midday, a miracle occurred. A bus drove up to the pavement; on the front of it was inscribed the magic word: CALAIS. Yes, we could take our seats; the trip would cost us five hundred francs. We should be at Calais by six in the evening.

We bumped and clattered over the suburban *pavé*, out into the country. The journey had assumed for me a nightmare, Kafka-like quality; I was dead-tired, and I hadn't had a proper meal since the night before last. Moreover, I had only about two hundred French francs left in my pocket.

We arrived at Calais at eight o'clock. It was bitterly cold. We drove up to the quayside: to our relief the Channel boat was in.

The purser met us at the gangway; he was red-faced, pompous and hostile. No, the boat didn't sail till tomorrow at midday. Go on board? Certainly not. It was clean against regulations. Where were we to sleep, we asked? The hotels in Calais were full – we had inquired on the way through. Besides, most of us were short of money.

The purser glared at us contemptuously. His orders were to let nobody aboard. It was no fault of his that we were stranded.

Nor, we pointed out as politely as we could, was it any fault of ours ... The argument proceeded with an incredible futility for a quarter of an hour. The purser became more pompous; we became less polite. The woman with the child from Palermo began to cry. A bitter wind pierced our thin clothes. I thought of Italy with complete incredulity; could it be only yesterday morning that I had left Florence?

With the pride of a true-blue Briton defending his frontiers, the purser stuck to his guns. I felt precisely as I had felt in the Army, arriving back late off leave, and confronted with my Company-Sergeant-Major.

Perhaps it was the woman from Palermo who finally worked the miracle; or perhaps the purser was getting bored with baiting us. At all events, he relented sufficiently to put the matter before the Captain.

We waited for another hour.

The purser reappeared at last; we could go on board, he said; but they could give us no food; we should have to wait till breakfast-time tomorrow.

We filed over the gangway, dumped our baggage, and tumbled on to the bunks in the first-class saloons. Even if there had been any food, I was too tired to eat. I finished the remains of a bottle of Chianti which Guido had bought for me, and which I had intended to take home; then, unwashed and fully-clothed, I dropped into a heavy, feverish sleep.

At Folkestone, I walked out of the Marine Station beneath grey skies, on to the deserted quayside. I ordered a taxi. We drove through the town, up the Canterbury hill past Sugarloaf and Caesar's Camp; the woods and fields seemed impregnated with a dripping, inexhaustible wetness. Squalid pink bungalows and tea-chalets slid past; forbidding-looking pubs with fast-closed doors;

hoardings, petrol-pumps, abandoned Nissen-huts. We passed through Hawkinge, Denton, and up the hill past Broome Park. Over the high plateau of Barham Downs rain-laden clouds swagged down the sky like funeral weeds.

Ridged and pocked with its earthworks and tumuli, the level downland lay drenched and desolate beneath the weeping clouds; here the Britons had buried their dead, here the Danes had fought, and the Romans camped; and here, too, in a remote, enchanted summer, the Big Rocket had swooped, unfulfilled, to its ignoble end.

PART SIX

Brick Horizons

My world has brick horizons,
A sprained and crippled frolic
And khaki garrisons:
O what a startled relic
Of my once merry ones.

LAWRENCE LITTLE

I

The building, once an Italian civilian hospital, had been recently occupied by a Basuto medical unit: the taint of their presence still lingered faintly in the air like the scent of fox or badger, suggesting an alien way of life – dark, incomprehensible, African. Little notices were pinned up all over the walls, in a transliterated version of the Basuto dialect; as a language, it seemed less than adequate: the frequent English phrases – watercloset, Orderly Sergeant, dressing-buckets – reminded me of the italicized 'five-o-clocks' and 'smokings' in an Anglophile French novel.

I was in no mood to appreciate this rather disquieting atmosphere: my release-group would be coming up next month, I felt that I was as good as out of the army already. But the services on such occasions are apt to behave with a dismal pedantry; officially I was still a soldier; and it seemed that the Army intended to enforce its claims upon me with an excessive, an almost greedy, insistence.

We had moved up from a big Adriatic port to a small town some miles inland: our unit was to be billeted with the General Hospital to which we were officially attached. As a VD treatment-centre we were, as usual, treated like lepers: hence our instalment in the ex-Basuto hospital. It was the early autumn of 1945: already the weather was growing chilly; half the windows were without glass, and there was no heating. For light, we had to depend upon hurricane-lamps; bats swarmed in the wards and treatment-rooms; there were no baths. Half the unit, moreover, was away on LIAP or Python; we were understaffed and over-worked.

I was put in charge of the office: I wasn't a proper clerk, and I knew very little about the work.

'You'll just have to manage,' said the Staff-sergeant. 'The Old Man's a bastard for work, but you don't want to stand none of *his* bullshit.'

Not only did I have to deal with all the routine-work – admissions and discharges, correspondence, acquittance-rolls – but the monthly returns were due as well. The 'Old Man', a Major Cohen, had been posted to us as CO only a fortnight before: being 'new', he was apt to be over-conscientious, and to demand impossibilities.

My only assistant was an Italian girl, one of the civilian employees we had brought up from the coast. She knew no English, but could copy out documents, parrot-fashion, on the typewriter. Her name was Assunta; she was a nice girl, though very ugly and almost half-witted. She would let out piercing screams if the least thing went wrong; and her feet smelt awful.

I chose a fairly intelligent patient to help with the admissions and discharges; Assunta typed out the correspondence. Then the typewriter broke down; it was not a mere matter of a worn-out ribbon or a loose screw or two; it broke down (being Italian) completely and hopelessly. Assunta screamed ineffectively; I went to the Staff-sergeant.

'The stationery office is shut for stock-taking,' he said, 'so you've had it. You'll have to take the stuff up to the hospital, after hours, and type it out on one of their machines.'

This wasn't nearly good enough; I went to Major Cohen. He knew the CO of a unit in the town, who might lend us a typewriter.

'Tell the Staff-sergeant to send a truck down this afternoon,' he said. 'I'll write Major Trilling a chitty.'

The effect of this message upon the Staff-sergeant was electrical.

'They crucified Christ,' he exclaimed dramatically, 'but I'm —ed if they're going to crucify me. No, chum ... I'm in Group 26, I ain't going to be no —ing Christian martyr. And what's more,' he added, more cogently, 'I can't make bricks out of —ing straw: what's he think *I* am? We ain't *got* no truck; the —ing General Hospital's got no truck neither; and if Major —ing Cohen wants one so bad, he'd better go and ask the Chief Rabbi for it.'

Further argument was useless; all the Staff would say was that he wasn't going to be crucified, not if all the wild horses in Palestine were to drag him to Golgotha; and what was more, he was meeting his *signorina* down town half an hour ago, and she'd create f— if he kept her waiting any longer.

So finally I had to waste a day hitch-hiking down to Major Trilling's unit, and hitch-hiking back again with an abnormally heavy typewriter. This meant working overtime on the monthly returns.

'I think you are fool,' said my friend Kurt Schlegel. 'You come out of the Army in one week, one month, and they make you work like nigger, the bastards. Why do you not say this to the Staff-sergeant?'

I told him I had already said all this and more.

'Then you go to the CO,' said Kurt who, being racially akin to Major Cohen, had perhaps more faith in him than the rest of us.

I said I'd been to the CO already.

'Ach, you are fool. I speak myself to the Staff-sergeant, I give him some *vino*, then he is putting someone else to work in the office, isn't it?'

With vague thoughts of the thirty pieces of silver, I dissuaded him. It was very kind, I said, but I didn't think, at the moment, it would be altogether tactful.

That night Kurt brought me some wine from the *trattoria* down-town, and I worked till midnight on the monthly returns. The hurricane-lamp flickered smokily, throwing vast dim shadows on the walls; bats circled in droves round the room; there was a faint but perceptible smell of Basutos. I kept coming on relics of their occupation: documents, articles of kit, dirty bandages. The notices stuck on the walls (nobody had bothered to take them down) irritated me with their fantastic gibberish. Over-worked, over-tired, I was reminded perpetually and unpleasantly of our black predecessors: their dark, improbable lives haunted me; and suddenly a vague, incongruous association clicked into place in some distant cavern of my mind ... I had a fleeting memory of giggling, secretive voices, talking a language I couldn't grasp – big, athletic women lounging on the lawn with tennis-rackets ...

'Dolly Matheson,' I muttered viciously, as though it were an imprecation; recalling suddenly the name of my sister's friend, with its hoarded suggestions of some mysterious life beyond my ken. It seemed, at the time, a perfectly adequate comment on the situation; though it was, I thought, a peculiar trick, on the part of the *id*, to equate poor giggling, hockey-playing Dolly with a Basuto medical unit.

Plainly, I was over-tired: I finished my bottle of *vino nero* and went to bed.

'This black man's got no religion,' said the patient who was helping me. He was writing-up the day's admissions, and was staring now, in perplexity, at the pay-book of a Swazi corporal. 'Shall I put him down as C of E?' he suggested.

'Better say "Pagan", ' I advised. 'It saves the padre a job if the bloke dies on us.'

'That sky-larking sheeny,' said the Staff (referring thus disrespectfully to the Commanding Officer), 'know what he's done now? Wrote to the Sergeant-cook, he has, and complained of the rations in the Officers' Mess. Can you beat it? I suppose' (he added meditatively), 'I suppose the grub they give him ain't proper Kosher.'

'I go to the Staff,' said Kurt, 'and I ask, quite polite, for some bandage from the store. And what does he say? He say: "It is odd of God to choose the Jews." Explain to me please: is this some English joke?'

'No, it's a Scotch folk-song,' I retorted, unsympathetically. I was too busy, just then, to enter into racial controversies.

'So, you make joke also. But I tell you' – Kurt's face flamed suddenly scarlet – 'if that is English humour, then I think it is pity that Germany lose the war.'

Then the typewriter broke down again.

'*Dio mio, che deastro,*' squealed Assunta.

'You've had it this time,' said the Staff.

So I had to go up to the main hospital-office and work after hours.

Next day sixteen Basuto patients arrived.

'We've got no room for 'em – send 'em back,' said the Staff.

'But I've brought them right over from Campobasso,' said the ambulance driver.

'Can't help that, mate. Major's orders are we can't take any more wogs. There's a Basuto wing up at Ancona – better take 'em on there.'

At this point the Major himself intervened.

'Let's have a look at them,' he said. 'H'm – yes. There's one here with a rather interesting extra-genital chancre ... H'm – yes. I think on the whole we'd better take them.'

'I'm joining the Mosleyites when I get home,' said the Staff, when the Major was out of earshot.

My patient-assistant was having a day off; so I had to stop doing the monthly returns and admit the Basutos. In the middle of this, a signal came through: all personnel in Release Groups 19 and 20 were to hold themselves in readiness to move off; release documents were to be completed forthwith.

'That's me,' I told the Staff.

'Well, what about it?'

'Who's going to make out my release papers – the hospital-office?'

'They won't touch nothing of ours – I asked the chief clerk yesterday. I expect they're afraid they'll catch the pox.'

'Well, who's going to do them?'

'You.'

'Me?'

'You want to get out of the Army, don't you? All right, then – get on with it. I'm just off down-town to see my bint.'

I managed to procure the release documents from the chief clerk. Leaving the monthly returns to take care of themselves, I wrestled for a whole day with the intricate procedure of getting out of the Army. Amongst other things, I had to have a medical board.

I asked the Staff about his: he went to ask the Major. When he came back, he said:

'Go on in, and he'll give it to you.'

'Give me what?'

'Your medical board.'

'He can't give me a medical board at a minute's notice, all by himself.'

'Can't he? That man wouldn't stop at nothing – except a rasher for his breakfast.'

So I went in to the Major.

When he looked at my release book he began to giggle.

'Not got VD, have you? All right, I'll put "No" against every-thing – I suppose my signature's as good as the next man's ... All the other officers seem to be on LIAP, anyway – if you *really* want to get out with your group, we'll have to cook it ... You won't be able to apply for a pension, but I don't suppose that'll worry you, will it?'

So the Major put 'No' against a long list of queries, and signed on the dotted line. By the end of the day, the documents were nearly completed.

'Ain't them monthly returns done yet?' asked the Staff. 'Old Ikey Isaacs wants 'em all squared up for the morning.'

'Then he can bloody well wait,' I exploded.

'*Scusi,*' Assunta chose this moment to interject, '*cosa significa, questa parola "bluddy-vell"?*'

'Oh Christ,' exploded the Staff, 'tell her it means her feet stink and for —'s sake get on with them —ing returns, before I land you on a fizzer.'

At last my movement-order came through: I was to report at the transit-camp next morning; from there I should go to Naples, and thence, by plane, to England. Now that the moment had really come, I couldn't quite believe in it: a sense of anti-climax pervaded the whole occasion. Somehow I couldn't summon the right romantic emotions: I had felt just the same when I left school.

I tried to think of England, of going home to my family, of lying in bed till ten, walking in the country, meeting old friends ... I thought of Bertie, Eric, Douglas: I had heard from none of them for ages; I didn't know where they were, even. And had Basil, I wondered, survived the War? Doubtless I should hear in time: but somehow it didn't at the moment seem to matter very much.

Things, people, places – all that was contained in the phrase 'Civvy Street' – seemed oddly unreal. The images they should have evoked wouldn't quite click into focus. The pre-war years had lapsed into a colourless vagueness: by contrast, the War, my time in the Army, seemed sharply-defined, tangible and 'real'. I had remained, as I thought, 'detached' from it: had made up my mind, from the first, that I wouldn't let the Army 'get under my skin'. Yet it seemed to have done so, in spite of all my efforts; soldiering had become a habit – or rather a whole complex of habits – of which I should find it hard to break myself. Perhaps, I thought, I should never break myself of it entirely: perhaps the mark of the soldier, like a tattoo, was indelible . . .

On my last night I went with Kurt and some others down to a *trattoria* in the town. We ate *pasta asciutta* and drank a lot of wine; we reminisced, sentimentally, about the past: Benghazi, Sicily, our peasant-friends in the Abruzzi. I went through the motions expected of one about to be 'released'; but without conviction. All I genuinely felt was an immense, paralysing fatigue; I should have liked to go straight to bed, and sleep for a week.

II

Next morning I reported at the transit-camp.

'It ain't no good you coming here today,' they said. 'Train don't leave for Naples till thirteen-hundred hours tomorrow. Better go back to your unit.'

So I went back to the unit.

'You must *like* the Army,' said the Staff, who had very reluctantly taken over control in the office. 'Now you're here, you can give me a hand with these 'ere discharges.'

'You've had it,' I told him.

That night, I said good-bye to the same people all over again.

'You'll be back again tomorrow,' they said. 'Nobody ever gets away from *this* —ing unit.'

It seemed only too probable. Next morning, I set off again: and at last found myself in the train for Naples. The journey took thirty-six hours: wedged, uncomfortably, between the other people's kit, on a hard wooden seat. A truck met us at Naples, and took us out to Lammie Camp. Vesuvius had erupted recently, and changed its shape; it wasn't anything like the pictures I remembered in my geography-book at school.

'Cor, here's some more of the poor —ers,' said the first people we met at Lammie.

'Why, what's up?' someone asked.

'Cor, you've had it chum. You'll never get away from here. Proper Belsen, this place is. They keeps you here till you rot, and then they goes on keeping you.'

'I been here five weeks,' someone else took up the tale. 'Without a word of a lie, mate – five bleedin' weeks.'

The camp was crammed: we could see that. There were hundreds waiting for LIAP or Python; hundreds more due for release. Mostly they were groups 17 or 18: we, being 19 or 20, were well down on the list. A few weeks ago, we heard, some Python blokes had started a riot; but they were still here, and likely to be.

'It fair sickens you with the whole —ing Army,' said one of the men in Group 17. '—ed around for six bleedin' years, and then when your turn comes up to get out, they starts —ing you around worse than ever. One thing, I'll be a conchy in the next war – too bloody true I will.'

Secretly I hoped it wasn't so bad as all that . . . The new arrivals were addressed by a jaunty young officer with a very OCTU voice.

'Well, you blokes,' he said, 'we're pretty overcrowded hyah, as you can see. It's not ah fault – it's the RAF: they won't run enough planes. But we'll get you all away as soon as we can. It shouldn't be mah than three or four days, at the most.'

This sounded better; we couldn't know, of course, that the same officer had been giving the same pep-talk for weeks past.

It began to rain: a sudden, drenching downpour. We queued for blankets, soaked to the skin; then staggered off, carrying blanket-rolls and kit, towards our tents. The tents weren't concreted, and there were no beds: only duckboards – one, about six feet by two, to each man. The tents leaked, the ground inside them was damp.

'Cor, if this is being demobbed, give me the —ing Army,' said somebody.

'Wish I was back with my unit,' said another.

We dumped our kit, and trailed down in the rain to the cookhouse for dinner. There was a queue nearly a hundred yards long. It moved very, very slowly. When we got to the cookhouse, they'd run out of meat and spuds, and we had to be content with cold bully and tepid beans.

The lists of plane-loads for the next day or two were posted on a board by the orderly room. We were warned to keep our eyes on them: nobody was allowed out of camp till after five o'clock, when the last lists were posted for the day.

'We'll be here weeks,' said a pessimist.

'The officer said only three days,' said an optimist.

'He's been saying that for weeks past – a bloke in 17 group told me.'

'Half the planes have been crashing – the pilots are all young blokes with about a half-a-dozen flying hours.'

'They won't let you draw no credits.'

'They're giving leave-blokes priority – it ain't right. Blokes on release ought to come first.'

'You wouldn't say that, not if *you* was goin on leaf.'

The camp was fairly cushy: once we'd handed in our kit, nobody bothered much about us. You had to do a guard or two; but another medical bloke and myself got out of this by volunteering to work in the M I Room.

For four days we never went for more than an hour without looking at the notice-board. But all we saw were the same lists that had been posted the day we arrived: no new ones had been posted, and the parties already briefed hadn't gone yet. They said in the orderly room that weather-conditions had prevented flying; but everyone knew that this was just bullshit.

After the fifth day, our hopes began to ebb. At the end of a week, we were almost acclimatized to the prevailing atmosphere of defeatism.

'Ain't there no boats?' people said. 'What about the *Queen Mary*?'

'Why can't they send us by M E D L O C?'

'What's the bleedin' Air Force doing, what I'd like to know. There was plenty of planes while the ——ing War was still on – what's happened to 'em all now, eh?'

'All been nabbed by the bleedin' officers for joy-trips, that's what's happened to *them*, mate.'

'*And* the Yanks – don't forget the bleedin' Yanks.'

Nothing in the Army, I though, had been quite so bad as the leaving of it: this interminable, pointless sojourn between two worlds. We were not out of the Army, and we were not yet in Civvy Street; the tough shell of endurance which, like crustaceans, we had carried about with us for six years, was cracking; we were left naked and quivering in an alien environment, and the least suggestion of Army 'bullshit' was like salt rubbed into a wound.

I found my temper suffering; the easy-going tolerance which I had long forced myself to adopt fell away from me; the monotonous cursing, the Army catch-phrases ('Roll on Christmas', 'It's a good life if you don't weaken'), personal tics and gestures, irritated me now past bearing.

I managed to scrounge a broken-down bed (the canvas sagged on to the floor, but it was softer than the duckboards) and lay on it for hour after hour, reading *Valmouth* and *Vainglory*, the two books which had accompanied me everywhere for three years – to South Africa, Egypt, Tripoli, Italy ... As always, with Firbank, I felt once again in contact with a sane, rational world, a civilized world in which I felt at home.

Sane, rational? Firbank, surely, was conspicuously lacking in these wholesome virtues; yet this was precisely the effect he had upon me. But perhaps my standards of sanity and reasonableness were abnormal. Lying on my broken bed, reading *Valmouth* and listening to the rain drumming on the canvas, I was haunted by a vague, unseizable memory: delphiniums wilting in a vase, Mistinguett on the gramophone, the taste of a Manhatten; and a shrill, feminine voice insisting: 'My dear, you *must* read Firbank.'

We stayed no less than three weeks at Lammie Camp. After the first week or so, even the authorities gave up the pretence that we were ever going to get a plane. Rules were relaxed, we were allowed passes into Naples, to Pompeii ... Pompeii reminded me oddly of Canterbury, where the blitz of 1942 had uncovered whole areas of Roman remains beneath the modern foundations: vestigial walls, mosaic pavements ... The friend I was with wanted to find the Roman brothel; but when we succeeded in discovering it, we found it closed: doubtless by order of the military authorities, who feared for our morals ... All over the ruins grew a familiar little orchid, the Autumn Ladies' Tresses, which I used to find on the Dover Cliffs and the hills near Folkestone. At Pompeii it was more robust, and flowered later, waiting, no doubt, for the rainy season.

At last it was announced that we were to go overland, by MEDLOC, instead of by plane. This meant another thirty-six hours in the train, another transit camp at Milan ... But we were light-hearted about it; if we weren't exactly 'on our way' (for they might keep us another three weeks at Milan), we had at least got away from that Slough of Despond, Lammie Camp.

When we arrived at the Milan transit camp, we were given good beds in comfortable barrack-rooms; there were hot showers, a complete change of clothes, good food. We should be three days there, they told us: and the words, this time, carried conviction. We felt that, here, the authorities were really doing their best for us; and in retrospect, our loathing for Lammie Camp became all the more intense. It was the old story: there was no reason why Lammie shouldn't have been as efficient and well-run, as the camp at Milan; it just wasn't; we had been mucked about for three weeks and more, unnecessarily. It was the Army all over.

Punctually, after three days, we left Milan, according to schedule. It was a rainy morning: Lake Maggiore was swathed in mist. Coming out of the Simplon, the north met us for the first time: green meadows, prim, square houses, solid unemotional faces – a Lutheran cleanliness, the northern protest against paganism. In spite of it all, I was sorry to leave Italy. One of my companions gave me an old *Daily Mirror* to read: 'Jane', 'Belinda', advertisements of Guinness, Zam-buk, Cuticura ... was I so glad to be going back to England?

Montreux and Vevey sped past, veiled with rain, looking almost like England. I drank the last of my Italian wine, and hoped English beer wouldn't be as nasty as I remembered ...

At Lausanne, people waved flags out of the windows: after all, we British had once been their main source of industry ... At Dieppe, that night, we re-encountered the 'English' climate – the unmistakable damp chill piercing the clothes at nightfall. The camp was ankle-deep in mud; the twilight seemed preternaturally long, lingering behind the high, misty tops of the elm-trees ...

At midday, next day, we went aboard the boat; the channel was calm, the day fine; England, when it emerged, looked precisely like one's idea of it: a cluster of pink houses (Newhaven) huddled beneath pale-green, cloud-shadowed downs.

The train was very comfortable; none of us had seen such a train for years. At the dispersal-centre at Reading, instructions were issued through a loud-speaker; 'One last announcement,' the disembodied voice shouted to our crowded, impatient ranks: 'Does anyone want to cancel his release and sign on for a further term of service?'

I have never heard anything like the howl of execration which went up at these improbable words ... I didn't howl with the rest; on the contrary, I felt a sudden, disquieting spasm of regret. For two pins, at that moment, I would have signed on again: only the fear of being 'different', the unanimous howl of the crowd, prevented me. Surprised at my odd reaction, I went to the barrack-room to which I had been assigned: it was like any other barrack-room; soldiers sat about on bed-cots half-undressed, there was the familiar mutter of obscenity, the old, changeless smell of piss and sweat and Woodbines. This was, I thought, my 'last' barrack-room ... Tomorrow at this time I should be out of the Army. Nostalgia possessed me; 'Roll on Christmas and let's have some nuts,' said an RE bloke on the next bed – high-polishing his boots, from habit, as though he were a rookie, and tomorrow was the Colonel's inspection ... There was still time to change my mind, I supposed; but I evaded the thought, and walked down to the canteen for a beer.

Next day we went to Guildford: the release-centre there was run most efficiently, and the actual process of demobilization took about seven minutes. While we waited, I read *The Listener* and *Picture Post* in a comfortable waiting-room; had a cup of tea in a canteen, where the wireless was playing softly: not, as one might have expected, a cinema organ or swing, but (improbably) Ravel's *Pavane pour une Infante défunte*. When our turn came, we filed past the long tables, handing over our various documents: the Army clerks called us all 'sir' impartially – other ranks as well as officers. We came to the last table, passed it: 'Good-bye sir, good luck,' said the clerk.

We were out of the Army.

III

'Munich' - weather: grey skies and a light, warm drizzle – I remembered 1938. But the atmosphere now was one not of crisis but of lysis: the slow, downward curve back to 'normality', back to the old rut.

I felt uneasy, uprooted, almost nostalgic; in the park, there were still soldiers in camp: I watched them crowding to the wash-house, queueing for grub; knowing that they were now strangers, and feeling half-sorry for it. A whole set of habitual compulsions had been suddenly removed: it was almost like having had a limb amputated – feeling the sudden twitch of a nerve or tendon which simply wasn't there.

I walked in the autumnal woods, still in my old, travel-stained battle-dress. I told myself that I wore it to 'save' my other clothes; but in reality I liked pretending that I was still a soldier. Lammie Camp seemed already almost unreal; I remembered only the good times in the Army, and the friends I might never see again. The brown woods dripped with a perpetual moisture; the last leaves fell, bronze against brown; I wandered, thinking of soldiers, through the thickets, still in my khaki: a brown thought in a brown shade.

I gathered fungi – not only field mushrooms, but others: blewits, parasols, puff-balls. At dinner, they reminded me of *funghi trifolati* at Naples. The spindle-berries in the hedges burst open, their orange seeds like sudden sparks glowing within their puce-coloured envelopes. In the fields, a pit here and there showed where a land-mine had exploded; the pasture was scattered with the burnt-out cases of incendiary bombs. Among them lay the immemorial flint-boulders of the chalk-country, strange twisted shapes like sculptures by Henry Moore; beside the rusted bomb-cases, they seemed like monoliths surviving among petrol-pumps.

I walked up to Barham Downs. At the top of the hill, almost unconsciously, from long-ingrained habit, I looked for the water-tower. It seemed to have gone. My heart gave a jump: one was prepared for almost any change after six years of war; but I wasn't prepared for this. I looked again: it was a grey day with bad visibility, and at last I saw it: the tank had been painted black (I remembered now) at the beginning of the war. By now, the paint was beginning to wear off, and hadn't been renewed: the tank showed dimly above the wood, a smudge of whitish grey – a burnt-out firework ... The dark, dangerous men had risen up at last from their underworld kingdom, and overrun the fields and wood-lands; the Mine of Serpents had discharged its freight of hoarded fires, and their charred remnants strewed the land. The tower was still there; but, like the past itself, it had become blurred, indefinite, almost without meaning; no longer, as once it had been, a landmark beckoning one on into unknown country.

Autumn turned to winter; the soldiers moved out of the park; one saw fewer troops about: I began to wear my civvy clothes.

I started to write again. Spring came, and the grey, dismal summer of 1946. I kept telling myself I was happy: three books of mine had been accepted for publication; I had money to spend; I made new friends; my affairs seemed to be prospering, financially and otherwise. But a curious undertow of depression invalidated, somehow, my contentment. All the things were there to make me happy: but for some reason they didn't 'add up', something seemed to be missing from the total. In the 'Munich' period I had almost longed for a war, as I had once longed for a definite 'illness' to break the vicious circle of hypochondria. Now the 'illness' had come, I had 'recovered'; but it seemed to have left me, like certain cerebro-spinal infections, with some functional deficiency.

Books, friendships, a newly-discovered orchid, a trip to Ireland – all these things lacked some transforming essence. *J'ai seul la clef de cette parade sauvage:* years ago, I had been able to say it with conviction. But now I seemed to have lost the key.

> Self-yeast of spirit, a dull dough sours. I see
> The lost are like this, and their scourge to be
> As I am mine, their sweating selves; but worse.

I went up to Three Barrows Down and found again the little green Helleborine: cleistogamous, self-loving, self-sufficient. The paths round the wood were deserted again: scabious and harebell waved undisturbed above the grasses, in the perpetual upland breeze. The soldiers had gone; only the dead remained, beneath the barrows, their bones embraced more closely, year after year, by the roots of the beeches.

I began to be haunted, again, as in the years before the War, by my old, obsessional landscapes: the monolithic uplands, the valleys clothed with beeches and haunted by the memory of ancient 'Druidic' ceremonies. I encountered again the yew-tree printing its dark signature against a spring sunset, the glossy ivy beneath the winter beeches. In the cottage garden, the Hellebore, which I had transplanted from the wood at Lydden before the War, raised its pale adder's heads, in February, above the iron-dark tents of leaves. Walking near Shorncliffe, I remembered, too, those rides over Dibgate, on winter afternoons, in the crisis-age – the cross-country runners strung out across the high, windswept

fields, the fauna of an alien country of which, a few years later, I
should have myself become a naturalized citizen.

I went to Dover: scarcely a house remained untouched by the
blitz. The Burlington Hotel towered above the ruined streets, itself
a ruin; the Grand, too, was a hollow shell. Granville Gardens had
gone, and most of Townwall Street, with its friendly soldiers' pubs.
Only the Castle and the barracks seemed apparently intact – these,
and the mysterious 'houses' built into the cliff-face. The elegant
early-Victorian terraces on the front were mostly in ruins; seagulls nested in their shell-shattered rooms, creepers covered the
boarded-up windows; the houses, such of them as remained, stared
out sightlessly, without hope, towards the sea: like old, crippled
people waiting for the final dissolution. Soon they would be pulled
down, to make room for something more up to date.

Unpretentious, dingy, rather grubby even in peace-time, Dover
had now sunk into a ruinous senile squalor. For me, the town had
always held a faint echo of old tragedy ('O Regan, Goneril!'); the
high, gull-haunted cliffs, the visible town merging into the mysterious inland 'underworld', had seemed the right background for
romance. Today, the gulls cried with a more poignant sadness;
'the vows, the tears, the slight emotional signals' had acquired a
quality more genuinely tragic. Yet the Dovorians retained their
tough, jaunty, proletarian gaiety in spite of it all; the pubs (such as
remained) were as full as ever. At the Royal Café in Bench Street,
Mme Nodiroli could give one something very like a pre-war
lunch; the Hippodrome, that source of Cyprian myth, had been
blitzed, but the bar was still open.

Bussing over from the country, I felt still, as always, that Dover
held the promise of escape: coming down Crabble Hill, into the
dingy, outlying streets, one felt that one had crossed a frontier.

One day, looking through some old copies of *The Times* which
my mother had saved, my eye was caught by a name in the List of
Fallen Officers: Major Basil R. Medlicott, the Royal —shire
Regiment. He had died on active service in 1944.

Afterwards, I heard that it was amoebic dysentery. Poor Basil, I
thought: even in his death he had missed being heroic ... I remembered him, now, merely as the man I had said good-bye to on
the first day of war, at Old England's Hole: the man who had

once, in my childhood, nearly taken me to *Razzle-Dazzle* or *To-night's the Night*. He should at least, I thought, have died in battle – if possible, leading a forlorn hope. But perhaps, after all, Basil had never really been a hero.

IV

Coming back from my Italian holiday in that summer of 1947, England seemed more than ever a 'country where nobody was well' –

> England our cow
> Once was a lady – is she now?

A well-known botanist, it was reported, had rediscovered the Military Orchid in Buckinghamshire; he refused, however, with a prim and self-righteous determination, to disclose the exact locality, even to his closest colleagues. So the quasi-mythical flower which had eluded me in childhood, and in the war years in Italy and North Africa, remained still unfound.

Dover, when I returned there, seemed to be lapsing into a state of permanent ruin. There was much talk of rebuilding, but nothing was being done. I hoped it wouldn't be: the town, even in ruins, preserved something of its almost Regency elegance amid the squalor. The creepers spread further over the shattered houses; rosebay-willowherb and the blitz-ragwort flourished on the demolished sites.

I bathed in the harbour with some soldiers from the Castle barracks, and had a drink with them in a pub.

> The Lion, the Rose or the Crown will not ask them to die,
> Not here, not now. All they are killing is time,
> Their pauper civilian future . . .

In the ten years or so since they were written, Auden's lines had become dated: we were all killing time now, the future would pauperize all of us. The soldiers, at least, had a definite function; their lives, moreover, were still lived to a traditional pattern – monastic, quasi-feudal. They warbled songs by Bing Crosby; but the bugles still uttered their archaic, melancholy calls from the Castle and the Citadel; poetry, exiled from Civvy Street, lingered on the barrack-square, and in scrubbed, naked billets: brown thoughts in a khaki shade . . . I remembered Hew Dallas, and wondered where he was stationed now.

Like a tattoo-mark, the print of the Army stained my mind, indelibly. The summer continued triumphantly, week after week of perfect weather. I felt fitter than I had felt for two years: and once again, like an adolescent, I was troubled by the old, perverse itch to abandon myself to something which I believed I hated. This time, however, there was a difference: it wouldn't be my first 'experience'.

Money was running short: the publishing trade seemed a moribund industry: a book took eighteen months to get through the press, where once it would have taken three.

> Patience who asks
> Wants war, wants wounds; weary his time, his tasks;
> To do without, take tosses, and obey.
> Rare patience roots in these, and, these away,
> Nowhere. Natural heart's ivy, Patience masks
> Our ruins of wrecked past purpose. ˵ ˵

From the sea, back-stroking lazily, out to the raft, I could see the blind house-fronts, swaddled in Virginia creeper. Above, on the cliffs, the mysterious outcrops of stone-work, like sham ruins of the Beckford period, were masked too with ivy or Traveller's Joy: 'ruins of wrecked past purpose' . . .

In London, I went to a literary party.

'You must meet so-and-so – he might fix you up on the Third Programme . . .'

'When's your next book coming; I've just got proofs of mine – they say it'll be another year before it's out.'

'I'll try and get you a review in *The Listener* . . .'

'Ring up Symons and mention my name . . . It's an awful paper, of course, but they pay quite well.'

'Cyril's so pontifical, isn't he? I still take *Horizon*, but I find I never read more than about one article . . .'

'*New Writing's* got quite un-Left, now.'

'Nobody will publish a war-book. My agent says wait another ten years and *then* try . . .'

'Did you hear Dylan on the Third? . . .'

'. . . so many *Lawrences* – one never knows. Lee, Durrell, Little. And I always think people mean D. H. when they mean T.E.'

'Isn't that Cecil Day Lewis over there?'

'When's your orchid book appearing? You ought to give a talk on the Third sometime . . .'

'We'll probably all be directed into coal-mines.'

'I sold the copyright outright. My publisher said something about its being a capital-payment, so I wouldn't have to pay income-tax on it.'

'Didn't you like the blurb? "This delicately-indelicate little cameo . . ." I wrote it myself, of course.'

The 'pauper civilian future' stretched ahead: the squalid, blitz-scarred vista of Civvy Street. But the sun still shone: serenely and impartially, on soldier and civilian, on the beach, the public-gardens, the hollow cliffs. There was still the sun: or bathing on wet days in a warm sea; re-reading Firbank or Proust: moments that could still keep the future at bay. The taste of red wine with a salad of chicory; laying down the pen at the end of a chapter, with the feeling that one had achieved one's purpose; or the first, sudden embrace of requited affection, sleeping together, the sense of one more quest coming to an end.

At Chatham I had a drink in a pub, and then two more. Then I went to the recruiting-office: only to make tentative inquiries, however. I wasn't quite prepared to commit myself – not just yet.

'Drop us a line when you've made up your mind,' said the Recruiting Sergeant. 'What job are you on now?'

'I'm a writer,' I said.

'Ship's writer?'

'No, just a writer. A journalist,' I added untruthfully, for the sake of being understood.

I took the train home: it was 'Munich' weather again, hot and thunderous, with periods of light drizzle. Instead of leaving the train at Canterbury, as I usually did, I went on to Bekesbourne. The station was silent and apparently deserted, isolated among

high, empty-looking fields. The rain fell gently; I looked across at
the line of woods on the horizon, and gave a sudden start of surprised recognition: there, protruding naked from the dark mass of
trees, gleaming with a tarnished whiteness against the grey sky,
was the watertower. I had scarcely ever seen it, before, from this
aspect: I was on the 'wrong' side of it, beyond the frontier-line of
the woods. Over there, on the other side, was familiar country;
mute, non-committal, the tower stood between two worlds, guarding the frontier: its white cap poised, like a silent, hovering bird,
between the future and the past.

JOCELYN BROOKE

THE
GOOSE
CATHEDRAL

To M.B.
with love from B.

Contents

> Thou hast committed –
> Fornication: but that was in another country,
> And besides, the wench is dead . . .

I DISLIKE burdening a book with a preface; but in this case, I think, a few words of explanation are necessary. *The Goose Cathedral* forms the third volume of what may loosely be called a 'trilogy' – though the chronology is not consecutive, and each book can, I hope, be read independently of the other two. The present volume, like its two predecessors, is neither entirely fictitious nor entirely autobiographical; by way of apology for this hybrid breed, I can only say that, as a method of composition, I happen to find it useful. To force my material into novel form would involve a Procrustean distortion of the theme which, for me at least, would make the book pointless, and not worth the bother of writing. On the other hand, 'straight' autobiography is ruled out for more obvious reasons – the law of libel being one. I have tried to solve these problems by presenting a blend of fact and fiction; but here a new difficulty arises, for certain personages and episodes exist on the border-line between truth and phantasy, and are consequently liable to cause confusion.

Let me, therefore, make it quite clear that the only sections of this book which are substantially 'true' are those which deal with the narrator's childhood (and even here a number of fictitious characters and incidents are interpolated); the remainder may be regarded, for all practical purposes, as 'fiction'. In so far as I have drawn on 'real' people, I have borrowed only certain aspects of their personalities: such characters as 'Esmé Wilkinson', 'Miss Bugle', 'Bert', etc, are composite constructions whose relation to the world of reality is so remote as to be negligible. As for the 'narrative', I can say only that it is, like the characters themselves, a composite affair: such things have happened, within my own experience, but in entirely different circumstances and (let me hasten to add) 'in another country'. I have used the town of Folkestone as my *mise-en-scène* merely because I happen to know it; and I should like to assure all residents of (and visitors to) that salubrious resort that the somewhat scandalous events which I describe as having taken place there occurred (in so far as they ever had any 'reality') in a totally different *milieu*.

The 'Goose Cathedral' itself does, indeed, exist, much as I have described it; but all reference to its past, or present occupants are entirely fictitious. 'Greylands House', Folkestone, was a real school (though I have changed the name) but exists, thank goodness, no longer. As for the 'I' who tells the story, it may be assumed for convenience (as Proust allows his readers to assume) that the narrator's Christian name happens to be the same as the author's.

'There are founde in the north parts of Scotland, & the Ilands adiacent, called Orchades, certaine trees, whereon doe growe certain shell fishes ... wherein are conteined little liuing creatures: which shels in time of maturitie doe open, and out of them grow those little liuing things; which falling into the water, doe become foules, whom we call Barnakles ...

'Moreover, it should seeme that there is another sort heerof; the Historie of which is true, and of mine owne knowledge: for travelling upon the shores of our English coast, between Douer and Rumney, I founde the trunke of an olde rotten tree which ... we drewe out of the water upon dry lande: on this rotten tree I founde growing many thousandes of long crimson bladders, in shape like unto puddings newly filled before they be sodden, at the neather end whereof did grow a shell fish, fashioned somewhat like a small Muskle ... which after I had opened, I founde in them living things which were very naked, in shape like a Birde; in others, the Birds covered with soft downe, the shell halfe open, and the Birde readie to fall out, which no doubt were the foules called Barnakles ...'

GERARDE Herball, 1597

CHAPTER ONE

Return Journey

I

There was no difficulty about the journey: I might just as well have been setting forth on an ordinary shopping expedition to the town. The bus trundled along the valley, through the familiar villages; it was an afternoon in mid-October, warm and sunlit still, but with an autumnal tang in the air. The light lay softly across the stubble fields, touching the far woods to a subdued brilliance of old gold; in the cottage gardens Michaelmas daisies and the last, frost-bitten asters smouldered like damp embers.

Between Elham and Lyminge there was a slight delay: a flock of sheep crowded the narrow road, their pullulating, woolly bodies milling helplessly between the hedges. The bus hooted, the boy in charge of the sheep scuttled to and fro, vainly attempting to divert this slow, ponderous flow of animate mutton. But the road was narrow, and the bus filled it; we crawled onward, at the sheep's pace, an ineffectual juggernaut – the driver tootling still, for appearance's sake, on his horn, the sheep baa-ing in melancholy chorus: it was we, not they (one felt), who were being led to the sacrifice.

'Disgraceful,' said a man in the next seat to me. 'They want to get organized, that's what they want.' A slick, bumptious townee, he had no patience with country ways – they needed 'organizing': but the woolly, baa-ing mass refused to be organized, we could only crawl helplessly in its wake. There were still moments (I thought) when Nature could interrupt the March of Progress.

At last the lane broadened, the sheep were driven on to the grass verge, and we drove on. The bus, topping the hill above Beach-borough, began to descend through the golden ruins of the beech-woods. The town lay below – a jumble of red and grey roofs smudged with chimney smoke and sea-mist. The hills guarded it, as ever, to the north: but their shapes were changed now, the smooth slopes were broken up by tank-traps and gunsites, the Bee Orchid and the Late Spider had become rare . . . Beyond the town lay the sea: a wall of tarnished silver against the bright, clear sky.

I left the bus at the squalid beginnings of Cheriton: a red suburb plastered with advertisements, fringing the wide, wind-swept plateau of the camp. I walked down Risborough Lane: canteens, 'soldiers' homes', outlying hutments – a no-man's-land which was still, technically, an outpost of 'Civvy street', but tainted, already, with the very smell of soldiering.

A few swaddies passed: all bullshitted up for the pictures or a piss-up in the town. I didn't know where the Company was quartered, and had to ask the way; but nobody else seemed to know either. I reached the confines of the camp, and took a path across open fields; a football-match was in progress: red and yellow jerseys mingling and shifting under the bright light, like figures in a ballet. Shouts and laughter came faintly across the fields: a single bugle sounded, remotely from somewhere beyond the garrison church.

More soldiers passed me: there were no civvies now – I had crossed the frontier, this was a soldiers' land. I asked the way again, and walked on – past the garrison church, towards the further boundaries of the camp and the cliffs above Sandgate.

When at last I found the company buildings, no one seemed to be about. I remembered the place, as one remembers something in a dream; it had once formed part of the old military hospital. Years ago, before the war, I had visited a friend of my brother's, Jack Fearnside-Speed, who had been in hospital with a broken leg . . . I followed an arrow which pointed to the orderly-room, knocked at the door and went in. A clerk sat at the table, struggling with a new typewriter ribbon; he looked browned-off. For a moment or two he didn't even bother to look up; then he raised his head and glanced at me with a faintly questioning air.

'You the bloke what's re-enlisted?' he asked.

'That's right,' I said.

'Cor, you must be crackers,' he said.

'I shouldn't wonder,' I replied.

The clerk's comment hadn't surprised me: it was exactly what I had been expecting. 'What do I do?' I asked.

'You better see the RSM – only he's gone to his tea, now, so you'll have to hang on a bit ... Tell you what, you could have some tea yourself, if you like.'

I said I thought some tea would be nice, only I hadn't any eating-irons yet, and I didn't know where the mess was.

'OK, I'll fix you up in a jiffy – I'm just waiting for my mate to relieve me. Then you can borrow his eating-irons, and I'll take you down.' He paused, and once again eyed me with a wondering curiosity.

'What you do it for?' he inquired. 'Trouble at home, like?'

I said no, I hadn't had any trouble at home. I just wanted a job.

'But why choose the soddin' Army?'

I said I didn't think Civvy Street was so good nowadays.

'Cor, they won't get *me* back, once I'm out ... What job was you on before, then?'

I explained that I was a writer.

'A sort of journalist,' I added, for the word 'writer' plainly hadn't registered. Probably I'd have been 'directed' into a coal mine, I said, if I hadn't done something about it.

'One of the spivs, eh?' said the clerk, eyeing me, for the first time, with something like respect.

'Just a drone, I expect,' I said.

'How long you been out, then?' he asked.

'Two years – just upon.' I added, with a bit of swank, that I'd got five and a half year's service in. The clerk, a boy of eighteen just conscripted, looked at me rather as a primitive tribesman might look at a sacred lunatic; his horror mingled with a certain superstitious awe.

'Cor, you must *like* the Army,' he muttered.

'I suppose in a way, I do,' I agreed.

He shook his head: sacred lunatics were something quite outside his orbit.

'Like to have a look at the paper?' he asked, and pushed over a copy of the *Daily Mirror,* well thumbed and folded very small.

I read 'Belinda' and 'Buck Ryan', and some paragraphs about Bruce Woodcock. Presently the clerk's relief arrived, I borrowed his eating-irons, and we went down to tea. It was good – fish and chips, well cooked and plenty of it. In my rôle of sacred lunatic I was treated with a certain politeness – almost as a sort of valuable pet. The unit seemed, from what I could gather, fairly cushy; I was lucky not to have been posted to Boyce Barracks, the Regimental Depot at Crookham.

After tea I was interviewed by the RSM.

'CO's inspection tomorrow,' he said. 'Stand-to-your-bed at oh-eight-fifteen. Ordinary days you parade on the square at oh-eight-thirty ... You better draw some webbing and get it blancoed ... What was your trade before – STO, eh? Well, you'll have to have a trade-test, of course – we'll send you to Woolwich for that ... All right, then – that'll be all.'

I came smartly to attention: it felt odd doing it in civvies. At the store, I drew a very incomplete kit: they were short of nearly everything. The corporal, who seemed nice, took me up to the barrack-rooms and found me a bed. I took off my civvies and put on the rough Angola shirt and battle-dress trousers. Then I went out to the Ablutions and started to blanco my webbing. The chap in the next bed to mine offered to give me a hand.

'You struck unlucky, coming on a Tuesday,' he said. 'Still, the CO's pretty cushy – as long as you've got your webbing laid out all right, that's all he's worried about.'

While my webbing dried I sewed the divisional flashes and medal-ribbons on to my tunic. The row of five ribbons looked, I thought, rather grand. I looked at the Italy star and remembered, suddenly, a farmhouse in the Abruzzi, the *padrone* pouring out wine from a big *fiasca*, and the *signora* cutting up the long strips of *pasta* at the table. But that had been a different Army ... In the barrack-room, the wireless was tuned in to the Light Programme: a talk for housewives on how to cook dried cod. Not surprisingly, nobody was listening to it; most of the room's occupants were getting ready to go out. Some were high-polishing their boots; a few lay back on their bed-cots, reading the *Mirror* or *Picture Post*. The chap next to me showed me the regulation way of laying out webbing: he was a Cockney, with a snouty face and a mop of black hair plastered down with grease; he seemed friendly, and showed no undue surprise at my having re-enlisted.

'You stayin' in tonight, or coming out to the pictures?' he asked. 'There's a smashing one at the Odeon – Dorothy Lamour.'

I thanked him, and said I thought I'd stay in tonight. Presently he went out: the barrack-room by now was almost empty. I had a wash, made my bed down, and lay back with my head against my kit-bag, reading an old number of *Picture Post*.

The wireless droned out a swing-tune; from the open window a cool wind, smelling of the sea, played over my bare arms and chest. I felt relaxed, free of responsibility, happy; I was back in the Army.

II

Reveillé was at six: but it wasn't like the reveillés I remembered. There was none of the shouting, none of the time-honoured cracks: 'Wakey-wakey, rise-and-shine, show a leg there'; the night orderly-sergeant simply stamped into the barrack-room, switched on the lights and the wireless, and stamped out again. The wireless was tuned in, full-blast, to the American Forces Network: a deafening blare of swing music, interspersed with announcements in the jaunty, get-together-boys voice of the campus. Reveillé had become an impersonal, mechanical affair, 'laid on' like gas or tap-water and with an American accent.

It seemed impossible that anybody should continue to sleep through such a din; yet most of the room's occupants showed no signs of stirring. Conscripts, for the most part, of nineteen or twenty, they belonged to a generation which had been 'conditioned' into an almost complete insensibility to noise. Reared in a quieter age, I did not share their immunity; soon I tumbled out of bed and made for the Ablutions. There were a dozen wash-basins between fifty-odd men: I had done well to come early. Soon there was a crowd: yawning, tousled, crapulous, they began to queue up for the basins; in the dim light their faces seemed reduced to a mere basic essence of maleness, indistinguishable one from another as a crowd of Japs or Eskimos. The water was icy, stinging the bed-warm flesh like the lash of a whip; jostled by my neighbours, I splashed my face and neck, and began to feel better. Individuals emerged, already half-familiar, from the vague, indeterminate mass of faces: my Cockney friend of the night before ('Wotcher mate, how yer liking it?'); a thin young man with straw-coloured hair; a boy with acne scars on his neck. Someone let a fart; there were laughs and cat-calls; one of the blokes began to sing – crooning, nasally, with a Yankee accent. It was, for me, a kind of rite of re-initiation – this crude, naked mass-encounter in the callow morning light. I hated it; yet it was a part of the life I had chosen. This first morning would be the worst: in a few days this frieze of blurred, formless countenances would have clicked into focus, separated itself into significant units – people I liked or didn't like, who bored me or made me laugh.

Back in the barrack-room, I folded my blankets, gave a rub to my brasses, swept my bed-space. The unit certainly seemed pretty cushy: there was no early roll-call parade. Once again I felt glad that I hadn't been sent to the Depot: Shorncliffe was a holding company for the Area; sooner or later – when I had had a trade-test at Woolwich – I should be posted; but I wasn't in any hurry to go; I lived, after all, only fifteen miles away.

The barrack-room windows looked out, over the cliff-tops, to the sea; somewhere out there, in the pale, diffused October sun-light, was Dungeness; below the cliff lay Seabrook and the coast-road to Hythe. The sea-wind, salt and chilly, blew in through a broken pane behind my bed; I stuck a piece of cardboard in the gap and, looking across the bay, had a sudden sense of home-coming: the view from the barrack-room was that upon which, in childhood, I had looked from the windows of my nursery.

Breakfast: rashers and mashed potatoes, and steaming mugs of tea. There was still a whole hour, before the CO's inspection, to tidy up the barrack-room. I arranged my webbing according to pattern; gave my new boots another polish; dusted the back of my bed and the top of my locker. Presently the orderly-sergeant called 'stand to your beds'. The CO came in, followed by the sergeant-major; when he reached my bed-space he said: 'Is this the new enlistment?' as though I were a parcel which had arrived by the morning post. The sergeant-major said: 'Yes-sir-short-service-en-gagement-of-three-years,' all in one breath. The CO looked at my medal-ribbons, then at my boots, then under my bed; and passed on.

'Report to my office after the parade,' said the sergeant-major.

The Cockney in the next bed-space was checked for dirty web-bing.

'No blanco in the store, sir.'

'Is that right, sergeant-major?'

'New consignment came in yesterday, sir.'

'Put him on a charge.'

After that, the CO went round the room rather quickly, looking bored; there were no more charges.

When we were dismissed I reported to the sergeant-major's room.

'Report in half-an-hour outside the CO's office,' he said.

I hung about for half-an-hour in the barrack-room; then I went back to the main building. I waited another half-hour. Presently the sergeant-major came past and looked at me vaguely, as though he remembered seeing me before somewhere.

'Your name Brooke?'

'Yes, sir.'

'Better go and have your Naafi-break. Come back in half-an-hour.'

I went over to the cookhouse, and drank a mug of tea. Then I went back and waited outside the CO's office. Presently the RSM came back.

'You the new enlistment?'

'Yes, sir.'

'All right, come back in twenty minutes.'

I went back to the barrack-room and gave my boots another brush-up; then I returned punctually to the office. This time the RSM was waiting outside.

'Where the hell have *you* been?' he said angrily. 'All right, hang on outside till I call you in.'

I hung on for another quarter of an hour; then the RSM opened the door and bawled 'Private Brooke!'

I marched in, came smartly to attention, and saluted.

'Private Brooke?'

'Yes, sir.'

'You've re-enlisted for a short-service engagement, eh?'

'Yes, sir – three years.'

'What was your job in civilian life?'

'Journalist, sir.'

'H'm – journalist, eh? What sort of papers did you write for?'

My mind went suddenly blank: I wasn't prepared for this. There was nothing for it – I should have to tell the truth.

'*Horizon, New Writing* and *The Nineteenth Century*,' I said, devoutly hoping that he hadn't heard of any of them.

As it happened he hadn't: so far, at least, as one could judge from his expression.

'Not much future in it, eh?' he asked.

'No, sir.'

Then he asked me about my former Army trade, I should have to have a trade-test, he said; till then, they could only give me five bob a day.

'But you'll get back-pay as from enlistment, when it comes through from Records,' he added, consolingly. Luckily I had just been paid a sixty-pound advance on a novel; but it didn't, at that moment, seem necessary to say so.

'H'm, yes – well, we'll have to find you a job . . . You seem to be an educated sort of bloke . . . Where were you thinking of putting him, sergeant-major?'

'They want someone in the store, sir.'

'All right, then – he'd better work there for the present. All right, er –' (he looked down at a note on the desk in front of him). 'All right, Brooke.'

I was marched out.

'Report to Corporal Bradnum in the store,' said the sergeant-major.

I reported to Corporal Bradnum. He was drinking a belated mug of Naafi tea with his mate.

'There's a drop left, if you'd like it,' he said.

We sat and smoked for half-an-hour till the tea was finished.

'What's to do?' I said.

'F— all, at the moment. There's a pile of eleven-fifty-sevens wants checking sometime, but that'll do after dinner.'

'I'm easy,' I said.

Corporal Bradnum settled down to the *Daily Mirror* crossword; his mate read a very old number of *Illustrated*.

'Word of seven letters beginning with C, meaning "heat to a high temperature",' said the corporal.

'Calcine,' I said.

'That's right – now I can get thirteen down – blank–p–blank: "man is descended from it." Cor, I dunno how these blokes think of these things.'

'Ape,' I said.

'I say, Corp,' said the other bloke, whose name was Andy, 'did you see that bit in this 'ere book about nudist camps?'

'Ay, I saw that. I wouldn't 'arf mind being a nudist, meself.'

'Some o' the tarts is proper smashing . . . It must be sort of queer at first – you'd think some of the blokes 'd get a hell of a – '

'Come on now,' the corporal cut in, 'let's get on with some o' them eleven-fifty-sevens.'

We started on the eleven-fifty-sevens: kit-lists of blokes who had just been demobbed.

'This bastard's diffy of one belt, web.'

'That's all right, there's that buckshee one you whipped off the bloke that went to Catterick.'

'Yes, but I thought I'd keep that – it might come in handy – you never know.'

'Proper QM you're getting – you better sign on.'

'Catch me . . .' The corporal suddenly turned to me. 'Say, are you the bloke that signed on again?'

'Yes, that's me.'

'Cor, stone a crow. What you do it for – was the police after you?'

'No – at least I don't think they were.'

'Come on Andy, get weaving.'

'It's half-twelve,' said Andy, who had lit a fag and picked up the *Mirror*.

'So it is and all – another morning gone,' said the Corporal. 'Sixty-six and a half days more before my demob – and by Christ,' he added, with a grin at me, 'they won't get *me* back.'

At two o'clock we came back; Andy had scrounged a jug of tea from the cookhouse, and we sat around for half-an-hour drinking it. Then we checked some more of the kits: several of them were diffy.

'You can't blame them,' said the corporal, philosophically, 'not when they're being demobbed.'

Andy went off at three o'clock to play football: the unit was playing the West Kents, and Andy was considered a very promising right-half.

'You can get off anything in the Army, if you play football,' said the corporal.

We checked the rest of the kits; then it was tea-time.

'They've got welsh-rarebit on today,' said the corporal. 'Ought to be worth trying . . . You know,' he added, looking at me with that expression of awe to which I was becoming, already, accustomed, 'you know, I can't make you out: an educated bloke like you signing on as a regular – it don't seem natural.'

'Probably,' I said, 'it's not.'

After tea I had a wash and lay on my bed for half-an-hour; then I walked down Hospital Hill to Seabrook.

It had rained in the afternoon: the tarred road and the roofs of the barrack-buildings gleamed in the dusk with a hard, steely brightness. The sea lay, faintly distinguishable, beneath a thickening pall of cloud; in the west, the clouds had parted, showing a yellow rift of sunset-light. In front of me, as I walked down the hill, the Military Canal caught the last, rainy brightness: a broad ribbon of tarnished silver stretching away towards Hythe and the Marshes. Dimly, between the road and the sea, I could make out a scattered cluster of buildings: a vague shapeless mass which must be the old police-station, and a smaller, more angular silhouette which I recognized as that of the lifeboat-station – that extraordinary Gothic structure, more like a Chapel than a boathouse, which we used to call the Goose Cathedral.

III

It must (I thought) have been my friend Eric Anquetil who, in some far-off summer, had thus oddly christened it. The name had stuck; and I could never, afterwards, refer to the boathouse by any other name. We called it the 'Goose Cathedral' on account of the geese which, at that period, waddled about the shingle patch surrounding it. Standing there, bleakly isolated, where the coast-road curves inland through Seabrook, the 'cathedral' had appealed immediately to Eric's taste for the odd and outlandish. Anything less like one's idea of a lifeboat-station it would have been hard, indeed, to imagine. Seeing it from a passing bus, one would have supposed it to be some kind of Nonconformist tabernacle – a spiky and ornate affair in pseudo-Ruskinian Gothic. Yet who, after all, would build a chapel just here, on this desolate tract of coast, within a few yards of the sea itself?

Over the Gothic porch was inscribed the date of its completion

– 1875. The walls were of a peculiarly forbidding grey stone, strongly built to withstand the south-west gales and the periodic assaults of the sea itself which, in winter, on days of high-tide, would flood the shingle patch and the road beyond. The slate roof was topped by a small turretted belfry; on either side of it protruded a pair of elaborately gabled windows. These struck a faintly anachronistic note, being small and circular and vaguely suggestive of portholes; one could fancy that the 'chapel' had been dedicated, originally, to some patron-saint of sailors.

In later years, I could appreciate the oddity of this chapel-by-the-sea; its incongruity was 'amusing' and at the same time rather sinister, like something in a surrealist picture. My friends laughed at it, and invented fantastic legends about its inhabitants; yet in my childhood there had seemed nothing specially odd about the boathouse; it was as much a normal part of the landscape as the neighbouring police-station, or the Fountain Hotel just across the road. To me it seemed no more surprising for a lifeboat to be housed in a chapel than for a snail to inhabit its shell; indeed, I should probably have been surprised (and perhaps a trifle shocked) if I had come across a lifeboat-station which was *not* built in the Gothic style.

Seeing it again now, looming dimly in the autumn dusk, I could hardly believe that it was indeed the true, the authentic Goose Cathedral which I was looking at. In the gathering dark it looked like the ghost of itself; and not less improbable, too, seemed the memories which, at the sudden sight of it, had flocked into my mind. Childhood memories – I remembered being taken to look at the lifeboat; memories of boyhood, botanizing on the shingle flats towards Hythe; and later occasions, when I had come back to live at Folkestone and had bathed, with Eric, from the beach below the boathouse. I remembered personalities and incidents that I hadn't thought of for years; it was like re-reading a forgotten, rather 'dated' novel, which had seemed plausible and 'true-to-life' at the time but which, with the passing of the years, had lost its power to convince.

I felt oddly saddened by the spiky, Gothic silhouette, and the ghosts which (itself a ghost, it seemed) the 'Goose Cathedral' had evoked. I walked along to the Fountain Hotel, that friendly Victorian pub which stands at the corner where the lane called Horn

Street branches off from the coast-road towards Dibgate and Peri-car Woods.

The bar at the Fountain was almost empty.

'Signed-on again, have you?' said the landlord who, an ex-gunner himself, was inclined to be sympathetic. 'You might do worse,' he said.

Yes, I thought, as I ordered another pint: I might do worse.

I went back early: my two new pairs of boots needed further attention before tomorrow morning. I was in bed before lights out. I listened to the Last Post, sounding remote and melancholy from somewhere on the heights above. Then I slept. It seemed no more than an hour or two before I awoke, deadly-tired, and with a sense of outrage at being roused in the middle of the night. I woke to a blaze of light: footsteps clumped heavily past my bed; a moment later, a raucous blare of sound filled the room.

'It's now six ack-emma, British time ... This is the American Forces Network, broadcasting to all American troops overseas ...'

CHAPTER TWO

The Wild Soldiers

I

In my early childhood, the Goose Cathedral (though its name, in those days, had yet to be invented) marked the limit – or nearly the limit – of our outings in that direction. Sometimes I would be taken to look at the lifeboat itself – an enormous blue-and-red prow protruding, like some captive leviathan, from the Gothic doors. The boatmen wore blue jerseys and chewed tobacco; I was given to understand that they were very brave. One of them fascinated me particularly because he wore small gold ear-rings, of precisely the same pattern as those worn by my nurse. He must, I suppose, be some kind of woman, though he didn't in the least resemble one in other respects. Such a fusion of the sexes rather upset my ideas: I had encountered the same anomaly in Kenny Meadows's illustrations to *Macbeth*, where the witches were shown with beards and moustaches.

But it wasn't chiefly the lifeboat (or even its androgynous attendant) which gave to our walks along this stretch of coast their peculiar quality of excitement. I was more interested, for instance, in the yellow horned poppies, which were abundant on the waste patch beyond the boathouse; I had also, on a memorable occasion, found coltsfoot there for the first time; and beyond the lifeboat lay vast, remote regions which I had never explored, but into which I hoped, one day, to penetrate.

On one occasion I had indeed found myself in the furthest hinterland of that unknown territory. 'Found myself' is the right phrase, for I had been taken by car, and this, I felt, didn't really 'count'. I had gone, with my family, to see the famous 'American Gardens' which some rich man had 'laid out' at, I think, Saltwood, or it may have been Sandling. I had no idea why they were called

'American'; in fact, I still don't know; but the name seemed appropriate to their remote situation. (I more than half suspected that the place we had come to was, indeed, America). As for the gardens themselves, they were rather dull – consisting entirely (so far as I can remember) of rhododendrons and azaleas. If these were American gardens, then I, for one, preferred the English kind.

The lifeboat-station, then, was a landmark and a limit; sometimes our morning walks would take us there, but more often we would set off in the opposite direction, towards Folkestone: either climbing the cliff-paths to the town itself, or (if we were merely going for a 'walk'), keeping along the 'Lower Road' as far as the toll-gate, or perhaps a little beyond – though we seldom went much further, because that end of the road was considered rather 'sordid' – a mysterious quality which was reputedly shared by the Hippodrome at Dover and (as I learnt when we went to London a few years later) by Madame Tussaud's and the King's Road, Chelsea. On the rare occasions when we did penetrate beyond the toll-gate, I was rather attracted by this dubious territory which, in the summer, became a kind of Luna Park, with a switchback, automatic machines and a Pierrot show called the Pom-Poms: all, no doubt, very 'sordid', but possessing, for me, the fascination of forbidden fruit; for I was not, of course, allowed to go on the switchback or to visit the Pierrots.

II

'Going shopping?' inquired my Aunt Ada, brusquely, one morning, just as we were setting out from the house. (She and my Uncle Arthur must, at that time, have been home on leave from India).

I shook my head, suddenly embarrassed, and quite unable to explain that we were not, in fact, going 'shopping', but were bound on quite a different errand.

Since I didn't answer her question, my aunt repeated it. In an agony of embarrassment, I managed at last to mutter, shamefacedly, that we were *not* going shopping.

'Well, where *are* you going, then?' my aunt insisted.

We were going, I whispered, to Pay the Books.

My aunt made that noise which, in old-fashioned novels, is indicated by the word 'Pshaw!' – implying, in this case, only too eloquently, that she didn't hold with such hair-splitting distinctions.

But for me the distinction was a perfectly definite one; and Aunt Ada's brisk assumption distressed me – implying as it did that I and my family belonged to the same world as herself, a world where, no doubt (among other peculiarities), little boys and their nurses were in the habit of 'going shopping'. I resented such simplifications: *I* was *I*, I belonged to *my* family, who lived at Number Nine, Radnor Cliffe, Sandgate, Kent, and were by no means to be confused with the families of those aunts and uncles who, periodically, descended upon us for visits, filling our house with their alien (and usually frightening) habits, and their loud, unfamiliar voices.

I don't know why the idea of 'going shopping' seemed to me, in some way, humiliating; but most certainly it did. Possibly it was an embryonic form of snobbery: most of our provisions were 'delivered' by the tradesmen, and we seldom had to go and buy things, ourselves, in the town. Yet I cannot believe that I was aware, at that time, of such social *nuances*: my distress, I think, was caused merely by an exaggerated, an almost pedantic awareness of the distinctions between things. I was extremely pernickety, for instance, about names: my family would enrage me by calling the riverside plant, *Typha latifolia*, a Bulrush – whereas I knew that its correct name, according to the books, was the Great Reed Mace.

It was the same with 'shopping': we were not going to Folkestone to *buy* things – unless it were a spongecake which, for a treat, I was sometimes allowed to bring away from Gironimo's, and eat on the way home. We were going to Pay the Books; I wasn't sure, exactly, what this meant; but the outsides of these 'books' were perfectly familiar to me: small, strongly-bound volumes like miniature ledgers, with the shopkeeper's name embossed in gilt on the cover. (The butcher's book had, in addition, a rather interesting picture of a cow). But Paying the Books was not, it seemed, an event which occurred in the alien, inferior world inhabited by my aunts and uncles; or if it did, it was not distinguished as a separate activity; it came, apparently, under the same category as 'shopping': which only showed, I thought, how different my world was from theirs.

I was, in fact, profoundly aware by this time of the gulf which separated me from the rest of mankind. I was fatally and incurably 'different'. I had suspected it for a long time; but recently I had begun to attend the Kindergarten at Gaudeamus, the girls' school in Sandgate where my sister was a boarder; and here my suspicions had ripened into certainty. I had known very few other little boys up till then – my brother was a decade older than I – and such few as I had met I had almost invariably loathed. They seemed to me of a different species: they talked of subjects about which I knew nothing, they were continually doing things which, even if I was able to do them myself (and I usually wasn't) seemed to me stupid and unnecessary. They jumped from high walls, they sprayed each other with the garden-hose, they laughed uproariously at the jokes in *Puck* and *The Rainbow*; they had, every one of them, a passion for ball-games and model railways, both of which I found hopelessly boring. On one occasion the young son of a friend of my mother's came to stay, and we were bathed together; by some curious *trompe d'oeil* I formed the impression that he possessed two penises, whereas I had only one. The fact didn't particularly surprise me; it merely confirmed what I had always known – that I was not like other little boys.

Plainly I was destined to develop, on sound Adlerian lines, as a victim of Organic Inferiority. Possibly I did – though, with all due respect to the psycho-analysts, I'm inclined to doubt it. I neither felt particularly inferior, nor, so far as I know, did I indulge in orgies of over-compensation. I was merely aware, with a sometimes painful acuteness, of being Different. This awareness of difference extended to my family: they were different from other people's families, and I resented all assumptions to the contrary. Other little boys from other families might, in the mornings, 'go shopping' with their nannies; I, on the contrary, went to Pay the Books with Ninnie.

Perhaps some early speech-difficulty had resulted in my calling her 'Ninnie'; but Ninnie she remained, and I fiercely resented any attempt, on the grown-ups' part, to call her by any other name. I loved her with a jealous and exclusive passion: with my mother and my brother, she completed the trinity of those whom, alone in all the world, I would admit to my affection. She returned my love: and the thought that one day she might leave us was one of the two major horrors which haunted my existence – the other being the prospect of going to boarding-school.

In my love I was to some extent a fetishist: Ninnie possessed, for example, some special embroidered aprons which she did not, on normal occasions, wear. They were laid away in the enormous domed trunk which contained the whole of her possessions, and were kept for 'best'. But whenever I was unwell – or 'not just the thing' – I would beg her to put on one of the cherished aprons, which had acquired for me a kind of symbolic potency, as though their smooth, goffered folds were a visible manifestation of Ninnie's devoted love and her magical power to console.

Once a year Ninnie went away for a holiday with her mother, who lived at Dover. For a whole fortnight I was deprived of her comfortable and reassuring presence. I dreaded these occasions; yet, I could, at times, be guilty of disloyalty in her absence. Thus, she would beg me not to eat cold boiled bacon while she was away; for as sure as fate, if I ate it, I should be afflicted with what she referred to as 'sand in my water'. Alas! Like some apostate Jew I would yield to the persuasions of my family; and devour my daily slice of bacon; with the result, of course, that I suffered from violent indigestion till the day of Ninnie's return. One glance at the tell-tale sediment in the *pot* was enough to enlighten her; I was promptly dosed with liquorice powder and put to bed: there to suffer all the agonies of remorse, coupled with the acuter discomfort caused by the liquorice. My unhappiness, however, had its consolations; for I knew that, when the liquorice had 'acted', Ninnie was sure to come and sit by my side, attired in the customary, the quasi-sacramental apron, and read to me *The Tale of Mr Tod* or a story from *Little Folks.*

III

On the days when we were not going into Folkestone to Pay the Books, we would go, merely, for a 'walk'. Usually this meant the 'Lower Road', which led from our house, along the undercliff, to Folkestone harbour. The undercliff, a tract of semi-wild land between the Leas and the beach, was for me a kind of substitute for the 'country'. Innumerable small paths traversed the bushy slopes; here and there, where the trees were planted more thickly, one could almost imagine oneself in a real wood. It was a manageable, a half-domesticated wilderness, where one could never wander far enough from the road to feel lonely or frightened. At night, certainly, it might have its terrors: my mother would never walk along it alone, after dark, for it was reputed (and perhaps justly) to be haunted by 'drunken soldiers'. In the day-time, however, there was no danger from the military or from anybody else: we met few people on our walks (at any rate during the winter months) and the undercliff became peopled, for me, chiefly with the personages of my own private mythology. Some of these, indeed, were inimical: particularly the Acorn-headed Tents, which I invested with such a potent atmosphere of horror that I lay awake every night for weeks, watching for their august and terrible forms to emerge from behind the nursery wardrobe. It was useless for Ninnie to assure me that these beings 'didn't exist'; I knew otherwise; had I not seen them, leaning rakishly against the wall of the toll-house, along the Lower Road? Ninnie's words, as it happened, far from consoling me, had the effect of increasing my terrors. The word 'exist' was new to me: and by its association, albeit a negative one, with the Tents, it acquired a terror of its own, suggesting to me, for some inexplicable reason, a kind of hair-net, such as Ninnie herself was in the habit of wearing. These sinister black webs thenceforward became associated with the Tents who, if they could speak, would probably (I felt) whisper sibilantly in my ear, as I lay in the darkness, the evil and minatory word: *'Exist'*.

The toll-gate lay at the further end of the Lower Road; the toll-keeper was a friend of ours – her name was Mrs Mawby, but from the time I could talk I called her Dadda-at-the-toll-gate. She wore a cloth cap; and this was enough to identify her, for me, with my father. Once, when Miss Trumpett came to stay with us, and had taken me for my morning walk, I had incurred her displeasure by hailing Mrs Mawby as 'Dadda'.

'But it's *not* your Dadda,' Miss Trumpett protested, in that rich, silky voice of hers in which, even at that age, I detected an exotic, almost indeed an erotic quality which never failed to alarm me.

'It is,' I insisted, obstinately.

'But it *isn't*,' Miss Trumpett repeated.

I was taken home in disgrace. It was my first experience of adult injustice: I was honestly convinced that my father and the toll-keeper, if not precisely one and the same, were at least aspects of the same divinity. Children are obstinately polytheistic; and not all Miss Trumpett's arguments could make me a monotheist. I drank my morning Bovril, gulping back my tears, and listening with an entire lack of comprehension to Miss Trumpett's flute-like and blandishing tones. Presently she left me to my disgrace; and I pretended, miserably, to look at the pictures in *Little Black Mingo*, in which the wicked Black Noggy seemed to me to bear a startling resemblance to Miss Trumpett herself.

But whether or not Mrs Mawby was my father (and the point, to me, didn't seem worth arguing about), it was quite certain that the Tents, which had inspired me with such horror, inhabited her house by the toll-gate. At first sight they had seemed quite ordinary tents; Mrs Mawby let them out to trippers at sixpence an hour; I must have seen them many times on the beach below our house. But leaning against Mrs Mawby's porch – tall, shrouded figures, with small black acorn-heads – they seemed to me evil beings, capable of wreaking their will upon myself. Night after night I pictured them hobbling along the undercliff towards our house – their white shrouds flapping, their acorn-heads nodding balefully one to another, conversing in high, squeaky voices like the voices of bats; nearer and nearer they came – in at the door, up the stairs . . . I would lie trembling, trying to be brave (because I had decided to be a soldier when I grew up), but compelled, at last, to call out to Ninnie, who slept in the big bed at my side. A moment later, the room was mercifully flooded with light: I was given some milk and a Petit Beurre biscuit and, as I lay listening to Ninnie reading *Mr Tod* for the hundredth time, I felt a blessed relief steal over me. The familiar words soothed me like an incantation; the Acorn-heads had vanished, defeated by a superior magic; Ninnie's voice became fainter and fainter; and at last I slept.

But the mythology of the Lower Road, apart from such notable exceptions, was not particularly alarming: for most of the creatures with whom I peopled it were, like the undercliff itself, partly domesticated.

There were, for instance, the wild soldiers (or airmen: I didn't distinguish very accurately between the two breeds). I cherished a secret and (I felt) somewhat discreditable passion for the Army (which included, at that time, the Royal Flying Corps); I wanted, when I grew up, to be a soldier or an airman myself; but in my heart of hearts I knew this to be a mere romantic phantasy; my profound and incurable 'difference' precluded me, I felt, from ever being a 'real' soldier.

I consoled myself by inventing a race of 'wild' soldiers – a tractable and harmless breed, smaller than the real ones (they were not more than two feet high), who could be kept as pets. They were easily tamed, and appeared to thrive in captivity: I fed them on Plasmon Oats and Robinson's Patent Barley. In the wild state, they nested among the bushes beneath the cliff; I recognized their nests – flattened, grassy patches among the denser undergrowth, bearing the recent imprint of their bodies. (No doubt these 'nests' were, in reality, the nocturnal retreats of loving couples; the official explanation, however, was that 'tramps' slept in them – and I was not allowed to examine them too closely, for fear of Picking Up Something).

The fauna of the undercliff included, also, a number of 'wild' variants of people with whom I was, or had been, in love. Among these were my brother's friend Basil Medlicott, and Alison Vyse, with whom I had fallen desperately in love during my first term at Gaudeamus: she was two or three years older than myself, and had given a brilliant performance as Puck in the school production of *A Midsummer-Night's Dream*. As for the 'real' people we met along the Lower Road, they were comparatively few. There was a pleasant lady who always smiled at us as we passed: she possessed a white terrier which was kept so scrupulously clean that it always appeared to have been bathed that very morning. This dog, for some reason, or other, became the basis of yet another of my private myths; he lived, I decided, somewhere up in the hills near the barracks, and I even invented a little tune, a kind of *Leitmotif* to accompany his appearances: it consisted of a single, rather melancholy phrase, reminiscent of a bugle-call. The terrier, I think, was a kind of dog-soldier, a distant relation of the 'wild' soldiers on the undercliff who, though 'human' in other respects, did, in fact, possess short white tails, like rabbits.

Sometimes we would meet Mrs Croker, the novelist; and quite often Sir Squire Bancroft would boom a genial greeting to us as he passed. With his bush of white hair and his black-ribboned monocle he was a somewhat terrifying figure; I felt more at ease with his red-haired Scotch parlourmaid, Rae, who often used to bob out of the 'Tradesmen's Entrance' of his house, as we went by, and offer me an 'Animal' biscuit – those fascinating confections made in the shapes of dogs, lions, rabbits and so forth. (Are they, I wonder, still obtainable?)

There was, too, at about this time or perhaps slightly earlier, a certain Mr Wells, who lived at Spade House: my brother and sister were invited to his children's parties, and would return laden with presents. One of these presents was passed on to me – a set of small and exquisite models of the Japanese fleet. I was too young to be invited to these parties – a fact which, if I was aware of it at all, must have been a profound relief to me, for I had a horror of all social functions. My relief, however, was tempered in after years by regret, when I learnt that the Mr Wells of Spade House was none other than the author of *Kipps* and *Mr Polly*.

Later, I became less interested in the fauna – 'real' or imaginary – of the undercliff than in its flora. It was not the 'country', and botanizing at Sandgate was a poor substitute for the real thing; only in the summer, when we went to our cottage in the Elham Valley, could I feel that the flowers I found were genuinely 'wild' ones: at Sandgate they seemed, like the local fauna, semi-domesticated.

The most exciting floral inhabitant of the undercliff was, for me, the Cuckoo-pint, or Lords-and-Ladies. There was, at this time, a rather grand prep. school at Sandgate, reputed to cater chiefly for the sons of the aristocracy. I have forgotten its name; but we often met the boys, in their scarlet caps, being shepherded, in a crocodile, along the cliff paths. They were known, locally, as the 'Little Lords and Dukes'; and Lords-and-ladies became, for me, arbitrarily associated with them. Not quite arbitrarily, perhaps: for the Cuckoo-pint, common as it is, has a certain quality of aristocracy, of being a 'cut above' its proletarian neighbours. To me, it seemed quite evidently not a 'weed'; and the pale spathe, with the purple or yellow spadix standing erect within its shade, seemed not only distinguished, but in some way exotic and rather sinister. I certainly hadn't learnt, at that time, the difference between a monocotyledon, and a dicotyledon; but most of the plants which impressed me by their beauty or strangeness were in fact monocotyledonous. The hyacinths, the lilies, the amaryllises – above all, the orchids – seemed to me naturally to take a higher rank in the floral hierarchy than mere dead-nettles, speedwell or cow-parsley.

One of the charms of the Cuckoo-pint was its habit of putting forth its earliest leaves in the middle of winter. In January or February – or even, in a mild season, as early as December – we would detect the first tightly-folded shoots pushing their way through the carpet of dead leaves beneath the still-leafless tamarisks or elders. Their brilliant shiny green had a flame-like, an almost praeternatural intensity: even in April and May, when their glory was diminished by the competition of other plants, the cuckoo-pint leaves still stood out bravely and assertively; but in winter, emerging solitary and naked from the brown, sodden leafmould, they had the breath-taking splendour of a fanfare of trumpets heard suddenly in a country silence.

From week to week we watched the glossy, sagittate leaves unfold: some immaculately green, others blotched and spotted like those of the Early Purple Orchid. Their thick, juicy texture made them seem edible and probably delicious; in fact, as I knew, they were 'deadly poison', and I wasn't allowed to pick them. I was infinitely disappointed: for weeks I was consumed by a passion of concupiscence for those bright and arrowy shapes. At last, unable to bear it any longer, I decided upon a method of satisfying my lust which, if not positively deceitful, had a certain jesuitical cunning. Might I not, I asked, pick *just one*? I had been reading about the ingenious methods by which the plant was fertilized; I wanted to examine its internal structure – which I couldn't do unless I was allowed to pick a specimen. I would take every precaution against its lethal properties; I would wear gloves; I would promise to keep my mouth shut all the time, lest the plant's devilish exhalations should overcome me . . .

Such a heartfelt plea in the cause of science could hardly be refused; my wish was granted at last. Had I asked to dig up a mandrake, there couldn't have been more fuss: wearing leather gloves, and (as though this were not enough) wrapping the leaves and spathe in a sheet of thick brown paper, I set to work with a trowel; and at last, in triumph, bore aloft the entire uprooted plant.

I duly dissected it, and afterwards kept it for a time in a pot of water; but (unlike my 'wild' pets) it didn't thrive in captivity, wilting, indeed, almost at once. But I was satisfied; I never wanted to gather another. Thenceforward I was content to observe the aristocratic, sinister plant *in situ*; alert, from late autumn onwards, for the first sign of those shrill green flames springing beneath the dead, crackling undergrowth, among the flattened 'nests' of the wild soldiers.

IV

Another plant, which not only appeared above ground, but actually flowered in midwinter, grew on sheltered banks round Sandgate. This was the sweet-scented Butterbur, or Winter Heliotrope. What I really wanted to find was the 'true' Butterbur, which was a native British plant, whereas Winter Heliotrope was one of those species which the floras dismiss, with a high-handed xenophobia, as 'aliens', or 'escapes from cultivation'. The native Butterbur, however, didn't grow near Sandgate (though many years later I found it by a stream at Postling, only a few miles away); I had to be content with *Petasites fragrans*, which I felt didn't quite 'count' as a wild-flower.

Its pink, woolly-looking heads smelt delicious – thrusting themselves out of the glacial winter earth with a hardiness which their delicate texture seemed to belie. Sometimes they would be in flower by Christmas, and I would gather them on our way back from Sandgate Church on Christmas morning. After the flowers came the round, dark-green leaves, very like those of coltsfoot.

Coltsfoot itself I had never found; I was mistakenly convinced that it was Very Rare. The rumour that it grew at Seabrook, beyond the lifeboat-station, haunted me for a whole winter; and one bright, windy morning in March we set out to look for it. I had been, of course, to Seabrook before – to look at the lifeboat, or, in late summer, to find the yellow horned poppy; but I had not, I think, been there so early in the year, and the occasion was in every respect a special one.

That stretch of road between Sandgate and Seabrook seemed to me then – and seems still – to evoke a sense of vastness, of enormous, airy spaces, and of being at the mercy of the elements. The sea here was not the tame, insipid sea which lapped on the Folkestone beaches; it raged and thundered upon the narrow shore, battering itself with an elemental violence against the sea-wall and, on stormy days, flooding across the road itself and into the basements of the houses beyond. The sea-wall was (and indeed still is) in a constant state of being repaired; the sea here is the enemy, a relentless monster forever threatening the land, and never quite to be propitiated.

On one side, the sea: on the other, gently-rising hills, scattered with villas, and smudged with the grey smoke of tamarisks. On the hill-top lay Shorncliffe Camp, its barracks and hutments stretching away towards Cheriton and the Downs. The bugles, in those days, haunted this stretch of coast perpetually: their sad cries drifting faintly seaward, as though answering the far, muffled booming of the foghorns, out in the misty distances beyond Dungeness ... Desolate, wind-swept, faintly melancholy, the sea-road had for me an exciting, a rather adventurous quality: it led to foreign territory, outside our customary ambience. Seabrook merged into Hythe (already remote) and beyond Hythe began the mysterious and endless plain of Romney Marsh: the nearest approach to infinity which I was able to conceive.

The road turned inland at Seabrook; we passed in front of the lifeboat-station, and took the rough shingle track which continued along the top of the sea-wall. Here the note of desolation was intensified: there were no more houses, and the sea-wall was in a state of advanced ruin. On this blustery March day, the waves thundered with an implacable fury against the broken masses of concrete and, sucked back by the tide through a series of miniature ravines and crevasses, retreated down the boulder-strewn beach with their 'melancholy, long, withdrawing roar'. The flying spray, laced with small pebbles, flung itself across the path in sudden icy showers: soon our coats were drenched. Presently we left the path and clambered down into the shingly waste which lay between the sea and the Military Canal. This was a kind of *Terre gastée*, a desolate strip of land which had been allowed to run wild, I suppose, since the building of the canal. It was here that I had come to find the horned poppy; and here, on this sunny March morning, after only a few minutes search, I found the coltsfoot.

Goodness knows, it's a common enough flower; but for me, at

that time, it had all the glamour of rarity, and its discovery was as much of a thrill as would be, today, the finding of the Blue Sowthistle or the Military Orchid. We walked back along the coastroad; the wind buffeted us so that we staggered to and fro across the pavement; the sun blazed down upon a sea of almost Mediterranean splendour, patched with bottle-green and peacock-blue, and flecked with a multitude of 'white horses'.

I was possessed by a bursting, irrepressible happiness; I wanted to laugh and sing, because of the wind and the sunlight, and because I had found the coltsfoot. I did sing: but not a triumphal paean, not a rumbustious, roaring ditty such as one might have expected. No: what I sang was one of Mendelssohn's *Lieder öhne Worte* – a melancholy, rather wilting little tune, very Mendelssohnian; I think it is Number 1 of the *Opus*. I had perhaps heard my sister play it at home, or had listened to somebody 'practising' it at Gaudeamus. It seemed to me perfectly to express the spirit of that particular morning: the sunlight, the wind, the shifting lights on the sea, and the yellow stars of the coltsfoot which I clutched, drooping already, in my hot, impassioned hand. The association remained, fixed indelibly in my memory; and to this day I cannot hear the tune without visualizing that same, identical complex of images which, on that March morning half a lifetime past, seemed to be so inseparably linked with it.

The problem of such musical associations is a knotty one; I have never come across any very thorough analysis of it. How much, I wonder, is musical appreciation based on such accidents? Are there certain harmonic modes or progressions which tend to evoke particular states of mind? Probably not; music, says Stravinsky, 'expresses' nothing. But there is more to it than the mere accidental association (such as the one I have described) between a given phrase or melody and a particular moment of time. A musical work which one has never heard before can immediately suggest certain images (there are some good examples of this in Proust); myself, I find that almost any Gregorian plainsong induces in me a vivid sense of the English countryside. Why? I never (being a Protestant) heard plainsong in my childhood; I came to it completely fresh, and its emotive power depended on no direct associations whatsoever. All I can suppose is that it suggested to me the work of certain English composers – Vaughan Williams, Ireland,

Delius – who sometimes use archaic modes, and whom I had already associated with a 'country' atmosphere.

Whatever theories one may hold about the matter, one thing is unarguable – the sense of absolute conviction which accompanies such associations. Nothing, for instance, will shake me out of my belief that there *must* be a genuine psychic correspondence between that tune of Mendelssohn and the coast-road near Seabrook on a morning in early spring. My conviction is a mystical one: in precisely the same way, I take it, is the mystic convinced of his apprehension of the Numinous. The experience is so vivid to him that its validity seems to him self-evident. Unlike the mystic, however, I don't propose to advance intellectual arguments in support of my own numinous convictions; I have read (or tried to read) too many such attempts. My arguments might, I myself believe, be quite as cogent as most of the others; but that, alas! is not saying very much.

v

It was more often, then, in the late summer that we made the expedition to Seabrook: our chief object being, usually, to look for the yellow horned poppy. This charming flower; common enough locally, was not my own discovery; it was showy enough to have impressed other members of my family who were, generally speaking, bored by botany. My sister had gathered it at Seabrook – doubtless on some school botany-ramble; and in Anne Pratt's little book on poisonous plants my mother had recorded (in pencil, above the coloured plate) the fact that she had found it at Aldeburgh in 1888. According to Anne Pratt, it was 'one of the handsomest plants of our sea-shores' – a remark which seems to me to damn the horned poppy with faint praise; I should be inclined, myself, to call it one of the most curious and beautiful plants in the British Flora. Like the Cuckoo-pint, it impressed me (though it wasn't a monocotyledon) with its 'aristocratic' air: I loved the big, silky-golden flowers, so delicately contrasted with the tough, sinuous stems and the coarse-textured leaves; I was fascinated by the leaves themselves, whose glaucous bloom seemed to have imitated the very colour of the sea. I gathered whole bunches with a

greedy enthusiasm; but the horned poppy is a disappointing plant
to pick – the delicate flowers almost always 'fall' before one can get
them home.

The poppy, however, was by no means the only interesting denizen of that waste-land beyond the lifeboat station. Samphire grew
there, and the clammy and evil-smelling Viscid Groundsel, as well
as such minor attractions as Sand-spurrey and Sea-blite. Samphire
had a literary as well as a botanical interest – it was 'in Shakespeare'.
(Though common enough near Dover, it does not, I think, grow
on Shakespeare Cliff itself.) The ubiquitous Pepperwort and Sea-
mallow were there too, and a number of other maritime plants;
the place acquired for me a curious fascination, and I could wander
there, happily, for hours at a time.

Occasionally our walks would take us into the hinterland
behind Seabrook; but these expeditions were few and far between,
and involved, usually, a whole day's outing, with all the para-
phernalia of sandwiches and Thermos flasks. On these occasions
we turned up the road called Horn Street, beyond the Fountain
Hotel, into what, by courtesy, might be termed the 'country'; it
wasn't 'real' country – it still counted, for me, as the 'sea-side' – but
in Pericar Woods there were wild foxgloves and, reputedly, yellow
irises. I was unlucky over the irises; they must have grown in the
vicinity, for the girls of Gaudeamus brought back sheaves of them
from their botany-rambles. I had admired them, in big jars of
beaten copper, in the green-tiled fireplaces at the school, where
they provided a natural counterpart to the *art-nouveau*, iris-and-
water-lily scheme of decoration which prevailed. My failure to
find the irises myself was galling: doubtless the girls who had gathered them in Pericar Woods had taken them entirely for granted,
whereas for me they would have provided a major thrill. It was
always the same – the most exciting things invariably happened to
people who couldn't fully appreciate them; I was resigned to the
fact, by this time, and had adopted, in such matters, an attitude of
rather cynical fatalism.

Horn Street led not only to Pericar Woods but also to the mysterious territory, where, as I was told, 'the soldiers lived'; bugles
called sadly over the hillsides, beyond the woods, and one was apt
to encounter, suddenly and without warning, groups of red-faced
men in khaki who would sometimes laugh at us or shout rude
remarks as we passed. They terrified me – but only for so long as

they were in sight; once we were safely past them, my terror gave place to excited imaginings: I liked to think of myself as one of those laughing, devil-may-care heroes inhabiting the high, wind-swept plateau of Shorncliffe Camp. How old did one have to be (I would ask) before one could be a soldier? At least eighteen, I was told. I was seven – I had eleven years to wait; my ambition, I felt, would hardly survive for as long as that. Besides (as I knew per-fectly well), I wasn't that *sort* of person: I was 'different'.

I resigned myself to less exacting phantasies; and the red-faced, swaggering heroes of Horn Street were duly translated into smaller, more manageable versions of themselves; nesting in the undercliff, or confined in wire cages in my private 'Zoo' – half human, half-animal, smooth-faced fauns with putteed legs and (protruding from their khaki-covered buttocks) small white tails like the scuts of rabbits.

CHAPTER THREE

The Goose Tree

I

Precisely at what period Eric Anquetil 'discovered' the Goose Cathedral, I cannot remember; but it must, I fancy, have been one summer in the early thirties, when he had come to spend his holidays at Folkestone. Thenceforward, the boathouse which, in my childhood, had seemed a perfectly normal feature of the landscape, became the breeding ground for a series of fantastic legends: an elaborate superstructure of nonsense not unsuited to the gimcrack, hey-nonny Gothic of the 'chapel' itself.

The boathouse, as it happened, had fallen upon evil times: soon after the First War it had apparently become, as they say, 'redundant', and had been converted into a private residence. Curtains hung now in the mullioned windows; the shingle patch was enclosed by an iron fence, within which three or four geese waddled up and down with a *dégagé* air, grubbing among the squalid remains of what had once, presumably been an attempt at a garden – a few stunted wall-flowers and Brompton stocks were all that now remained of it. The place must have changed hands several times since its 'conversion'; it seemed chronically dirty and unkempt, and exhaled a curious atmosphere of desolation – as though its inmates had fled before some threat of war or pestilence.

We never, I think, caught a glimpse of the 'chapel's' real inhabitants; but if they didn't (visibly, at least) exist, we were quite prepared to invent them, and during that summer, sunbathing on the beach below, we elaborated a whole mythology centred about the 'Goose Cathedral'. It was inhabited, we decided, by a mad archdeacon named Vindables, who had been unfrocked in consequence of his untimely conversion to Mithraism (he had attempted, with a notable absence of tact, to sacrifice a bull on the high altar at Canterbury). He was also a good amateur alchemist, and had (like Cardinal Pirelli) a marked tendency to transvestism; he had married, in later life, a Rumanian from Bessarabia who, besides being a noted witch, and the leader of the local coven, conducted as a sideline a highly successful *bordello* catering exclusively for the needy and deserving clergy ... As for the geese themselves they were undoubtedly, said Eric, Barnacle-geese, hatched from the fruit of the legendary Goose-tree (he had written, a few years before, a learned little paper on this topic for the *Oxford Outlook*). Doubtless Mrs Vindables employed them for her own dubious purposes; probably they were her familiars.

Mythology quite apart, the Goose Cathedral became for us a minor aesthetic *culte*: it was an admirable example of *le style* Betjeman, and a perfect monument to the age which produced it. As such, we considered, it ought to be preserved by some antiquarian society, or bought for the National Trust. A boathouse disguised as a Gothic Chapel – it was a *reductio ad absurdum* of all that was commonly implied by the word 'Victorian'; it became for us a symbol, in fact the very archetype, of all that we condemned so fiercely, in those days, as 'bogus'.

The word was fashionable at that period – the late twenties and early thirties. It was a useful word; and perhaps the Goose Cathedral was a useful symbol. So much could be included in the context – not only the obvious 'bogosities' like Tudor petrol-pumps and Scots-baronial cocktail bars, but all those other, more insidious counterfeits: a pretentious prose-style, for instance, a fake-cubist picture or (even) the refined accents of suburbia. Bogosity, indeed, was ubiquitous; it wasn't only a question of art or architecture; it was linked up (we considered) with snobbery: a symptom, merely, of the same pernicious and deep-rooted disease. We were all snobs of one kind or another – social, intellectual, sexual, athletic or what have you. The virus of bogosity, like the influenza-bug, infected all of us sooner or later; it was, we decided, a peculiarly English disease: no other country, for instance, could have produced anything quite so fantastically perverse as the Goose Cathedral.

At this time – I was still in the early twenties – I was much preoccupied by the problem of my own bogosity. The disease appeared to be incurable: ever since my childhood I seemed to have been afflicted with a chronic *bovarysme*, a perpetual mania for escaping from 'reality'. In my last year at school I had envisaged myself as a sort of modified Huxley character – an oh-so-disillusioned Gumbril or Francis Chelifer; at Oxford, I had been the *poète maudit* of the nineties, modelling my personality (very inaccurately) upon that of Verlaine. Since then, however, my *personae* had tended to become polymorphous and confused – I was never quite sure which, at any given moment, was uppermost. I would have liked to evolve a brand-new one; I contemplated desperate remedies – I would become a communist, or join the Army (*n'importe où, hors du monde!*); but these particular Transformations of the Libido threatened to be rather too exacting. Besides, I wasn't quite sure how one set about becoming a communist: I knew nobody, alas! who could direct me to that 'small club behind the Geisha Café' where, it seemed, most of my contemporaries were congregating.

I decided, instead, to become a Business-man; and was conveniently offered a job in my father's business at Folkestone. Not Emma Bovary herself could have been more unfitted for her chosen rôle than I was for mine. I realized it; but I continued to wear a checked cap, drink a great deal of beer, and cherish an incipient moustache – perfectly aware, all the time, that beneath this unconvincing disguise lurked the old, ineffectual *poète maudit* of my Oxford days. I lived in hopes, however, of a 'change of heart'; if only one observed the forms of piety for long enough (so my Catholic friends assured me) one finally acquired Faith. Something analogous, I felt, might happen to myself in my father's office: I would in time (so I devoutly hoped) develop the authentic, the indispensable characteristics of the business-man. (Why I should have supposed a business-man to be nearer to 'reality' than anybody else, I cannot attempt, after so long a lapse of time, to explain.)

Poker-faced, with the stiffest of Stiff Upper Lips, I tried my best to cultivate the virtues of Efficiency, Initiative and Commonsense. Alas! I was never a very good actor; and the stiffness of my upper lip was seriously impaired by my total inability to grow a really convincing moustache. Like Theodore Gumbril's (and in spite of vaseline), it remained incorrigibly mild and melancholy.

> And I must borrow every changing shape
> To find expression ... dance, dance

> Like a dancing bear,
> Cry like a parrot, chatter like an ape . . .

I tried hard (in spite of my moustache) 'to keep my countenance', to 'remain self-possessed'; but alas! my efforts were
doomed to failure. I would hear too often that

> worn-out common song,
> With the smell of hyacinths across the garden
> Recalling things that other people have desired . . .

I developed, in fact, a cult of nostalgia – that easiest of all escapes
from a hostile environment. Not that this, for me, was anything
new: I had always, I suppose, been in love with the past – even in
my childhood. But now my nostalgia became deliberate and self-
conscious: I had not read my Proust for nothing, and I excused
what I sometimes felt to be a weakness by telling myself that *les
seuls vrais paradis sont les paradis qu'on a perdus.* One day I was
going to write a Proustian masterpiece of my own; I owed it to
myself, therefore, to keep (so to speak) my sense of the past in
working-order. And if the lost paradise of the past was the only
true one, I felt, also, that nowhere but in the past could I escape
from my chronic *bovarysme,* and encounter once again my 'real'
self – so, at least, I liked to think; in fact, I was rather sceptical
about this 'real' self lurking beneath the successive layers of my
assumed *personae.* Did it, in fact, exist? Had it ever existed? Sometimes I suspected that it hadn't. In any case, my contemporary
'personality' was, I was convinced, irretrievably bogus: a mere
façade of wishful phantasies, a kind of Goose Cathedral of over-
blown whimsy and pretension.

In one respect, my cult of nostalgia assumed an outward and
even a 'practical' form: for almost the first time since I had left
school, I rediscovered the pleasures of botany. True, I went about
it in a half-hearted – even a rather shame-faced – manner; for
since I 'grew up' I had come to regard botany (like fireworks and
tame grass-snakes) as an occupation unworthy of my mature years,
and particularly unsuited to one who was dedicated to a romantic
and Baudelairean career of self-destruction. I compromised, however, with my career, to the extent of going for a series of long
walks at week-ends: I preferred to think of them as romantic ex-

peditions *à la recherche du temps perdu*, which indeed they incidentally were; none the less, I had retained a lively interest in botany for its own sake (whether I approved of it or not) and it was noticeable that my walks took me, with an increasing frequency, to places where I was likely to find interesting plants.

Thus, in the early spring of this year, I had walked out to Seabrook, to that waste patch beyond the boathouse where I had once, so memorably, found the coltsfoot. The March morning was still haunted, for me, by that slow, sentimental melody of Mendelssohn; but the coltsfoot itself, unaccountably, had vanished. Common on every bank round Folkestone, and the bane of local gardeners (why had I never found it elsewhere but at Seabrook?) it had gone from the one place to which it could still, for me, lend a certain enchantment. I searched in vain: other former denizens were still there – I saw the leaves of the horned poppy – but no coltsfoot. Some silting of the shingle, perhaps, had occurred, or the soil had become too salty; but the plant's absence seemed to me, somehow, to have a more esoteric significance ... So much, I thought, for the *recherche du temps perdu* – it didn't do to try and salt the tails of one's private myths.

I walked, also, over the Hills – those chalky knolls behind Folkestone, once so rich in orchids, where I had wandered on so many summer afternoons with Ninnie. There were still orchids – but not so many as formerly, for educational 'reform' had progressed considerably since those days, and now every summer brought its hordes of botanizing schoolchildren to despoil these hills of the Bee Orchid, the Dwarf and the Late Spider.

But I wasn't, particularly, in search of rarities; unaccustomed, of late years, to botanizing, I could feel a thrill of delight in encountering even the commonest, the most ordinary of plants; and today, in memory, that summer at Folkestone is enshrined for me in a flower which in former days I would have passed over as an uninteresting weed: the common purple vetch, *Vicia sativa*.

I had walked, on an afternoon in May, across the fields behind Cheriton and Shorncliffe, towards the hills; in the rough patches at the edges of the fields, the vetch was just coming into flower, its winged petals gleaming suddenly among the ox-eye daisies like small, crimson flames. Walking up to the hills I hummed to myself Reynaldo Hahn's setting of Verlaine's poem:

> Le ciel est pardessus le toit
> Si bleu, si calme . . .

and the melancholy little song became, like the vetch, indelibly imprinted upon my memory.

> Qu'as-tu fait, ô toi que voilà,
> Pleurant sans cesse?
> Dis, qu'as-tu fait, toi que voilà,
> De ta jeunesse?

The words, I felt, were all too relevant to my situation: what indeed had I done with my youth? Listening, in the evenings, to Ninon Vallin's charming performance of the song, on the gramophone, I was bowed down by the weight of a vast, indefinable sadness, a tragic sense of the *lacrimae rerum* which (to be honest) I found highly enjoyable . . . If only I wasn't a business-man, if only I were free every day (as I had been today, since it was Sunday) to walk the hills and play the gramophone, I should have been, I felt, almost happy. But alas! I was committed to my *bovarysme* – I had chosen to become what I was, and there was no getting out of it. Self-condemned to 'office-hours' and to the cosy, bourgeois ambience of Folkestone, I cursed myself for a fool; and pulling forward the typewriter which I had borrowed from the 'office' (on the pretext that I wanted to learn to type for 'business' reasons), I settled down to type out my latest batch of poems.

These were, without exception, exceedingly bad – essays in the 'New Country' manner, without a spark of individuality. But I was going through a phase when I would seize upon the mannerisms of any modish writer to 'body forth my own vacuity'. I wanted to write a Proustian *roman fleuve* – but I was far too tired, when I came home in the evenings, to feel like doing anything except have a drink. The most I could do was to attempt an occasional poem: full, in nearly every case, of the fashionable images – pylons and kestrels and ruined farms – and of curt monosyllables like 'death' and 'stripped' and 'chum'. I didn't really find the cult of homo-communism very sympathetic; but having borrowed its accents, I found myself borrowing, also, a modified and extremely corrupt version of its ideology. I became, in fact, something of an inverted snob – not only in my poems, but also, to some extent, in my social life as well; it was an affection which, amid the burgess respectability of Folkestone, was liable to be misinterpreted.

It was, of course, just another symptom of the disease from which I was suffering – a *hyperbovarysme* with complications. On Sunday evenings, when a day's freedom had restored some of my normal power of self-analysis, I was able to diagnose my complaint only too easily. The prognosis seemed extremely gloomy; I could see no prospect of a permanent cure. But I knew, at any rate, that I wasn't and never would be a 'business-man'; nor, for that matter, was I likely to be a poet-*maudit* or otherwise – judging from my recent efforts. I was (in the fashionable phrase) 'overcompensating', with a vengeance. But overcompensating for what? Aware of abysses yawning at my feet, I drank beer with moustached hearties in Prince's Bar or the Esplanade, and wished that I had the courage to flee, like Rimbaud, to Abyssinia. The fact that none of the people with whom I consorted had ever heard of Rimbaud gave me immense satisfaction. I felt, in some obscure way, that in such company I was nearer to what I still, with a singular naïveté, called 'Reality'.

II

On certain other occasions I approached (so I liked to think) even nearer to that chimeric and delusive entity. Often I would take a bus over to Dover, on a Saturday night, and drink beer in the squalid, cheerful little pubs in Snargate Street. I liked the workmen and soldiers whom I met there; and I liked the town itself – the tough, vicious, sea-port atmosphere overlaid by a seedy, early-Victorian elegance. I had never been to Dublin, but in Dover I thought I could detect a quality which evoked for me the *mise-en-scène* of Joyce's *Dubliners* and *Portrait of the Artist*; nor was I, in fact, so very far wrong.

But even this weekly dose of 'reality' didn't really satisfy me; I would return to my rooms as disgruntled and melancholy as ever; there to sit morosely over some book which I felt I 'ought' to read – usually it emanated fom the Left Book Club – or to play, over and over again, my favourite gramophone records.

The sole compensation, I found, for being a business-man, was that I had (for the first time since I left Oxford) a Room of My Own. True, I wasn't doing any writing – which, I felt, was the proper function of a Room-of-one's-own. But at least I could play the gramophone and contemplate my future masterpieces without being disturbed.

The Room was at the top of a tall, gaunt apartment-house called 'Glencoe', in one of those big, rather *déclassé* squares in the 'West-end' of Folkestone. My brother inhabited two rooms on the ground floor, where we took our meals together; but apart from this we kept religiously to our own quarters. Besides the gramophone, I had collected together my few other possessions – books, and one or two reproductions (Cézanne and Sisley); and the mere fact that I was thus able, even to a limited extent, to create my own 'background', gave me an illusory sense of freedom. The landlady, Miss Bugle, was tolerant and unobtrusive – a negative, dim-featured woman whose conversation was mainly restricted, like that of Mr F's aunt, to occasional utterances of a sibylline obscurity, such as (when it was a question of some bit of local gossip) 'There's some in this town could tell a different tale,' or (àpropos of nothing in particular) 'kind words butter no parsnips' ... She could maintain an almost unnatural calm in the face of misfortune: once, for instance, when an accident with the geyser had all but blown her sky-high, her only comment was: 'Oh well, it'll all be the same in a hundred years, I suppose.' The rise of Hitler (it was 1933) seemed to her less alarming than the rise in prices: 'Tuppence-'alfpenny-on-the-meat-and-everything's-awful,' she would announce, in dazed and hopeless tones. Life, one could imagine her thinking, was an unavoidable misfortune; she would rather have been dead, but there it was; and what she was going to give us for dinner that night the Lord only knew, unless it was a little bit of done-up ... Yet, surprisingly, she was quite a good cook; and the 'bit of done-up' would prove, as often as not, to be excellent.

There were few other lodgers in the house; I could play my gramophone without fear of disturbing anybody, and of this I took full advantage: putting on record after record, well into the small hours, drugging myself with music to dull the sharp edges of my unhappiness and my sense of frustration. ('These fragments I have shored against my ruins.') I bought more records than I could afford: mostly modern works, and mostly chamber-music. I fell in love with Poulenc's Trio for Oboe, Bassoon and Piano, finding its crisp yet nostalgic gaiety a good corrective for my own costive moodiness. There was, too, Ravel's Piano Concerto, that curious, febrile work which seems to embody all the sensations of hyperpy-rexia – the quickened pulse, the hot skin, the nervous twitching of the limbs. And there was Ireland's 'Cello sonata which, for me, became inextricably associated with winter evenings by the sea: the sunset flaming yellow in the west, the last rainy light gleaming in the puddles on the cliff-paths, and the sullen thudding of the waves on the beach below.

I found the same quality in other works by this composer – in some of the piano works, for instance: *Month's Mind, Soliloquy, Ballade*; a bracing, 'open-airish' feeling combined with a rather austere note of nostalgia, an awareness of 'old, unhappy, far-off things'. Probably I was mistaken: but Ireland's music became one of my *cultes*, I associated it with my own love of certain country-scenes which I felt to be haunted by Druidic memories and the 'forgotten rites' of a pre-Christian civilization.

III

My flirtations with the Left Book Club were brief and unre-warding – as indeed they deserved to be, for my intentions were far from honourable. What I wanted was the passing thrill of 'conversion'; I had no real intention of tying myself down to anything more permanent. Before long, the last, paper-bound pamphlet had been returned to the library, and, by way of giving myself a holiday, I took to re-reading all the books which I really liked. Proust, the early Huxley, *To the Lighthouse, Howard's End* – how refreshing they seemed after all those wodges of facts and statistics! I had cured myself, at any rate, of one of my *bovarysmes* – I should certainly never become a communist.

Happy in my new-won freedom, I abandoned myself to even worse excesses: I began to burrow, with delight, through old piles of school-magazines, copies of *The Isis*, manuscripts of abortive novels which I had begun at school. What talent I must have possessed in those days! But alas! the stream had dried up; my 'writing' had been no more, perhaps, than a disease of ado-lescence; it was high time I faced the facts, and settled down to be a Responsible Member of Society.

I turned out, among other relics, an old copy of the *Oxford*

Outlook, containing Eric's article on Barnacle Geese. It was extremely erudite, and full of quotations (with page references) from obscure authorities ... That same night I had a curious dream: I was on the beach at Seabrook, near the 'Goose Cathedral'; night was falling, but the Gothic façade was perfectly recognizable against the darkening sky. From the centre of the roof, where the bell-tower should have been, rose a vast tree, from whose branches hung clusters of inky-black shells, shaped like mussels, but very much larger. Perched upon the tree's boughs, or fluttering around it, were a number of plump white geese; some of them had descended from the tree, and were waddling rapidly along the beach where I stood, or had taken to the sea, and were floating among the foam-crests in the shallows. I knew, obscurely, that I had to catch one of these birds: somebody had just been explaining at great length the best method of doing so. My father stood on the edge of the sea-wall, urging me on: outlined against a stormy, threatening sky, he kept shouting at me: 'Wake up, Brooke! Run for it!' as though I were fielding in a cricket-match. But I was paralysed, I couldn't move: the birds waddled by me, close to my feet, yet I stood motionless, possessed by an increasing terror and a desperate, annihilating misery. Suddenly the whole company of geese took wing, like a drove of rooks, and the sky was darkened by their enormous wings. They swooped upon me, I felt the wind of their onrush, I saw their yellow beaks and their small, evil, black eyes ...

I woke up to find that I had, literally, been weeping in my sleep: my face was wet with tears, and for several minutes the sense of that desolate, heart-rending unhappiness persisted. Like so many bad dreams, this one left a slight hangover the next morning: a faint, unpleasant taste in the mouth, a curious feeling of uncleanness. It haunted me, in fact, for some days, and attached itself to my waking thoughts: the geese, it seemed to me, had been a kind of manifold projection of myself, they were my innumerable *personae,* one at least of which I must capture and cling to, or I should be lost.

The idea, I thought, would make rather a good poem; I sat down with paper and pencil; but perhaps, I decided, I should write a better poem if I went out and had a drink first. ('Malt does more than Milton can', etc. – I was an adept, in those days, at discovering literary justifications for my behaviour). It was a Saturday night; I walked down to the Clarendon in Tontine Street. There I picked up with some acquaintances; it was not till some hours later that I sat down again to begin the poem. By the time I had finished it, it was nearly two o'clock. I went to bed; the poem, I thought, was a good one, and I felt a profound satisfaction at having completed it.

Next morning I took up the scrawled pages with a certain eagerness. Alas! Malt might justify God's ways to man, but it didn't, I felt, so easily justify the ways of Auden, Spender and Day Lewis. The poem, in fact, was no better than any of the others I had written lately: it was very bare, very stark, and full of phallic symbols. It had almost nothing to do with my dream; the geese, it was true, did make a brief appearance; but from the context they might just as well have been kestrels. It really wouldn't do, I thought. I tore up the poem; it was a fine Sunday morning in May, and I decided to take a bus up the Elham Valley to the park where, in my childhood, I had found the Monkey Orchid.

I searched the park for a couple of hours; but there was no sign of the Orchid. I hadn't really expected to find it; it had not been seen in the district for at least ten years. The sky was clouding over; a chilly wind blew across Barham Downs, bringing with it a spatter of rain; I hurried up to the main road and caught the next bus into the town.

CHAPTER FOUR

Tea on the Quarter-deck

I

On those days, when, instead of merely going for a 'walk', we made the expedition to Folkestone (either to Pay the Books or on some other domestic errand), we would mount the cliff, more often than not, by a steep track known as the 'Cow Path', through those thickets of elder and tamarisk where, if I was lucky, I would be able to identify the 'nests' of wild soldiers, and where, too, in early spring, would be delighted by the dark-green, maculate spears of the cuckoo-pint.

Sometimes, however, if the weather was bad, we would take one of the funicular lifts which plied between the Lower Road and the Folkestone Leas. The lift was an alarming affair: a cross between a train and an aeroplane. Having a bad head for heights, I could never quite accustom myself to the sight of the Lower Road falling dizzily away into the sea as we ascended; but the attendant was a fatherly, reassuring man, and I learnt, in time, to trust to his steersmanship. Arrived at the top, and once more on *terra firma,* I would look down at the lift 'station' (built of red-brick in the Edwardian villa style) with a sense of triumph at having achieved, once again, the perilous passage.

Walking along the Leas, I would observe, narrowly, the promenading crowd for familiar faces. In those days, Folkestone possessed an unrivalled collection of eccentrics; it wasn't surprising, for the town catered, principally, for elderly *rentiers*, retired Colonels and invalids. On almost any morning one could observe some of these oddities; they tended, indeed – at least in the winter months – to be in a majority ... Hobbling, dancing, lolloping along the asphalt paths, they formed a fascinating spectacle: some twittered or grimaced at us as we passed, some muttered or sang to themselves, some peered myopically from the hooded darkness of bath-chairs ... There was, among others, a tall, rather distinguished-looking old man with a long beard who, in other respects apparently quite normal, would at every third step give a little hop-skip-and-a-jump, as though remembering the gay polkas of his youth. Often, too, we would encounter the lady who 'painted' – an almost unmentionable aberration in those days; probably she was perfectly virtuous, but she was surrounded, for me, by the glamour of 'immorality' – a word which, though I hadn't the faintest idea what it meant, seemed to me thrillingly evocative ... Most memorable, however, of all these odd, aberrant figures was the elderly dame who flaunted the proud title of 'Archduchess'. I suppose she was harmlessly mad – certainly she was no more an Archduchess than I was; but she seemed to have succeeded, to some extent, in imposing her private myth on her fellow-townsfolk, and was never referred to by any other title. Her morning promenade along the Leas had almost the quality of a Royal progress: people would stop to stare at her with a frank curiosity which, no doubt, the 'Archduchess' thoroughly enjoyed. Bowling along in her bath-chair, she would glare malevolently to right and left from beneath a fantastic 'Merry Widow' hat; her neck was encircled, on most days, by a kind of Elizabethan ruff of pink chiffon, and, tied to her ankle was, invariably, a dishevelled fragment of coloured silk which, trailing negligently along the ground, became constantly entangled with the wheels of her chair.

I was fascinated by those curious, derelict offshoots of humanity; but perhaps I didn't find them quite so odd as they would seem to me today. For I was, after all, accustomed to them: they were, for me, merely the indigenous fauna of the Leas, and as such I took them for granted. Once in the town itself, the people we passed became less extraordinary; though even here the crowd would always include a few of those strange anthropoids, strayed from their grassy Mappin Terrace on the cliff-top.

Mostly our transactions were confined to the Sandgate Road, that broad *bourgeois* thoroughfare which traverses the modern 'west-end' of the town. Here I was familiar with the odour and atmosphere of almost every shop: there was, for instance, Gironimo's, the pastrycooks', where sometimes I was allowed to buy a sponge cake. From the door, as we entered, came a hot waft of air, laden with a breath-taking, paradisiac mingling of odours: newly baked bread, hot chocolate, cakes fresh from the oven. Or there was Cave's Café, in whose window was displayed a fascinating machine rather like a steam-engine, which belched and rattled and hissed, and (as we entered the doorway) assailed our nostrils with the delicious scent of roasting coffee. Clements' the shoe-shop, Heron's the grocer, Maestrani's restaurant – each of those establishments had for me its particular emotive flavour; some of them we visited, others not – Maestrani's, for instance, was for some reason forbidden territory, and I could only judge its charac-ter by the spicy, vinous odours which escaped from the constantly swinging glass doors.

Sometimes, too, on rather exceptional occasions, we would pay a visit to 'The Office'. This was, in fact, the name by which we invariably referred to my father's wine-business; and not only 'we' – the family – but every member of the firm, from the directors down to the lowest cellar-boy. To have called it the 'shop' would have been a solecism not easily forgiven. And indeed, when one entered it, one would have supposed it to be a bank or an estate-agent's office, rather than a wine-merchant's. Severe counters, with grilles; a bevy of neatly dressed clerks; etchings on the walls – it seemed highly unlikely that one could enter these grandiose premises and buy a bottle of ginger-beer; not only buy it, for that matter, but take it away under one's arm! Yet such, indeed, was the case. In point of fact, nobody ever did anything of the kind – except for a few misguided 'trippers' in August (and these were not encouraged); the correct procedure was, of course, to 'order' one's wine (or, possibly, even one's ginger-beer) which was, in due course, 'delivered'.

The smell of the 'office' was characteristic – a faint odour of leather, of fine cigars and (but this was the merest *soupçon*) of port or sherry. Usually we would go into the 'Inner Office' to see my father, who as often as not would be tasting wine – his thin, kindly face poised over a claret glass, his aquiline nose delicately wrinkled. He would sniff; take a sip; and then, disappearing behind a screen, spit discreetly into the sink provided. Sometimes, for a treat, I would be given a biscuit – a very thin, very dry bis-cuit, intended as an accompaniment to sherry. I was not, however, given any sherry, and the biscuit rather reminded me of the one which the Red Queen gave to Alice, in *Through the Looking-glass.*

*

'Going to the Office' was rather a solemn business altogether: I was unpleasantly reminded of going to church. Far more interesting and more memorable were our periodic visits to the Miss Hodsells. These were two sisters, a twin-archetype of that mysterious section of the community known, generically, as 'my-little-woman-round-the-corner'.

They were, in fact, seamstresses and dressmakers on a small scale. My mother patronized them regularly; partly because they were useful and partly because they were poor. They inhabited a very dark, very small and very overcrowded little room over a shop in George Lane, the alley-way leading off Rendezvous Street. The entrance was next door to Scott-the-Dyer (where we also sometimes called: the name, for me, had a mythical quality – I associated it with such hero-figures as Herne-the-Hunter or Hereward-the-Wake). The door led into a kind of area or lobby, roofed with glass; just inside was a sort of wire basket, standing upright on four legs, in which grew a few wilting, depressed-looking ferns. The place had a pungent and characteristic odour, compounded of stale urine and escaping gas; the gas predominated; there must have been a permanent (and considerable) leakage. A flight of stone steps led up to the Hodsells' room; perhaps there was more than one room – they must have slept on the premises – but if so, I never discovered it. Their work-room exhaled, but more faintly, the same odour as the lobby below; here, however, it was mingled with a slight taint of onions, and with that complex, indescribable smell of rooms in which the windows are never opened.

The place was crowded, not only with the Hodsells' private possessions, which were numerous, but with the implements of their trade: three or possibly four (I cannot be certain) enormous sewing-machines, of that type which is worked, like a harmonium, by means of a treadle. As one entered, one was greeted by the busy whirr of these august and rather terrifying engines; and one detected, as one's eyes became accustomed to the gloom, two intent, black, seated figures, like Fates employed at some interminable and mindless juggling with destiny.

The machines at last would stop; and the two Miss Hodsells would rise to greet us. One was a great deal older than the other: emaciated, grey-faced, with false teeth which rattled in her bony jaws, and a high pile of frizzy white hair. The younger sister was plumper and pinker and wore pince-nez: she was known as Miss

Jenny Hodsell, to distinguish her from her sister, whose Christian name I never knew.

The elder of the two was, I imagine, the leading partner in the firm: she chattered away endlessly, her teeth clicking and rattling an accompaniment like castanets, and her gnarled, delicate fingers always busy with something – threading needles, rolling a tape-measure, gathering together little piles of odd 'snippets' which mustn't be wasted.

They must have been extremely poor; yet they always seemed to have more commissions than they could deal with. Sometimes they would come down to Sandgate for a day's work – machining, fitting, or any odd jobs in their 'line' which might need doing. And once, on an extraordinary and unprecedented occasion, they came over, in the summer, to our country cottage. This, I think, was purely a holiday for them; we took our tea out into the woods: and I was immensely impressed by the sight of the Miss Hodsells, dressed in their habitual, funerary black, sitting on a path among dense thickets of bracken, and drinking tea out of the tops of Thermos flasks. I hope they enjoyed that day; but I cannot help feeling that it seemed to them – as it seemed to me – an incongruous and rather embarrassing occasion. Sitting there, in their black clothes, among the bracken, they appeared disconsolate and *dépaysées*; they seemed to me, in such surroundings, to be birds of ill-omen. I liked them well enough – in their own special ambience; but I wasn't prepared to cope with them here, on a hot summer afternoon, among the silent, fly-haunted thickets of Gorsley Wood.

II

A visit to the Hodsells, to the 'Office' or (on very rare and special occasions) to Upton Bros., the toyshop – our mornings in Folkestone seldom lacked some element of interest or excitement ... We would return, punctually in time for lunch, along the Lower Road; alert with hunger and a slight, rather pleasant fatigue, I would be, on those occasions, abnormally receptive to familiar sights and sounds. The undercliff, apart from its real and mythological inhabitants, abounded also, for me, with a number of inanimate fetishes. At one time, for example, I was much attached to a felled tree which resembled, so I imagined, the funnel of a railway-engine; and I never failed to pause in front of a certain house whose gate-posts were surmounted by two large balls, bristling with iron spikes ... Objects such as these had for me a profound mystical significance, and I couldn't pass them without an act of homage. More potent still – because it seemed to me entirely inexplicable – was a large iron bolt, in the shape of the letter S, let into the garden-wall of the house next to our own. I wondered for a long time what it was for; but I was an incurious child in some respects, and usually preferred to invent myths about the things which puzzled me, rather than inquire too closely about their true nature. If well-meaning grown-ups insisted on 'explaining', I would pretend, as often as not, that I knew all about it already.

This intellectual snobbery became, at a somewhat later date, rather inconvenient: as, for instance, when the headmaster of my first boarding-school gave me a little talk about the Facts of Life. Such, at least, was his intention; but his embarrassment was even more acute than my own. 'I take it,' he began, 'that you know about the – er – process of *reproduction*?' I blushed; I realized that he meant something to do with babies. I had evolved a vague idea that these were excreted, like *faeces*, from the anus; but beyond that, I was abysmally ignorant. However, I wasn't going to admit it, and, in answer to the headmaster's question, I said yes, I did know. He proceeded to inform me that Certain Parts of my body were Sacred – though he did not, apparently, think it necessary to explain which parts, or why. We parted with a mutual embarrassment: I was a good deal more puzzled than I had been before, and for the first time in my life developed an active curiosity about sexual matters. Thenceforward, I was not satisfied until I had plumbed the mystery to its depth.

The undercliff possessed also, in addition to these visual landmarks, its habitual and familiar sounds: the wailing of gulls, the muffled thud of the waves and (in misty weather) the far booming of fog-horns ... There were other noises too, more homely and localized: the shrill 'ping-ping' of the Sandgate school-bell, or the incessant yapping (as we passed her home) of Lady Bancroft's prize Pomeranians; and if we were returning earlier than usual, we would be sure to hear the voice of the fishmonger, Mr Jarvis, intoning his monotonous litany outside the 'Tradesmen's Entrances'; 'Nice fresh codling, lovely mackerel, all alive! All alive!' Every day he came with his barrow-load of fresh fish from the fishmarket, crying his wares along the Lower Road, and finishing up at Sandgate, where, later in the day, one would recognize his empty barrow, parked outside the doors of the Military Tavern. For Mr Jarvis Drank: it was disgraceful, and the residents of Radnor Cliffe would have liked to discourage him; but then his fish was so much fresher than any one could get elsewhere ... Once he didn't appear for nearly three weeks; on the morning of his return, he explained that he had been suffering from 'that nasty influenza'; but we all knew that he had, in reality, spent the period in gaol for being drunk and disorderly and (it was said) for beating his wife.

Some years later, when the war was over, my mother attended an Armistice-day service at Sandgate; it was held in the open air, by the war-memorial, which stood at the corner of the road just opposite the Military Tavern. Eleven o'clock struck, the traffic stopped, and everyone stood awkwardly and self-consciously to attention for the two-minutes' silence. It was a quiet, windless November morning: no sound broke the stillness but the faint, far murmur of the sea, and the distant crying of gulls. The crowd stood solemn and immobile, remembering the dead of Ypres and Passchendaele ... Suddenly the silence was rudely shattered; round the corner, from the direction of the sea, came a clattering of wheels, and a voice – loud, ringing, stentorian – bawled out the only too familiar but, in the circumstances, blasphemous and appalling words: 'All alive! All alive!'

From the Lower Road, our house looked undistinguished enough: semi-detached, and faced, rather depressingly, with grey cement. The front door was painted green, with a brass knocker; the bell was at the side – one of those old-fashioned bells with a large knob which had to be jerked (with considerable muscular effort) from its slot, and smartly released again. An extraordinary noise of clanging and rumbling ensued somewhere in the bowels of the house; to me, returning famished from my morning 'walk', the sound seemed a kind of extension of the rumbles in my own empty stomach. At last the door would open and we would be sucked forward, as though into a vacuum, by the rush of air thus generated – for, as often as not, the door of the dining-room and the french windows beyond would be open as well. The hall seemed filled, perpetually, with the sound and smell of the sea: entering the house, it was as though one were passing, merely, through a kind of tunnel from one 'out-of-doors' world to another; the sun blazed in one's face, the wind rushing in from the windows lifted the hall carpet and flapped the tiger-skin hanging on the wall. The whole house seemed, in its 'coign of the cliff', to be perilously suspended between two worlds – the tame, 'country' world of the undercliff, and that other, uncharted universe – inimical and frightening – of the sea.

If there was time before lunch, I would run into the drawing-room, through the small greenhouse, and down the wooden steps to the garden where, if it was morning in spring or early summer, I would find my family assembled under the 'verandah', waiting for the luncheon-bell.

The house was built, as it were, on two levels, so that the 'ground-floor', which one entered from the Lower Road, became the 'first-floor' when viewed from the garden. An iron balcony, partly roofed with glass, projected from it, forming a kind of enclosed terrace below, on the basement level. Even in winter, on a sunny day, it was possible to 'sit out' here in comfort; the sun's warmth seemed to be concentrated into a thicker, an almost palpable element, seasoned with an odour which I could never quite identify, but which was perhaps compounded of crushed privet leaves and the piles of last year's bulbs, which were laid out to dry on the window-ledges. The balcony was supported by pillars, wreathed with jasmine and honeysuckle; and in the corner, by the boundary hedge of thick-set privet, grew an enormous barberry-tree which, at the end of April, showered its multitudinous fading blossoms upon the pinkish stone of the terrace, and upon the edge of the lawn.

Unimpressive from the Lower Road, the house, on the seaward side, offered a complete contrast: virginally white, with its green *persiennes* and projecting balcony, it resembled some Mediterranean villa. For me, it seemed then (as indeed it seems still) the very archetype of all houses, and I cannot, to this day, hear the word 'house' without visualizing, instantly, our old home on Radnor Cliffe; nor, for that matter, can I encounter, in Southern

Europe, some green-shuttered villa perched on its terrace above the sea, without feeling a curious sense of homecoming, as though this 'foreign' and outlandish building, inhabited by strangers, were a kind of distant cousin of the house in which I spent my childhood.

The terrace below the balcony gave on to a small lawn – half the size of a tennis-court and, so far as games were concerned, only suitable for clock-golf. At the end of it, beyond a narrow flower-bed, rose a wooden frame over which clambered a carmine-pillar rose. Flowering in May – or even, in a mild spring, at the end of April – the frail, vividly-crimson blossoms had for me a special poetry of their own: they should by rights, I felt, have flowered in June or July, like other roses; instead, they chose to appear with the pheasant-eye narcissus and the first tulips. Charming inter-lopers, dressed unsuitably for the season, they were like girls who, in earliest spring, if the weather is fine, will daringly assume their thinnest summer finery. Spring flowers – English ones at least – have a marked tendency to be white or yellow: reds and purples are comparatively rare 'before the roses and the longest day'. Perhaps it was this fact which made me fall in love, at an early age, with the Purple Orchis – and which, for that matter, many years later, would invest with the same poetic nostalgia the common vetch of the May-time hedgerows.

From the 'lawn' the garden descended, in terraces, to the beach: steep flights of steps led from stage to stage, and the journey to the beach and back was an arduous one, not lightly to be undertaken by old ladies, or by the numerous tribe of aunts, who seldom went further than the second terrace, which we called the 'Quarter-deck'. This was a kind of look-out post, furnished with a rustic seat and a summer-house; below it lay the 'rose-garden' – though I remember it less for its roses than for the purple irises which, with a perversity equalling that of the carmine-pillar, unfurled in late April their aestival and unseasonable splendours. To see the first blackish-violet bud bursting through its tight green sheath was an event to which, each spring, I passionately looked forward: violet became for a time my favourite colour, and any object even faintly tinged with it acquired in my eyes a disproportionate value. Flowers, particularly: Purple Orchis, Purple Loosestrife, Purple

Gromwell occupied, for me, a special and distinguished rank in the botanical hierarchy.

On afternoons of spring and summer, if we had not gone to the cottage, and if the weather was reasonably fine, we would have tea on the 'Quarter-deck'. From here the 'view' was uninterrupted: one looked out directly across the bay towards Dungeness. For most children it would have been exciting, I suppose, to live thus with the sea at one's back door; yet I was indifferent to it – at times, indeed (if it was a question of trying to make me bathe), I positively hated it. All my desires, all my romantic imaginings, were turned towards the country; and the winter months at Sandgate were spent, by me, almost wholly in looking forward to the time when we should go to our cottage in the Elham Valley.

The Quarter-deck, however, had for me attractions quite other than that of the 'view' – which, though it might appeal to the grown-ups, left me comparatively cold. There was, for one thing, the summer-house: a small, 'rustic' building impregnated with a pungent odour of creosote and paraffin. In it was kept a miscellaneous collection of objects – garden tools, balls of string, a 'Beatrice' stove, cups and saucers (for a special tea-set was reserved for tea on the Quarter-deck: thick, white cups and tea-pot, embellished with the pale-blue 'rose-and-thistle' pattern). One of my favourite sensations was to bury my nose in a ball of 'tarred' garden string, whose aromatic, rather acrid odour seemed to hold the very essence, the irreducible spiritual reality, of the scene about me. Just as a seashell, held to the ear, seems to contain the sea itself, so, in this ball of creosoted string, were implicit for me the green arbour of tamarisks, the irises, tea-on-the-quarter-deck, the whole sunlit, miraculous April afternoon; and on more than one occasion, years later, when I was enduring the hell of my first boarding-school, I would sniff, by accident, this magical scent again, and would be overcome by a sudden and inexplicable happiness, a conviction that life was worth living after all.

Often, if we were at Sandgate in the summer, people came to bathe from the Quarter-deck: friends, mostly, of my brother and sister. I would watch them romping and laughing in the sea below, at once thrilled and appalled at the thought of their valour and their nakedness. At tea-time we would signal to them; and with mackintoshes over their bathing-suits, they would come running up the steps to the Quarter-deck, where, sitting on deck-chairs beneath the tamarisks, they devoured crumpets and sandwiches, with heroic appetites. Their 'heartiness' repelled and fascinated me: so did their bare legs and chests, and the shameless pleasure which they seemed to take in their bodies . . . The thing I dreaded most (apart from Ninnie leaving us, or my going to boarding-school) was being made to bathe. It didn't often happen; but the threat was always there, and when there were bathing-parties, I kept, as much as possible, out of the way.

I might, now and again, be threatened with 'bathing'; but there seemed little immediate prospect, at this time, either of Ninnie leaving us or of my going to boarding-school. (Both those events would, I suppose, occur sooner or later: but, like Death, they remained for me mere intellectual abstractions; I didn't 'feel' them, as D. H. Lawrence would have said, in my solar-plexus.) I was, however, shortly to leave my Kindergarten, and go to a new school – a Real Boys' School: Greylands House, at Folkestone. Only as a day-boy; but the prospect filled me with alarm. Would it, I wondered, be like the school-stories in *Little Folks*? I hoped not; at the same time, my alarm was tempered by a vague, heroic excitement: I began to imagine myself as a 'schoolboy', just as I had imagined myself (rather half-heartedly) in the role of a soldier. My life was to include both experiences, as it happened: but one couldn't, as I realized, be a soldier at the age of seven (a fact for which, in my more unheroic moments, I was profoundly thankful); one could, on the other hand, most decidedly become a Schoolboy. I viewed the prospect with mixed feelings:

> Through my reins, like ice and fire,
> Fear contended with desire. . . .

I should, presumably (amongst other things), have to play football; this was all very well in the school-stories, but lately, walking along the western end of the Leas, I had seen a real game in progress, and had formed a rather different impression of it. A war, when one takes part in it, has seldom much in common with the thrilling accounts of wars in history-books; and the same was true, I suspected, of football. The crowd of scuffling, barging men, muddy and sweating, with their bare knees and open shirts, filled me with terror; yet I felt at the same time, a curious, rather guilty excitement creep over me. I wanted to play football; but I cherished the desire like some secret vice which I would have died rather than publicly admit.

III

Tea on the Quarter-deck had something of the quality of a picnic; true, the tea-things were kept ready in the summer-house, but the eatables had to be carried across the lawn and down a steep flight of steps to the terrace; Quarter-deck teas were not popular with the parlour-maid, who, at four o'clock, would mince disapprovingly down the garden carrying a silver dish of crumpets and one of those curious wicker-work contraptions, like portable pagodas, perilously laden with plates of cakes and sandwiches.

These outdoor teas, moreover, were apt to be unpopular not only with the maids but with the family too: little green spitinsects dropped out of the tamarisks into one's cup, and the tea itself tended to have a slight flavour of paraffin or creosote; moreover, the terrace was usually either too hot or too cold; one's deckchair was apt to collapse; why have tea uncomfortably out-ofdoors when you could have it comfortably in the drawing-room? But my mother would listen to none of these objections: dispensing tea from the summer-house, she enjoyed, like Marie Antoinette in her dairy, the sensation of doing something faintly adventurous and a bit messy. 'And besides,' she would insist (while the rest of us shivered in the chilly June breezes) 'it's such wonderful *air*.'

So far as I was concerned, tea on the Quarter-deck had one major advantage: when it occurred, my mother would usually be 'not at home', so that one felt safe from callers. Tea in the drawing-room, on the other hand, was fraught for me always with a slight apprehension; and nothing could exceed my horror when (as often happened) the door opened and the maid announced Mrs So-and-so from along the cliff, who had come to 'call'. My shyness was almost pathological: I was on awkward enough terms with our own relations – even, indeed, with my immediate family circle; with strangers I became no better than a cretin.

However, once the 'how-d'you-do's' were over, I would, more often than not, be left in peace; and sitting, unnoticed, on the tuffet by the corner of the fireplace, I would listen to the obscure, prolix and fascinating stream of talk which flowed above my head. Grown-up conversation struck me as being a kind of game played for its own sake: people didn't, it seemed, talk about the things which really interested them; they talked, rather, as if it were a question of filling up the time, or as though someone were perpetually listening to whom they didn't want to give anything away. When I was first taken to a 'grown-up' play, I recognized the technique: the actors talked in just the same way, and even with the same accents. They went on talking until something 'happened' – usually somebody was kissed, or perhaps there was a quarrel, or (if the play happened to be a musical one) the characters suddenly burst, without warning, into song. But in the drawing-room at home none of these things happened: people just went on talking.

None the less it fascinated me, this endless and apparently aimless talk; and sometimes it would rouse in me desires which obsessed me for weeks afterwards: for example, the height of my ambition, at one time, was to be taken to a 'show' at the Pleasure Gardens Theatre, which I had heard much discussed; or I would develop a craving to go to an enchanted land called the 'South-of-France', where my Uncle Hewlett lived (he was reputed to be rather wicked), and whence, at intervals, he would dispatch enormous crates of mimosa or carnations to my mother.

Sometimes, after tea, my mother or my sister would play the piano; I preferred the things my mother played, on the whole – chiefly the ballads and 'pieces' which she had learnt in her girlhood. I knew these 'pieces' by the pictures on the covers, and associated the music, in each case, inseparably with the picture. My sister, a proficient pianist, was more ambitious: the things she played seemed to me mostly rather dull, and, moreover, they usually didn't have any pictures on the cover – unless, indeed, they were 'selections' from recent 'shows', which she would rattle out in her more low-brow moments. These I found extremely exciting: there was a musical play called 'Betty', for instance, the piano-score of which had a cover-photograph of a man in evening-dress leaning over a beautiful lady on a sofa. I fell hopelessly in love with the lady; but alas! when 'Betty' came to the Pleasure Gardens Theatre, I was not allowed to go, for it was considered, apparently, to be slightly 'improper'.

Yet some of these 'pieces' which my sister played, if they seemed at the time too complex or 'grown-up', acquired for me none the less, in after years, an extraordinary power of evocation. They became, like the Mendelssohn 'Song Without Words', arbitrarily associated with certain moods, and possessed for me a poetry which had little or nothing to do with their purely musical qualities. Thus I cannot (for instance), to this day, hear Debussy's First Arabesque without visualizing our Sandgate drawing-room on an afternoon in summer: an impression of outdoor heat and of coolness within, the room bathed in a greenish, subaqueous twilight, the sea-breeze stirring the potted plants and flapping the green sun-blinds which shaded the verandah . . .

The drawing-room fascinated me, at that age, probably because my visits to it were comparatively infrequent, and because, when they occurred, I acquired the honorary status of a grown-up, and was expected to behave like one. I developed an almost religious awe for certain of my mother's treasures – in particular, for a gilt Empire mirror which hung over the long-tailed, rosewood piano. In its depths appeared a rounded, concentrated duplicate of the room, more 'real', it seemed to me, than the reality. The chintz-covered sofa and chairs, the gilt-framed watercolours, the pot of weeping smilax on its tall, mahogany pedestal – all these appeared in the glass, but with a heightened vividness: their colours seemed brighter, their shapes more elegant, the refractory planes and angles of their surfaces were softened into baroque curves and swelling rotundities.

But the real room, if less compactly beautiful than its mirrored duplicate, had its own charm: though small, it gave an impression of spaciousness, a sense of being suspended in some windy eyrie between sea and sky. French windows led into the greenhouse, from whose outer door a flight of steps descended to the garden; standing in the doorway, one seemed to be perched above an abyss, an immense void of air and sunlight. Below lay the garden, with its grey-green clouds of tamarisk, and beyond and below the garden, the enormous sweep of the bay – the sea rising like a wall against

the sky, the gulls wheeling in the empty air. Here, more than
anywhere else, I would be aware of those two worlds – the known
and the unknown between which our house seemed always to be
maintaining its perilous equilibrium ... From behind me came
the sounds and smells of my own limited and familiar universe –
the tinkle of the piano, the faint odours of pot-pourri and tobacco-
smoke; before me lay the *au-delà*, a chasm of blue air from which
small, disembodied sounds emerged like distant echoes of themselves, fraught with terror and strangeness: the remote, iterated
bark of a dog upon the beach, the chug-chug of a pleasure-boat
plying up the Channel and, far below, the soft thud of the summer
waves upon the sun-baked shingle.

I turned back to the familiar, the 'indoor' world – fearful of
such remote limitless prospects ... The greenhouse was a translucent cage in which scarlet geraniums, fragile and sour-smelling,
lolled like jungle-blooms in a green shade; beyond the french
windows was the drawing-room, where the grown-ups were sitting, still, in the tranquil aftermath of tea, listening to my sister
who, at the piano, was playing one of those interminable and complex 'pieces' which I could never recognize, because there was no
picture on the cover ...

Back in the world which I knew, in which I felt at home, I wished
passionately that nothing would ever change. I was a true-blue, a
positively last-ditch Conservative: I could hardly bear even the
necessary, day-to-day alterations in my environment. Only recently my bedroom – or nursery, as it was still called – had been re-
papered; I found the new pattern intolerable, it seemed to me
that, in stripping off the faded green-striped paper which I had
known all my life, the paper-hangers had torn away some surface-
layer of my very self, leaving me flayed and smarting from the loss.
And now, in September, I was to go to Greylands – a further stage
in that process which I so feared and hated, but which I was
powerless to check; a process which, cruel and inevitable as the
passing of time itself, was removing me every day, every minute
even, a little further from that closed, familiar world where the
piano tinkled on in the green twilight, and the round glass
reflected a vision of the drawing-room as I remembered it and
wished it forever to remain: fixed in a moment of time, the long
lucid pause before sunset at the end of an afternoon in summer.

CHAPTER FIVE

The Breede of Barnakles

I

Eric Anquetil took one look at my moustache and burst out laughing.

'It's no good, Jocelyn,' he said, 'you'll never make a business-man. You might just as well give up trying.'

Eric had come down to spend his summer holidays at Folke-stone. I was pleased enough to see him; but I found his presence, at this time, somewhat embarrassing, for I realized that he had seen through my 'business-man' pose and (very rightly) refused to take it seriously.

Our friendship dated from Oxford: he was the only person I had 'kept up with' from that period, perhaps because we made so few demands upon each other. Our relationship, in fact, was of that enduring kind which is grounded firmly on a basis of frivolity, dissipation and a shared sense of the ridiculous. We were quite unable to take either each other or (when we were together) our respective selves *au grand sérieux*. It is, I suppose, as good a foundation for friendship as any other; better, perhaps, than most.

'I wouldn't in the least mind dying tomorrow,' Eric had once said to me in the early days of our acquaintance. It wasn't just an undergraduate affectation; I could tell when Eric was merely word-spinning, and on this occasion he indubitably wasn't: he meant exactly what he said.

I was less fatalistic: I didn't mind the idea of death (who does, at that age?) but I viewed with a certain disfavour the idea of dying. It was apt, I felt, to be rather messy.

'I should like,' Eric had said, on another occasion, 'to fish up some unknown *dix-huitième* poetaster, and write a "definitive" biography of him – with lots and lots of footnotes.'

The poetaster had yet to be found, and the biography written; meanwhile, Eric had contented himself with 'writing up' the Barnacle Tree (as well as a number of other recondite natural phenomena) for the *Oxford Outlook*. When he came down from Oxford, he had taken a job on a London evening paper, for which he had written gossip-paragraphs about totally fictitious personages and events; at the moment, he was a schoolmaster – 'We sons of the manse all take to drink and pedagogy,' he said, 'it seems inevitable.'

A parson's son, he professed, as he put it, 'a vapid interest in cults', and in fact, while still at school, had shocked his headmaster by reading a paper to the sixth form on the more lubricious and unsavoury aspects of Hinduism.

'I was born to be a pedagogue,' he declared, as we sun-bathed on the beach at Seabrook. 'I have a kind of niggling pedantry which makes me find it rather *sympathique*. Besides, though I loathe small boys, I get on quite well with them, because I remember what it's like to *be* a small boy. Most people forget.'

My first meeting with Eric, at Oxford, had perhaps been significant. Tea in my rooms had merged into an impromptu cocktail-party; having demolished the best part of a bottle of gin between us, we spent an hour happily boring holes, with a screwdriver, in the tin dishes which had held muffins and tea-cakes; after that, we had walked arm in arm down St Giles and the Cornmarket trying to think of as many synonyms as we could for the word 'prostitute'. In a sense, the evening had been typical of our subsequent relationship, in which drink, destructiveness and a certain rather pedantic pornophily had all played their part.

Also, on the same evening, we had discovered that we both wanted to Write.

We exchanged the manuscripts of our unpublished works: I admired Eric's taut and sophisticated prose, so different from my own vapourings (which might have been described as by Huxley out of Hugh Walpole). I even admired his hand-writing – so admirably formed and characteristic, whereas mine was still naïvely round and schoolboyish. The difference between us, I decided, was the difference between the professional and the amateur; nor have I ever changed my opinion.

*

But Oxford seemed a long way off, this summer at Folkestone; we both felt immensely old, and very *rusés* and sophisticated.

'I wonder what's happened to all those people we knew,' said Eric, with an obituary note in his voice. 'Hew Dallas, for instance – he seems quite to have faded.'

I said I had seen Hew once at the Blue Lantern.

'Oh, *that* place ... And I haven't seen Basil Medlicott lately, either ... You know, I'm becoming completely provincial, nowadays. Not that I much mind – but I wish, sometimes, that I'd some of your opportunities for urbanity. You're lucky, really.'

'Am I?' I echoed, rather bleakly.

'I only wish,' said Eric, 'that *I* had a nice comfortable family business to go into. What good is it, I ask you, to be a parson's son? One might as well be the son of a greengrocer.'

Eric spent his time bathing and sunbathing: I joined him when I could – on 'early closing day' (Wednesday) and at week-ends. We went to the Seabrook beach because it was clean and comparatively unfrequented: nobody went there much in those days except the soldiers from the camp, who were marched down periodically for bathing parades. Sometimes a party of troopers from a cavalry regiment brought down their horses to cool them off in the sea. Sitting naked astride their beasts, they rode them into the shallows, or trotted up and down the beach: I meditated a poem about centaurs, but decided that it would be a mistake; I had not forgotten my last attempt at verse – though I would have preferred to if I could.

'*Je suis victime de mes propres désirs*,' declared Eric lazily, àpropos of nothing. We both had a silly habit of using French as a kind of safety-valve: things tended to sound funnier in it than in English – a fact often enough exploited by Firbank, whom we were still reading at this time; we would take the 'slim', rainbow-coloured volumes down to the beach, and quote the funny bits aloud to each other. Sometimes, however, it would not be Firbank but Baudelaire, Mallarmé or Laforgue. Eric's attitude to poetry was cautious in the extreme: so much of it, after all, was 'bogus' ... My own taste became, I think, to a great extent modelled upon his. I, too, demanded the Latin clarity, and found most English verse woozy and shapeless. By a tacit agreement, formed long ago, we both felt committed to puncturing, whenever possible, each other's pretensions; I might confess, for instance, to a taste for Housman, but at my peril: I could foresee the ironic gleam in Eric's eye, his faint satiric giggle.

That August was fine and hot: we sunbathed at Seabrook, read our Firbank, and added occasional glosses to the saga of Archdeacon Vindables. We pub-crawled in the Folkestone fishmarket – a congeries of pleasantly squalid pubs long since pulled down. Sometimes we went to Dover; and now and again we were invited, by friends of my brother's, to the various officers' messes in the neighbourhood; I derived a curious pleasure from penetrating into the mysterious confines of Shorncliffe Camp or the Citadel Barracks at Dover – places which, in my childhood, had seemed the haunts of legendary heroes.

Once I took Eric up the Elham Valley, to visit the village of my childhood; we walked up through Gorsley Wood to Langham Park, a region which to me had seemed always to exist on the edge of the known world: beyond lay an unknown land into which it still seemed to me almost foolhardy to try and penetrate. Eric's proposal that we should walk on as far as Upper Hardres rather shocked me: it was as though he had suggested crossing the frontier into some alien and savage territory from which we might never return.

The papers were full of Hitler, and I began to wonder what I should do if there really was another war. I supposed that I should enlist immediately: conscientious objection had become, I felt, like so many other things, rather 'bogus'; besides, I had no genuine scruples about fighting – I was merely frightened of it. A war, at any rate, would provide an escape from my present situation; and at times I found myself looking forward to it with an almost pleasurable excitement. Walking up Horn Street, beneath the windy levels of Shorncliffe Camp, I remembered the ambitions of my childhood: there seemed every chance that I should be able, during the next few years, to fulfil them.

II

Sometimes our trips to Shorncliffe or Dover were varied by visits to Esmé Wilkinson, a somewhat pea-green old gentleman widely known to his acquaintances as 'Pussy'. I had few friends in Folkestone with whom I was on visiting terms; and I cultivated Pussy Wilkinson, perhaps, for no better reason than that I had known him since my schooldays. He never became a close friend of mine; yet the memory of that summer at Folkestone will always, I suppose, both for Eric and myself, be haunted by his ghost, and by the ghost of his curious *protégé*. They were to recur, these improbable phantoms, with a singular persistence in after years; and the happenings of that summer, which in ordinary circumstances I should long since have forgotten, acquired, for me at least, the 'archetypal' and haunting quality of some private myth.

Pussy Wilkinson had first settled at Folkestone while my family were still living at Sandgate, and I had on several occasions, in those days, been taken to tea with him by my brother. At that time, I had been rather impressed by his 'culture' – a quality which, on the whole, was lacking in most of the people we knew in Folkestone ... 'Pussy' Wilkinson played the piano, and possessed a considerable library of gramophone records; moreover (and this I found especially sympathetic at that age) he had read *Antic Hay* and *Crome Yellow*.

At a later period I found his 'culture' less impressive; but he remained of interest to me for another reason: he was a perfect period-piece – a man of the nineties who had managed to preserve the authentic aroma of that (to me) still fascinating decade. He had known Robbie Ross and Reggie Turner, and had even, on one memorable occasion, been introduced (at Dieppe) to none other than 'Sebastian Melmoth' himself. He seemed, though not notably wealthy, to have more than a genteel sufficiency: at any rate (one gathered) he had never found it necessary to adopt a profession.

Eric, like myself, found Pussy of considerable period-interest, and during this summer we frequented his house a good deal. Sometimes we would persuade him to show us his treasures –

signed photographs of celebrities (mostly musicians or opera-singers), rare editions of Wilde or Dowson, or the unexpurgated version of Beardsley's *Under the Hill*. Pussy himself was a plump, dapper little man, nearer sixty than fifty, with an urbane manner which just (but only just) stopped short of preciosity; he resembled, we decided, an elderly choir-boy. Everything about him was neat and orderly; his movements had an exquisite precision – the mere lighting of a cigarette was for him a small but important ritual which demanded his whole attention for its proper performance. His habits of neatness and exactitude extended to his household; meals were always punctual to the minute, every ornament had its exact and immutable place, one didn't dare to drop one's cigarette ash anywhere but in the trays provided.

Pussy inhabited a rather grand, pink-and-white Edwardian villa in the Shorncliffe Road. Over the front door hung a large wrought-iron lantern of vaguely *art nouveau* design; inside the door was a mat with SALVE stencilled upon it. The house was furnished in that rather cautious style which seems to indicate a horror of 'bad taste' rather than any more positive predilection on the owner's part. There were a lot of rather boring 'antiques', and some expensive-looking lacquer tables and cabinets; the walls were hung with unexceptionable etchings and a respectable painting or two, including a reputed Cuyp. At the back of the house was a garden full of bird-baths and rockeries, and a small greenhouse in which Pussy cherished a few rather dispirited cattleyas and cypripediums.

Pussy, one felt, had 'measured out his life with coffee spoons'; he had never married, and, apart from his piano, seemed to have no particular 'interests'. (He was a proficient if rather dull pianist, and if asked to play would usually treat one to interminable transcriptions of Italian opera, Bellini or Donizetti for preference). His reading, apart from novels, was largely confined to the reminiscences of exiled Royalty – a form of literature which fascinated him. One would meet him, of a morning, punctually trotting down the town to W. H. Smith's, to change his library-book: accompanied usually, by his two Sealyhams, Aucassin and Nicolette. He had a number of friends in the town – mostly women, whom he would entertain periodically to what he called, with Edwardian raciness, a 'tea-fight'.

Eric and I avoided these functions, which were inclined to be fussy and rather formal; sometimes, however, we were invited to what Pussy referred to, rather archly, as a 'little gathering': these entertainments were of quite a different character, occurring, normally, rather late in the evening, and confined almost exclusively to Pussy's male friends.

'I *may* be old-fashioned,' he would remark, 'but I'm afraid I do *not* like to see a pretty woman under the – um – influence.'

The phrase 'pretty woman' made us giggle: it summed up, we felt, Pussy's whole attitude to what he himself would have called 'the sex'. He romanticized his feminine acquaintances quite shamelessly: one visualized a company of gracious Edwardian dames who were all 'the dearest of creatures' and all stunningly beautiful. (In point of fact, the women one met at his house were mostly hard-faced, bridge-playing old harridans who could have probably drunk Pussy under the table if he had given them half a chance.)

Pussy might disapprove of hard-drinking females, but he had no such prejudices where his men-friends were concerned. His evening 'gatherings' were, in fact, distinctly gay, and sometimes revealed aspects of Pussy's character which were, to say the least, surprising. The evening would start sedately enough; but sooner or later, under the influence of a double whisky or two, Pussy would decide that the moment had come to let down (as he invariably expressed it) his back hair. To new acquaintances this proceeding was apt to be disconcerting, and even, on occasion, alarming – as, for example, when Pussy was persuaded into giving his celebrated imitation of Sarah Bernhardt . . . On these occasions he would retire to his bedroom, to return, after some considerable delay, draped in a jaguar-skin and quantities of tulle. Thus attired, he would assume a throaty falsetto, and declaim the speech from *Phèdre* beginning '*Mon mal vient de plus loin.*' It was a notable performance; his voice rose to an astonishing pitch, his gestures became more and more dramatic until (and this was the climax) he reached the famous line:

C'est Vénus toute entière à so proie attachée,

when he would, without the least warning, pounce upon the nearest person in the audience and, with an alarming realism, 'attach' himself to his startled (and sometimes, indeed, terrified) victim – who would, as often as not (such was the force of the impact), overbalance and fall flat on the floor, with Phèdre, *toute entière*, on top of him.

Nobody, certainly, who had seen Pussy promenading down the Leas with Aucassin and Nicolette, or fussing into the library for the latest E. F. Benson, would have supposed him capable of such uninhibited gaieties. They were, one suspected, a throw-back to his ninetyish youth; and Eric and I would sometimes encourage him to recount some of his more dubious past exploits. But Pussy's reminiscences remained always upon an impeccably polite level.

III

Pussy was a stickler for convention – so much so, that his odd freaks of behaviour seemed all the odder by contrast. One such peculiarity was his refusal to employ women-servants: no woman, he would declare, had any sense of 'responsibility' in household affairs. Ever since I had known him he had employed menservants exclusively – apart from a daily charwoman, of whom he lived in terror, lest she should break his precious specimens of Wedgwood (which in fact he preferred usually to dust himself).

At present, he was being looked after by a young man known as Bert: a somewhat ambiguous character, whose presence was liable to disconcert the more conventional of Pussy's acquaintances.

Bert, as it happened, was by way of being a friend of mine: indeed, I saw rather more of him, this summer, than I did of his employer, for Bert was a first-rate swimmer, and often came down to bathe at Seabrook with Eric and myself. His status in Pussy's household was somewhat ill-defined: half-servant, half-*protégé*, he reminded one rather of some poor relation, or one of those 'companions' employed by rich old ladies. A certain air of mystery surrounded him . . . As it happened, I had been at least partly (and quite by accident) let into the secret. Some months earlier I had called on Pussy uninvited, and had been surprised to find him entertaining, at tea, a young private soldier in uniform. The soldier seemed nice – a red-faced, blond-headed Cockney, with the torso of a boxer and, when he smiled, a mouthful of strong, very white teeth. I gathered (when Pussy, on my departure, accompanied me to the door) that the young man had been in some kind of trouble, and that Pussy had befriended him. The whole story, as I heard it, was rather vague: exactly what had happened, and how or where Pussy had originally picked him up, I was never told; but not long afterwards I was astonished to hear that Pussy had bought his *protégé* out of the Army, and engaged him as a kind of chauffeur-valet-companion.

It was, certainly, an odd enough *ménage*; but it seemed, from Pussy's account, to be an eminently satisfactory one. According to Pussy, his generous gesture had been amply rewarded, for Bert was not only a good cook, but, in addition to his other duties, made himself extremely useful at such odd jobs as mending fuses, repairing leaky taps and so forth. He was in fact – so Pussy alleged – something of a mechanical genius, and his ultimate ambition, it seemed, was to get some kind of job in the wireless-trade. Pussy, however, was reluctant to part with him – not surprisingly since, owing to Bert's efficiency and good-will, he had been enabled to dispense with his chauffeur and even (much to his relief) with the charwoman.

I was still, I suppose, something of an inverted snob, and perhaps derived from Bert's company the same sort of pleasure which another man would have obtained from hobnobbing with a lord. None the less, I found Bert likeable in himself: he had a pleasant disposition, a lively Cockney humour and, though 'clever' above the average in some ways, possessed a kind of child-like naïveté which I found refreshing. His company was unexacting – rather like that of a highly-intelligent dog; and I was reminded of the 'wild' soldiers whom, in my childhood, I had 'tamed' and fed on Robinson's Patent Barley . . .

Bert was almost embarrassingly fair-minded: he would never accept a drink unless he could afford to buy the 'other half'. He was also, I guessed (at least where his employer was concerned), scrupulously honest. Yet he didn't, for all his good points, seem particularly well-fitted for his present job; and his patent incongruity caused a certain amount of amusement to Eric and myself. Bert might be, as Pussy alleged, a mechanical genius, and the victim of 'unfortunate circumstances', but his appearance and manners were hardly calculated, one would have thought, to endear him to prim old gentlemen of Pussy's temperament. Pussy, however, obviously adored his *protégé*, and would hear no word against him.

Once or twice Bert had accompanied me on my expeditions to Dover; and I noticed that he was apt, once he had a drink or two inside him, to become obstreperous and even violent. Sometimes, too, he would give vent to disrespectful and even hostile remarks about his employer: I took no notice of these, but I couldn't help feeling slightly apprehensive on Pussy's behalf. Much as I liked Bert, he was quite capable (I thought), in certain moods, of behaving in a manner highly inconvenient to his 'protector'.

Both Eric and I were tickled by Pussy's *protégé* and Bert, for his part, seemed rather to enjoy our company. For some reason or other he conceived a limitless respect and admiration for Eric: at first he had been painfully shy, imagining goodness only knew what aristocratic background for my friend. Once, in the middle of a conversation, he had broken off suddenly, and eyed Eric with profound awe: 'I suppose,' he muttered at last, having apparently made up his mind on the point after prolonged meditation, 'I suppose you're what they call a *gentleman*?'

After this embarrassing episode, however, he seemed to accept Eric as not more alarmingly blue-blooded than myself; and proceeded to ask him a series of minute and penetrating questions about Oxford College, an institution which had, apparently, an almost morbid fascination for him.

He would entertain us, in return, with some of his adventures in the Army – amorous and otherwise. His attitude to sex was wholly *terre-à-terre*: 'You got to get rid of it somehow,' he would say. Nor, it seemed, was he above turning an honest penny by his exploits: 'I've known dames what'd pay for it,' he told us 'Coupla quid I got orf one of 'em – and she was a Real Lady, too.' He would relate such episodes – and others even less creditable – with a disarming air of *naïveté*. 'And that's nothing,' he would add, 'to what some of the swaddies get up to – some of them guardsmen, they'd do any-bloody-thing for ten bob.'

Bert, I think, was a bit of an exhibitionist: he was impressed by our 'Oxford education', but he liked to impress us, in his turn, not only by his scabrous tales (which were partly, no doubt, invented), but by his physical prowess. He would show off all the latest strokes, and turn elaborate cart-wheels on the shingle: his muscular, athletic body was a source of great pride to him, and if there were any women on the beach he showed off more outrageously than ever.

Calling on Pussy Wilkinson one day, Eric and I were greeted by the news that his sister was shortly coming down to stay with him for her annual fortnight's holiday. Pussy was immensely excited: this visit from his sister was an event to which he looked forward for months beforehand. They were devoted to one another: the sister was a widow, and I had once asked Pussy why they didn't set up house together. Pussy, however, was quite definitely opposed to such an arrangement – and so, he said, was Moira. 'We *quite* agree about it,' he said. 'Dear creature as she is, it would really *never* do. Brothers and sisters should *never* live together.'

I had met the 'dear creature' on one of her previous visits. She was, in fact, a very pretty, extremely elegant and entirely silly woman of about Pussy's own age: I could quite imagine that, though charming, she might not be the ideal housemate for Pussy.

A few days after her arrival Eric and I were invited to tea – not one of Pussy's 'tea-fights', but (which was a great compliment, coming from Pussy) 'Just ourselves.' Pussy's sister was as elegant and charming as ever: I could imagine that she fitted perfectly Pussy's idea of a 'pretty woman'. She possessed that rather rare kind of beauty which the 'fluffy' blonde occasionally acquires in middle age: a 'well-preserved' elegance, in which the stigmata of age are, for a certain type of man, an added attraction. The 'fluffy' type too often becomes faded or blowsy: Moira Wemyss was one of the rare exceptions. In her dress, she affected mostly pale greys and mauves, with wisps of pink chiffon depending vaguely from improbable places; I noticed that she almost always – however unsuitable the occasion – wore a hat. Enveloped in an aura of extremely (one guessed) expensive scent, and laden always with half-a-dozen totally useless bags, 'reticules' and *châtelaines*, she exhaled an almost overpoweringly feminine charm tempered by complete idiocy, which both Eric and I found sympathetic.

'My dears, how lovely of you to come to tea with an old woman like me,' she greeted us. 'Esmé *does* always manage to have such nice, charming friends – I adore them all ... You can't *think* how lovely it is to get down here after Town – *such* a rush and of course

I'm always terribly busy, and really, when you get to my age, it *does* take it out of you – sugar *and* milk? – and of course, I cannot *resist* the theatre – I expect you've seen that delicious play at the St James' – yes, Esmé, dear, I think there is just a *teeny* draught from that window – but Edith Evans is *always* good, isn't she, in any part? . . .'

She chattered on, with an unbelievable tattiness, for an hour or more: the whole occasion had, for me, a quality of nostalgia – Moira, exhaled, to perfection, that atmosphere of Edwardian drawing-rooms which was (though he seldom achieved it nowadays) Pussy's natural ambience. Moira was the kind of woman who inevitably reminds one of one's mother – or, if not one's own mother, of motherhood in the abstract. Moira herself was, in fact, childless – which no doubt made her all the more maternal. Her husband (who, one gathered, had been 'well-connected') had made a fortune in South Africa, and had left her extremely well-off – which was, one felt, very right and proper; one couldn't for a moment imagine Moira being 'poor'.

Later, when tea was over, Bert made his appearance. I had been wondering what attitude Moira would adopt to her brother's *protégé*; as it happened, she took the fairly obvious course of treating him exactly as she would have treated a small boy. Moira, one felt, was capable of 'mothering' the Archbishop of Canterbury if occasion offered; and in Bert's case, his youth made him an obvious target. She positively cooed over him: one almost expected her to offer him a rattle or a teddybear. Bert, for his part, seemed (rather surprisingly) to have developed a slavish affection for her: doubtless, I thought, she reminded him of his mother.

Pussy, as it happened, went out with Bert a few minutes later to settle some domestic problem in the kitchen, and Moira took the opportunity to express her admiration of her brother's generosity.

'He was always the same,' she declared, 'even when he was quite a little boy, he'd give his last penny to a beggar. And, of course, he's always been so fond of soldiers, you know – he had a *great* friend, a charming boy, who was killed in the Boer War, and he says Bert reminds him of him . . . I'm so glad to think he's got such a nice person to look after him – and it gives him quite an *interest* in life, too, if you see what I mean. Like a dog or a cat, you know, only it's so much better when they can *talk* isn't it? . . . I must say, I think Bert's a charming boy – such *natural* good manners you know, really quite presentable. I tell Esmé, he must let him come up to Town one day, and I'll take him to Madame Tussaud's. He's never been to London, it seems, and the waxworks are the *one* thing he wants to see . . .'

'She's the perfect Oedipus-object,' said Eric, on our way home. 'The mother-to-end-all-mothers. Did you notice how she gushed over Bert? She looked just as if she'd like to eat him . . .'

We agreed that Moira Wemyss was just like all the mammas in autobiographical novels, from *Sinister Street* onwards: the classical 'Artist's Mother', in fact, though hardly Whistler's.

'It's just as well she had no children,' said Eric. 'If she had, they'd all have been queer or literary or gone over to Rome.'

IV

Eric and I developed a slight *culte* for Moira Wemyss: we took her to the theatre and to tea at the Grand, and rather enjoyed being so prettily gushed over. Her affection for Bert, too, had become almost embarrassingly maternal – a circumstance which pleased Pussy immeasurably. As for Bert himself, whenever Moira appeared, a kind of holy look would come into his eyes; one almost expected him to climb into her lap to be cuddled. When not actually in her presence, however, he seemed less susceptible, and even, one day when he was bathing with us at Seabrook, made some slightly bawdy remarks about her. The fact that she was wealthy impressed him, of course, enormously: 'It's surprising she don't marry again,' he said.

Miss Bugle, our landlady at 'Glencoe' had conceived for Eric a passion which almost exceeded the limits of decency. She would, so he alleged, sidle into his bedroom on the most slender of pretexts, and, once inside, would stand there 'leering' at him, and commenting diffusely upon the pattern of his pyjamas or the state of his complexion.

'I think Mr Ankytil's ever such a nice gentleman,' she said to me. I felt, vicariously, quite flattered: none of my other friends had ever had a comparable success at 'Glencoe'. Miss Bugle excelled herself, while Eric was there, in concocting 'bits of done-up' which she thought would please him. Nothing was too much trouble where he was concerned: he was, as she once confided to me, her Ideel of what a Perfect Gentleman should be.

'He tells me,' she said, 'that he's going to write a book one of these days. I expect it'll be ever so exciting. I do like an exciting book, myself – something with lots of murders, you know.'

I said I didn't think Eric's book would be quite like that; but Miss Bugle's ideas about Authors were derived exclusively, it seemed, from an article she had once read in *Everybody's* about Edgar Wallace; and she proceeded to build up a similar myth about Eric's future as a Literary Gent – not omitting the dressing-gown and the outsize cigarette-holder.

'Did you see,' she asked us, one night at dinner, 'did you see in the paper where somebody's saying there's bound to be another war in five years?'

We admitted that we had, in fact, read the article in question.

'Do you think it's true?' asked Miss Bugle breathlessly, with an unholy gleam in her eyes. 'Do you think there reelly will be a war?'

'Undoubtedly,' said Eric.

If he had announced the millennium, Miss Bugle couldn't have looked more delighted.

'Well, of course,' she said, paying tardy lip-service to a convention for which, obviously, she hadn't really the least respect, 'of course, nobody *wants* a war. But if you ask me, there's some people in the world – *and in this town too* – who could do with a bit of shaking up, and I don't mind who hears me say so, neether.'

One afternoon, calling upon Pussy Wilkinson, we found him in a state of acute nervous excitement. Moira, it seemed, had a close friend who was a director of one of the big wireless-firms, and she had promised to use her 'influence' for the benefit of Bert. The outcome, it seemed, was almost a foregone conclusion: the firm in question (Moira happened to know) was taking on a lot of new employees, and there seemed every likelihood of an opening for a young man like Bert who was really 'keen'. This very day, as it happened, Moira had gone to London, and taken Bert with her: they were to pay the long-promised visit to Madame Tussaud's.

'Of course,' said Pussy, fretfully, 'I should be the *last* person to stand in the way of his advancement. He's really most *keen* on that kind of work, you know, and I think he really has quite a *genius* for it. At the same time, I shall *much* regret it if he decides to go to London. *Quite* apart from losing a charming – um – ah – companion, one doesn't feel quite happy about letting a young man loose in London nowadays ... So *many* temptations, you know, and the poor lad is really still so young and – um – innocent.'

I said I thought that Bert was more than capable of looking after himself, and that it would be an extremely good opportunity for him. But Pussy, I could see, was fundamentally opposed to the whole scheme, though he didn't quite like to admit it. Bert had become a kind of habit with him; moreover, he was extremely useful, and saved Pussy (who was inclined to be mean in such matters) a great deal of domestic trouble and expense.

A few days later, as it happened, we met Bert himself, who was treating himself to a drink in the Queen's bar. He looked, I thought, rather depressed; and it was not long before we discovered the reason. Moira, it appeared, had seen her friend of the radio-firm, and he had as good as promised Bert the job; but Pussy, driven into a corner, had proved unexpectedly obstinate, and advanced a number of quite specious arguments against the project. Moira, for her part, had displayed a surprising adroitness in countering his objections, and Pussy, finding himself beaten on points, had adopted a purely emotional attitude. He had appealed, in fact, to Bert's 'better nature'; wasn't Bert being a little selfish, a little ungrateful?

Poor Bert was obviously in an extremely delicate position: he was honestly fond of Pussy, and grateful for his protection; at the same time, he had his future to think of. Moreover, Moira was entirely on his side, and might well be offended if he didn't accept her offer.

'Cor, she's proper smashing, that sister of Pussy's,' Bert confided to us. 'Yer know', he added, his face suddenly breaking into a rather naughty grin, 'Yer know, I could almost fancy 'er meself – I could and all. You'd say she wasn't a day over thirty-five, to look at 'er and as nice a pair o' legs as you'd see in a day's march ... Cor, I do wish old Pussy'd be more reasonable, though. It's a bit 'ard when a bloke 'as a chance to better 'isself and can't take it up, like.'

Both Eric and I advised him to disregard Pussy's blackmailing tactics and take the job. We had several more drinks; Bert was already half-tight, and by the time we left him was in one of his sullen, obstreperous moods, cursing his luck and speaking (I thought) in rather a menacing way about his employer.

'If you ask me,' said Eric, 'I think Pussy's going to have trouble with that young man. I can't say I'd blame Bert, either – Pussy's really been rather silly about the whole business.'

I agreed; and remembering Bert's sudden fits of drunken violence, felt a qualm of apprehension. It seemed only too probable, as Eric said, that, with Bert in his present mood, Pussy's little idyll might soon be brought to an untimely end.

Eric's prophecy, as it happened, was fulfilled with a startling promptness. The very next morning, Pussy rang me up in great agitation, and poured into my ears a confused and largely unintelligible story, the essence of which seemed to be, so far as I could gather, that Bert had done a bolt. I was hardly surprised – and rather irritably told Pussy so, over the telephone. That evening Eric and I went round to investigate, and found Pussy almost in tears and looking quite ten years older. He could hardly bring himself, at first, to tell us what had happened, and could only repeat over and over again, that he had 'nourished a serpent in his bosom'. Presently, under the influence of a very large whisky and soda, he became calmer, and we heard the distressing details.

Bert, apparently, had returned late on the previous evening, after Pussy was in bed. ('No doubt he had been *drinking*,' said Pussy, pronouncing the word with a spinsterly primness, and fortifying himself with a large gulp of whisky.) In the morning, Pussy had come downstairs, at nine o'clock, to find the house empty. The drawing-room was a shambles; beer stains on the sofa, a picture (the precious Cuyp) torn from the wall, and cigarette-ash all over the carpet. Pussy's little *escritoire* had been broken into, and all the money in it taken – about seven pounds in all.

'He must have emptied the ash-trays *deliberately* on the floor,' moaned Pussy, who, with his passion for tidiness, seemed to find this the most poignant part of the whole affair.

'I suppose you've informed the police,' I said, rather maliciously – knowing very well that he had done nothing of the kind, for Pussy suffered from a superstitious terror of policemen.

'Good *gracious*, no,' he twittered, his agitation overcoming him afresh. 'The whole affair is *quite* unpleasant enough, without making it *worse* ... I blame myself,' he added, after a pause. 'I quite see now that I must have seemed a trifle – um – *unreasonable*. But even so, I should never have thought him capable of such – um – ah – *monstrous* ingratitude.'

'It might have been better,' said Eric, rather unkindly, 'if you'd let him take that job in the first place.'

'Don't *talk* about it, dear boy, don't *talk* about it,' whimpered Pussy, who seemed likely, at any moment, to burst into tears again.

Had he, I asked, rung up his sister? (It had struck me, suddenly, that if Bert had gone to London, he was quite capable of flinging himself on Moira's mercy.)

Pussy admitted that he had rung up Moira, who had, however, heard nothing of the fugitive; she was, said Pussy, much distressed, and had even suggested that she should come down and look after him. Pussy, however, had refused this well-meant offer – preferring (one gathered) to endure his grief in solitude.

It was not long before there was news of the runaway: Bert, it appeared, had gone straight up to London and, having (presumably) had a roaring time for a couple of days on Pussy's seven pounds, had then turned up (as I had suspected he might) penitent, dishevelled and very hungry, at Moira's flat. Moira, after (as she reported) giving him a 'good scolding', had finally taken pity on him, and forthwith arranged an interview with her friend of the wireless firm. This, it seemed, had proved satisfactory; and Bert had written a long letter of apology and explanation to Pussy, enclosing seven pounds (in cash), and imploring his forgiveness.

As for Pussy himself, he seemed to be suffering from a kind of delayed shock; the affair had entirely prostrated him, and, as he told me the story, he could hardly restrain his tears.

'It's all been *most* unpleasant and distressing,' he sniffed. 'But one can't help feeling,' he added, with a long-drawn sigh, 'that perhaps, after all, everything's happened for the best ... One hates to admit it, of course, but one does feel, sometimes, that one's getting just a *leetle* too old for such – um – ah – youthful companionship ... And although our friend was a charming person in many ways, one couldn't deny – could one? – that there was a certain strain of *coarseness* in his character ...'

A few days later, I encountered Pussy trotting, as usual, down to

W. H. Smith's, with his two Sealyhams; he asked Eric and myself to tea, and we spent a decorous hour listening to dull transcriptions of *Norma* and *Lucia di Lammermoor*.

Pussy seemed to have made at least a partial recovery. He had secured the temporary services of a certain Miss McPhee, who had once been employed by his sister, and had now settled in Folkestone. Miss McPhee was not the least of Pussy's present misfortunes:

'I don't doubt,' he said, 'that she's an excellent woman in her way, but I'm afraid, dear boy, she will *never* make a good cook. I've shown her over and over *again* the proper way to make an omelette, and *every* time, in some *mysterious* way, it turns into scrambled eggs. It's really *most* vexing – but then, of course, say what you like, the Scotch are *not* really a civilized people.'

As for Bert, it was obvious that Pussy preferred to avoid the subject: he couldn't even bear to mention his ex-*protégé* by name, but referred to him, darkly, as 'A Certain Person'. We gathered that Bert was to start his new job shortly, and that Moira had behaved 'most generously' over the whole affair. It struck me, however, that Pussy spoke of his sister with a trifle less than his usual enthusiasm; perhaps he felt that her 'generosity', in this case, had been somewhat misplaced.

v

In retrospect, that summer seems (as so many past summers seem) to have been perpetually hot and sunny; doubtless it wasn't, but during Eric's visit I bathed and sunbathed with him at every opportunity, and the memory of those weeks is indissolubly linked with afternoons at Seabrook: the August sun grilling our bodies, sandwiches on the beach, fragments of Firbank read aloud, the cavalrymen like centaurs prancing in the surf.

Among other *niaiseries* of that silly season, we collected *graffiti*: Eric proposed publishing an anthology of the better ones.

'Or *you* might write a little monograph,' he suggested. ' "Mr Brooke's acute and penetrating little study, dot-dot-dot".' (We were both fond of quoting from reviews of each other's future works.)

We collected other *curiosa*, too: Eric had a magpie's eye for oddities. There was a firm, for instance, with the pleasantly suggestive name of Hayward and Paramor: 'So much better than just "and Co.".' said Eric. There was, also, the bus-company which advertised itself as 'Luxure Coaches': no doubt, we decided, each coach was provided with an assortment of *petites dames* for the delectation of its passengers.

'I'm glad poor Bert cut the painter,' Eric remarked. 'I hope he likes being mothered by Mrs Wemyss. She begged me to call on her whenever I was in London – or rather, what she actually said was "when you come to Town".'

'Snob,' I said.

'You're an inverted one, anyway.'

'And will you go?'

'I daresay I'll ring her up.'

'You mean you'll "phone" her.'

'I bet she calls her drawing-room "the lounge".'

'I expect we're being rather unkind. I like Moira – she asked *me* to go and see her too.'

' "... lissom as a glove, lively as a kid, and as fond of tippling as a Grenadier-Guard",' quoted Eric, who was reading *Valmouth*. 'Incidentally, Moira herself can put back a fair amount – I saw her drink three of Pussy's enormous Sidecars without batting an eyelid. She and Bert ought to get on like a house-on-fire.'

It was the last Sunday of Eric's holiday: tomorrow he would be returning home, *en route* for the prep-school which employed him. We were spending the whole day on the beach, with sandwiches and a bottle of claret.

'How lucky you are,' said Eric, 'to divide your time between selling wine and drinking it.'

I found the remark depressing – emphasizing, as it did, the fact of my servitude which, on such days as this, I preferred to forget. The troopers from the cavalry regiment had brought down their horses again: pink and white centaur-trunks welded to dark, prancing steeds, they shouted and laughed in the calm shallows.

'I'd rather,' I said lazily, 'be almost anything than a wine-merchant. I'd as soon be one of those soldiers.'

'*Housman*,' said Eric, warningly.

'It's not Housman in the least. I should rather like to de-intel-
lectualize myself – '

'*Lawrence*,' snapped Eric. 'And you couldn't anyway,' he
pursued, taking a draught of St Emilion 1924 from the bottle.
'Even if you joined the Army, you'd only write poems about it.'

'I wonder,' I said, and fell silent: looking through the thumbed
pages of *Valmouth*, which Eric had abandoned. ' "Indeed she looks
a squilleon",' I quoted.

'You're incurably literary,' said Eric, 'whether you like it or not.'

'So are you.'

'I never denied it. That's why I'm a pedagogue – the refuge of
the *poète manqué*.'

'There's always the BBC,' I suggested.

'Thank you, I'd rather keep my independence, such as it is.'

'You'd better discover your poetaster, and write the definitive
life ... "Mr Anquetil's delightful and scholarly monograph" –
dot-dot-dot *New Statesman*.'

'*You'd* better write a book on orchids – or fireworks. "Sheer
delight" – dot-dot-dot *Woman's Journal*.'

' "*Ce livre honteux de M. Anquetil doit être instamment sup-
primé*' –"

'A wine-merchant and a pedagogue,' said Eric, reflectively. 'I
wonder how long it'll last?'

Presently we bathed again: the sea was warm, and calm as a
lake. The soldiers and their horses had gone back to the barracks;
the beach was nearly deserted. When we came out, the sun was
getting low; we sunbathed for another ten minutes, then dressed
and, feeling pleasantly limp and deflated, climbed to the top of the
wall.

'I do like the Goose Cathedral,' said Eric. 'It's so *echt* what it is,
if you see what I mean – the triumph of the *Kitsch*. By the way, I
found some rather good *graffiti* this morning – I forgot to tell you.
One was about boots.'

'Oh, I know that one – it's in Bouverie Square.'

We bussed home through the late afternoon sunlight, had a
hasty dinner at 'Glencoe', and then set out (since it was Eric's last
night) for Dover. It was a gay evening: there was a fair on the
seafront, and we spent a lot of money on the roundabouts and
charaplanes. Afterwards, in the Prince Regent, we met a soldier-
friend of Bert's, whom I had been introduced to on a former oc-

casion. The soldier was rather tight, and disposed to be confidential.

'That Bert,' he told us, 'he wouldn't stop at nothing – a proper lad he was, in the regiment. 'E'd have been in trouble, if that old toff 'adn't bought him out.'

We asked what kind of trouble: and were treated to a number of details about Bert's Army career which he hadn't seen fit to reveal himself. Among other indiscretions he had (it was rumoured) put one of the officers' wives in the family way; the affair had been hushed up, but Bert had boasted about it quite shamelessly, and even alleged that he had blackmailed the lady in question.

'But you couldn't help liking him,' his friend added. 'He'd do anything for his own pals – I've known him fork out his whole week's pay for a bloke what was in trouble. And he was clever, too – real deadly, he was, on the gunnery course, and there wasn't nothing he didn't know about wireless. He ought to do well at that new job of his.'

VI

Some weeks after Eric's departure, I went to London for a few days: I was to visit the cellars and offices of a famous firm of wine-shippers, as a further stage in my 'business' training. I hung about the premises for several days, trying very hard to be brisk and efficient, and to learn something about the shipping of wine; but I learnt, alas! nothing. Secretly I was convinced that I should never be a successful – or even a reasonably efficient – wine merchant; and I was trying to screw up my courage to tell my father so.

While I was in London, I decided, in a rather sentimental, Oedipus mood, to ring up Moira Wemyss, and invite myself to tea. Moira was delighted: I must go, she insisted, that very afternoon.

Her flat was in Earl's Court: very cosy and Edwardian, just as I had imagined it, with lots of white paint, gilt-framed water-colours, and cinerarias in brass pots. When I entered the drawing-room, a young man rose from a chair to greet me – rather a large young man, very smartly-dressed and prosperous-looking.

'Hullo, Jocelyn, it's nice to see you,' he said.

I looked again, and to my amazement recognized Bert. Never

would I have believed such a transformation possible: it was only a few weeks since he had left Folkestone, yet in that short space he had become a different person. Chiefly, of course, it was the clothes; in former days, he had affected rather tight-waisted suits of blue serge, with wide-bottomed trousers; now he wore a smart lounge-suit with a shirt and tie which came, probably, from Hawes and Curtis. But it wasn't entirely his dress which altered him: his manner was more confident, he was fatter, and even his accent was becoming modified – he was rather careful, I noticed, not to drop his aitches.

He seemed, so far as Moira was concerned, to have assumed the status of an old family friend. He called her, now, by her Christian name; and both of them called each other 'my dear' – a form of address which, meaningless in itself, seemed to have acquired, in this case, a special significance. Bert, I thought, must be on very familiar terms with his protectrice; and I couldn't help remembering occasions at Folkestone when his appreciative remarks about her had taken on a tone distinctly more Aristotelian than Platonic.

'So delightful of you to come,' Moira was gushing. 'I knew Bert wanted to meet you again, and I just managed to get hold of him at his rooms. So lucky it was a Saturday – he works terribly hard, don't you?' she said fondly, turning to Bert, who gave an embarrassed grin.

Swathed in tulle and chiffon, and positively bathed in scent, Moira prattled away in her usual artless manner. Presently I asked Bert how he liked his job: it was smashing, he said, and he was dead-keen on the work. It was well-paid, too, he added, and he'd be getting a rise before long. I thought he seemed a trifle embarrassed as he spoke of his salary: it was fairly obvious that he couldn't be earning enough, as yet, to pay for such clothes as he was wearing. I noticed, on his wrist, an expensive-looking watch; and he offered me a cigarette from a case which hadn't, I guessed, cost less than ten pounds. There couldn't be much doubt, I thought, as to who had provided those luxuries; nor did it seem unlikely – knowing Bert – that he was willing enough to repay them in kind. Watching Moira's fond glances resting on her *protégé*, I could well believe that she was finding the bargain, on her side, eminently satisfactory.

Soon I rose to go.

'You two boys must have a night out together sometime,' said

Moira, with a matronly archness, as I left the flat. Her manner, I thought, was precisely that of a newly-married woman, anxious to show her husband's friends that she wasn't going to be a 'possessive' wife.

A few evenings later, having arranged a rendezvous with a friend of mine, I walked into a pub off Charlotte Street. I was slightly early for my appointment, and, as I entered, noticed with some astonishment that Bert was sitting at the bar, apparently very much at home, with a pint of beer in front of him.

Seeing me, he appeared, at first, a trifle embarrassed, but soon recovered his self-possession. I was offered a drink – 'Anything you like,' said Bert, 'double-whisky? Gin-and-It?' I said I would have a bitter; and noticed, as Bert pulled out his note-case, that it was well-filled with pound-notes.

We had several drinks: Bert was waiting, he said, for a bloke he'd promised to meet, but it didn't look as if he'd turn up. My own friend, too, was late; and after another twenty minutes wait, I decided that he must have forgotten, and agreed to accompany Bert to another bar.

It was a very beery evening. Bert seemed to know all the pubs in the district, and was plainly bent upon spending as much money as he could before eleven o'clock. In the Fitzroy he was on nodding terms with all the habitués, and appeared, moreover, to be extremely popular there. I wondered how he had introduced himself into such circles: a few weeks ago, I remembered, his one ambition in London was to visit Madame Tussaud's.

Towards the end of the evening, he became more confidential, and (I noticed) more like his old self. I began to suspect, from certain things he said, that Moira was not his only benefactor. There was, for instance, a Real Titled Lady, who had asked him out to supper; and he related to me, also, a rather confused story (for he was pretty tight by now) about a Rich Bloke who wrote Books; this personage, it seemed, had asked him down to his 'place' in the country. Did I, he asked, think it would be worth going?

I advised, prudently, against the Bloke who wrote Books. Bert, I thought, seemed to have acquired a pretty accurate idea of his own value; and I wondered how much Moira knew or suspected about the circles in which he was moving.

We parted when the pubs closed; Bert was tight enough, by now, to have dropped all pretences: he was going round, he said, to say good night to Moira. In a sudden access of bonhomie, he asked me to accompany him: I refused politely, adding that I should hate to intrude.

Bert gave a grin in which a certain slyness was mingled with an immense self-satisfaction.

'Cor, she's a real peach, Moira is,' he confided; and proceeded to add a number of intimate details about her amorous proclivities. 'You'd never think,' he finished, with something of his old *naïveté*. 'You'd never think she was fifty-six last birthday.'

I parted from him with a curious sense of finality – it seemed unlikely, now he was living in London, that we should ever meet again.

I returned to Folkestone: it was mid-October, but the weather was still warm and summer-like, and I went down to bathe, for the last time, at Seabrook. The sun was hot, the sea warm; but the beach was deserted, now: the soldiers no longer came down with their horses, and the last trippers had long since departed. As I passed the boathouse, I observed it for signs of life: but the Goose Cathedral looked as desolate as ever. Curtains of a rather arty orange-colour hung in the windows; a few nibbled and squalid-looking asters lingered in the trodden flower-garden. The geese waddled rather dispiritedly round the shingle patch, eyeing me malevolently as I passed. I remembered my dream of the Barnacle Geese: the darkening winter shore, the sense of desolate, annihilating misery. Inimical birds, images of my own *personae*, they hovered still, like waiting vultures, in the dark places of my mind.

CHAPTER SIX

King Minimus

I

Greylands House, Folkestone, was generally considered to be a very good school: its snob-value, as they say, was considerable. I suppose it was, in fact, no worse than most preparatory schools; and I have met, in my time, quite a number of its ex-pupils who seem to have survived with their bodies and brains more or less intact.

In my day, I suppose, the school must have entered upon a period of decadence. Partly, no doubt, the war was to blame: all the younger masters had joined up, and the remnant were elderly, vicious and mostly quite irresponsible. The Headmaster himself was a young man; somehow he had managed to get himself exempted from military service. He hated me at sight, and I hated him.

At the time, owing to some digestive trouble, I was forbidden to eat meat. It was arranged, therefore (for I was to take my midday meal at school), that I should be given a 'vegetarian' diet. This, in effect, consisted of my being helped, at dinner time, to such vegetables as were being served, with a spoonful of washy gravy poured over them. No supplementary dish was provided in lieu of meat; and as the 'vegetables' usually consisted of boiled rice, or a mess of flaccid turnips and fibrous, half-mummified carrots, it was hardly surprising that my 'vegetarian diet' didn't agree with me. Day after day my stomach would turn at the tasteless rice, the translucent corpse-like turnips; I thought of the good food at home, and tried to fight down my tears. Often I only prevented myself with difficulty from being physically sick. The other boys didn't fare much better: the meat had a curiously grey, slimy appearance, as though it had been fished from the bottom of a stagnant pond; yet I was so hungry that I would gladly have eaten it, had I been allowed to – even at the risk of being subsequently afflicted with 'sand in my water'.

On the morning of my arrival, I was delivered into the hands of the Headmaster, who conducted me to the classroom where I was to work. The mistress in charge (a Miss Greenhalgh) had not yet arrived; the boys sat in rows at their scarred and ink-stained desks – there seemed to me to be hundreds of them, all of a uniformly brutal and degraded cast of countenance. The Headmaster muttered an inaudible word or two, and retired. I was left alone with my enemies.

No sooner was the door closed than the assault began. There was a chorus of shouts, mostly unintelligible, directed at myself; paper pellets and 'darts' showered around me. I sat at my desk, paralysed with terror, and wishing that I were dead. Presently, from the chorus of shouting, one remark emerged – it became, that is to say, recognizable by insistent repetition, though I still couldn't understand what it meant.

It sounded like 'What's your paper?' Apparently I ought to have brought some kind of paper with me, but nobody had told me so. At last I realized that the word was not 'paper' but 'pater'; I still didn't understand, until one of my tormentors happened to repeat the question in English: 'What's your father?'

I thought for a moment; persecution had already made me cunning. I had once or twice overheard the grown-ups saying that a wine-merchant was not considered, by snobbish people, to be quite a 'gentleman'. At that moment I passionately wanted my father to be a gentleman: I would have lied like a trooper in the cause of his gentility.

'What's your father?' they shouted in chorus.

'A lawyer,' I said, and blushed all over my face.

It was, in fact, a half-truth: my father had read law at Oxford, and was qualified to practise as a solicitor, though he had chosen, at an early date, to enter the family business. My persecutors, at any rate, seemed satisfied. A moment later Miss Greenhalgh made her appearance: a twittering, stringy woman with an air of rather careful elegance. Class began: I was safe, at any rate, till the eleven o'clock 'break'.

The classroom looked out over the playing-fields towards Sugarloaf and Caesar's Camp – those hills were (but how long ago it seemed!) I had wandered, with Ninnie, on hot June afternoons, looking for the Bee Orchid. Tears sprang to my eyes: an intolerable homesickness swept over me. Staring through the dust-grimed windows at the distant hills, it seemed to me that, if I prayed hard enough and with sufficient faith, God himself would probably appear and (having struck the rest of the class dead), bear me up with him into the blue sky above Caesar's Camp. I stared with a hypnotic intensity at the flag-staff on the hilltop, which I could just discern; and waited for the heavens to open.

By 'break' time, however, God had still not appeared: peradventure, I thought, he sleepeth; and, with terror in my heart, followed my companions down to the playground.

I must have been the only 'new bug' that term: at any rate, I was the centre of attention. My own classmates and a crowd of other, older boys surrounded me. They made jokes about my legs, which were thin (I was known thenceforward as 'Matchsticks'); they commented on my clothes, which were, of course, 'wrong'; they played tricks: 'Do you collect stamps? All right, then, here's one' – stamping violently and painfully on the toes of my boots. They used a whole vocabulary which was as alien to me as a foreign language – there was the word 'Kay-vee', for instance, which, since I had as yet no Latin, terrified me by its mysterious potentialities. Gradually the less abstruse terms they used became intelligible: 'bug-grease' was hair-oil, 'sausages' were *faeces*, 'lemonade' was urine. ('Do you like lemonade? All right, come to the bogs and I'll give you some.')

After the break, God still delayed his appearance: nor did he appear next day, or the next. I soon gave up invoking him. I must have been, for my tormentors, a particularly satisfying victim: they gave me no respite. At 'break', at meals, in the interval before tea, they kept it up tirelessly. I went about in a perpetual state of near-weeping. Did my family really *know* what it was like, I wondered? Presumably they did; in which case, it was useless to complain. In any case, when I got home at night, I was too relieved at escaping from the day's horrors to want to talk about them.

I might have accustomed myself to the teasing and bullying; but football was, for me, an even lower and less bearable circle of the inferno. I was hopeless at it to begin with; and the jeers of the others made me worse. Once a peculiarly shrill whistle sounded in the middle of a game; but nobody had warned me that this was the signal for an air-raid 'practice', and, instead of following the crowd to the shelter, I made my way to the changing-room. This, of course, was an excuse for a new campaign of persecution: I was made to feel that my mistake had been not only stupid, but disloyal and unpatriotic into the bargain.

Among my tormentors there was one, in particular, who emerged as my special and implacable enemy. His persecution of me was almost professional in its ingenuity and single-mindedness.

His methods had a certain subtlety: from the first he had assumed, intermittently, an air of friendliness to which, of course, I fell an easy victim. So naïve was I that, for so long as I remained at the school, I never failed to react in the expected manner to his 'friendly' overtures. Once, for instance, I had caught a moth – a yellow underwing – which I was going to take home for my collection. Professing an amiable interest, King Min. (for such was his name) asked me to show it to him. I held out my hand: in an instant he had dashed my treasure to the ground and trodden on it.

'That'll teach you to go bug-hunting,' he shouted. 'Don't you know it's cruel, to kill butterflies?' And thereupon he treated me to a long diatribe against 'cruelty-to-animals'; whether his irony was intentional I don't know; I suspect that it wasn't: for small boys are quite capable of such inconsistencies (as indeed are plenty of grown-ups).

King Minimus – he was the youngest of three brothers, all at the school. The abbreviation, King Min., had for me a sinister ring – it sounded vaguely Chinese. He was a grubby-looking boy with sandy hair, freckles and pale, pinkish eyes. His tie was perpetually slipping down to reveal his collar-stud, which was a cheap and tarnished brass one. This, more than anything else about him, I found repellent: for I had conceived a curious horror of collar-studs, cuff-links and similar minor appendages of male costume. It was not a question of mere personal association: I loathed having to wear a collar-stud myself, and could hardly bear to touch it. The least one could do, I felt, if one had to wear such a repulsive article, was to keep it covered up; and I was scrupulous about the set of my own tie.

King Min., however, naturally scruffy, displayed his brass stud with a shamelessness which nauseated me. He also, as I discovered in the changing-room, wore a medal on a chain round his neck: so did his two brothers. I gathered that they were Roman Catholics; and this fact, if it did not entirely account for their general depravity, was no doubt a contributory cause of it: for Roman Catholics, as everyone knew, were Dirty and Dishonest, and worshipped the Virgin Mary. The three King brothers were, I decided, typical of the degraded and superstitious religion which they professed. I became, for the first time in my life, consciously and militantly a Protestant.

Much has been written about fetishism; but has anyone investigated that complementary aberration which, for want of a better name, might be called anti-fetishism – the passionate and quite irrational loathing for perfectly harmless objects? I cannot remember a time when I did not possess this hatred for collar-studs; I loathe them still, and will, if possible, always wear shirts which *button* at the neck. My loathing extends to cuff-links, Catholic 'medals', and even rings and bracelets: I would never wear a ring myself, and to this day can hardly bear to touch anybody else's. I can think of no feasible explanation: Freudians, I suppose, might see in the collar-stud a phallic symbol, and interpret my feeling as a sexual phobia. I cannot say they would be wrong, for I am in no position to judge, without allowing myself to be psychoanalysed; but I very much doubt whether my peculiarity can be so easily explained.

The force of my repulsion varied, somewhat, according to what *kind* of stud people wore; the least disgusting seemed to me that made of bone or ivory, and this was the only type I would ever consent to wear: brass or nickel ones were altogether beyond the pale, those who wore them (such as King Min.) were not less repellent, to me, than people who had lice or suffered from 'bad breath'. In fact, I would have found it less disgusting to handle their excrement than to touch their collar-studs.

II

That winter of 1916–1917 was a hard one: snow fell heavily and often, the roads were ice-bound for weeks at a time. For me, at Greylands, the weather had one advantage – it sometimes put a stop to football. Unfortunately, however, it favoured another form of activity which I hated almost as much. A long strip of ground was cleared at the edge of the playing fields; water was thrown over it at night; by the morning it was smooth and slippery as an ice-rink, and a perfect place to 'slide'. In every break the boys assembled there in force: the idea was to take a run at the ice, and to try and 'slide' from one end to the other, without falling over and without touching the edge of the track. I was not so much scared of hurting myself as shy of being laughed at; I avoided the 'slide' as much as possible. It was not, however, particularly easy to avoid, for the Headmaster himself was a keen 'slider'; and made himself personally responsible for my instruction. He was a quiet-mannered, shifty-eyed little man; he seldom lost his temper, but he had a genius for making sarcastic and wounding remarks.

'Come on, now, Brooke,' he would say, 'let's see you put on a really good show this time.' I would venture, feebly, on to the track, and, of course, fall over immediately. The slight pain was enough to release my hoarded tears, never very far from my eyes: I sobbed, helplessly, beneath the cool, contemptuous regard of the Head. 'That's enough now,' he would snap at me. 'Brace up and try and be a man – we've no use for mother's darlings here, you know ... Or Nannie's darlings either,' he would add, as an after-thought – for I had failed to conceal the humiliating fact that I still had a Nannie.

The boys tittered obsequiously. I slunk away to the edge of the crowd, hoping I should be forgotten; and stood there, shivering and wretched, in the glacial afternoon. I was developing a chronic blink from the effort to fight down my tears; and I suffered, too, from a perpetual slight nausea, caused no doubt by the disgusting and inadequate food. I saw no possible end to the hell which I was enduring; I was only eight, and the oldest boys were thirteen or even fourteen. Six more years of 'sliding', of football, of King Min.

... I supposed (with a gleam of melancholy hope) that I should probably die before then. Or perhaps I should be taken away and sent to a boarding-school; this prospect, which had always seemed to me the ultimate horror, a Fate Worse Than Death, began actually to seem attractive. It couldn't, I decided, however dreadful, be any worse than being a day-boy at Greylands House.

Perhaps the worst periods of the day were the intervals before meals – half-an-hour before dinner and half-an-hour before tea, during which the whole school assembled in the Big Schoolroom, to await the sounding of the gong. There must have been, I suppose, some master on duty; but he seldom appeared; and my memories of those pre-prandial half-hours are of a complete, unbridled anarchy. Bad food and lack of discipline had reduced these boys to the level of savages – though this, in fact, is a mere *façon de parler*, for very few primitive tribes are addicted to that demoniac cruelty-for-its-own-sake which is found in its worst form only among English schoolboys. They were not, perhaps, by nature worse than other small boys, who are all potential demons, anyway; but at Greylands this potentiality was given every possible encouragement. Naturally, I was the favourite victim, as always; and King Min., my self-appointed tormentor-in-chief, was well to the fore in every assault which had me as its object.

There was no escape: my only hope of being at least temporarily overlooked was to climb up, by means of a radiator, to a high, deep window-sill, and sit there, making myself as small as possible. The window was some five feet from the ground: with luck I might be unnoticed there for five or ten precious minutes. I could look down from my perch, with a certain detachment, on the milling crowd of boys; or, more often, I would turn away and stare through the steamy windows at the falling snow.

The snow fell heavily and interminably: big, feathery flakes, coming down in dense clouds and whorls, as though a series of feather beds were being ripped open somewhere up in the opaque, brownish sky. I watched the flakes emerging from each gusty, descending swarm, taking individual form, hovering and whirling against the window like falling leaves ... The playground, the playing-fields were nearly invisible: blotted out by the grey, feathery darkness of the snow. Yet somewhere, I thought, beyond the fields, lay the railway; beyond that, Cheriton and Shorncliffe; and beyond that again, the Hills: those beloved hills where I imagined it as always summer – a perpetual afternoon in June, haunted by bees and the scraping of grasshoppers and the remote, melancholy crying of bugles from the camp. And over the hills – far, far away, beyond Lyminge and Denton and Elham, was 'our' village, where we went to live in the spring and summer. Would the spring ever come, I wondered? The winter seemed, like my own life at school, to be unrelenting and probably eternal.

But I was seldom left for long in peace upon my window-ledge. Sooner or later someone would spot me – more often than not King Min. He would seize my dangling foot and pull; usually I was quick enough to kick out at him, and, as he recoiled, make my descent in safety; on at least one occasion, however, he took me by surprise: grabbing me by the legs and pulling me bodily to the ground – a drop of five feet. I fell on my head, and was for a minute nearly unconscious; I had also twisted my arm rather badly. A few seconds later, a master happened to come in – one of those ineffectual old boobies, too old for military service, of whom the teaching staff mainly consisted. I decided, quite coolly and unemotionally, to Sneak. I had never sneaked before: being restrained, perhaps, more by fear of worse torments to follow than by any real respect for this most hallowed of schoolboy taboos. But things had gone too far: I had no scruples left, and no recriminations could be much worse than the hell which I was already suffering.

I went to the master; he called King Min. up to him.

'You've no business to bully a younger boy than yourself,' he said.

'But he's *not* younger,' said King Min.

And indeed it was true: we were both eight years old; my birthday, in fact, was a month earlier than King Min's.

The master, having established these important facts, looked at me with some contempt; then turned to King Min., whom he warned (but in the mildest terms) not to repeat the offence. At that moment, fortunately for all concerned, the tea-gong sounded.

I never sneaked again – not because I felt ashamed, nor because I was made to suffer for it afterwards, but simply because I was convinced, by my single experience, that it *didn't do any good*. I had, I suppose, imbibed even at this age some abstract idea of Justice; but concluded, after this episode, that 'Justice' was one of those vague, beautiful things that the grown-ups encouraged one to believe in, but which didn't really exist – like Father Christmas, or God. I had 'seen through' Father Christmas some considerable time before; and more recently – in my first week or two at Greylands – I had seen through God as well (for plainly, if He existed, he would have appeared to me, over Caesar's Camp, on that first homesick morning). Now Justice had gone to join God and Father Christmas, in that limbo of myths and fairy-tales in which one no longer 'believes'. My unscrupulous 'sneaking' had at least taught me this much; and the knowledge so gained was of the greatest use to me in after-life – more particularly in the Army, for which profession, indeed, no better training could be imagined than that provided at Greylands House.

The winter ended at last – rather to my surprise. The summer-term came, cricket replaced football, there was no more 'sliding', and the half-hours before dinner and tea were usually spent out of doors, where it was easier to efface oneself.

I felt chronically unhappy and (owing to the food, which didn't improve) rather ill. But the summer-term promised to be slightly more bearable than the two previous ones – or so I thought. I had forgotten that horror which, even in previous summers at home, had always lain in wait for me, a recurrent threat. Should I, I asked myself with secret terror, be expected to bathe? I was not long left in doubt: on the very first warm day, the school was marched down to the sea-water baths by the harbour. There was no escaping it. Naked, I felt, as always, more vulnerable, and the jeers of the Headmaster were more wounding, even, than on previous occasions. Not surprisingly, my phobia about 'bathing' became intensified, and lasted, indeed, until I was fourteen, when I went to Bedales. (Here I was at last taught to swim, by R. E. Roper: the kindest person I encountered during my schooldays, and one of the most admirable men I have ever known. Once I had learnt to swim, I developed a passion for bathing; it became for me one of the major pleasures of life, and has remained so to this day.)

III

One afternoon in May – it was, in fact, 25 May 1917 – Ninnie had come to meet me, on my way home, at the bottom of Earl's Avenue. We walked up the tree-lined road in the warm, May sunlight: the day was cloudless and without wind. Suddenly we heard sounds of gun-fire: we didn't take much notice, for there were a number of practice-ranges and gun-sites round the town, and we were habituated to the continual explosions. As we walked on, however, the firing became heavier and more continuous. We looked up: and there, in the brilliant blue sky, to eastwards over the town, we saw a number of little smoke-puffs like swabs of cotton-wool. Probably they were only practising; but we began to walk rather more quickly. Just as we reached the corner of the Leas, by the Burlington Hotel, a familiar figure emerged into view – twittering at us excitedly from the edge of the pavement, in an effort to gain our attention. It was the eldest Miss Hodsell.

'*Such* a noise,' she gabbled, her teeth clacking like castanets, her cheap little boa dangling from her shoulders, her hat awry. 'I was quite scared – I thought it might be an air-raid, you know, but I've just asked those soldiers over there, and they say it's only "practice".'

Meanwhile I had been peering upwards into the dazzle of sunlight. The guns were firing again more heavily than ever: cluster after cluster of little white puffs appeared in the sky. Between them, I suddenly detected something else: half-a-dozen tiny, brilliant points moving northwards, in a triangle. They flashed silvery in the sun: between the bursts of gunfire, I could hear a deep, remote drone, which seemed to fill the wide blue air.

'Only practice (click), only practice,' Miss Hodsell was insisting. At that moment, an explosion like a near clap of thunder burst upon our ears; Ninnie grasped my hand, we ran into the Burlington where, in the entrance hall, an excited crowd was already collected, staring skywards and pointing at the high silver birds. Somebody had succeeded in dragging Miss Hodsell in after us: she stood, dithering, on the hotel steps, still insisting that it was 'only practice'.

Another thunderclap and then another, further away ... Presently the gun-fire diminished, and finally ceased. We walked home through the still-bright sunshine, down the steps by the Grand Hotel, and along the Lower Road. At home everyone was very excited: my father had been in Folkestone, so had my mother; our maid, Alice, had been walking along the Lower Road. Everyone was congratulating everyone else on being alive. My heart swelled with pride: I had been in a Real Air-Raid.

Next morning, walking down Earl's Avenue to school, I saw the results of that first explosion, which had so inconsiderately interrupted Miss Hodsell: a big house on the corner of Jointon Road had been completely demolished. When I reached Greylands, I found everyone in a state of mingled excitement and awe. A bomb had fallen on the edge of the playing-fields, and the school-gardener had been killed instantly. We spent the 'breaks' that day picking up bits of shrapnel in the playground. I had scarcely ever spoken to the gardener, but I shared the prevailing mood of rather pleasurable gloom occasioned by his death. All the same, I felt inclined to regret that the bomb had been wasted on somebody who, after all, had done me no harm; I would have preferred the Fire from Heaven to descend, more suitably, upon the Headmaster or (better still) upon King Min.

The summer dragged on: there was to be a school concert at the end of the term, consisting of selections from *The Gondoliers*. All through the preceding weeks, for an hour or so every day, we bawled out those catchy chorus-numbers; after a month of it, I knew the score almost by heart.

But I was not, as it happened, destined to take part in that end-of-term concert. Three terms of bad food and constant persecution produced, at last, the results which might have been expected; my body finally rebelled, and I was overtaken by a series of violent retchings and vomitings. Dr Percy Lewis, our family-doctor, was called in (he was a practitioner of the old school, and never visited a patient, even in the middle of the night, without assuming his full regalia: frock-coat, top-hat and buttoned-boots). He was shocked at my symptoms; I was suffering, he declared, from starvation – nothing more or less. (Nowadays, I suppose – so refined have we become – it would be called 'malnutrition', but Dr

Lewis had the *démodé* habit of calling a spade by its proper name.)

I was kept away from school till I recovered; shortly before I was due to return, we heard that chicken-pox had broken out. My family were away, and Ninnie took the law into her own hands: she refused to send me back. In vain did the Headmaster write, in vain did he telephone: Ninnie was adamant.

Convalescent, I began to write a series of little 'books': sheets of writing-paper sewn together in brown paper covers, with the titles painted on the outsides in emerald-green and crimson-lake: *British Orchids, British Butterflies* and so on. I illustrated them with my own water-colour drawings. I was, I suppose, in a numb and lifeless sort of way, happy.

In August we were to go and stay at Camberley, to be near my brother, who was at Sandhurst. Before we went, however, the D'Oyley Carte Company visited the Pleasure Gardens Theatre, and I was taken to a *matinée* of *The Gondoliers*. It was only my second 'theatre' – the first had been *Peter Pan*. Not even my memories of the Greylands 'concert' could diminish the paradisiac delights on that afternoon; for the rest of the summer I hummed the tunes without respite, much to the annoyance of my sister, who begged me to sing something else for a change. Every scene in the opera was imprinted clearly on my mind; in bed at night, I would stage a private 'production' for myself, and go through the whole score from Opening Chorus to Finale. For years after this I was privately convinced that *The Gondoliers* must be one of the world's masterpieces; I longed for an opportunity to go to it again. This did not, in fact, occur until I was nineteen, and at Oxford: I duly went; and was so profoundly bored that I spent the whole of the second act in the bar.

It was while we were at Camberley that I was told the stupendous, the breath-taking news: I was not to go back to Greylands. Of course I was relieved; yet not so profoundly as perhaps I ought to have been. I seemed to have lost some capacity for feeling; it was as though virtue had gone out of me: I felt limp and flaccid, like a piece of elastic which has been stretched too tight and has lost its resilience. I botanized happily enough on the heaths round Camberley; and, when we returned to Sandgate at the end of August, resumed my usual life as though nothing particular had happened.

For the rest of the holidays, however, I was 'looked after' with greater care than usual; I needed fresh air and 'feeding-up', said Dr Lewis. We made an expedition to the hills – those hills which, from the window in the 'big' schoolroom, I had imagined, lapped in their perpetual summer, beyond the curtain of falling snow ... The Bee Orchid was over now: but we found the Lady's Tresses, with its little spiral spike which smelt of lilies-of-the-valley. The sunburnt turf was gay, too, with other late-summer flowers: Devil's-bit Scabious, Felwort, Carline Thistle. The bugles sounded, remote and melancholy, through the long, hot afternoons; the months at Greylands seemed as remote as a bad dream; I hummed to myself the Duke of Plaza-Toro's song from *The Gondoliers*, and persuaded myself that I was happy. But Greylands, though its horrors were already becoming dim in my memory, remained in my system like an infection which I couldn't quite 'shake off'. I was aware, with a certain vague disquiet, that the moments when I felt consciously 'happy' lacked some of their old intensity; I had a sense of straining after some higher pitch of delight to which I had once been able to attain, but could achieve no longer. Perhaps, I thought, I should never feel genuinely and absolutely happy again.

We walked along the Lower Road; we went to Folkestone, to see the Miss Hodsells (they were still brooding, with a ghoulish delight, over the air-raid of 25 May); and towards the end of September, just before I went to my new school, we made, once again, the expedition to Seabrook.

It was a grey, melancholy day; the sea lapped gently against the wooden groynes and the broken-down wall. We reached the lifeboat-station, and stopped (for the doors were open) to look at the lifeboat. The man-woman with the ear-rings was in attendance: he greeted us with a friendly grin. As we lingered to speak to him, a column of soldiers approached along the coast-road, from the direction of the camp. They carried packs and kit-bags, and, as they marched, they sang: *Tipperary, Goodby-ee, A Long, Long Trail.* There must have been several battalions of them – the marching column seemed as though it would never end. We stood there till the last file had passed: watching them till they were almost out of sight. The last notes of *A Long, Long Trail* died away, mingling with the soft hissing and thudding of the waves.

'No doubt where *them's* going,' said the boatman. 'Poor blighters, they'll be in France before nightfall.'

We turned away, and walked on towards the sea-wall; skirting a clump of grey, wind-tossed tamarisks, and making for the desolate, shingle tract beyond, where, beneath the heavy sky, the last summer flowers still lingered: fleabane, the sticky sea-ragwort and the fragile, golden cups of the horned poppy.

CHAPTER SEVEN

The Triumph of the Moor

I

I decided, at last, that I should never make a successful business-man, and announced the fact to my long-suffering family. Returning home, to Blackheath, I settled down with a grim determination to write; and did actually succeed (rather to my own surprise) in getting an article accepted by the *New Statesman.* Alas, the article was a mere flash-in-the-pan; rejected manuscripts continued to flop, with a depressing monotony, upon the doormat; it didn't seem as though I should be any more successful as a writer than as a wine-merchant.

After a year or two my health broke down, and I went abroad: first to Switzerland, then to the South of France. It was while I was at Geneva, staying with a family at Chênes-Bougeries, that I received an excited letter from Eric. He had at last, it seemed, discovered his *dix-huitième* poetaster – somebody almost totally unknown and quite *sympathique.* Eric had lately abandoned schoolmastering for a copy-writer's job in an advertising agency; in the intervals of writing advertisements for toothpaste and soap-flakes (he enclosed some peculiarly excruciating examples), he was engaged in running his obscure quarry to earth at the British Museum.

'He seems quite uncharted,' Eric wrote, 'and I find all this niggling research quite sympathetic – I suppose I'm one of Nature's pedagogues, after all. William Penycuick' (such was the poetaster's name) 'seems to have divided his time between writing mild pastoral lyrics, vaguely Cowperish, and poisoning his aunts with arsenic. He had a passion for "Follies", too – I ran to earth a small Vestal temple, still called Penycuick's Folly, not far from Shaftesbury. I shall probably have to go to Sicily, where P., it seems, ended his days: nothing is known of his goings-on there, but he seems to have developed an interest in Black Magic in later life, and there are hints that the *milord inglese* was not *bien vu* at Palermo.

'But enough of my boring pedantries. Who do you think I saw the other day? None other than Bert – I never knew his surname, and still don't, but you know the one I mean. He seems a regular frequenter of Fitzrovia nowadays, and looks very fat and prosperous. His job seems very money-making – though I imagine *la belle* Moira also helps to keep the wolf from the door. Probably not only Moira, either – Bert seems to be steeped in the highest philosophy. I wonder what view she takes of his popularity in "musical" circles.

'Otherwise, London's very dull – everybody getting so serious and political, and no parties like the old days. There's apparently a new cult called Mass-Observation – everybody spies on each other's bathroom-habits, and counts the aspidistras in suburban windows. It sounds enthralling. I gather the Mass-Observatory is at Blackheath, so perhaps you'll enrol yourself when you return.

'I thought I saw Hew Dallas in Piccadilly the other day, but couldn't be sure. Incidentally, your brother (whom I saw briefly in the Carlton Bar – "Sunshine" sent her love to you, by the way) tells me that Pussy Wilkinson has become very dim and decrepit lately. I suppose he misses his precious Bert – and it seems he's not on the best of terms, nowadays, with his sister. He consoles himself, your brother said, with politics, and apparently he's turning into a kind of second Lady Houston.'

I was glad about Eric's poetaster, and wished I could discover someone of that kind myself. Switzerland depressed me; yet the thought of returning to England was even less exhilarating. I went to Cassis, where Eric afterwards joined me (he was on his way to Sicily, where he was spending his holidays in pursuit of the elusive William Penycuick). I stayed on for some weeks after his departure, then moved to the 'Welcome' at Villefranche. It was here that I received another letter from Eric, who had returned, some time before, to England, where he was busy still with his forthcoming biography. William Penycuick, it seems, had become in his latter days a kind of *dix-huitième* Aleister Crowley, and his experiments in the occult had apparently rivalled, in their horrific ingenuity, those of Gilles de Rais himself.

'But to revert,' Eric went on, 'to our contemporary muttons, what do you think? Sir Henry Griddle has finally married the hog-faced gentlewoman – in other words (believe it or not) our friend Bert has made an honest woman of *la belle* Moira. I saw it announced in *The Times*, yesterday. Can you beat it? I suspect, myself, that Moira was afraid of his slipping through her fingers, and wanted to make sure of him. Bert stands to do pretty well out of it, anyway – she must be sixty if she's a day, and I imagine she's otherwise unattached, except for Pussy. The situation strikes me as being Proustian in every possible sense of the word.'

I returned at length to England – an England where 'nobody was well', the England of the crisis-age. As Eric had said, everybody seemed to be becoming 'serious' and boring; mere old-fashioned futilitarians like ourselves were looked at rather askance; to be *chic*, to be in the movement, one had to have an axe to grind: Communism, Anglo-Catholicism, Pacifism – it didn't much matter what 'Cause' one embraced, provided it was a cause of some kind – even Mass-Observation would do, at a pinch. For light relief, there was always the latest gossip about Mrs Simpson or (in Bloomsbury) the perennial topic of X., the Communist poet, whose persevering (though painful) efforts to become heterosexual were a source of much innocent fun to his acquaintances.

II

Soon after my return, I went to stay at Folkestone; while I was there, it so happened that my brother invited Edward Hoopoe, the distinguished lawyer and writer, down for the day.

Ted Hoopoe has been described, with some justice, as the last of the English Eccentrics. Certainly, he was a fantastic and (at times) an overwhelming figure ... Physically, he was immensely stout, and his clothes seemed always several sizes too large for him; often he forgot to shave or cut his nails, and one guessed that he seldom, if ever, took a bath. His mind, however, like that of Edward Lear, was 'concrete and fastidious': his spiritual home, one felt, was in the clubs and coffee-houses of Georgian London; yet there clung about him, also, a faint but perceptible whiff of the nineties ...

'He's a sort of cross,' Eric Anquetil had remarked on a former occasion, 'between Dr Johnson and Oscar Wilde.'

My brother and I were both acquainted with him: but the ostensible reason for his visit to Folkestone was to taste some rather special clarets and old brandies. We lunched at the Burlington Hotel – all palms, plush and Edwardian comfort; the ambience, one felt, was suitable. Ted Hoopoe was in one of his most genial and expansive moods; we drank, I think, a Château Lafite 1875, following it with a vintage port and several different kinds of brandy. By the end of luncheon our guest had an impressive row of glasses still in front of him – my brother having taken particular care that none of them should remain empty. Ted Hoopoe proceeded to 'orchestrate' (as he put it) the remaining samples one against another; a sip of brandy, a sip of port, a draught of claret.

'Extraordinarily interesting,' he pronounced. 'And this cheese is really excellent ... Nobody, of course, knows how to mix a salad in this country – with the exception of myself ... You must lunch with me, both of you, at the Athenaeum, and I shall give a demonstration.'

Presently he expressed a desire to revisit his old school, Greylands House: today, he said, happened to be a special occasion – he wasn't quite sure what, but he believed it was speech-day, or prizegiving, or something of the kind ... I had not been inside Greylands since I left it in 1917; to revisit it with an ex-alumnus so distinguished (and so formidable) might prove, I felt, to be a memorable occasion.

And so, indeed, it did. We arrived at the school about half-past four; the 'special occasion' turned out to be a cricket match – Fathers *versus* Sons – and on our arrival we were escorted out to the playing-field. It was a grey, bitterly cold afternoon in June; tea was laid out on trestle-tables, but we were rather late for it, and the school servants were already piling the dirty cups and removing the stacks of uneaten rock-cakes. The tea-stained table-cloths flapped desolately in the glacial wind; a few small boys (they all looked exactly like King Min.) were stowing handfuls of buns and biscuits into their trouser-pockets; I wondered if the food was still as bad as it had been in my day.

Presently the Headmaster appeared: the very same who had made my life miserable twenty years ago. He looked somewhat taken aback, as well he might: for the three of us – my brother, myself and our guest – could hardly have appeared in a suitable condition to judge the finer points of cricket. Ted Hoopoe, indeed, presented an appearance which, even in less conventional surroundings, might have attracted notice: his tie had slipped from his collar, his hair was rumpled, and in his eyes was that far-away look of a man who has drunk at least two bottles of claret and several bumpers of brandy and vintage port. The process of 'orchestration', in fact, was beginning to have its effect.

'Delightful, quite delightful,' he was bumbling to the Headmaster. 'Yes, I should adore some tea. Nothing like tea on such occasions. So delightfully English ... No, no, please don't put yourself to the trouble – ' there was some difficulty about finding a clean cup – '*this* will serve the purpose quite excellently.'

Whereupon, before the glazed eyes of the Headmaster, the distinguished visitor seized with both hands upon a vast china slop-basin as large as a chamber-pot and, pouring into it a couple of pints of stale tea and half a pint of milk, raised the gargantuan draught to his lips.

I met the eyes of the Headmaster; they were pale and shifty, as I remembered them; but there was also, at this moment, a look in them which I did not remember – a look of such outraged bewilderment that I really feared, for a moment, that my ex-tormentor was about to burst into tears. I returned his glance as coolly as I could: it was important, I felt, to remain perfectly detached and self-possessed; but all my efforts were in vain – I began, helplessly, to giggle.

'Excellent, excellent,' said Ted Hoopoe. 'And *now* I should like to make a tour of the school.'

'Certainly, Mr Hoopoe – only too delighted,' burbled the Headmaster; and without further delay we set forth. It was a curious progress: the Headmaster trotted in front, Ted Hoopoe stalked majestically behind him, and my brother and I brought up the rear. We visited the dining-hall, which, in my childhood, had seemed so vast and desolate; now it seemed unbelievably diminished, almost poky. The 'big' school-room, too, seemed less big, but was otherwise unchanged; there was the green-baize door leading to the Headmaster's study, there was the window-ledge from which I had been dragged by King Min. . . .

'Most interesting, *most* interesting,' the visitor declared, studying the tablets on the wall inscribed, in gold paint, with the names of old boys: his own was included, but not, I noticed, mine.

Then we went to the chapel.

Perhaps Ted Hoopoe was tired; perhaps he had indigestion; or perhaps it was merely a further, delayed result of that too-elaborate 'orchestration' at the Burlington ... Whatever the cause may have been, I noticed that his manner, as we reached the chapel, had become far less genial; he smiled no longer; he pouted; he looked, I thought, like a sulky little boy.

Suddenly he began to speak: his words were obscure, he stumbled over them, one could grasp no more than the vaguest outline of what he was trying to say; but there was no mistaking the tone in which he spoke; seldom, indeed, have I heard the human voice embody so unequivocally the feeling of pure, concentrated malice.

'Ridiculous,' he mumbled, 'perfectly ridiculous. Look at those windows. How do you expect the boys to read the small print of an ordinary prayer-book by that disgustingly inadequate light? I can't think what the architect was up to – or the headmaster. It was in your predecessor's day, of course ... I'm surprised at him, I really am ... Doubtless you don't realize that the structure of the retina in a child of prepubertal age – '

'Perhaps you'd like to go and have a look at the match?' the Headmaster interrupted, in a feeble attempt to stay the onrush. But Ted Hoopoe swept him aside like an importunate fly; he was getting nicely into his stride, and it would have taken far more than a nervous usher in a Folkestone preparatory school to stop him. Period after period rolled thunderously (though indistinctly) from his lips: what was more important than the eye? How many physiological (yes, and psychological) disasters could not be traced to astigmatism in early life? Much research had been done, in recent years, upon the subject: most of it, of course, in Germany, where education was taken seriously. Naturally, one didn't expect an English schoolmaster to be interested in theories of education ... None the less, the Headmaster should, if he had the welfare of his boys at heart, yes, he really *should* consider the matter seriously. He ought at least to read the literature on the subject: there was, for instance, an interesting work on the psychology of astigmatism by Herren Fuchs and Schytte, of Bonn University – a really valuable contribution ...

At last, with considerable difficulty, we dragged him away. The Headmaster, by this time, was becoming almost hysterical; his eyes gleamed dangerously with suppressed rage ... Our farewells were said with the barest, the most perfunctory politeness. We escaped at last: my brother and myself in the last stages of a giggling fit which had threatened, for the last half hour, to disgrace us publicly and irretrievably.

'A delightful afternoon,' said Ted Hoopoe, as we made our way to the station. 'Perfectly delightful: and such a sensible headmaster. I'm sure he'll take my advice about that chapel.'

I looked back at the ugly, sprawling buildings of the school, mean and squalid-looking under the grey afternoon sky. Exhausted by suppressed laughter, I could no longer feel vindictive towards the place or its inmates; for I was aware that, vicariously and on a small scale, but none the less effectively, I had at last, after twenty years, taken my revenge.

During this same visit to Folkestone I had another odd encounter. One day, walking down the Sandgate Road, I noticed, standing in the gutter outside the Esplanade, a little man in a black shirt, selling copies of Mosley's paper *Action*. I wasn't surprised: for Folkestone had always been a home of lost (or unpopular) causes. I should have passed by without another glance, had not the hawker suddenly hailed me by name. I looked at him again – and nearly burst out laughing, for the little man in the black shirt was none other than Pussy Wilkinson.

He had changed almost out of recognition: he was nearly bald, his face (once so plump) had fallen in – he had, I discovered, had to have most of his teeth out; he looked scruffy, undistinguished and rather pathetic.

He greeted me, however, with all his old amiability. I concealed my surprise at his 'conversion', and he invited me round for a drink that evening. He had given up his house (which, he said, he could no longer afford), and taken a flat over a shop in Bouverie Road. It proved to be poky but not uncomfortable: most of his old possessions, which I remembered, had been squeezed into it. Pussy was a little shy, but I did my best to 'draw him out': what, I asked, had made him decide to join the Fascists? He looked down modestly at his plump, white hands – an old mannerism of his; the nails, I noticed, were not quite clean.

'Oh well,' he murmured, 'one feels, nowadays, that one must do *something*, you know, for one's country.'

After an interval, I ventured upon the delicate subject of his sister. Her marriage, it was evident, had shocked Pussy profoundly: he considered Moira hopelessly *déclassée*, and I gathered that he had flatly refused to attend the wedding. I suggested, rather timidly, that it might at least be a very good thing for Bert.

Pussy looked at me reprovingly, as though I had made some indecent remark.

'I have no wish,' he said, 'to discuss the fortunes or misfortunes of that – um – *tiresome* individual.'

Miss McPhee, I learnt, had become a permanency; Pussy appeared to be resigned to the fact – perhaps he regarded it as a mortification. Her cooking, he said, had never really improved – she still seemed quite incapable of making an omelette, and had, apparently, an unnatural passion for boiled mutton and caper-sauce, a dish which Pussy detested.

I never saw Pussy again. When war broke out, he retired to North Wales; in 1940 he was detained for a time (on account of his 'Fascist' activities) under the 18B regulations. He was soon released as harmless: but the experience had been too much for him. He returned to Wales, and died soon after, fortified by the comforts of the Roman Church – to which (true to his ninetyish traditions) he had undergone what amounted, almost, to a death-bed conversion.

III

The dismal, uneasy decade drew towards its end: Edward VIII abdicated, and it was as though some tribal totem had been removed, to make way for a new, imported cultus. The Archbishop anathematized the King's friends – 'they stand rebuked' – and one felt that he was rebuking all of us. The New Puritanism gained ground every day: poetry became more and more stark and minatory; novelists, if they wanted to be taken seriously, were obliged to confine themselves to topics which were considered 'socially significant' – in other words, they had to write about the poor. The currency of language seemed to have become suddenly debased: a competent slickness prevailed; books, like cars, became 'streamlined', any writer with a personal, idiosyncratic style was condemned as 'dated'. To be fashionable, one had to be 'tough': there was a vogue for books by ex-burglars and spivs, and American novels (*école de* Hemingway) flooded the market. There was a boom in travel books, too:

> For we are obsolete who like the lesser things,
> Who play in corners with looking-glasses and beads;
> It is better we should go quickly, go into Asia
> Or any other tunnel where the world recedes ...

There were plenty of tunnels to choose from: the most *chic* was the Spanish War – if one couldn't fight in it, one could at least write about it, and in either case one had the comforting feeling of being ideologically orthodox. (The more widespread conflict which followed was never, for some reason, considered really *chic*, even in its earliest stages – possibly because England was directly involved in it; Auden – soon to acquire American citizenship – had proved a far better recruiting-sergeant, in certain circles, than Chamberlain.)

Some went to Asia (there was another war there), some to Iceland; a few lingered, disconsolate, at Trou-sur-mer. Myself, having failed to embrace a 'Cause', stayed at home and read their books; or went to the ballet or to French films at the Academy – but haunted, always, by a curious uneasiness, a feeling that the world I knew was in some way chronically corrupted, the 'good things' turning to 'poison and pus':

> The excess sugar of a diabetic culture
> Rotting the nerve of life and literature ...

Massine in *Petrouchka*: the ballet seemed to me (as it must have seemed to so many at that time) a projection of my own predicament and that of most of my friends. Petrouchka was doomed, the Moor always won in the end: the tough-guy and the twister, King Min. and the Average Bloke – these were the ones who came off best.

Coming out of the theatre, I went into a bar in the Strand to have a beer and a sandwich. Suddenly I was hailed by a red-faced beery person in the uniform of a RAF officer. I thought at first that he must have mistaken me for somebody else; then I looked again, and saw, to my utter astonishment, that it was Bert – Pussy Wilkinson's ex-*protégé* who had, incredibly, married Moira Wemyss.

'Why, fancy seeing you, Jocelyn,' he said. 'Have a drink ... Gosh, this is absolutely wizard. Where are you living nowadays? You left Folkestone, didn't you? Two double whiskies, miss ... Well, this beats the band. Moira was saying only the other day she wondered what had happened to you.'

Recovering from my first surprise, I managed, at last, to ask him what he was doing in Air Force uniform.

'Well, you see, Jocelyn, it's like this. The Company I was working for was getting sort of stuffy – they're a good enough firm, but I didn't see eye to eye with them over certain things, if you get my meaning ... Well, with all this war-talk, it looked like I'd have more chance in the RAF, so I talked it over with Moira, and she was all for it – very patriotic, Moira is, and she was ever so thrilled the first time I put on the uniform. I've been damned lucky, too – fell for a wizard job, right up my street. I can't tell you what it is – it's all very hush-hush – but you can take my word for it, if old Hitler does have a go at us, we'll be ready for him.'

We had another drink. Bert had grown into a burly, thick-set man whom, if he hadn't been in uniform, one might have taken for a heavy-weight boxer. His face, always inclined to plumpness, had taken on an almost middle-aged rotundity; the nape of his neck bulged over his tight collar, and he wore a very spruce little toothbrush moustache. It wasn't surprising I hadn't recognized him – even his accent had changed beyond belief; it was what might be called (for want of a better name) technocratic – the accent of the future: a hybrid affair in which the native intonation – Cockney, in this case – is overlaid with a quasi-'Oxford' blah-blah tempered by an American twang.

He was very full of himself, and inclined to be rather patronizing. He was, he said, stationed down at Uxbridge, and Moira had taken a nice little place down there, so as to be near him. I must go down one night and take pot-luck: Moira would be ever so pleased. Later on, they hoped to have a flat in Town as well: perhaps sometime we could all meet and do a show together. Moira, said Bert, was ever so fond of a nice play.

'Well, Jocelyn, I'll have to love you and leave you. It's been wizard seeing you again. How's old Eric? You ought to bring him along one night ... Well, so long – I've got to meet a bloke at the Standard, up Piccadilly way. Don't forget to phone Moira.'

I left him, and walked along towards Charing Cross, to catch my train home. The evening papers were full of war-talk; there seemed a curious lack of gaiety about the homing crowds. The station, when I reached it, was full of soldiers: evidently some large-scale troop-movement was in progress. The meeting with Bert had made me vaguely depressed: people like him, I thought, were the ones who mattered nowadays; Bert and his kind were almost a historical necessity. The fortunes of all of us lay in their hands: tough-guys, clever with gadgets, with nice little places near Uxbridge – the technocracy of the future.

The Moor always won.

I had half-intended, for sentiment's sake, to accept Bert's invitation, and ring up Moira at Uxbridge. But other, more important matters supervened, and I postponed my visit indefinitely. Then, one day, I came across a paragraph in the *Daily Express:* 'Fortune for Flying-Officer', it was headed. I should scarcely have bothered to read it, had my attention not been caught by the adjoining photograph, which showed a young man in Air Force uniform. Incredulously, I recognized the face of Bert; I read the caption printed below – Flying-Officer Albert Edward Hunwick. Surely, I thought, there must be some mistake; and then remembered, out of the dim past, that this had in fact been Bert's name. I read the paragraph, and learnt that Moira had died suddenly, of heart-failure, a few days before, leaving her entire fortune to her young husband. Written in the jaunty, telegraphic style of the *Express,* the story had, for me, a curious unreality: it was as though I were reading the last chapter of a novel which I had begun years ago and never finished. But there, after all, were the facts: poor, silly, elegant Moira was dead – I should never, now, be able to ring her up at her 'little place' near Uxbridge; and Bert – Flying-Officer A. E. Hunwick, ex-chauffeur-gardener and *protégé* of Pussy Wilkinson – had inherited a fortune which, even when death-duties had been deducted, would amount (said the *Express*) to not much less than five thousand a year.

IV

I went, once again, to Folkestone, and Eric came down to spend a Saturday-to-Monday with me. His 'Life' of William Penycuick was finished, and due for publication in the spring. Sitting in my rooms, we corrected the proofs together: the sight of the title-page, with Eric's name on it, made me extremely envious, though I didn't say so. The height of my ambition was still, I suppose, to publish a 'book' – any sort of book, provided I could hold it in my hand and look at the title-page and think: '*I* wrote this.' It was an ambition whose fulfilment seemed, nowadays, further off than ever. I had started a novel a year or two before, and kept recasting and rewriting it perpetually: somehow it wouldn't come right. Once, how many years ago, I had envisaged a vast, Proustian *roman fleuve*; but I realized, now, how bogus that particular am-bition had been. Nowadays I wrote (or tried to write) largely from habit or a sense of duty: I still thought of myself as a 'writer', and I felt impelled to produce some kind of 'book', if only to settle my debts with the past. But I seemed to have lost, nowadays, the one faculty which, for me, was essential: the capacity to *enjoy* the process of writing. My health was still poor; and my own malaise seemed to extend itself to the world around me. The function of the writer seemed to have become invalid: successful poets and novelists of my own generation were already discredited, and nobody seemed to be taking their places. Publishers, said Eric, were taking no risks (it was Munich year); he had been lucky to get anyone to accept William Penycuick: most of them would look at nothing but thrillers.

Folkestone seemed a curiously dead town that autumn: the threat of war had already touched it, one saw more and more men in uniform. Most of the people I had once known were dead or departed. The weather was warm, with a perpetual ceiling of grey, immobile cloud. One morning Eric and I walked along the coast-road to Seabrook: nothing had changed, yet the whole landscape seemed dead with a more-than-wintry deadness. The sea lapped gently on the brown shingle; from the Camp, as always, came the far crying of bugles. When we reached the Goose Cathedral, a surprise awaited us: the old boathouse had been transformed into a tea-shop. A painted board, spanning the steep roof, bore the legend: 'The Boathouse Café'. Over the Gothic door hung a sign: TEAS WITH HOVIS. The garden had been tidied up, and the fencing repaired; otherwise, the place seemed unchanged.

There it stood: our old symbol of 'bogosity', haunted still by all the legends we had woven about it. I felt more than ever, nowadays, that its air of pretentious whimsy was a kind of reproach: my own bogosity could still make me blush; and I hadn't, now, even the courage of my own *bovarysmes*.

'What a come-down,' said Eric. 'But perhaps it's really rather suitable, after all ... I'm surprised they didn't call it Ye Olde Gothicke Tea-rooms.'

We stood for a few minutes by the sea-wall, opposite the boat-house: half-consciously from force of habit, my eyes travelled round the fenced enclosure, searching for some familiar feature which I associated with it, but which seemed to have disappeared. Suddenly I remembered what it was.

'They don't,' I remarked, 'keep geese any more.'

'Nor they do – I thought something was lacking. I expect,' said Eric, 'Mrs Vindables took them with her when they moved to Sicily.'

'Did they move to Sicily?'

'Yes, they settled at Cefàlu, in the villa of a Lesbian *professoressa* from Girton. The archdeacon was a descendant of William Penycuick, of course, so it was all eminently suitable.'

We continued to discuss the fortunes of the Vindables family as we walked down the road into Seabrook. At the corner by the Fountain Hotel, a column of soldiers, coming from the Hythe direction, was left-wheeling up Horn Street: we watched them march up the lane, under the disused railway bridge, towards the remote, mysterious land beyond Pericar Woods. Then we turned into the Fountain for a drink.

'Here's mud in your eye, old boy,' said Eric, raising his glass and assuming his best 'hearty' manner. 'I suppose,' he added meditatively, 'we'll all *really* be talking like that in another year or two. War's a great leveller.'

Eric's words, for some reason, made me think of Bert, and I mentioned my last meeting with him.

'I wonder if he'll stay in the Air Force now he's so rich,' I said.

'He'll probably have to,' said Eric. 'And anyway, knowing Bert, he'll probably run through his fortune in six months or so. I wish *I* could find a rich widow.'

We left the pub, and started to walk back towards Sandgate. It was high-tide, and the waves were thudding against the sea-wall below the boathouse. As we passed it, a sudden gust of wind flung the cold, salt spray in our faces, and, almost simultaneously, a heavy rain began to fall. We waited on the pavement for the Folkestone bus: the Goose Cathedral, beneath the downpour, looked more than ever malign and sinister.

'We ought to go and have tea there, one day,' said Eric. 'I'd rather like to see the Casa Vindables from the inside.'

We promised ourselves that we would duly take tea at the 'Boathouse Café' before Eric left; but for one reason or another we never did, and the mysterious interior of the Goose Cathedral remained, after all, unexplored.

CHAPTER EIGHT

Roll on Christmas

I

The parade at 8.30 was said to be cushy; there was an inspection, but no one bothered much, so long as your boots were clean and your hair short. This morning, however, the RSM had other ideas; instead of dismissing us after the inspection, he gave us 'Right turn – by the left, quick march'; we began to march down Hospital Hill.

'He don't often do this,' said the man next to me. 'Must have been on the piss last night.'

'*Playing at soldiers,*' said the man on my other side, with infinite contempt (I was in the centre of the file).

We continued to converse in undertones, through immobile lips; from time to time the RSM rapped out a word of command, but usually on the wrong foot: he had no idea of drill, people said, owing to being a clerk by trade.

'Working in the store, ain't you?' said my left-hand neighbour. 'Cor, some blokes has all the luck.'

I didn't think I was particularly lucky, and said so.

'They'll be making you up, I daresay,' he added, with a side-glance at my medal-ribbons.

The morning was grey, with a chilly freshness in the air: we marched down the hill, and struck across the road by the Goose Cathedral. Seen by daylight, it seemed almost unchanged by the War; it was still, apparently, a café: the same signboard ('Teas with Hovis') hung over the entrance. The garden was rather less tidy than it had been ten years ago; the whole place looked a little grubbier; but there was no substantial alteration. The chapel-by-the-sea preserved all its old air of rather sinister incongruity; but it seemed now a monument, merely, to a past life in which I had almost ceased to believe.

We marched along the new motor-road, above the sea-wall: the wall itself had been rebuilt again. But the patch of waste ground on the landward side had suffered a sea-change; either from natural causes, or (more probably) owing to anti-invasion measures, the rich maritime flora which had once adorned it seemed to be nearly extinct. Even the horned poppies had vanished: the single tract had become a waste land indeed. I remembered, suddenly, a walk I had taken recently over the hills behind Folkestone – those hills whose very shapes had changed since the war. There, on the areas of naked chalk which had been tank-traps and gun-sites, a new flora had established itself: sea-cabbage, viper's bugloss and horned poppy. A puzzle for botanists, this sudden invasion of the hills by plants from the sea-shore had struck me as strangely disquieting; to find the Horned Poppy on Caesar's Camp seemed as improbable as finding the Spider Orchid on the beach at Seabrook. It was as though the fixed categories of my childhood were becoming, in some way, unstable and invalid; the 'sea-side' world had encroached upon the world of the Hills – itself a frontier-land, part 'sea-side' and part 'country'. I could hardly have felt more disturbed if the sea itself had overrun the land, flooding the levels behind Cheriton, creeping past Etchinghill and Postling, and flowing at last, a devastating tidal river, up the Elham Valley.

But the waves lapped tamely enough, this morning, beneath the new sea-wall. We marched as far as the outskirts of Hythe, then turned and marched back: past the Goose Cathedral, up Hospital Hill, towards the Camp.

In the store, we scrounged some tea and made ourselves comfortable.

'Play by Shakespeare – seven letters,' said Corporal Bradnum. 'Must be *Hamlet* – that one that was on at the Odeon. No, that's wrong: Hamlet's only got six letters. It's got two L's in it, too. What's another play by Shakespeare?'

'Try *Othello*,' I suggested.

'That might do . . . How d'you spell it?'

Soon it was time for Naafi break. We sat around for half-an-hour outside the cookhouse, drinking tea. I could feel myself slipping into the old, familiar rhythm of the soldier's day: the long tracts of time arranging themselves round certain fixed points, thought and feeling plotted like a graph. There was the zero-hour of reveillé: the intolerable trauma of rebirth to a new day; then the nude, squalid turmoil of the wash-house – the steel-cold splashing of water, the pissy reek of maleness, the farts and curses exploding obscenely in the thin, pure air of morning. Then the first small peak of happiness – breakfast; the graph rising, but dropping sharply again for the 8.30 parade. Then a level tract of boredom, sloping up abruptly towards the ten o'clock Naafi break; then more boredom, till dinner-time; then the heavy post-prandial oppression, lifting gradually, during the afternoon, as tea-time approached. Then tea itself: a peak-period of happiness, the day's duties finished; a wash (or a bath, if the water was hot); relaxing, half-dressed, on one's bed, with a whole evening of freedom ahead ... Warm with tea, relaxed and contented at the day's end, I could think calmly of reveillé and the morning's bullshit; the day arranged itself into a pattern, a framework within which happiness could spring into sudden, unexpected bloom, like a flower from the bare rock: a tentative, frail growth, resistant to cultivation, requiring a coarse soil and a hard climate.

II

That evening, I took a bus into Folkestone, and visited a friend in the town. I felt fitter, happier than for a long time: the flower which had lain dormant in the lush climate of Civvy Street had blossomed once more – springing from this thin, dry soil, as the horned poppy had sprung, incongruously, from the naked chalk of Caesar's Camp.

I had a few drinks, and went back early. The barrack-room was nearly empty: I turned the wireless low, and settled down to correct the proofs of my new book. The task, which would once have given me a certain pleasure, now seemed tedious and unimportant: I soon gave it up, and took out my shoe-cleaning materials. A highly-polished toe-cap or a highly-polished style: was there so much to choose between them?

'You're incurably literary,' Eric Anquetil had once said, sitting on the beach, years ago, below the Goose Cathedral. But was I? It was true, I liked writing; but I tended, nowadays, to be rather bored by literature. I didn't, certainly, feel any regret for the companionship of 'intellectuals'. Among literary people I found myself at a disadvantage: their conversation scared me, consisting, as it too often did, of a perpetual scoring of debating points. Recently, too, I had been made aware of the embarrassing gaps in my education: I had never read *War and Peace*, nor Wordsworth's *Prelude* – nor, indeed, had I any serious intention of ever doing so. I had hardly so much as heard of Lermontov; I found both Kafka and (though I scarcely dared admit it) Henry James almost entirely unreadable. As for my own writing, I enjoyed it well enough, but I was unable to take it with a proper seriousness. To spend hours, like Flaubert, polishing a phrase, was for me an impossibility; I would rather polish a pair of boots.

The prospect of becoming a professional *littérateur* depressed me; I preferred to remain an amateur. I knew the booksy racket too well: a *succès d'estime* with a first novel; reviewing for the *Statesman* or the *Times Lit. Supp.*, a talk or two on the Third Programme. Then another book: not so successful. ('I confess to being disappointed with Mr X's new novel . . .'); more reviewing, more talks; an essay or two on some obscure minor writer for the *Cornhill;* and then the gradual decline, through anthologies, 'introductions' and light middles, to a weekly *causerie* in *John O'London* or a staff-job in the BBC . . . No, no, I thought: I would as soon be helping Corporal Bradnum with his crossword; or sorting out eleven-fifty-sevens and one-oh-eights; or marching, in the chilly autumn mornings, along the top of the sea-wall, past the Goose Cathedral and the police-station, to the waste land where once the yellow poppy had grown, and might one day, perhaps, bloom again.

Next morning I put in a thirty-six-hour pass for the week-end. The sergeant-major gave me a dirty look.

'I'll put it in for you,' he said, 'but I don't think for a moment the CO'll sign it. We've got to detail fifty per cent of the unit for Garrison Church-parade on Sunday. They say Monty's coming.'

The next day was Saturday. After the 8.30 parade the RSM told me to stand fast.

'You'll go on coal-fatigues this morning,' he told me. 'Draw a suit of denims from the store, and report to Corporal Westrup.'

I interpreted this to mean that the CO either had signed or in all probability would sign my pass; it was the RSM's way of getting his own back.

Had he but known it, I was rather pleased at being put on coal-fatigues: the store-job was tedious, and I needed some exercise. I drew my denims, and reported to Corporal Westrup: our job was to fill a truck with coal from the coal-store, and take it round to the various offices, barrack-rooms, married quarters, etc. The morning was sunny: we worked in our shirt-sleeves, shovelling the coal leisurely on to the truck; there wasn't any hurry – we had the whole morning for the job.

It was the sort of job I liked in the Army; but being a first-class tradesman (subject to re-trade-testing) and – worse still – an 'educated bloke', I should invariably be condemned (when not working at my own trade), to the very jobs I detested, such as clerking and store-keeping. Dirty and sweating in the still-warm October sun, I wished I hadn't a 'trade' or a bourgeois accent.

When the truck was full, we made a trip round the company lines, filling the scuttles in the offices and barrack-rooms. Then we started on the married quarters: prim, red houses, most of them, built on the cliff-side below the barrack-buildings. The sea gleamed palely in the thin, golden light; birds sang among the tamarisks; out in the misty Channel a foghorn boomed. I had a curious feeling that, for the first time since childhood, I really 'belonged' to this landscape; as a civilian, I had been a mere spectator, a tripper, bearing no genuine relation to it. As a soldier I was an integral part of this land: I was possessed by it, and at the same time possessed it.

'Roll on Christmas,' said the Cockney from my barrack-room (his name was Ron Eley) who was cheerfully shovelling coal at my side; tousled, untidy, with his shirt gaping open to his waist, he worked with a kind of despairing violence. He looked, as usual, far dirtier than anybody else; he also seemed happier – though he was feeling sore, this morning, about having been checked at the Wednesday morning inspection.

'Seven f—g days CB,' he exclaimed. 'It ain't right – there weren't no f—g blanco in the store, not when I went to get it. Never come in till five o'clock – and that bastard bleeding well

knew it.' He spat, expressively, over the side of the truck. 'Roll on
my next leaf,' he added. 'And after that I've only got two months
more in the f—g Army.'

At twelve-thirty I went to the RSM's office to ask for my pass.
The clerk handed it to me without comment: it had been duly
signed by the Company Officer.

I went to dinner; then took the bus up the Elham Valley to my
home. The fine weather persisted: a thin, warm sunshine fired the
woodlands to a dying blaze of crimson and gold; the hedges were
hung with a multitude of spindleberries – lurid purple bursting
into fiery orange. In the space of three days, the land appeared to
have undergone a subtle alteration; the change seemed to me
more than merely seasonal: the familiar hills and fields had taken
on a new freshness, colours and contours seemed suddenly more
vivid and emphatic; it was as though I were seeing the country,
today, through the eyes of a child. Perhaps, I thought, the
difference lay not in the land but in myself.

At home I looked through the *New Statesman*: the world with
which it dealt seemed oddly remote. News from nowhere ...
Recent novels by Waugh and Huxley: a batch of new poets; a
book on Kafka. Skimming the reviews, I felt rather as I used to
feel in my childhood, listening to the diffuse, interminable conversation of the grown-ups: they spoke always of a world to which
I didn't belong, and to whose affairs they seemed to attach an
exaggerated importance.

A batch of letters awaited me, too: there was one from Eric
Anquetil.

'I hope' (he wrote) 'that your reswaddification proceeds
smoothly. Everybody, of course, says: "I suppose Jocelyn is doing
a little T. E. Shaw" – just as one would have expected. How
obvious people are. Nigel said he'd always suspected you of being
an inverted snob, to which I retorted that I preferred the inverted
to the upright variety – such as himself.

'Did I tell you I'm giving a talk on the Third next Friday? It's a
re-hash of that quasi-erudite blather I wrote for the *Outlook* – do
you remember? I'm entitling it "The Breede of Barnakles". How
we return to our vomit – "taller today, we remember similar even-

ings". The oddest part is, I'm being produced by – who do you think? None other than Hew Dallas, my dear – who's "bought himself out" of the army (sounds vaguely Thomas Hardy), and is now a Talks Producer. Apparently he quite enjoys it, though he says it's apt to be rather too convivial. We had a mild giggle about old times, and agreed that the situation was *echt* Proustian.

'Hope the book is selling well. I found "Penycuick" the other day in a bookshop, "remaindered" at five-bob. Depressing, rather.

'Oh, and another ghost – I was almost forgetting. The other day, at a rather dim party, I was hailed by a fat, bald, middle-aged person with a sub-Cockney accent. I had no clue at all, until he announced himself. You'd never guess who it was – none other than Bert, the boy-friend of that pea-green old fascist at Folkestone. We talked amicably but dimly of the past – I gathered there wasn't much left of Moira's fortune. However, he looked excessively prosperous, and in fact asked me to dinner at Claridge's (of all places – I suppose he still thinks I'm a "gentleman", and hoped to impress me). I couldn't go, anyway. Apparently he has some quite high-up and important job in Radar research and seems to be longing for the next war. He asked after you – when I told him you were in the Army, he assumed that you were at least a Lieut-Col., and thought I was joking when I told him you were a private . . .'

Eric's letter, like the *New Statesman*, seemed to come from some remote, alien universe. I felt again, as I had felt more than once lately, that I had picked up some novel of an earlier epoch, which had once seemed 'true-to-life', but had now become 'dated' and unconvincing. Bert, for instance – was it credible that the prosperous middle-aged man whom Eric described was really the same person as the young soldier 'adopted' by Pussy Wilkinson? Even Eric himself seemed now (though I had in fact met him quite recently) no more than a character in the same diffuse, improbable chronicle. Yet Eric did, indubitably, exist – a successful *littérateur*, and Assistant Editor of a highbrow weekly. There, in my bookshelf, was his *Life* of William Penycuick – a fat volume bulging with footnotes and appendices: a real 'book' such as I myself should have liked to write. My own books never seemed to me quite 'real' – partly, perhaps, because they had appeared since the War, and were therefore produced in conformity with 'economy' standards; whereas Eric's *Life* was printed on fine paper and lavishly illustrated.

Not only the *New Statesman* and Eric's letters but the very ambience of my home seemed infected with the sense of unreality; I passed the week-end in a daze of sleep and over-feeding, and returned to Shorncliffe on Sunday evening. I arrived about nine o'clock, to find that Ron Eley, thinking I might come in after lights-out, had made my bed down for me.

'That's all right, tosh,' he said, when I thanked him. 'You'd have done the same for me.'

I was rather touched; and wondered, with a disquieting conviction of my own selfishness, whether I should, in fact, have remembered to 'do the same' for him. An act of kindness can, on occasion, be more disturbing than an act of cruelty; perhaps because (and especially nowadays) one is less prepared for it.

III

I continued to work in the store; most days there was little or nothing to do; now and again, however, there would be a bunch of postings or a new intake, and we had a pile of kits to check. Andy played football nearly every afternoon; Corporal Bradnum and I would settle down with a jug of tea and a pile of illustrated papers and enjoy ourselves. I was slipping comfortably into the routine: rejoining the Army had proved an easier process than I had expected. It seemed to me as good a life as any other.

The frieze of red, animal faces in the wash-house was separating out into individuals: I knew their names and their peculiarities, greeted them at meal-times and at the Naafi break. There were one or two regulars among them who, like myself, had got browned-off with Civvy Street and signed on again. We swapped war-memories: Africa and Italy, wogs and Eye-ties, the bints of Sister Street, booze-ups in Cairo or Syracuse.

On Friday evening I stayed in to listen to Eric's talk on the Third Programme. The barrack-room was nearly empty, so nobody objected. Eric's voice sounded, like so many of one's friends' voices on the air, unfamiliar: dry, formal, rather donnish, with a slight drawl.

'I s'pose that's the Oxford accent,' said Ron Eley, who was stopping in too that night. 'I got a cousin lives at Oxford, but f— me, he don't talk like that. Cor, I'd 'ave his f—g ring, if he did.'

I remembered some of Eric's erudite cracks from the article in the *Outlook*: his talk was tactfully embellished with quotations from Baptista Porta, Gerarde, Butler's *Hudibras* and Drayton's *Polyolbion*. I envied his neat marshalling of facts, his polished professorial phrases; Eric could still, as always, make me feel rather bogus (I remembered his *juvenilia* at Oxford, so pointed and competent by comparison with my own woolly meanderings). No, decidedly I was not born to be a Literary Gent.

'But the Breede of Barnakles,' remarked Eric, concluding his talk on a dying fall, 'is alas! extinct.'

I burst out laughing: I had suddenly remembered the geese at the lifeboat-station in those summers before the war. The breed was indeed extinct: I wondered if Eric would even remember the Goose Cathedral.

Ron Eley, high-polishing his boots at my side, looked at me in astonishment.

'What yer laughin' at, for Christ's sake?' he exclaimed. 'I can't see nothink funny – sounded like a lot of balls, to me.'

I switched over to the Home Service for the news: it was all about the rounding up of spivs and drones – categories which, one felt, included almost everybody not engaged in 'heavy industry'.

But I, at least, was safe.

Another week passed; I heard nothing more about my tradetest at Woolwich. The Army moves slowly in such matters; for my part, I was not in any particular hurry.

One night I went to have a drink in a pub in Sandgate. The bar was fairly empty: a woman sat alone in a corner. When I had bought my drink, I glanced across at her, curiously. She returned my glance: plainly she recognized me, yet was unwilling to believe the evidence of her own eyes. (I wasn't surprised at this: it had happened several times since I had gone back into uniform.)

I looked again: and suddenly recognition flashed upon me. It was our old landlady at 'Glencoe', Miss Bugle.

'Good Lord, fancy seeing you,' I exclaimed. 'It *is* Miss Bugle, isn't it?'

'Well, it is and it isn't,' she coyly replied. 'You see, I'm married now. Boatwright's the name.'

'*Married?*' I said, showing my surprise rather rudely; Miss Bugle, I thought, must have been well over fifty in the days when I used to live at 'Glencoe', and that was over fifteen years ago.

'And whatever *are* you doing in that uniform?' she asked. Her surprise was perhaps no less than my own; I explained as well as I could, but she didn't seem altogether satisfied.

'Well, you could have knocked me down with a feather, when I saw who it was,' she said.

I offered her a drink – she was drinking Guinness (which she called 'Guin*ness*'); while I bought it, I took another look at her. Never had I seen anybody so changed: it was little wonder that I hadn't recognized her at first. Gone was the drab, mousy little woman with the straight hair and steel-rimmed spectacles whom I remembered; in her place, I saw a well-turned-out matron with permanently-waved hair beneath a smart hat. Her face was obviously (though not blatantly) made up; her nails were reddened; even her steel-rimmed glasses had been exchanged for a smart pair of horn-rims.

We settled down to gossip like old friends; I told her my news (such as it was), and she told me hers. Mr Boatwright had been the commandant of a first-aid post where she had worked early in the war: he was a widower, and comfortably off. They had married in 1941. Obviously the war, for Miss Bugle, had been one long glorious party: she had thoroughly enjoyed it, and was still happy in the aftermath. Before the war, she had accepted disaster as her birthright, and gloried in it; her sole pleasure had been in prophesying worse misfortunes to come. The war had succeeded in satisfying even her appetite for horrors: if I had let her, she would have continued, till closing time, to give me lurid details of the air-raid casualties with which she had helped to deal. I managed, however, to deflect her from this topic.

'Do you remember my friend Eric Anquetil?' I asked.

'Why, as if I'd forget Mr Ankytil! He was talking on the wireless only the other night.'

'Oh *you* heard it, did you? That's what made me think of him.'

'He's ever such a good speaker, isn't he? And such an interesting talk – all about geese. My old granddad was a great one for keeping geese – we had one every Christmas, regular as clockwork. Lovely birds they was, too.'

We drank another Guinness.

'Now mind you remember me to Mr Ankytil,' Mrs Boatwright reminded me, as I left her. 'I always thought of him as a friend more than a lodger, if you see what I mean – though he was always my Ideel of the Perfect Gentleman.'

Soon after my meeting with Mrs Boatwright, I was sent, at last, to Woolwich, for my trade-test. It wasn't very alarming: I was given a *viva voce* by two MOs and found I remembered the stuff fairly well.

A very nice major named Boyle gave me a 'practical': I had to set up a microscope for dark-ground examination, and read a slide for *Treponema pallidum*. I couldn't find the spirochæte; but the Major only grinned.

'I expect it's because you're not used to the mike,' he said. 'It's not a very good one, anyway.'

A week or so later the result of my trade-test came through from Records: I had passed it, and was therefore eligible for a higher rate of pay.

'You won't be staying *here* long,' said Corporal Bradnum.

The RSM said the same:

'We'll be posting you to Barming, I daresay,' he said.

I put in for a posting to Woolwich: if I was stationed there, I should be able to get a sleeping-out pass and live at my mother's house at Blackheath. But I was in no hurry to leave Shorncliffe; the unit was cushy, I could get home most week-ends, and Corporal Bradnum and Andy were very nice to work with.

I was, in fact, 'settling down' to the Army; it seemed to me as good a life as any other nowadays, and I didn't in the least regret the loss of my 'liberty'. For a born outcast like myself, unattached and socially irresponsible, the Army had, after all, a number of advantages: one was relieved of responsibility and of the burden of *Angst*, one's capacity for worry was canalized, expended in the ritual performance of trivial acts: tomorrow's barrack-room inspection loomed larger than the threat of war. It was freedom of a

kind: perhaps, in the long run, the only kind worth having. At the
same time, the Army could give one a comfortable (if delusive)
sense of 'belonging' to the social order. One accepted the military
Weltanschauung rather as one accepts a system of theology: some
of its tenets seemed laughable, but it was easier, on the whole, to
swallow such gnats along with the camel. One even found oneself,
after a time, developing a certain fondness for the gnats ... *Credo
quia absurdum* – and why, after all, not?

IV

The weeks passed: I still wasn't posted. The weather had turned
colder: there were fires in the barrack-rooms. I finished correcting
my proofs and sent them off to the publisher. The unit continued
cushy: occasionally, on the 8.30 parade, the RSM would take it
into his head to have a little squad-drill; or we marched down
Hospital Hill to Seabrook, and along the coast-road past the Goose
Cathedral.

One day, after dinner, I was lying on my bed, looking at the
strip-cartoons in the *Daily Mirror*. It was only twenty-past one: I
wasn't due back in the store till two o'clock. The wireless was
tuned into the Light Programme: a sextette was playing MacDow-
ell's *To a Wild Rose*. Ron Eley, allergic to the BBC's ideas about
popular culture, was singing happily to himself in a nasal, Cockney
whine:

> *When* this *blink*ing war is *o*-ver,
> *Oh* how *hap*py I shall *be*!
> *When* I get my civvy *clothes* on,
> *No* more soldiering for me. . . .'

Someone else took up the dreary, Sankey-and-Moodyish tune:

> '*No* more church-parades on Sun*day*,
> *No* more asking for a pass;
> *You* can tell the Sergeant-*ma*jor
> To *shove* his passes up his arse.'

Suddenly the barrack-room door flew open; the company-
runner appeared, breathless and distraught.

'Private Brooke!' he shouted.

I leapt up; my posting must have come through at last. I couldn't help feeling rather sorry: there were worse places, I thought, than Shorncliffe.

'That's me,' I said.

''Phone call for you – company office,' the messenger gasped, white-faced and trembling from the effort of running up the slope from the orderly-room on top of his dinner.

''Phone call?' I queried, bewildered. One didn't get telephone-calls in the army; that was one of its many advantages. 'Are you sure it's for me?' I added, rather stupidly.

'That's right – Private Brooke. Sounded sort of urgent: they're hanging on, so you'd better double down quick.'

My heart sank: it could mean only one thing – something had happened at home; someone was seriously ill, or had had an accident. One wasn't rung up, in the Army, for anything less.

I doubled down to the company-office, my heart beating painfully. By the time I got there, I could hardly speak.

'Know who it is?' I asked the clerk. He was the same who had been on duty the day I arrived; he was looking at me now, as he had looked then, with an almost superstitious awe.

'I couldn't catch the name,' he said, 'but it was Squadron-leader Somebody.'

'*Squadron-leader?*' I gasped. 'But I don't know any Squadron-leaders.'

'Well, he seemed to know *you*,' the clerk retorted; adding ironically: 'Not thinking of transferring to the RAF, are you?'

'Hullo,' I said into the receiver.

A bluff voice replied:

'Is that Jocelyn?'

'Yes,' I said, breathlessly. 'This is Jocelyn Brooke speaking – Private Brooke, that's to say. Who's that?'

'Squadron-leader Hunwick here – you haven't forgotten me, have you?'

'Squadron-leader *what*?' I queried, still hopelessly at sea.

'See here, Jocelyn, this is Bert Hunwick – you must remember me, surely?'

The name meant nothing to me: plainly there was some mistake. I was still convinced that a telephone-call must mean disaster of some kind at home; but in such cases, I told myself, one was hardly likely to be rung up by totally unknown Squadron-leaders called Bert Hunwick.

The bluff voice was speaking again:

'I heard you were at Shorncliffe – old Eric told me. I thought I'd look you up – I had to come down to Hawkinge on a job.'

The truth flashed upon me at last.

'D'you mean you're *Bert*?' I said, stupidly.

'That's right. I was wondering if you could get out and have some tea – I've got to get back to Town later on, otherwise I'd say have a drink.'

'I suppose I could get out about five,' I muttered, rather help-lessly. My brain was so benumbed that I could think of no excuse for refusing; I was confused, moreover, by the sudden realization that the man at the other end, whatever his origins, was a Senior Officer, who probably expected to be called 'Sir'. It was a problem in etiquette which was, I thought, probably unprecedented.

'OK, then,' the voice replied. 'Where'll I see you?'

I remembered, suddenly, that I had promised to 'stand-in' for somebody on fire-picquet from six o'clock onwards.

'I'll have to be in by six,' I said, still uncertain about how Bert ought to be addressed.

'Tell you what,' came the bluff, slightly Cockney voice, 'there's a café-sort-of-place just down below where you are – they call it the Boathouse Café, or something.'

In my confused state, the name rang no bell at all.

'Boathouse?' I queried – then realized, suddenly, what he meant. 'Oh, you mean the Goose Cathedral.'

'That's right – where we used to bathe from.'

'All right,' I said. 'I'll meet you there at five o'clock' – and rang off. My hand shook as I replaced the receiver; I had envisaged at least a death in the family, and my nerves had behaved accord-ingly; to be rung up by an ex-valet with the present rank of Squad-ron-leader was, if less distressing, not exactly calculated to soothe my agitation.

The clerk stared at me owlishly, as well he might: it was not customary for privates to be rung up by senior officers (even Air Force ones) and asked out to tea. Meeting his glance, I felt myself beginning to blush: plainly I had exceeded, this time, even the licence allowed to sacred lunatics.

'Pal of yours, eh?' said the clerk, in the sort of nervously ironic tone in which one might address somebody who had just been rung up by Lord Montgomery or Winston Churchill.

'Just a bloke I used to know,' I replied.

V

Just a bloke I used to know ... The words were, I supposed, strictly true: in some remote, unreal past, I really had known Squadron-leader Hunwick; moreover, Bert was indubitably a Bloke – the word described him with perfect accuracy. Yet the case seemed one of those in which more than merely factual truth is involved: Bert, though a Bloke, was also something more; and the fact that I had 'known' him had acquired a kind of symbolic significance.

I passed the rest of the afternoon in a curious, almost hallucinatory state; Bert's voice, heard over the telephone, haunted me disquietingly, like a voice from some other world, vivid yet unreal: it was as though one had been rung up by a character from Tolstoy or Proust.

At a quarter to five, I set off to keep my strange appointment. It was a grey, chilly evening, threatening rain; by the time I reached the bottom of Hospital Hill, it was quite dark. Dimly-lighted, the Goose Cathedral loomed through the blackness; I crossed the road, and approached the back entrance, facing towards the camp. A small conservatory or 'winter garden', like some salvaged fragment of the Crystal Palace, had been built on to this side: I entered it, and looked round unhopefully (I was slightly early) for any sign of an Air Force uniform. None was in sight: the glass annexe was occupied only by a couple of civilians seated at separate tables – a middle-aged man and a young woman; the man was apparently still waiting for his tea, but the woman, I noticed, was eating hot buttered toast with an extreme rapidity, as though she had a train to catch.

I passed on, into the building itself; just as I crossed the threshold, I heard a quick step behind me, my arm was seized, and turning round, I found myself looking into the face of the man who had been sitting by himself outside.

'Hullo, Jocelyn, old boy,' he exclaimed. 'It's fine to see you again

– for the moment, I didn't recognize you: there's nothing like a uniform to disguise a bloke, is there? And of course, we're none of us any younger, are we?'

I stared full into the stranger's face; now I came to look at it, there was something vaguely familiar about the eyes and mouth: I was reminded of somebody, I couldn't quite remember who ... Why, of course – the person I was trying to think of was Bert: the very person I was expecting to meet. It was an odd coincidence; but who was this bald, fat creature who had greeted me as an old friend?

'. . . hope it was OK phoning you,' the stranger was saying. 'I was a bit pushed for time, 'cause I've got to get up to Town. It's grand to see you again after all these years.'

It was Bert: reason assured me of the fact, but the evidence of my senses flatly contradicted it. Was it possible that Bert had grown into this gross, middle-aged man whom I should never, even if I had spent an hour in his company, have recognized?

'I'm sorry,' I said at last, rather lamely. 'I didn't notice you – it must be the light.'

'Come on in, and let's have some tea . . . It was like this, you see, I had to run down to Hawkinge on this job, and old Eric had told me you were at Shorncliffe, and I said to myself, "Well," I said, "I can't go back to town without looking up old Jocelyn".'

'Very nice of you,' I said – and then, my former confusion once again overcoming me, I added: 'Sir.'

'Aw, cut it out, Jocelyn – we don't want none of that bullshit between old friends ... And anyway, I'm in civvies ... Well, what's it to be? The old char and a wad, eh?'

By this time, we had sat down at a table. In the faint electric light, the interior of the café seemed enormous, barn-like: I had a curious sense of dissolution, as one feels sometimes on waking, suddenly, from a dream. Down the sides of the room were placed a number of solid, mahogany tables: the light gleamed vaguely on their polished surfaces. The place seemed almost empty: two elderly, dowagerish women sat in one corner, eating crumpets with an air of infinite refinement; and a black cat sidled aimlessly between the tables. Eric, I thought, would have immediately identified the cat as one of Mrs Vindables' familiars: and once again the sense of insubstantiality overcame me, as I realized that I was sitting, at last, beneath the roof of the Goose Cathedral – that sinister and sacrosanct chapel-by-the-sea where, in my childhood, the enormous blue-and-red lifeboat had couched, mysteriously, like a sea-monster in its lair.

Bert, meanwhile, was chattering away nineteen-to-the-dozen. It had been grand seeing Eric again – he had met him at a party, a real posh turn-out (Eric's description of this function, I seemed to remember, had been rather different); it was funny how people turned up again after all these years. Eric seemed to be doing pretty well – editor of a paper, or something: he was always a brainy chap, was old Eric – and brains counted, nowadays, too bloody true they did.

'Of course, I've been damned lucky myself,' Bert went on. 'I'd have been out in Group 18, but I saw I'd got a good chance, and I signed on again. It's paid me, over and over – they're still crying out for regulars, and of course, the job I'm on's a pretty skilled one: a bloke that's just called up and does his two years doesn't have time to get more than a smattering ... See here, Jocelyn, I don't want to sort of ask leading questions, but what's the idea of you signing on as an OR, eh?'

'I suppose I prefer it,' I said.

'I should have thought a brainy chap like you could have found something a bit more cushy ... Mind you, I don't regret my time in the ranks, but for an educated bloke, like you, why, it's obvious you ought to have a commission.'

'Why is it obvious?' I asked, rather irritably, looking across at the coarse, red face, the receding hair, the bristling moustache. Bert was much fatter and coarser than he ought to have been at his age; he must, I conjectured, be round about thirty-six, but he looked fully ten years older. Probably, I thought, it was too much good living: doubtless he had enjoyed running through his wife's fortune, and obviously he didn't take enough exercise.

Bert looked embarrassed by my question. Self-satisfied and patronizing as he was, he couldn't, it was evident, quite forget his origins. His plump cheeks took on a darker tinge, and he busied himself with pouring out the tea, which had just arrived.

'Hang it all, Jocelyn,' he said at last, 'you know what I mean – the way you were brought up, an Oxford education and all. You ought to be something better than a – an ordinary swaddie.'

I laughed, suddenly taking pity on him.

'I suppose I just happen to like it,' I said.

Bert grinned across at me, rather shyly: his vulgar, cocky self-confidence seemed suddenly to have vanished, and as he smiled I recognized once again the naïf, rather charming boy whom Pussy Wilkinson had bought out of the Army.

'Well, Jocelyn, it's all right, I s'pose, as long as you're happy ... I always thought you wanted to write books.'

'I have written one or two,' I said.

'Have you, now? Well, *I* never knew you had. The fact is, you see, I don't get much time for reading.'

We drank our tea and ate crumpets: I could not, even now, quite rid myself of the disquieting sense that the whole odd occasion was part of some dream. Even the two old ladies in the corner seemed phantasmal images: hoary old dames with dateless hats perched upon high-piled Edwardian *coiffures*, they might have been people I had encountered in my childhood, on the Folkestone Leas, during my morning walks with Ninnie.

Presently Bert announced that he would soon have to go; I, too, had to return shortly, to 'stand-in' for my friend on fire-picquet.

'You know, Jocelyn,' Bert said, still with a certain shyness in his manner, 'I was real keen to see you again – I was always sort of fond of you and Eric.' He had leaned forward, and now, rather to my embarrassment, placed a hand, affectionately, on my knee. 'I'd just like to say – if I can ever help you any way, just to let me know. And if ever you're in Town, just phone up my place – I've got a nice little flat up Russell Square way, with a spare bedroom, so I can always put you up. I'd be real pleased if you'd come – just turn up any time.'

It had plainly, I thought, cost him something to say this. He still looked slightly embarrassed; and, as I rose to go, he added:

'You know, Jocelyn, poor old Moira was ever so fond of you – I know she'd have been pleased to think you was still a pal of mine.'

Bert paid the bill, and we left, crossing the road to the bus-stop, where Bert was going to catch a bus to Folkestone. A fine rain was falling, and the road gleamed like metal beneath the arc-lamps. The buses were infrequent: it was time I started for the camp, but I was seized by a kind of paralysis of the will, and lingered impotently, making conversation, till Bert should have departed.

At last the bus arrived: Bert climbed on to it, and, as he waved to me from the step, I came smartly to attention and saluted. His broad, red face grinned back at me, half-mocking, half-embarrassed, as the bus bore him away. When he was out of sight, I was suddenly overcome by a helpless fit of laughter. The Moor had won again, I thought: the realization had flashed across my mind at the moment when I saluted Bert's departing figure. The gesture had given me, for some reason, an infinite satisfaction: I realized that, in my heart of hearts, I had always wanted the Moor to triumph. Yet my laughter was not provoked, entirely, by that parting salute: it seemed, rather, an outlet for some deeper emotion which I couldn't, at the moment, quite identify. It was as though, in the shadowy, haunted spaces of the Goose Cathedral, the whole of my past, the whole, carefully built-up structure of my life and personality, had collapsed like a card-house. My innumerable *personae*, my *bovarysmes*, lay scattered like shot birds about the spiky, turretted pile of the boathouse; the breed of barnacles was, as Eric had said, extinct at last.

The coast-road seemed more than usually desolate; as I turned up Hospital Hill, a couple of soldiers passed me, walking down towards the Fountain Hotel. A bugle sounded, remote and melancholy, from somewhere up in the Camp: beyond the road, below the newly-built sea-wall, the waves thudded softly on the shore.

MORE ABOUT PENGUINS
AND PELICANS

For further information about books available from Penguins please write to Dept EP, Penguin Books Ltd, Harmondsworth, Middlesex UB7 0DA.

In the U.S.A.: For a complete list of books available from Penguins in the United States write to Dept CS, Penguin Books, 625 Madison Avenue, New York, New York 10022.

In Canada: For a complete list of books available from Penguins in Canada write to Penguin Books Canada Ltd, 2801 John Street, Markham, Ontario L3R 1B4.

In Australia: For a complete list of books available from Penguins in Australia write to the Marketing Department, Penguin Books Australia Ltd, P.O. Box 257, Ringwood, Victoria 3134.

In New Zealand: For a complete list of books available from Penguins in New Zealand write to the Marketing Department, Penguin Books (N.Z.) Ltd, P.O. Box 4019, Auckland 10.

MEMORIES AND IMPRESSIONS
Ford Madox Ford

As a child, 'Fordie' frequently heard loud arguments between William Morris, Rossetti and the other Pre-Raphaelites; he was well used to finding Swinburne dead drunk in the bath; he sat on Turgenev's knee and offered a chair for Tolstoy. As a young writer he was companion to Henry James; comforter to Crane; collaborator with Conrad; friend and then enemy of H. G. Wells. Fattish and fiftyish, he was universal uncle to 'the arts'; patron of Ezra Pound; first guide of D. H. Lawrence; employer of Ernest Hemingway. Later still he turned, like Horace, to his garden, living off his own smallholding in Provence and preaching the holocaust to come.

These essays, anecdotes and autobiographical passages create a fascinating picture of his life in England, France and America, and an intimate glimpse into the lives of many of the literary giants of the century.

THE LETTERS AND JOURNALS OF KATHERINE MANSFIELD
Edited by C. K. Stead

Katherine Mansfield was one of our most gifted, and tragically short-lived, writers, whose relatively small output has nevertheless exercised a powerful influence on modern fiction – indeed, Virginia Woolf confessed that hers was the only writing she was jealous of. Although these letters and extracts from Katherine Mansfield's journal deal with the 'tremendous trifles of life' – the funny, the ridiculous, the exasperating – they also inhabit a dimension that transcends the everyday as their author comes to terms with the problems of living and dying, with pain and fear and loneliness, with her own creativity, with friendship and, above all, with the great and enduring love she had for her husband.

THE HEAT OF THE DAY
Elizabeth Bowen

Wartime London; and Stella's lover, Robert, is suspected of selling information to the enemy. Harrison, shadowing Robert, is nonetheless prepared to bargain, and the price is Stella.

Elizabeth Bowen writes of three people, estranged from the past and reluctant to trust in the future, with the psychological insight and delicate restraint that have earned her a position among the most distinguished novelists of the century.

'Rarely, to my knowledge, has the late flowering of love in wartime been more poignantly described in fiction; and never, perhaps, more effectively presented as an integral experience, shared equally in all its aspects by a man and a woman' – John Hayward in the *Observer*

VALMOUTH/PRANCING NIGGER
CONCERNING THE ECCENTRICITIES OF CARDINAL PIRELLI
Ronald Firbank

Beneath soft deeps of velvet sky dotted with cognac clouds lies the world of Ronald Firbank.

There her ladyship languishes on the jaguar-skin sofa, robed in jewelled pyjamas; a negro boy roams the gold city streets, searching for sherbet but dreaming of butterflies; there, closeted in a chasuble, his Eminence baptizes the blue-eyed police-pup of the Duquesa DunEden . . .

Ronald Firbank's short novels have been compared with those of writers as various as Joyce, Evelyn Waugh and Ivy Compton-Burnett; they may be Impressionist or perhaps Surreal – certainly they are vibrant, colourful, comical and, literally, fantastic.

'A world, in the last resort absolutely original; one that causes a cavalcade of wish-fulfilment myths to sweep gaily past the reader's vision' – Anthony Powell